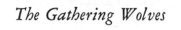

The Gathering Wolves

ALSO BY ELIZABETH DARRELL

The Jade Alliance

The GATHERING WOLVES

Elizabeth Darrell

COWARD, McCANN & GEOGHEGAN

NEW YORK

Library of Congress Cataloging in Publication Data

Darrell, Elizabeth.
    The gathering wolves.

      1.   Russia—History—Revolution, 1917-1921—Fiction.
I. Title.
PR6054.A697G37   823'.914   80-19605
ISBN 0-698-11061-7

Printed in the United States of America

For my father—who was there

Author's Note

The Russian Revolution and the subsequent Civil War were historical dramas that drastically changed the European political map. But there is a little-known aspect of the great Russian upheaval that is as bizarre, exciting, and tragic as any other.

From early 1918 until October 1919, the arctic forests of North Russia were occupied by troops of an astonishing variety of nationality and purpose. Starting as a revival of the war on the Eastern Front when the Russians made a separate peace with Germany in the midst of the Great War of 1914–1918, the struggle took on an unexpected and complex nature when the Armistice was signed in November 1918. Former enemies became friends, old allies became hostile.

In those forests throughout the dark frozen winter and short summer of perpetual daylight were British, French, Italians, Czechs, Canadians, Americans, Finns, Karelians—and Russians, of course. Red Russians, White Russians, partisans, counter-revolutionaries, starving peasants, political refugees, released convicts, mercenaries—all fighting for the future of Russia and all with different aims.

The North Russian Campaign appears to have been scantily recorded, and many details would seem to be lost forever beneath the arctic snows along with the men who fought there. The reason for this is probably in the nature of a campaign that necessitated the use of small, isolated groups operating all over inhospitable terrain with little or no means of contact with each other, and language barriers of no mean proportions.

The lifeline of this campaign was the railway running from Murmansk to Petrograd, and along its single track were posted engineers whose task it was to keep that line open. *The Gathering Wolves* tells the story of what might have happened to one of them.

I should like to offer my grateful thanks to all those gentlemen, military or civilian, who gave their professional knowledge to help me re-create what must now be only a dim memory in the minds of those few remaining today who were there in North Russia during those desperate days.

The Gathering Wolves

Prologue

Alexander Ivanovich Swarovsky came face to face with his young brother Vladimir for a few shattering moments during the great retreat of 1915. They met in a devastated village where dragging, broken regiments converged to cross by the only available bridge over the river, and it was a miracle that they should have recognised each other in that mêlée.

The sun blazed from an early summer blue sky that made the scene below all the more heartrending. What had once been a serene settlement of wooden houses surrounded by wild, sweetly perfumed roses and vegetables in neat rows was now a smoking, charred ruin. The road and gardens were pitted with shell craters, cornfields were blackened and strewn with the debris of death. The trees, still in their early green foliage, lay uprooted or broken and twisted, their great branches ending in jagged white splinters that resembled the shattered bones protruding through the flesh of many wounded troops.

Along the road, across the ruined fields, up through the black and lifeless copse swarmed the retreating Russians: men staggering in fatigue and pain, carts rumbling and lurching behind beasts almost beyond their endurance, gun-limbers rolling into craters amidst clanging metal and surging out again with a rush of heavy wheels when dragged and pulled by desperate men and animals; ambulance-waggons, bearing the red cross of mercy upon their canvas sides, creaking beneath the overloading of men, some of whom were already lifeless from the cruel journey and jostling their companions in grim competition for space.

Soldiers made no pretence at marching; the time for military precision had passed. They came in thousands, dark swaying lines against the summer landscape, shuffling in dazed pursuit of the man ahead or drooping in the saddles of their half-living mounts. The officers maintained a little of their dignity, but they, too, were morose and exhausted as they rode with the retreating horde.

Here and there could be seen a feminine face, those courageous nurses who served in the front line beside their menfolk. But their courage had reaped a harvest of anguish and years that sat upon faces of girls and

9

made them old women. There were other women also—mothers, sisters, wives of the village that had once existed here. They watched with eyes full of fear and hatred. During the Russian army's advance some months before, these same soldiers had broken the peasants' lives as theirs were now being broken.

All the men of the village had been taken to swell the ranks, fill the trenches, feed the cannon. They had been tied up and dragged away—even old men, and boys with the soft petal mouths of youth. The women had been used by the soldiers for sport, and when the lust had dimmed, these soldiers had departed with all the food they could carry from the village. Now, they were seizing the few things that were left in that place of devastation, and the peasant women were left to find what refuge they could from an advancing enemy who would show even less mercy.

But there was no time for compassion or humanity. The senses had become dulled, the emotions frozen. Eyes looked, but no longer saw. Ears heard, but no longer listened. Man had become animal . . . and yet, when brother saw brother in the midst of that depredation, life came surging back. There in the din and dust of retreat, the sight of a dearly loved face brought emotion to choke the throat and tears to mist the vision. Both men forgot all else and fought through the criss-cross of movement to reach each other. Without a word they gripped hands, then fell into a fierce embrace, weeping unashamedly for what life and they had become—a man just thirty and another not much more than a boy.

The elder recovered first from that moment when each found the other blessedly still alive, yet the horror, the humiliation of defeat had never seemed more overwhelming than when he looked into that boyish face and saw it written there.

"*Slava Bogu!*" he said huskily. "Thank God, it goes well with you, *bratishka*."

"If you mean that I still live, yes, it goes well with me," was the unsteady reply. "But it is no thanks to God. He has forsaken us—forsaken Russia."

"Valodya, I am ashamed to hear such words from you! Where is your faith and trust? Are you my brother, that such foolishness masquerades as wisdom?"

The rebuke made the boy defiant. "It is not easy to see His wisdom, at the moment. We have no bullets for our guns, no bread for our stomachs, no men to replace the dead." He looked around wildly at the scene. "If He does watch over us, He must weep at what He sees." He gripped his brother's arms. "Sasha, where has it all gone, the pride and the greatness?"

At that moment a mounted officer rode up to touch Valodya on the arm with his riding-whip. "Vladimir Ivanovich, you must come immediately. It is our turn to cross the bridge, and there can be no delays."

He had to go or lose all touch with his regiment. The flush had receded, leaving his face pale and fatigued, and Sasha felt the parting more acutely than when they had said goodbye at a railway station at the outset of the war. There had been no time to comfort Valodya, no time to study his face in case he might never see it again.

"The pride and greatness are still there," he called after the slender figure pushing through the crowd, but his voice was husky and did not carry far enough. All he could do was raise an arm in farewell as Valodya waved, and murmur, "May God go with you, *bratishka*."

It had been so brief, hardly more than a heartbeat in their lives, yet the encounter with his brother left Sasha strangely strengthened. Despair dropped away. Soon, they would turn and make a stand against the enemy. The flower of Russia's youth could not be allowed to die so easily. There were always reverses in war; a soldier had to expect that. But when they had re-grouped and re-armed, the retaliation would be fierce and deadly. Sasha knew his moment would come, and every blow he struck would be for his brother and those like him.

But the retreat continued and more men died. Those who brought up the rear tried to stem the oncoming Austrians and Germans, in desperate battles. They ran out of bullets, so they used their rifles to swing like clubs at the enemy, and when the rifles broke, they used their bare hands. They died from fever, starvation, and neglect. They also died from their own officers' bullets. Sasha shot four of his men who climbed from the trenches and ran from the enemy. It was the same all along the line. More and more appeared at the field hospitals with self-inflicted wounds. There was no food for cowards. There was no food at all!

Winter, Russia's greatest ally, brought a short lull. Sasha managed a short leave at home in Moscow and enjoyed his reunion with his two sisters and ailing mother. He enjoyed even more his reunion with Lyudmilla Zapalova, the darling of the ballet. She had been his mistress for five years and he came near to truly loving her during that Christmas leave, but the time flew, and they surrendered each other again.

That surrender became final one day about five months later when Sasha emerged from three pain-racked days to find himself in a hospital bed, being tended by a girl of no more than eighteen, who represented the antithesis of all he had left behind on the battlefield. Throughout his long recovery, she was there with her sweet smile, giving quiet encouragement when pain prevailed and filling his mind with the sanity of love amidst the madness of the past two years.

But her nursing skill was too good. He was back on his feet far too soon for his heart's liking, but he knew she regretted her devotion to duty that was shortly to send him back into hell. The tide had turned and Russia was advancing again, but the forward rush killed as many as the retreat had done. He grew desperate as the day of his discharge drew nearer and even contemplated faking a relapse. There was so little time.

Then, fortune favoured him. An outbreak of a contagious disease forced a period of quarantine throughout the hospital, and he used the delay impulsively. They married and spent two days together in an apartment loaned by a kindly doctor, before Sasha left to rejoin his regiment. But it was better now. There were letters to write and receive, her photograph to kiss each night, and a future full of brightness.

It was still raining. For a week it had hardly stopped. It made day very little different from night. With the high mud walls of the trenches obstructing the view, and the pall of storm-clouds darkening the sky, those fighting desperately for possession of France had lived in sessions of complete darkness followed by others of half-darkness all through the first part of November 1915.

Second Lieutenant Paul Anderson stretched his neck in an automatic gesture, but the movement gave him no relief from the sodden collar. He had forgotten the last time he had been completely dry, the last time the sun had shone. The old hands said things were no better when it did.

Paul pushed such thoughts from his mind and tried to think of home. Summer, in England. It was his favourite way of blotting out this present reality. A red brick house like all the others in his street but stamped as individual by his mother's touch in house and garden. Being on the corner, number seventeen was larger than the others. The garden was surrounded by a high wall that allowed them to make it anything they wished it to be. Mrs. Anderson said it was the Florentine Garden and that through the gate in the back wall lay the remainder of the estate. She was fascinated by the royal family, and all nobility, and lived in a dream of stately homes, carriages at eleven, and garden parties with marquees on the lawn and croquet.

Paul's sister Nora, at thirteen, roamed the grassy paths through lupins, love-in-a-mist, and tea roses, wrapped in a trailing lace curtain and dreaming of knights, paladins, and Billy Daniels next door.

Paul had spent his summers in that garden wrapped in dreams of his own. There had never been a moment when he had wavered from his determination to become an engineer. School holidays had been spent in that garden with books from the library, sheets of plain paper bought at the corner shop owned by Mr. Dobson, pencils, a ruler, and a rubber. He had drawn bridges by the hundreds, starting with copies of the pictures in library books, then progressing to his own designs from earnest calculations.

He was the brainy member of the family; the unexpected product of two kindly, hardworking, but ordinary people living in a railway depôt town in Wiltshire. His parents were very proud of him, embarrassing himself and all those who listened by singing his praises on every possible occasion. They scrimped and saved to send him to Oakwood, the school whose fees were normally beyond the pockets of people like the Andersons, and attended prize-givings dressed in their Sunday best to watch their son walk off with several each year. They were not only academic laurels that Paul won, for he had inherited the athletic prowess of a father who was in his works' football and cricket teams. A good all-rounder, the schoolboy's outstanding talent was for swimming, and Paul had swum for his county at fourteen.

The recollections faded, as they always did when guilt stepped in to drive them away. He gazed miserably at his men, who were detailed to strengthen and extend some earthworks put out of action by enemy shells. They all stood knee-deep in mud whilst more slid down the sides of the broken trench; they shovelled impotently in the drenching rain. Paul knew it was futile and ridiculous, but he had been told to see that it was done and had no option but to make his men go through the motions.

Thank God his mother could not see him now! He could still remember the pain on her face and the quiet desperation of her words when he had told her his decision.

"Paul, no, you can't do it, son. Isn't it enough that your dad is out there fighting?"

"The army is appealing for more men," had been his dogged answer.

"*Men*, yes," she had cried, "but you are only a boy of seventeen. You don't have to go—no one can make you."

"It's too late. I signed on this morning."

She had begun to cry. "Ever since you were a little boy, you wanted to be an engineer. Dad and me scrimped and saved to send you to Oakwood. We were so proud of you. And now this! Oh, Paul, how could you do such a thing?"

"But I shall be an engineer, Mum," he had stammered. "They've taken me into the Sappers."

So he was—a subaltern in the Royal Engineers who stood watching a group of men shovelling mud in the middle of France. He had not the heart to tell his mother what his work entailed. His letters home were full of shamefaced inventions that would shore up her pride. Since his father had been killed, the lies were more than ever necessary.

He was jerked back to the job in hand by a voice at his elbow. "Mr. Anderson, it's no good. The stuff's just running back to the bottom as fast as we shift it."

He shrugged farther into his sodden greatcoat. "I think it's coming, slowly but surely," he told the man with false cheeriness. His own voice sounded very youthful in comparison with that of the sapper who was digging. "I think we're getting somewhere, you know."

Suddenly, there was a familiar whine followed by a shuddering crash nearby, and his reflexes sent him headlong into the mud along with the others. It choked him, coated his face, stung his eyes, and he turned his head sideways to avoid being suffocated.

"Blimey, that was a close one," gasped a voice as the owner spat the mud from his mouth.

But the next was even closer. A great spout of ooze shot into the air, and the roar beat against Paul's ears in agonising waves. He was momentarily deafened, but the hand he pulled across his eyes cleared his vision enough to see young Vincent disappear under a wall of rain-softened earth no more than a few yards away. The men were clawing their way toward the transverse trench that would take them back to the main force, but he flung himself forward in a shocked frenzy of action and began shovelling like one possessed in the spot where the young sapper had disappeared. He could still see the face before it sank beneath the covering of slime: it had been white and terrified.

The air was full of thunder and flying pieces that whistled overhead. The day seemed to have grown darker, and mud that had reached his knees was now up to his thighs. It was tugging him down, trying to prevent his digging. A hand touched his arm, another took away the spade.

"Sir, come away . . . He's a goner."

"You don't know that. You can't be sure." It was high-pitched, almost a scream, and he had to fight to bring down the level of his voice. "Get back to the line—all of you. I'll bring in Vincent." He gave the N.C.O. a push. "Do as I say, damn you," he shouted wildly.

From then on he dug with his hands. The blood pounded in his ears, and the rain fell on his tin helmet like bullets—or maybe it *was* bullets! The earth shook and shuddered all around him. He had never felt so lonely. Dear God, let Vincent be alive so that he would not be the only living man out there in that wilderness. His body ached with the weight of mud now caked on it: his hands had become shapeless masses of a brown sticky substance. But still he tore at the mound covering one of the men for whom he was responsible.

There was another noise. It was himself sobbing with fear and exhaustion. He was beginning to shake all over. All hell had been let loose, and he was in the midst of it. Perhaps it was the end of the world.

The ground began to move. His heart lurched. Someone was alive beneath his feet. Clawing, scraping, his hands contacted rough serge, then something pliant and slimy. Vincent was barely living, but the sheets of rain washed away the mud as his face emerged from his living grave. The boy began to retch and cough, clinging to the officer who was no older than himself. Paul pulled out his own handkerchief and wiped the mud-splattered mucus from the other's mouth and nose until Vincent was able to breathe in regular rasps.

With a strength that somehow returned to him, Paul managed to free the body and began dragging Vincent along the trench toward the transverse way that led to the rear. In that trench were duckboards to make walking possible, but the effort to reach it cost him dear. Struggling, falling, inching his way along, Paul was four feet from the entrance when a shell exploded almost directly overhead. Vincent was torn from his grasp and hurled into the air like a broken rag doll. Paul was flung back in a somersault that left him sobbing with the futility of it all, when pain brought blessed darkness.

The weeks he spent in the base hospital passed too quickly. Paul was young and strong; his wounds healed easily, and the shock to his system was less damaging than it was to many men as old as his father who shared his ward. But the boy of eighteen suffered from an affliction that did not touch the older men. Her name was Lila Reynolds.

The days when Nurse Reynolds was on duty were golden. When she was not flitting about the ward, Paul was restless and depressed. He was almost completely inexperienced where girls were concerned. Oakwood had been a boys' school, so he had missed the growing-up companionship of schoolgirls enjoyed by other lads in his town. His sister's friends had been little girls her own age, and Paul had been the big brother who mended toys and bound up cut knees for them. Lila was altogether different.

She was a redhead of twenty-one with a shape he found very much to his liking. Indeed, he was certain his temperature rose when she leant over his bed. But there was more to it than that. He admired her tremendously. Nothing seemed to shake her calm patience. Whether the men were crying with agony or swearing with the frustration of immobility, she maintained the same sweetly grave expression and soothed with gentle words and hands. After a week he began feeling jealous of every other patient in the ward, caught himself measuring the time she spent with each man and trying to keep her by his own bed for longer than any other.

He was not very successful. She was too efficient, he was getting better too quickly, and he was far too shy to know how to handle the situation. He wished for the *savoir-faire* of Micky Knott, a pal he had made whilst in the ranks. Micky could get any girl interested with just a word, a wink, or a glance from beneath his ginger lashes. It was Micky who had been responsible for Paul's first and only sexual adventure, with a girl in a small French village soon after they had landed.

The "girl" had been nearer thirty than twenty and attractive in a too-obvious way. Urged on by Micky, he had gone off gamely enough but emerged feeling rather like a fly who had been lucky to escape the spider. It was not that he had not enjoyed the experience—once he had got going, it was wildly exciting—but his partner had seemed all set to eat him for breakfast, and her astonishingly large bosom had been more than he could cope with. He had not exactly fallen out of her door, but his exit was too fast to be nonchalant, and Micky had told the others, who had ribbed him about it for days afterward. That night had left him with a hunger, but also with a fear of making a fool of himself. He could still hear the woman's laugh as he had scrambled hastily into his clothes and made his escape.

Two weeks of hospital life passed, and he grew more and more smitten with Lila Reynolds. His jealousy made the situation worse. When she did eventually approach his bed, he was almost surly in his responses to her enquiries. Once or twice she raised her eyebrows at him and said, "My, we *are* in a bad mood today," which did not help one bit!

Then, after another week, she changed to night duty, and Paul found it almost unbearable to lie in the intimate glow of one lamp, the only person in that ward awake with her, yet unable to make communication. He grew feverish for a day or two and had the further torment of ministrations from her when his body had to be sponged in the long night hours. Then a fresh batch of wounded arrived and took all her attention.

It was over one of these cases that things came to a head. He was an officer in the Artillery, no older than Paul, who had been brought in with a stomach wound and shell shock. He suffered from bouts of madness—sitting up in bed and screaming that the enemy was coming—but the stomach wound demanded minimum movement, so an orderly was constantly at his side to hold him down. One night when the patient appeared quiet, the orderly slipped out to relieve himself, leaving Nurse Reynolds watching beside the bed.

Paul was watching through sleep-heavy lids, wondering desperately how he could get to know her better, when disaster occurred without warning. The man flung himself sideways with such force, screaming that they were coming in the hundreds, that he fell from the bed and lay writhing in his madness on the floor. Pandemonium ensued. Medical staff came running from all directions as the young nurse knelt on the floor trying in vain to hold the boy still.

Paul sat up horrified as Lila's apron grew dark with blood and the patient's mad screams changed to cries of agony. A doctor arrived, followed by a stretcher party, but the young subaltern died before they could pick him up. They carried the body from the ward, and the doctor turned to the nurse and snapped, "I shall want an explanation of this—if anyone *can* explain how she let a patient die from negligence."

Something exploded inside Paul's chest as he watched the girl automatically begin to strip the bed, then abandon the task and run from the ward to disappear into the sluice-room at the end. Getting from his bed he followed her, hardly hearing the comments from the other patients, who had all been woken by the noise, and giving no thought to the fact that he was only in pyjama trousers.

She spun round when he accidentally brushed against some bed-pans stacked near the door. "What are you doing out of bed, Mr. Anderson?" she whispered, fighting for control of herself. "Go back at once."

"You're crying," he accused, tight with emotion. "That doctor was beastly to you. I saw the whole thing, and it wasn't your fault."

Her head moved from side to side. "It wasn't anybody's fault, the doctor knew that. He's overtired and overworked. They all are. It wasn't what he said."

He moved closer hesitantly. "Was it because he died?"

She shook her head again. "It was inevitable. He had no hope, you know. I suddenly felt the futility of my work, the waste. I came out here to heal people, but what can any of us do against such destruction? For a moment I just felt like walking away and never coming back." Her pale eyes appealed to him. "Does that sound terrible to you?"

He was profoundly moved. "No," he said through a lump in his throat. "I have felt that way many times in the trenches. I think everyone does—even the Germans. But we don't do it, do we? That's the important thing."

There was another long pause while she studied him, then a faint smile broke through. "It's always the quiet ones that are the most interesting."

His colour rose as a thrill went through him at what her words suggested. But he had no idea what to say next.

"I'll be glad when this strapping comes off," he said swallowing hard. "It's damned uncomfortable."

Efficiency took over. "Well, it won't improve if you keep hopping out of bed when you should be asleep. Sister will be round in a few minutes, and you'd better be back in by then."

"I'm not afraid of Sister," he boasted.

"I am," she told him with a gleam in her eye. "Now go back, and I'll come in a few minutes to tuck you in and make you comfortable."

With hammering heart he heard himself say, "And kiss me good-night?"

Her hasty attempt at starched disapproval melted quickly, and she said in a soft voice, "If it will make you sleep, all right. But it's strictly against the rules, so it had better be here where no one else will see."

Happiness was too good a healer, and Paul left for the Front again within two weeks. When he said goodbye to Lila, he asked if he might write to her.

"Yes, of course, if you'd like to," she said.

He took one of her hands. "I think you are the most wonderful person in the world."

She let him kiss her rather experimentally, and then she wished him Godspeed as he climbed into the truck with leaden feet.

Her letters kept him going all through the grimness, horror, and savagery of the following months in the trenches that seemed to stretch across the whole of France. He fought through bombardments of shells, through bayonet attacks, through grenades and bullets, and through deadly layers of poison gas, and Lila was the only sweet thing in his life.

Then, six months after his return to duty, his company was in reserve in a gutted town barely twenty-five miles from the base hospital, and he was given twenty-four hours leave. Normally such leave was something of a farce, but this time he knew exactly what to do with it. Enquiries revealed that a medical officer was leaving to visit the hospital and would give the young subaltern a lift there and back. Paul was almost sick with anticipation as he sat in the car imagining what it would be like to see her again.

He never did. Where the hospital had stood was a pile of wreckage. Only the night before the town had been the target for fierce bombardment by German forces who had broken through on the right flank. The whole place had been devastated. More than half the medical staff had been killed, including Lila Reynolds.

Paul felt nothing except a violent urge to return to the trenches. He stopped a truck in a convoy on its way to the Front and used his rank to commandeer a seat in it. The driver soon gave up all attempts to make conversation with him.

The road was pitted with shell holes and churned into mud by the constant stream of heavy vehicles, tramping boots, and the hooves of horses still so necessary to an army on the move. The truck lurched and bumped through a struggle of marching men and animals, past guns and transport-waggons, alongside a troop of cavalry, drab in khaki greatcoats and a sad comparison with their glittering ancestors.

Then, the pattern changed and disintegrated as German aircraft swooped low and machine-gunned the length of the road. Men dived for cover in the ditches and hedgerows, horses shrieked with terror as they reared and jostled each other from their orderly lines, ammunition packed in the waggons exploded in great roars of sound that hid the screams of those who had been in the firing-line. Smoke and flames billowed wherever one looked. Khaki-clad figures were writhing in the road or lying still, oblivious of riderless horses that galloped madly over them. All semblance of humanity had gone.

The aircraft had turned and were now rushing low over the distant trees to strafe the road from the opposite direction. In the next few minutes, dozens more would be dead. Paul opened the door beside him and jumped down into the mud that was part of his life now. Then he was running, running along the road to meet the overhead menace. His head was back and he saw them through a dazzle of tears. There was thunder in his head and body as he screamed abuse at the dark shapes passing overhead—shapes that went by in a flash of noise and spurting flames and left madness behind.

"You bloody murdering bastards!" he screamed at them, but when he tried to repeat it no sound would come. The screaming went on in his head instead.

Two soldiers sheltering under a nearby hedge saw him standing totally vulnerable in the middle of the road, head thrown back and shaking with sobs.

One snorted with disgust. *"Officers!* We're expected to follow bloody fools like him."

The other, older and more perceptive, looked with compassion. "He's no more than a boy, Bert. They expect him to be an adult before he's been young. If this war goes on much longer, he'll be an old man all his life. That's if he lives beyond today, poor devil."

O n e

Paul stood in the middle of the railway track, dwarfed by the great pines that surrounded him. The last puffing of the departing train had died away: the rails no longer sang with vibrations.

He let his gaze follow the majestic outline of long, straight trunks disappearing into a spread of green-needled branches that reached so high, only by tilting his head fully back could he see the gently swaying tops. The beauty of dark conifers against vivid blue sky held him as he stood for some minutes, then he closed his eyes, the better to enjoy the sharp, sweet smell of pine needles and the clean air warmed by midsummer sun in the arctic circle. The silence was glorious.

If only the whole world could be like this, he thought, and opened his eyes again to make sure he was still in the same place. Yes, there were the armies of trees on each side, and the single-track railway cutting through them until it curved away out of sight half a mile from where he stood. He began walking along it, finding himself altering his stride so that he should not step on the sleepers. A slight smile touched his mouth at the remembrance of that childhood game, but he continued unselfconsciously playing it. He did not hurry; there was nowhere to go. This was to be his home for as long as it took to do the job.

For some while he strolled, boots crunching on the shale between the track, as he thought about the coming months. It was a challenge. It was also a compliment to his ability as an engineer that he should have been selected to command such an important operation—a command that surely reflected the confidence of his superiors in his professional skill.

Lost in thought, he stepped over the rail and entered the gloom of the dense forest. There was no real path, but the sun-shimmer on the lake beyond guided him in the right direction. Pine needles formed a carpet that muffled the sound of his heavy tread, and the sharp smell of conifers increased in that dim interior. There was a small settlement beyond the lake, but he had no interest in it except as a source of additional food supplies or labour. The thought of the inhabitants held no charm for him.

His deep bitterness over the manner in which the Russians had walked away from their trenches during the war, leaving the Germans free to fling extra battalions against those on the Western Front, had left Paul with a feeling akin to hatred, and it had not been any wish to help these people that had prompted him to volunteer for service with the British Relief Force. The terrible straits the Russians now found themselves in had been brought on by their own treachery, he felt, and was no concern of his. They had walked out on him and his comrades in 1917; he felt no compunction to come to their aid now.

Breaking through the trees to the shingle shore of the lake, he found his whole attention was taken once more by the visual beauty before him. The forest rose in the background on all sides, giving a dark green corona to lighter green grassy slopes possessing that lushness and vividness of colour seen in lands where snows only melt for a short while to expose the turf beneath to a benevolent sun. Near the edge of the water, grass gave way to rounded rocks leading to the beach of pebbles. The lake itself lay still and beautiful, reflecting the surrounding nature in perfect reproduction. Wild ducks sat on the surface in the peace and warmth, enjoying the solitude as much as the man who watched them.

Charmed, Paul sat on a smooth rock and took off his uniform jacket. It was very warm where he sat, the sun making him shade his eyes to look out across the water. He sighed with satisfaction and relaxed his tense body. The decision he had made had been the right one.

Four years of war had left him with the desire for beauty and tranquillity, but he had not found it in England. Last November, when the Armistice had been signed, he had still been in France, and it had been more than a month before they had returned him to England on leave. It had taken him a mere two days to realise he could never go back to the life he had once known.

Mrs. Anderson had grown selfish and complaining; Nora, his sister, now fully developed, had shocked him with her obsession with men. All she spoke about was the fun she would have "now the boys are home," and she plastered her face with cosmetics that made her look common. He soon realised his mother and sister had little understanding of life beyond their front door. It was not their fault, he knew, but there was no trace of the boy who had been one of them in the man he had now become. He had travelled and seen things they would never understand. The gulf between them was too wide, and if they should wish to bridge it, he could not. If he spoke of France, his mother quickly said it was all over now and best forgotten. But Paul knew he would never forget, nor would any man who had been there.

After a week he had taken to going for long walks in the nearby countryside, but peace was not to be found there when he knew he must return to his home. The atmosphere worsened. Mrs. Anderson began pestering him to find civilian work. Things were not easy, she said, and it was time he took over the responsibility of breadwinner. She helped a local nurseryman four days a week, and Nora had a job in the end grocery shop, but it did not bring in much, and the nurseryman had warned Mrs. Anderson that he would have to give her job to a man returning from the war. There would be thousands seeking employment.

So Paul found. He also discovered that it would be hopeless to try to settle in that red-brick corner house with a self-absorbed widow and a fast young woman. There was really only one answer: to stay in the army. It was his best hope of fulfilling his ambitions as an engineer, and it gave him the escape from something he could not face. He placated his mother by promising to send her the greater part of his pay each month and added that there would be one less to feed if he was not living there. She did not appear heartbroken. The son who had once been her pride and joy had turned out to be a great disappointment, after all.

Having promised a set sum for those at home, he then found himself broke halfway through the month. Small wonder he had jumped at the chance to earn more by volunteering for North Russia—a posting that was considered hazardous enough to warrant financial inducement. On top of that, he was, at last, to realise his ambition to build bridges.

A jab of excitement went through him. This was his job—his alone. Leaning back against the warm stone, he reviewed the project anew. From the port of Murmansk, where he had disembarked, a single track railway ran down to Petrograd, and thence to Moscow. It had been built in a hurry—sixteen months or so, he had been told—and for the most part through dense coniferous forest. The Russians had not made a good job of it. Rather than blast through obstacles, they had gone round them and over them. In consequence, the track twisted and curved, crossed innumerable bridges, and ran up and down small hillocks. The bends in the track were often insufficiently scarped and ballasted, the wooden bridges crossed rivers so rapid the frail supports were constantly being swept away by swollen spring waters, and many of the inclines were so steep the trains were unable to climb them at first attempt and had to roll back in order to get up more steam. Paul had seen all this for himself when he had come down the line during the past four days, and it had not improved his opinion of the Russians as a people.

The British and their allies had moved into the northern ports of Murmansk and Archangel soon after the Russians had treated for a separate peace, over a year ago. Still at war with Germany, the Western Powers had a threefold reason for landing troops: to prevent stockpiles of arms and supplies sent to aid the Russians on the Eastern Front from falling into German hands; to stop the Germans from using the ice-free port of Murmansk as a submarine base for attacks on shipping in the

North Sea; and to stop the flow of German troops from Russia to France and Belgium, where the war was still bitterly raging. They succeeded on all three counts.

But by the time the European war was over, revolution had struck, starting a civil war in Russia. Bolshevik troops had begun attacking the Allies in their country. Suddenly, the struggle in North Russia took on a different guise, and it seemed politic for world peace that the Allies should fight back. Reinforcements were landed to aid those White Russian loyalists who were making a desperate stand against Lenin and his regime. Britain's old allies against Germany now became her enemies; the hostile White Finns now joined forces with White Russians to fight the Bolsheviks. The pattern was changing and confused. Battles were being fought all over Russia—not only between opposing armed forces, but between soldiers and peasants, workers and nobles, intellectuals and politicians, and between anyone who wanted something and the person from whom he could take it.

Paul did not care about any of them. He was not here on a crusade, but to repair and rebuild a railway. The rest was none of his concern. Let them all kill each other, if they wished. He was doing what he had always wanted to do, at last.

But however much he might wish to isolate himself from the general situation, it was not possible to ignore the cause of his present command. A British armed force had succeeded in pushing the Red troops south and had set up a forward base at Lake Onega, two days down the line. It was planned to build an airstrip and seaplane harbour, and to maintain the base it was essential to bring supplies and possible reinforcements down the railway from Murmansk. The Reds were well aware of this, and the single track had become of vital importance to both sides.

Sections of the railway had been allocated to various groups to repair and improve so that fast and easy access to the south would be possible. American engineers were tackling the more northerly sections, and Paul was one of several Englishmen coping with the other stretches.

The single track had, of necessity, sidings every twenty miles or so to allow trains to pass each other, and it was in one of these that Paul had just been left with a small supply train with a Russian engine-driver, a corporal of the Royal Engineers, and his own batman. He was in sole command of the operation and the prospect thrilled him, but there was one drawback. To do the labouring he had been assigned a body of Russian soldiers led by a Tsarist officer who had fled north when the Bolsheviks took over the government of Russia and murdered the royal family. They were due to rendezvous with him sometime that evening.

The thought put a damper on his pleasure, and he got restlessly to his feet. He wanted no involvement with them or their revolution. He was there to build bridges, level track, and strengthen escarpments, that was all. They must be made to realise that at the outset, or he could foresee trouble ahead.

The small company had been on the march for most of the day when it broke through the trees to the side of the lake. The men made a run for the water and fell on their faces to quench their thirst, scooping it up and over their heads further to refresh themselves.

Sasha rode down to the foreshore to let his horse drink, got thankfully from the saddle, and accepted a cup of water that his orderly offered him. The water was cold and clear, fed by the melting ice of early summer, and refreshed his spirits as much as the scene before him. His heart swelled. Was there any more beautiful country than Russia? Its range of desert and mountains, snows and sun-drenched valleys, peasant villages and cities of immense grandeur, lakes, plains, and vast green forests all combined in one great territory acquired by the tsars of successive generations.

The people of Russia were as varied and exciting as the land in which they lived—Oriental, Asiatic, Middle Eastern, European, Slavic, and Scandinavian strains were all to be found—each bringing cultures, music, religions, and temperaments that often clashed but always fascinated.

He sighed heavily. The present madness resulted from this. How could the *Bolsheviki* hope to succeed when they gave power to the people willy-nilly? Did they not understand that such power would be interpreted by the Russian people in diverse ways, according to their heritage? Did they not realise that power was a potent weapon that should only be used for good? Right now, all it was doing was destroying—destroying a nation already broken by war with Germany.

The reminder served to end his halt by the water's edge. Giving orders to bivouac at the rim of the trees, he remounted and set off along a rough track toward the railway siding he had been told was there. He would not know if the train carrying the British officer had arrived until he reached it, but since there was no sign of life at the lake, it was to be supposed that his own company had reached the rendezvous first.

It was a surprise when the thinning trees gave him a sight of the siding where an engine and four trucks already stood. He reined in at the far side of the main track and scanned the scene. Beside him was the tall water tank and the hut housing the point levers. Across the track, between it and the siding rails, was a platform of stout wood where several boxes were piled and broken open. The train consisted of a small donkey engine, two open trucks filled with shingle ballast, a long flat-car piled with lengths of rail, and a closed truck at the end with a heavy bar and padlock on the sliding door.

Movement caught Sasha's eye. At the end of the platform three men sat on upturned boxes around another, which they were using as a table for their evening meal. Beyond the platform on a small patch of open ground, a tent was pitched. At the entrance, a man in khaki uniform sat at a folding table, eating. There was a bottle and glass beside his plate. He was undoubtedly the officer with whom Sasha must rendezvous.

Sasha urged his horse forward across the track, a smile lighting his face. The man glanced up and rose too hastily, knocking over the glass and its contents, so that the liquid ran down the leg of the table. As Sasha leapt from the saddle, he had only a brief impression of a startled face and dark eyes before his fervent gratitude won an emotional victory over protocol.

"Welcome to my country," he said in English, finding his voice thick with the import of the moment. "The sons of Russia salute you." He took the Englishman in an embrace of brotherhood, kissing him on both cheeks and clapping his shoulders with hearty enthusiasm several times. "My brave ally, no words can express the gratitude of all loyal Russians for coming to our aid at this desperate time—a brave ally and valiant friend."

On the point of further demonstrating the warmth of his comradeship, Sasha found the other man stepping back to avoid the embrace and he cast a quick glance toward the men on the platform. Sensitive to something he had no time to identify, Sasha took refuge in military formality. Snapping his heels together, he gave a hint of a bow.

"Lieutenant Colonel Alexander Ivanovich Swarovsky, at your service."

The response was unpleasantly surprising. An expression of flushed disapproval already on the other's face slowly changed to livid anger.

"*Lieutenant Colonel!*" He almost choked over the words. "You can't be . . . I mean, I understood . . . They told me there would be only 'one small contingent,' not even a full company of Russians coming here."

"I *have* only a small contingent. In the Tsar's army I had a regiment. Now, I lead any loyal man who will follow."

The Englishman looked in danger of exploding. "*In the Tsar's army!* Are you telling me you are now a partisan—a mercenary?"

Cohesive thought was returning. Sasha realised the fellow in khaki shirt and breeches was only a year or two more than twenty. His welcome had been made to an ill-mannered subordinate.

"Who is in charge here?" Sasha demanded with icy superiority, making it clear he was used to dealing only with men his equal.

"I am. Captain Paul Anderson, Royal Engineers." It was delivered like a challenge.

Furious by now, finding the situation incomprehensible in its unexpectedness, taking a violent dislike to the youngster before him, Sasha treated him to a derogatory optical appraisal.

"You are very young to be a captain," he said in a tone that suggested it could not possibly be true.

The flush emphasised the freckles scattered across tense angry features. "Promotion was quick in the trenches of France. To stay alive even six months made a man top in seniority, and I survived four years. *To the bitter end.*"

"I, too, fought for four years, but our bitter end is still to come," snapped Sasha. "We do not find it easy to fight our own countrymen."

"You did not find it easy to fight the Germans. We had to finish them off for you."

Sasha almost struck him around the face, as he would have done one of his subordinates, but shock held him motionless. This "boy," no older than his brother Valodya, had spoken of something that would fill Sasha with shame and heartbreak for the rest of his life. He had spoken to Alexander Ivanovich as if he were of no account. Where was the ally, the friend of his country, the true soldier who had landed in the North to support a cause that dare not be lost, the man prepared to risk his all in defence of a nation in danger?

"Where is your superior officer?" Sasha demanded imperiously.

"Four days by train to the north, two to the south. I am the only English officer for hundreds of miles," was the tight-lipped reply. "I am in sole command of this project."

The news shook Sasha, but he responded immediately. "No. I hold senior rank and must, therefore, command."

"Lieutenant Colonel in the Tsar's army, you said . . . but it no longer exists, does it?"

The question was full of contempt, and all Sasha's agony returned in a moment. As he looked at that young face full of hostility, he thought of the many young faces that would never smile again and spoke with returning emotion as memories overcame him.

"You may never know what it is like when those you think of as good, loyal men spit in your face as they hold a bayonet against your throat; when they tear the insignia from your jacket and trample them in the mud; when they cut to pieces your fellow officers, cursing their families as they do so. You may never know what it is like to be left in the trenches surrounded by humiliated and dying officers, knowing your country is almost lost. A man cannot fight an enemy on his own, Captain. I think even you would not have survived your four years under those circumstances."

For long moments they stood in silent confrontation, taking stock of the situation. Perhaps they should have done so at the outset, but Sasha's heartfelt gratitude to the allies who were showing staunch support to the White Russians had led him to approach the rendezvous with emotional eagerness, little expecting hostility.

Then, the Englishman turned to indicate the bottle on the table. "I have no vodka, but I can offer you a brandy."

It was armed neutrality, and there was no choice but to accept. They had to work together in the coming months.

"Thank you," Sasha said stiffly, but he felt heavy-hearted as he took the proffered chair and watched while one of the soldiers came forward with a box for the English officer to use as a seat.

Nodding his thanks, the young man said, "Stevens, this is . . . Colonel . . . Swarovsky. Think you can rustle up something for him?"

"Ow d'yer do, sir," said the soldier, standing stiffly to attention. Then his eyes swivelled to his own officer. "There's plenty of stores, sir. Dinner's all gone, but I can get something underway for Colonel Svar . . . Svaro . . . for the Colonel, sir," he finished.

"I need nothing," put in Sasha swiftly. "My servant is preparing dinner down at the lakeside at this moment." He waved a hand at the soldier. "You may go."

"*Thank you, Stevens. That's all.*" The tone was meant to override the Russian's dismissal, and Sasha took a pull at the brandy to mask his anger.

"You have a batman," commented the other. "Does that mean your soldiers have settled down at the lake?"

"Naturally. Why else would I be here? I have forty men bivouacking beside the lake—men who have remained loyal and answered the call to arms, who will offer their lives to help free Russia of the madmen who now hold sway. Men from the fields and villages who have flocked to the cause."

The Englishman stared at him, glass half-raised to his lips. "Do you mean there are no trained soldiers, just peasants in uniform?" he asked in strangled tones.

Sasha glared back. "Did you not have such men in your army, Captain? You, yourself, must have gone to war straight from the schoolroom. Were you a trained soldier? No, but you are very quick to speak of the years you fought as one."

Sasha's opponent got over that by taking a long pull at his drink. When he lowered the glass to the table, he attacked in another direction.

"Your men cannot bivouac by the lake."

"They have already done so."

"Then they will have to move. The train is up here, and that *cannot* be moved. There's really no alternative."

Leaning forward and rapping his glass on the table, Sasha said, "I think we have already acknowledged that my seniority must prevail here.

Nothing will be achieved by your taking your present attitude. I must accept your hostility, but fail to understand it. Everything you have said and done suggests you hold Russia and her people in contempt. Why, then, are you here?"

"To perfect a railway. I am an engineer." Paul got to his feet. "I have fought my war and won. Now I want to follow my profession to the best of my ability. What you people do to each other does not concern me. I am here to do an engineering job, and nothing is going to stand in my way—not politics, revolution, and civil war . . . nor a rebel officer leading forty uniformed ruffians. My superiors gave *me* this command, and that is the way it has to be or we might as well forget it." His anger was mounting again. "In this train I have explosives, guns, ammunition, food, medical supplies, and a great deal of money. From what I hear of this country at present, all those things are considered worth killing for. In view of that, I want everyone in this venture gathered where I can see them—*all the time.*" He nodded toward the soldiers on the platform. "Those two are my own men whom I know and trust, but forty ill-assorted peasants I do not."

Sasha was about to speak when the other put his foot on the box he had used as a seat and leant forward to emphasise his next point.

"As far as military etiquette is concerned, I am not sure how a British captain stands when faced by a lieutenant colonel of a disbanded army who is in charge of an irregular body of armed peasants. I will address you as 'sir' if you insist, but in no way will I consider myself under your command."

Sasha rose filled with something of the pain he had felt when his men had hurled insults at him and walked away after humiliating him in the most terrible manner. But all the inborn pride of his background was in his voice when he said, "A brave speech by someone who thinks he holds all the cards. In fact, I hold the ace, Captain. I accept that without your knowledge the work on the railway cannot be done, and with no superiors in easy reach you cannot be relieved of your command by a word from me. You hold us in contempt—you have admitted as much—but we are fighting not only for our lives but for our future. When one is desperate, all else must be pushed aside. We need you, but let me point out that despite your astonishing self-assurance you will be hard put to deal with an irregular body of armed peasants, as you so cuttingly call my men. Since you have made no attempt to speak to me in Russian, I take it you know nothing of our language. I, on the other hand, speak yours fluently. If you intend to command this operation, I suggest that you also need me, or your orders will fall upon uncomprehending ears. You cannot build your railway without me, Captain Anderson. You must see that."

At that moment a volley of shots was heard nearby, and Sasha noticed with grim amusement the nervous reflexes of the British officer as he spun round, reaching instinctively for the revolver strapped around his waist.

"Not revolutionaries, Captain, just my men shooting wild duck, I suspect. They are excellent marksmen, having been hunters all their lives."

Thinking how very like Valodya he looked—Valodya pale, strained, and sickened by what he had seen in battle—Sasha saw the young man hesitate, then drop his hand from the gun.

"Very well, Colonel. For administrative purposes I will accept that you must command your own men, but where the railway is concerned what I say goes. When they are working under my guidance, orders must be obeyed without question. Is that agreed?"

Tired, disappointed with the hope that had been bruised, thinking of his young brother who had been trapped in Moscow, Sasha turned away to mount his horse. "I came here in the expectation of bowing to superior technical knowledge. It is a great pity your arrogance has forced us to take so long to reach that point, Captain Anderson." He swung into the saddle and sat looking at his opponent. "I will order a rota of guards for your train, who will stand duty all night. They will do their best to protect your stores, but as you have just stipulated, anything to do with the railway is your responsibility, so if you do not trust my 'armed peasants' you have no alternative but to stay awake all night and keep your eye on them."

He turned the horse and rode it at a walk across the track and through the trees toward the lake. Tilting his head back to look up at the great pines that had stood for as long as Russia had existed, Sasha prayed to that God the *Bolsheviki* had banished from the lives of his people. The fight promised to be long. Surely He would not let it be lost!

Paul did stay awake all night. Although he shared guard duty with Corporal Banks, he found himself unable to sleep even when relieved of his post. It was easy to blame the Russian summer night that hardly darkened from day, but he knew inside that it was the encounter with the Colonel that was to blame.

The pride and pleasure he had felt at being given the command of this project seemed tawdry now. He thought of his arrival at the siding, his delight in the beauty and peace of his surroundings, the feeling of escape from the mud and horror of France. His body grew hot as he recalled how he had been serenely eating his dinner in the pine-scented stillness when a figure had broken from the trees on a horse—a *horse* in the midst of a dense coniferous forest—and had proceeded to hug and kiss him in full view of his men. Acute embarrassment had led to shock when he had discovered the new arrival was of higher rank. In the Russian Army a lieutenant colonel was only one rank higher than a captain, but still Paul felt cheated by his own superiors, completely let down. This coveted command looked as if it were slipping through his fingers to a Tsarist aristocrat, of all people. He had been led to expect a small company of Russian infantry led by an inexperienced junior.

Swarovsky's attitude had not helped. There had been too much damned Slavic melodrama about his patriotism and devotion to duty. How would his countrymen have fared in France if Paul had babbled on about "the sons of England" and "men from fields and villages who offered their lives to free their country from madmen" instead of getting down to the job of fighting? Dammit, the Russian had been on the verge of tears when talking about the ruffians he had brought with him. It seemed a little overdone, when one considered the facts. If trained regular troops could drop everything in the middle of a war and go home, just on the promise of getting a share of the nobles' wealth and land, what hope was there that ignorant villagers, given a rifle and food, would not instantly do the same? This time they were being asked to fight other Russians!

However, the feeling that he had handled the confrontation badly stuck in his throat all night. His point had been made at the expense of appearing arrogant and unfeeling. The Russian had gone off like a martyred nobleman. No doubt he had suffered but, by God, had he been gassed, buried beneath mud, machine-gunned from above? Had he? Sure, it must have been terrible to find his own men bayonetting officers and tearing off their badges of rank, spitting in his face. But surely there was something wrong with an army whose officers could not hold the allegiance and respect of their men?

By morning all his wakeful hours had not made the problem any easier, and Paul washed and shaved at his canvas washstand more intent on his next meeting with Colonel Swarovsky than on the smell of bacon frying or the beauty surrounding him. After breakfast he went back into his tent to don his uniform jacket, but first he strapped around his waist a money-belt, hiding it beneath his shirt. There was a large sum for which he was responsible, and he was determined not to let it out of his sight now. It was allocated for the purchase of supplementary supplies from the local settlers or to hire extra labour when needed. He had yet to visit the settlement on the far side of the lake and did not hold out much hope of co-operation from the inhabitants of such a primitive place.

Buttoning his jacket and taking up the gun-belt, he pushed open the tent flaps and went out to where the ten Russians who had taken last watch of the guard were lolling about the platform. They looked a villainous bunch, most with dark blank eyes and thick beards, dressed in high boots, khaki trousers, and overshirts held in by hefty leather belts. Their headgear did not conform to a pattern, being so shapeless as to take on any style to which the wearer pulled it. Any one of them looked capable of selling his mother to the highest bidder, and Paul did not trust them to a man.

Waving his arm in the direction of the lake, he said loudly, "Duty over. Go back to your comrades."

The use of the word comrade, which they would surely understand, together with expressive movements of his arm, should have told them what he wanted, but they merely looked with interest at the trees, as if expecting their friends to appear from them.

"Damned idiots," swore Paul under his breath, and he called the Russian engine-driver over. "Yagutov, tell them to join the rest of their company, will you? And make sure they do it right away."

Yagutov grinned and shouted in Russian, shaking his fist as he did so. They moved quickly enough then. Paul asked what he had said, but the man just grinned wider. "'Tis secrets," he said in thick accents. "The Captain is pleased?"

"Yes . . . So long as you didn't tell them I'd shoot any man who disobeyed," said Paul absently.

Yagutov's face fell. "How that you guess?"

"Eh . . . *what?*" cried Paul. "You told them *that*? A fine way to instil their trust in me!"

The Russian spread his hands. "Trust? Who trust anyone these day? Better they afraid of gun. You safers."

Paul gave up and turned to his own two men. "I'm going down to the lake, Corporal Banks. You're to guard that truck until I get back. With the Russians all down there with me, it should be safe enough."

The Corporal was a man well into his thirties, a soldier of long years and experience who knew how to obey orders.

"Yes, sir. There's none of 'em will get past me."

Paul smiled. "Good man. But Stevens can back you up. He can be stationed inside my tent, and at the first sign of suspicious movement, he'll fire three shots. I'll be back double quick." He turned to his batman. "That clear, Stevens?"

"Yessir."

Paul laughed. "Don't look so worried, man. I am only taking precautions. They are on our side, you know."

"Well, you wouldn't rightly be sure to look at them, Captain Anderson. I never seen a more bloodthirsty lot than them that was here all night."

"Ah . . . not all of them, Sapper Stevens," put in Corporal Banks with a straight face. "Some of them can be quite affectionate. Isn't that so, sir?"

Acknowledging the sly dig with a rueful grin, Paul retaliated with, "I just hope you don't find yourself on the receiving end one day, or you might be hugged to death."

"True enough, sir," said the short, slightly built N.C.O. with a return grin. "I wouldn't mind one of their buxom peasant girls, but another man . . . No, sir, that'd be too much like a sandwich that was all bread and butter."

Satisfied that his train was safe enough, Paul set off with Yagutov for the lake, and Colonel Swarovsky. It was important that the work begin right away, and he strode through the trees telling himself that personal feelings must be put aside. The railway was of first importance; it must remain that way.

The railway and everything else were forgotten when he broke through the trees and the first sight that met his eyes, a short distance past the troop bivouac, was a slender figure in a long dark skirt and pale blouse in the act of hanging over a branch something that looked like a petticoat and other items of female underwear. Angry colour suffused his face. By God, surely Swarovsky had not brought camp followers on this project!

Swinging round to Yagutov, Paul told him to ask the nearest soldier where he would find the Colonel. Words were exchanged, and the engine-driver explained that His Excellency was on the far side of the lake catching fish for his breakfast. That information angered Paul even further. Did he think he was on a bloody camping holiday?

"Who is that woman?" he demanded hotly, pointing to the spot where he had seen her. The clothes were blowing in the breeze as if to mock him, but the woman had gone.

The information came. "His Excellency's sister."

"His . . . *sister!*" Paul was taken aback, but no less angry. What had possessed the man to bring his family with him? Was he on a military mission or a family fishing-trip? With Swarovsky on the other side of the lake somewhere, Paul determined to find out what was going on and began making his way through a straggled bivouac that ruined the beauty of the previous day. Yagutov wisely remained with the soldiers.

The improvised washing line was a little distance beyond and apart from the troops. He could see someone moving about in a large khaki tent pitched at the edge of the tree line and bore down on the unsuspecting victim of his wrath. She was in the midst of putting pins in her hair, apparently so engrossed in the task that the sound of his footfall on the pine needles did not disturb her. It gave him time to register the scene quite clearly, and what he saw left him flabbergasted. The interior of the tent was like something out of the *Arabian Nights*. Camp beds were covered with beautiful soft rugs of Turkish-style design, two polished wood chests served as dressing tables and bore silver-backed brushes, cut-glass perfume bottles, and jewel cases of fine tooled leather. The ground was partially covered with Afghan rugs, clothes hung from a cord strung across the tent, and the girl was engaged in dressing her hair with the help of a gold-framed mirror of eighteenth-century French design.

"Good morning," Paul said thickly, his anger swamped by a daze of disbelief, and she spun round in surprise, the swathe of hair falling loose past her shoulders as her hands lowered. Large grey-green eyes looked at him with no hint of embarrassment.

But he was acutely embarrassed. The girl was no more than twenty-one and strikingly lovely. She was also looking at him with the air of a lady about to interview a servant. He felt the back of his neck grow warm, and the warmth creep round to his face.

"I came to talk to your brother," he said awkwardly, feeling large and clumsy standing in the doorway of that luxurious tent. "I am in charge of the railway. The Colonel is going to work with me on the project." He cleared his throat to cover the uncomfortable silence. "My name is Anderson. Perhaps your brother mentioned me last night."

Brightness lit her eyes. "Ah yes, Captain Anderson. Sasha spoke of you at *great* length."

Paul grew hotter, and aggression returned to bolster him up. "No doubt. There is a great deal of work to be done, but I find your brother has gone *fishing*. I suppose he does intend to return before supper."

The sarcasm was evident, but she studied him with composure before she replied, "We are not a comfortable army, sir. It is impossible to bring supply waggons through such terrain. What we eat we catch for ourselves. My . . . brother is getting our breakfast."

Supremely conscious of beribboned petticoats fluttering from a nearby branch to his left, Paul grew more awkward. "I have been given supplies to cover your needs. There is plenty, and more will come down the line with passing trains." Feeling he should make his authority felt, he said with what he hoped was official sternness, "Of course, there is no provision for women. I mean . . . this is a *military* operation. What made Colonel Swarovsky expose his sister to such a life?"

"I am a trained nurse, Captain. An army has much need of such a person."

His glance travelled over the opulent interior of the service tent and finally over her dainty figure. His pulse beat increased. "Soldiers usually need more than ointment and a smile, you know. I hardly think . . . "

"You do not approve of my brother, I understand," she remarked, cutting into his protest.

He stiffened. "Perhaps I don't understand the Russian way of doing things, but I am here on a vitally important job which should have been started by now."

A slight smile touched her mouth, making her lovelier than ever, he thought. "Sasha said you were highly efficient . . . and more than a little truculent."

That the man should have discussed him so freely with this dainty young creature who appeared to be playing a game of Oriental camping sent a flash of temper to sharpen Paul's tongue.

"Miss Swarovsky, I . . . "

"Swarovskaya," she corrected gently. "A woman takes the feminine version of her name in Russia."

Thrown off his stride, he went on with rough impatience, "Whatever reason your brother has for bringing you here with his ramshackle army, I have to say I will be obliged if you will remain down here out of the way. There is a great deal of work to be done—some of it highly dangerous—and I cannot be responsible for your safety."

Her eyes widened provokingly. "But my brother will take full responsibility for me, Captain Anderson. Should you or any of your men be hurt doing this highly dangerous work, it might be that you will need my services."

The scent of pine needles beneath the shade of overhead branches, added to the sweet perfume that wafted to him every time she moved, was affecting his wits. Now, the suggestion of her hands touching his body with healing ministrations did something drastic to his system. Full of the fascination of pale shimmering hair, a mouth beautifully curved into a shape he found irresistibly exciting, and eyes so clear and expressive they turned a classic face into one of provocative beauty, he struggled to hold his own.

"I don't think that will be necessary, Miss Swarovskaya," he said huskily. "I have medical supplies and enough knowledge to cope with minor injuries."

She moved nearer, which was fatal. "And if there are major injuries, Captain?"

"I . . . They will be sent down the line to the base hospital," he said in the manner of a drowning man.

The moment was broken by the arrival of another woman, holding a bundle of wet cambric adorned with pink ribbons. The newcomer's flow of Russian was halted when she saw him. Completely bewildered, he took in the compelling quality of brown hair drawn up to reveal a face mobile with passions as yet unexpressed, darkest blue eyes, and a tall voluptuous figure in a dark skirt and pale blouse. It was instantly clear that this had been the woman he had seen hanging out the washing.

He turned swiftly to Swarovsky's sister for an explanation, but she was smiling at the newcomer. "Captain Anderson of the British Army has called to introduce himself." She smiled at Paul. "May I present you to Olga Ivanovna, Colonel Swarovsky's sister."

Another sister! The whole operation was turning into a Viennese operetta—something that had become out of control! The two girls were exchanging words in Russian and smiling in his direction. Then, the dark-haired one held out her hand.

"How do you do, Captain Anderson. My brother told us about you last night."

"Did he?" It sounded hollow and faraway.

"I'm afraid you have been under a misapprehension," she continued in her throaty accent. "You have been speaking with Irina Karlovna, my brother's *wife*."

The pines seemed to crowd in on him. The combined perfumes of the women made his head start to spin. He felt as if he were standing naked before them and there was nothing on hand with which to cover himself.

"You said you were his sister," he accused hoarsely.

The lovely eyes were full of amusement. "No, Captain, *you* said I was Sasha's sister."

"But . . . you let me believe . . . " He almost choked. "Why did you let me go on with . . . ?"

She struck a pose with feet astride and lowered her voice in mimicry. "*I am in charge of this railway project, and there is a great deal of work to be done.*" Her sweet laughter could no longer be suppressed. "You were so very *serious* and *earnest*, and so angry because Sasha was catching fish instead of looking at your railway track."

The blood began to drum in his ears. They thought him a figure of fun, a huge joke. Colour flooded his face.

"So it was all lies. It is *she* who thinks to heal the wounds of an army." His voice was lashing and bitter as he pointed to Swarovsky's sister.

"No, Captain," said Olga Ivanovna. "I help, but have had no training. Irina Karlovna worked throughout the war in front line hospitals. Even under enemy fire she was there. There is nothing she does not know about nursing an army."

He looked back into the grey-green eyes, now shining with innocent delight at the success of her joke, and knew in a flash that she had the power to hurt him beyond reason. She had just ridiculed him, taken away his dignity . . . and yet he would have no peace of mind from now on.

The two women stood laughing, arms lightly around each other's waists, and he could take no more. Turning on his heel he walked out into the sunshine washing the shoreline, hearing their laughter even when well out of earshot. He saw no one, heard nothing except her voice. "You were so *serious* and so *earnest*." All he wanted was to get on his train and put himself as far distant from this place as possible. The work he had to do would take several months to complete and had to be finished before the arctic snows crept southward. Somehow he must build his bridges and remain immune, but plunging into the forest on the way back to the siding, he knew it would be impossible. *Damn the Russians to hell!*

T w o

It was late in the evening when Sasha returned. He brought with him a supply of tinned food, two bottles of brandy, and a collapsible wash-stand for use in the field.

"From our reluctant ally," was his brief comment. "His English sense of chivalry demanded that he surrender some of his comforts, along with his tasteless tinned meat, to the ladies. It was all done with tight lips and an air of disapproval which nevertheless managed to suggest he was issuing an order not to be disobeyed."

"Is he a bachelor, Sasha?" asked Irina, opening the box containing tinned food.

"We did not discuss his private life, but I imagine there is no room in it for anything but railways. We went right up the line to the next siding, and he hardly paused to draw breath as he pointed out all that had to be done." Sasha sank down heavily into a folding chair beside his sister, but it was to Irina that he addressed his remarks. "There are some faults, I admit, but I think it is not necessary to make it the best railway in the world."

She looked up from her task. "He probably cannot do it any other way, if there is no room in his life for anything else."

Sasha just grunted and took a cigar from his box. Losing interest in the gift of food, Irina studied her husband as he lit the cigar and took the first few contented pulls at it. He looked older than his thirty-four years and bore the strain of past and present horrors. Somewhere behind those blue eyes and sharp features was the man who had captivated her in that hospital ward, but she had not seen him for some while. Time had dulled the hurt, the sense of having lost before she had won—time, and the knowledge that countless women all over the world were facing the same problem. War took men away, whirled them all into a vortex of horror and pain, then threw them out again to live as best they could.

At best, it broke their lives; at worst, it broke their minds and bodies. The women who had known them before tried to understand and accept. Not many succeeded. Irina was lucky. Unlike the majority of women of her class, she had also gone to war. From the age of seventeen she had lived a life dominated by men, not in the sense of domestic subservience to the male members of the family, but in that those years were spent nursing soldiers. Apart from her sister nurses, only men surrounded her, in their thousands—men of all kinds and ages, from all walks of life, but sharing one thing in common: pain.

If she had not begged and pleaded, then finally defied her father to do what every instinct dictated she should do, Irina would have led the spoiled, pampered life her sisters had experienced. She had lived half their normal lifetime in those four years. Now, at almost twenty-two, there was little she did not know or understand about men. Apart from a day-to-day familiarity with their naked bodies, she had a deep knowledge of their naked souls.

A man will reveal to a nurse things no other woman would ever hear from him. He will trust her implicitly, adore her, regard her with reverence, cling to her like a child. He will swear at her in his agony; sob his thanks when it is relieved at her hands. All this Irina discovered and her compassion was all the greater because of it, but those years had robbed her of the bubbling champagne moments of youth—the time of nosegays and blushes, ardent billets-doux, ballrooms, troika races across the snow, hesitant trembling kisses. She had never been young.

There seemed no chance of it yet. The war had turned into one against her own people. It was tragic, destructive, agonising, but she knew why it was happening. Sasha did not. He was a fine man, brave, loyal to a fault, full of all that made Russia great—but he was blinded by his own beliefs. Because of that she had lost him. Sasha held that the British captain had no room in his life for anything but railways, but *he* certainly had no room for anything but Imperial Russia.

They rarely quarrelled; he protected her with his life. But Russia was now his mistress and Irina could well have been his sister, as she had pretended that morning.

Returning from her thoughts, she found him looking at her curiously.

"Where were you then, Irusha? So many miles away, it seemed."

She smiled, shaking her head slightly. "No, I was just thinking that the efficient Captain Anderson so far forgot himself as to send us tins, but no tin-opener. Still, there are other ways of opening tins."

He seemed to accept the lie. Holding up a tin, he said, "I suppose I must resign myself to this unpalatable mixture. *Gospodi*, the British soldier eats most unwisely!"

"The Russian soldier eats only *kasha*," put in Olga with sudden intensity. "He would consider this a feast."

Sasha sobered immediately. "He would not know what to do with it. His belly is used to simple fare."

"Not any longer. The soldiers in Moscow are eating their fill from the cellars of rich nobles—from *our* cellars, Sasha. They will never be content to go back to *kasha*."

"They have no idea what they are doing," was the passionate answer. "Their heads have been filled with ideas of greed and disloyalty. It needs only the destruction of the Bolshevik madmen to bring them back to their senses. They cannot be blamed."

"No?" flashed Olga. "Can they not be blamed for murdering the Tsar, the Tsarevich, and the Grand Duchesses? The Tsarina was German and deserved to die—an enemy of Russia and puppet of Rasputin the Devil. But not those sweet girls, and a little boy in delicate health." She got to her feet in anger. "Do you say those murdering soldiers cannot be blamed? Do you truly believe that all it needs is a word from people like you for them to abandon all they think they have gained and go back to serfdom?"

Her brother looked at her sadly. "You speak with such heat of things you do not understand. Serfs were freed many years ago, *sestrushka*. What can you know of social and political matters when you spent your time nursing our dear mother until she died?"

Olga rounded on him. "Those wasted years! Tied to an invalid when you and Valodya and Ekaterina were free." Sasha made a move, but she was in full spate. "Yes, wasted years of my life. But I read, I listened to the servants, I watched from my prison window . . . and I saw the truth." She pointed across the lake. "It is there, out in the open, but you will not see it. You live in a dream, Sasha, a dream that is broken and turned into a nightmare. They will not be content with the Imperial family. They will not rest until they have killed everyone who represents what they were . . . and that includes us. When are you going to accept it?"

Irina got to her feet, knowing she must intervene, but her husband remained where he was. The lines of strain on his face had deepened.

"I trust you will never say such things within the hearing of those men out there, foolish girl. They are willing to give their lives for you in this fight for our cause."

Olga dropped as if exhausted. "The cause . . . always the *cause*!"

"Nothing will be helped if you two are always seen to be quarrelling," put in Irina quietly. "Since we are here to assist with the building of a railway, let us do it for Russia. Surely that is cause enough? Whatever his faults, Captain Anderson has left his homeland for our sakes. Shall we let a foreign ally do what we are too pugnacious to achieve?"

Sasha scowled. "He did not leave his homeland for our sakes. We may all kill each other with his blessing."

Irina was profoundly shaken. "He said this to you?"

"With some force. He is governed by professional self-interest and the determination to force his command on us. I think I have never come upon such an insufferable whelp."

She pondered that for a moment, then asked thoughtfully, "Is it merely his youth that you hold against him? Professional efficiency and the powers of command are traits you normally praise. Would you accept him more readily if he were your own age?"

He seemed irritated by her argument. "Age does not come into it."

"But if it were Valodya in his place, holding such responsibility in a foreign country, would you not then say he was a young man of skill and ability?" Irina asked.

"You are suggesting I overlook his pompous aggression?" asked Sasha angrily.

"No, Sasha, that would serve no useful purpose. To try to understand it might be better. He is a young man who has experienced more than his years can accept. Some go mad; others lock themselves away inside. I think that is what he has done."

"There is one thing you have not mentioned, *sestritsa*," said Olga, using the nursing title derisively. "All the experience you say is locked away inside him does not include knowledge of women. If petticoats hanging over a tree and two girls teasing him send him off covered in blushes, there is a lot he has yet to learn in that direction."

Sasha laughed sourly. "Do you plan to teach him, Olga? A hard lesson might do him good . . . and keep him off my hands."

"No," said Irina quickly. "I think that would be very foolish at this particular time."

Olga's blue eyes blazed as she looked the other girl over. "I am not the nurse. Perhaps my duties on this project are to provide something you cannot with your bandages and soothing words. Let us see how arrogant he is when faced with something he has *not* experienced."

Irina slipped away after supper and made her way through the forest to the siding. She had meant to go, anyway, but now she felt it was necessary before any more time passed. As she walked, her skirt trailing in the pine needles, Olga's words echoed in her mind. Oh, yes, Irina had certainly seen that the young captain was unused to female company, but she had seen more than that. Only when it was too late, only when he was turning away had she seen how much they had hurt him with their lighthearted laughter. Then, she would gladly have wiped away those minutes and begun again.

Since morning she had felt disturbed and uneasy over what she had innocently done. It was one thing to deflate a thick-skinned puffed-up egotist; quite another to ridicule a sensitive and highly vulnerable man. The thought she had given to what Sasha had told them about his first meeting with the English officer, and what she had seen for herself, told her an all-too-familiar truth. She had met men like him by the hundreds during her years at the military hospitals, and her heart had gone out to them.

This time she had acted without thought. Sasha had given her a picture of such an objectionable character that when he had appeared so unexpectedly that morning, full of bravado and calling Sasha her brother, the impish streak within Irina had led to the deception. How could she have known . . . but she should have, she told herself yet again. Had her experience taught her nothing?

Four years of war must have meant he was just a boy from school when he went off to fight. Four years of living with men. No time for flirtations or emotions that cracked the heart but soon mended it again. On reflection, the same was true of herself, but the Englishman had lived four years with his own sex; she had done the reverse. Whereas he was unsophisticated about women, she understood men too well for her peace of mind.

At some point during the day she had decided to approach their young ally, and his gifts had given her the perfect opportunity. Olga's words had made her mission more vital. Uncertain whether the girl had been serious or not, Irina had been alarmed. At twenty-four, Olga was now free after being tied to her invalid mother throughout her dream-youth years, but the young men who should have been pursuing her were all taken by the revolution. She was a deep and devious personality, with a passionate nature. If she really did intend to experiment with emotions—hers and the inexperienced young officer's—she had chosen the wrong time and place. If there had been another Russian, rather than an English, officer with them who knew exactly how to keep things under control, Irina would have given Olga her blessing. But a foreigner with no defences was a dangerous target for that kind of experimental dart.

As she broke through the trees, her approach caught the attention of a slight, short-statured man in British uniform who was standing on top of stacked lengths of rail on a flat-car attached to the train. She heard his low warning.

"Lady approaching, sir."

The subject of her thoughts was bending over some papers at his table, apparently deep in concentration, but his head came up quickly and he rose, almost falling over the chair when he saw her.

He came across quickly, meeting her at the edge of the track. The look was still there in his dark brown eyes, although the whole of the day had passed since he had walked away so abruptly from her tent. He would need careful handling, and she was almost afraid to begin.

"Good evening, Captain Anderson."

He barred her way, a tall, broad-shouldered man in khaki shirt and breeches, and high, polished boots.

"I believe I asked that you and your sister-in-law stay down by the lake," he said jerkily.

"I came to thank you for the supplies. It was most thoughtful of you."

"I believe I mentioned that I had been given enough for those I was to meet."

"But we were not expected and did not deserve any."

He swallowed. "Your husband said all that was necessary."

She tested him with a smile. "I'm glad he did."

The test was a failure, so she sidestepped him and walked across to the train, feeling he would not go to the extreme of physically removing her from the vicinity. When he caught up with her she was not so sure.

"Madame Swarovskaya, I really must . . ."

"No, please," she said softly, "since we are to spend some time here, you cannot go on calling me so. Irina Karlovna is quite correct and formal enough to satisfy your English good manners."

Having halted him in his tracks, she seized the opportunity to peer into the truck. The floor was strewn with straw, but there was little open space. Boxes were piled high at both ends, several small barrels stood beside them, and there was a long wooden crate containing all manner of labouring tools. But her gaze moved back to the crates and small barrels that had printed on their sides: HIGHLY DANGEROUS—KEEP AWAY FROM NAKED FLAME.

She swung round to face him. "You have a great deal of explosive material here."

"Yes. I told you a lot of the work would be highly dangerous. That's why I . . ."

"I had not realised. You see, I do not know much about building a railway." Leaning back against the rough wood of the truck, she ventured into unknown territory. "Your army must think very highly of you to entrust such a project to your sole command, Captain Anderson."

There came again the slow flush that touched her all the more because his face was not the smooth, cherubic one of adolescence. The faint colour crept over square features that had been untouched by laughter for too long, across a brow and cheeks with a scattering of freckles, and over a chin that showed a faint bluish shadow. With a small shock she realised he was definitely not an insufferable whelp. Now that she saw him away from the dimness of her tent, in casual dress, without the cap that had hidden his dark curly hair, it was evident he was an extremely attractive man in the most physical sense. Her unease about emotional games increased. Out in a forest clearing where one's senses were heightened by the pine fragrance and clear air, and where it was difficult to sleep during nights as bright as day, such games could bring unexpected results.

The flush was already receding as he said, "You must excuse me. I am very busy."

He was stiff, unfriendly, on the defensive. It was plain he thought her compliment false, a further attempt at ridicule. More than ever she felt it imperative to win him over. She knew the signs. He was hurt and was hitting back.

"Sasha says there is a great deal to be done," she said, strolling past him. They drew level with the folding table, and she stopped to study the books and papers on it. Columns of figures, diagrams, and tiny sketch-maps showed what he had been working on, and she was genuinely interested.

"So much work! What does it all mean?" she asked, bending to look closer.

"It is not something that can be explained in two minutes."

"But it is all so neat and careful. How does one ever understand such things?" Tilting her head sideways and upward to look at him, she knew with dismay her visit had done no good. It was written as plainly as possible in his expression that he believed her to be gushing like an empty-headed schoolgirl who had been dared by her silly friends to lead him a merry dance. But he was not to be bitten twice.

"I have to get this finished tonight, ready for an early start in the morning," he told her with a muscle moving in his throat. "Goodnight, Miss . . . Madame Swarovskaya."

"Irina Karlovna," she reminded him, knowing it was pointless to remain any longer. "I did not mean to detain you, Captain." Looking across the clearing, she said in a tone she hoped he would not ignore. "Will you assist me to the edge of the trees?"

He went, albeit unwillingly, and she obliged him to steady her as she crossed two lengths of track she had managed without difficulty before. But he remained stiff and silent until he stopped at the edge of the pines.

"From now on I trust you will heed my request that you should stay out of the way by the lake."

Something about his lingering expression made her try one last shot. "I really came to apologise for my behaviour this morning. Please forgive me. Our future is so uncertain and there is so little laughter in our lives, we tend to play silly jokes. But our laughter should never be at the expense of someone we hope will be our friend."

The temptation to turn back had to be resisted, but she would have given anything to know what effect her last words had had on him.

For four days, everything went smoothly, after an initial tussle or two between the two officers. Paul adamantly refused to let the two women anywhere near the train or the site where they would be working.

During that first day, Paul had gone to the settlement with Yagutov as interpreter to see what he could buy in the way of fresh food from them and to sound them out about possible labouring help with the cutting of trees for sleepers. Paul, and those who had sent him there, did not know the first thing about the hardy folk who endured life in the arctic coniferous forests. There was virtually no soil in which to grow crops of vegetables, except along the riverbanks during the brief summer season. There was no question of there being any surplus for sale. With no pasture to graze animals, they lived by trapping the creatures of the forest and lakes and were extremely hostile because the soldiers had been firing guns and frightening the animals off. It was always the same with soldiers, they said, and the *starosta*—the headman of the settlement— shook his fist at Paul. They would get no help from his people, he vowed. They had no use for money and were being robbed of their food by the nobleman and his *rota* of troops.

Paul, addressed as "the nobleman" because officers in Russia mostly were of that class, decided to withdraw before they grew nasty, and he wondered what he was going to do with the money he had strapped around his waist beneath his shirt. It was a hell of a useless commodity in this part of the world, it appeared.

Paul knew his job when it came to the work in hand, and he began where the work was most urgently needed. There was a curve on a slight incline where the track had been insufficiently banked, with the conse- quence that trains tended to tilt dangerously toward the outer curve when travelling at comparatively slow speeds. Heavily or awkwardly laden trucks were at great risk when drivers attempting to make up speed after a series of difficult bends came upon the hazard too quickly to take precautionary action.

Paul was in touch by telegraph with the chief engineers at Murmansk and Lake Onega, who informed all those working on the railway when trains were being sent through. With that information, Paul was able to plan his work shifts, which, with practically no hours of darkness, meant he could go non-stop until the imminence of a passing train meant they must return to the siding.

The through trains all stopped to take on water and logs, the southbound ones dropping off supplies to those isolated parties working along the line. It was from these visits that news of the war reached them. The Russians crowded round the men on the trains, excited, voluble, jostling each other for room as they heard of the successful advances of the White armies under General Denikin. They cheered, hugged each other, sobbed openly. But Paul was too busy checking the off-loading of stores, studying his manuals, or taking a well-earned rest to show any interest in war bulletins.

He was beginning to revive from the disaster of that first day and enjoy the sensation and satisfaction of following his profession out of reach of gunfire. There were no whistling shells overhead, no chattering machine-guns from aircraft, no strident blasts on whistles warning of gas attacks. There was no mud, no smell of rotting corpses, no rancid meat stewed between bayonet attacks. He ate well, concentrated on the job in hand, drove himself mentally and physically to ensure that he slept, and all around was the silent, peaceful forest.

There was also Irina Karlovna. Paul said the name over and over in his mind during those occasional times when he was unoccupied. He remembered the softly accented way she pronounced his name. He remembered the white blouse with a high frilled collar and how the softness of the material had emphasised that lovely blonde fragility of expression. He remembered looking up and seeing her stepping across the rails with a grace that was arresting in such surroundings. He remembered how she had put out her hand for his supporting one as she pretended to find the return crossing difficult to negotiate. He remembered those beautiful eyes as she had apologised and spoken of friendship. He remembered . . . oh, hell, he remembered too much for his own good!

His order that the two women should stay at the lakeside, although bitterly contested by Swarovsky, had ensured that he had not seen her again, and the absorption of his work kept him from thinking about her too much. But he knew what had happened to him and was violently jealous of the man who claimed her as his wife. It did not help the general situation, but Paul took particular delight in every point he scored over the Russian.

Each time his train was on the move, Paul would sit in the open doorway of the truck, leaning on one upbent knee, and gaze at the passing scene that never failed to fascinate him. Where some men found the everlasting forest monotonous, Paul gloried in the vast silence and peace and clarity. It entered his soul and began to chase away the trench horror he had lived with so long. He dreamed; he imagined this place in winter, the ground covered in white, the pines standing proudly still, unbowed by the snow trimming, the lakes frozen into shimmering mirrors. He dreamed of the great creatures of the forest, deer, bear, wolves, and of men in furs, their beards glistening with frost. He imagined this same railway stretching across the land, sturdy and everlasting, and trains puffing through the icy stillness, pushing the snow aside with their pointed snow-ploughs, going where man with beast could not and linking communities separated by winter.

The thought stirred him. Come December, when arctic night lasted twenty-two of the twenty-four hours, great iron wheels would roll over track he had strengthened and laid, across ice-coated bridges fording frozen rivers—bridges he had built—and along embankments created from his figures and calculations. When polar cold seized this place, his work would ensure that the link remained.

Once, his Russian companion had broken into his reverie by asking, "You find it beautiful?"

"Yes."

"It is Russia in only one of her guises. If you could also see her others, you would understand why we fight to save her."

Paul had said nothing. War did not come into his dreams of this place.

The work progressed. After initial difficulties and attempts at shirking by the Russians, they accepted the routine of shifts, so that work could go on right round the clock whilst there were no trains on the line. Paul designed the shifts so that the men did equal stints at heavy and lighter tasks and had adequate rest periods. But the peasants were obstinate men and caused immediate trouble when told they were to drink no alcohol whilst working. Paul had a heated session with his counterpart trying to get across to the soldiers that there was plenty of water in the barrels if they were thirsty and that the beer sent down the line by courtesy of the Murmansk garrison was purely for their off-duty hours.

Colonel Swarovsky had tightened his lips and barked a tirade at the committee of grumblers, ending by slapping a couple around the face and pushing them bodily toward their fellows. Paul had watched open-mouthed. Striking a subordinate was a court-martial offence in his army. But the matter appeared settled, so he went uneasily to his own tasks. These peasants with whom he could not communicate except through Swarovsky were an incomprehensible lot. How long would they stand for such treatment before revolting?

But Paul did not attempt to interfere. The railway was his command; he had ceded Swarovsky the right to administer the soldiers in his own fashion. But Corporal Banks had also noticed the severe discipline meted out to the Russians and commented on it to his own officer. A sociable little man, Banks had integrated with the Russians very quickly, even picking up some of their phrases.

"Come in useful, they will, sir," he told Paul with a smile. "It was bad enough not knowing half the time what the Frogs were saying, and this lot I trust even less. If they start whispering together, it'll be as well if one of us knows what's being said—besides Yagutov, I mean."

"Yes, I think Yagutov could be a bit of a rogue," said Paul.

"Oh, I don't know, sir. He seems a decent enough chap. What he don't know about engines is nobody's business."

"I agree, but I'm never certain he will pass on the exact meaning of my messages," Paul had told him with a grin. "I suppose I should learn some Russian myself . . . but I'm not keen to ask the Colonel to teach me."

"Perhaps one of the ladies, sir."

It was said innocently enough, but Paul felt it was a subject to be avoided and walked off without another word.

By the fourth day, the job was so well advanced Paul decided to go several miles up the line to have another look at his first big improvement project, knowing it would soon be time to tackle it. When the Russian officer announced his intention of accompanying him, Paul felt it would look churlish to refuse. Since the party was now working well, they left the N.C.O.s in charge and went on the footplate with Yagutov as he took the engine up to the problem spot.

It was an area covered by sharp undulations where the track first swung in a tight left-hand curve, immediately into a longer right-hand one that formed almost three-quarters of a circle, then back into another tight bend to the left before running straight for several miles.

It was at the end of this straight stretch that Yagutov brought the engine to a halt in a cloud of steam to allow the other two to get off. Paul walked ahead, cutting off from the track to climb through the trees over the central area through which he intended driving a cutting. It was immediately dark beneath the pines in a semblance of night that he had almost forgotten after two weeks of Russian "white nights." But he walked across the tangy carpet underfoot with his mind more on the problems than the beauty of the place, for once.

For an hour or more he walked the area, studying the formations and squatting to dig away small areas beneath the trees. Until he ascertained the composition of the rock beneath, he was unsure of the size of the problem, and time was all important. If a cutting was to be made at all it must be done properly and efficiently, but there were other problem spots on the line and all the work had to be finished before winter caught them all up. If he were in an area with roads and easy accessibility, there would be any amount of mechanical equipment he could use. Stranded in the middle of a forest, he realised that his means were limited. But it was a challenge that excited him.

Looking once more at the point where he hoped to link up with the northerly stretch of track, he knew that the slightest mistake would be fatal. Unless he broke through dead on target, it would mean costly delay and a bungled piece of engineering. There was no time or room for error. He caught the Russian looking at him and decided the man was unwillingly impressed. "The whole thing might have to be scrubbed if it looks to be too massive a project," Paul commented.

Swarovsky wore a frown. "You will make this decision yourself, without consulting your superiors?"

"Naturally."

"Then you must be very highly rated, Captain."

Paul shook his head. "Not at all. The man on the spot always has superior knowledge of what can or cannot be done. It is a foolish commander who tells him what he should do from hundreds of miles away."

The Russian began walking back to the engine waiting on the track behind them. Paul followed, smiling to himself.

Yagutov saw them descending the slope and put away his rags. He was forever cleaning his beloved engine, fussing over the iron "baby" with tenderness not even glimpsed in some mothers.

"You finishes?" he asked Paul cheerfully. Patting the side of the engine he added, "I tell her soon she go straight instead so much ins and outs. She smiles, so." He gave a wide smile that stretched his mouth almost from ear to ear.

Paul laughed. "Tell her to wait until it is finished before she smiles, then we'll all smile with her."

"That is funnies," was the reply as Yagutov swung onto the footplate and began unwinding the handbrake, prior to making the short run back to the remainder of the party.

They arrived in the midst of a crisis. Paul thought at first glance that there had been a mutiny, for no work was being done and the men all stood in a large circle over the track. Then, from his elevated position on the footplate, he saw the cause of the trouble. Two men were on the track itself, one holding the other down so that his throat was against the iron rail, and there was nothing playful about the way the aggressor was putting his weight into the attack.

"My God, he'll kill him!" Paul cried, jumping to the ground before they had come to a halt, but his companion was ahead of him, barring his way.

"This is my concern, I think," Swarovsky snapped. "I order you to remain here."

Paul halted, still appalled at the situation that had developed in so short a time. But it was nothing to what he felt a moment later as the tall Russian strode toward the scene, drew his pistol, and fired at the couple on the line. The shot made his nerves jump, and he fully expected to see the soldier on top twitch and fall lifeless. But the aim had been excellent. Shingle flew up as the bullet hit the sleeper nearest the pair and ricochetted harmlessly into the trees.

It did the trick, drastic and dangerous though Paul thought it, and some of the soldiers rushed to drag up the man whose windpipe must be severely bruised if not broken by the rail. But Paul's attention was taken at that point by Corporal Banks, who appeared beside him.

"Christ, I thought he was a goner, sir!"

"Yes," agreed Paul tautly. "How did all this happen? Everything was all right when I left."

"Sorry, sir. It all happened very quickly. There wasn't anything I could do on my own, and it was their quarrel, when all's said and done."

"I'm not suggesting there was anything you could or should have done." Paul's reply was sharp, reflective of his unease over the sudden suggestion of violence in the Russian ranks. "Do you know what caused it?"

"Not exactly . . . Well, I caught a word or two here and there that made me suspicious. From what I could make out, it was revolutionary agitation started it."

"*Revolutionary agitation?* What are you talking about, man?"

Banks's pointed face stayed completely expressionless, as if the whole incident were nothing out of the ordinary. "Time came to change shifts, and one man complained about the food. Some of the cooking isn't very good, sir," he explained. "It seemed to bring on a general air of dissatisfaction, and that Sergeant Gromov gave some of them a bit of a poke with the handle of a pick." The scanty eyebrows rose. "They didn't like it, sir, and rounded on him quite suddenly. Then, they started a real slanging match all round. What were they doing this for, they said. The railway workers had all downed tools for more money, and now they were doing their jobs for them with chance'll-be-a-fine-thing for payment. It wasn't right, they said. They had volunteered to fight because they had been promised life would be better for them and their families, yet all they were doing was labouring on the railway for a bloody foreigner." Banks cleared his throat. "Sorry, sir, but I'm only repeating what they said."

"All right," said Paul irritably. "So how did those two get fighting on the track?"

The Corporal shifted his feet and began to look uncomfortable. "Well, sir, one pipes up and says they'd all be better off with the Reds. Their soldiers were allowed to help themselves to anything they fancied—including women." He swallowed. "Course, this is a bit of a monastic life, I suppose, and they pricked up their ears at that. Down in Moscow, says this agitator, his cousin is living in a noble's house, enjoying the pick of the storeroom and cellar—and the pick of their women. Women like those two back at the lake. The Colonel's wife and sister."

Paul felt himself grow hot. "My God, they didn't . . . ?"

"Oh, no, sir. The ladies are well thought of by the men, and some of them began to lose their spark at that. But Sergeant Gromov went sort of mad, hurling himself at the one who was doing most of the yelling, grabbing him round the throat. Next minute he had him down over that rail. Thank God you came when you did, or I swear he'd be dead by now." Banks let out his breath. "I've never seen anything like it, sir. I mean, if we went on like that, it'd be a right free-for-all. You can't have N.C.O.s choking the life out of any soldier who upsets them."

"No," agreed Paul forcefully.

"Of course, that Sergeant Gromov was with the Colonel in his old regiment and thinks he's next in line to the Almighty, so to speak. I saw some of our chaps go berserk in France, but that was as if they didn't know what they were doing. This one knew, all right. It was cold-blooded murder he had in mind."

The whole incident had left Paul off balance and proved his initial distrust of Swarovsky's men in a way he had not foreseen. He blamed himself for going off and leaving the site.

All he could say was, "You did very well to understand all that, Corporal."

Banks looked embarrassed. "I told you my bit of Russian might come in handy one day, sir."

"You certainly seem to have been an apt pupil." It was said rather vaguely because Paul's attention was caught by the Russian Colonel, who was leading the half-fainting victim toward the trees. The medical kit was in the train. Surely the man needed some kind of attention?

The two figures disappeared, and almost before Paul had begun to walk forward, a shot rang out from inside the forest. Nobody but Paul moved, and shock sent him running like a madman toward the sound, feeling a pressure in his throat similar to that which the rail must have made on that other one.

The Russian officer emerged just as Paul reached the edge of the trees. Paul saw that his face was grey and set as he replaced the pistol in its holster, and a flood of sickness filled his own stomach.

"He never stood a chance. You dragged him in there half-dead." It came out rasping and dreadful as he fought for breath. "My God, it was bloody murder!"

The other looked at him with contempt. "You are in command of the railway, Captain Anderson. That is all. This is my affair."

"But . . . but you just shot him down," he shouted.

"He was a traitor to the cause."

"He should have stood trial."

The Russian's face twisted. "Do you think his people hold trials? They murder by the thousands, including those whose only crime is to be alive and breathing the same air. Get out of my way and go back to your game of trains. You have no idea what this is all about."

Paul was suddenly icy cold and determined. "I know what death is all about, believe me, but I only ever killed those who were trying to kill me.

When my enemy was unarmed, I made him my prisoner." He raked the man with a withering look. "I think I now understand why your soldiers all deserted you. The kind of army you run is like no other I know."

Paul made to pass him but was stopped by an uplifted hand.

"Where are you going?"

"To fetch the body."

"Leave it where it is. The wolves will find it good company."

Paul's feeling of sickness increased. "I intend to give him a Christian burial."

The face twisted again. "He and his Bolshevik masters are no longer Christians. They have renounced God. Didn't you know that? But no, you are contemptuous of our fight against evil, are you not? You wish to have nothing to do with it. Then stay immune . . . *if you can.*"

He walked off, shouted at his men in Russian, and they went back to work.

Three

A volley of shots rang out in the stillness around the lake.

"He told me ammunition was precious and shouldn't be wasted," commented Sasha dryly. "That is the biggest waste of all."

Neither of the women made a reply, just continued to ride beside him around the edge of the lake. The horses needed exercise after their prolonged halt, and since a rest day on the railway had been declared, Sasha had suggested a ride. Irina and Olga had swiftly agreed. They were glad of his company. Time passed slowly at the bivouac with only a few orderlies to wait on them, and a small group of soldiers left behind because of sickness.

But Sasha had another reason for suggesting the ride. He wanted them to forget for a moment why they were there and what was taking place that morning. The whole thing merely made him angry and impatient with the young Englishman, but they were both unhappy over the affair. Olga looked strained and nervous; Irina had a faraway look in her eyes.

When the train had returned to the siding in the early hours of the morning, the tale had had to be told. There was no point in evading it, for the men were talking of nothing else in the excited aftermath. Olga had immediately burst into one of her passionate declarations of imminent death for them all: her fear now had her tense and afraid of her own shadow. Irina, his too-wise young wife, appeared more distressed over the incident itself than the political implications.

They had all argued loud and long. His dark, secret sister who saw drama in everything had walked restlessly up and down vowing they would all be murdered as they slept, by this rabble calling itself an army who, she said, were like corn in the wind, bending in a new direction at the slightest pressure. This was only the beginning. How long did Sasha believe they would be safe? All over Russia people of their class were being murdered, women raped and humiliated. Would he only believe the truth when the gun was at his throat, and herself and Irina spread across the ground naked? Irina had pointed out that it was not only Reds who murdered and raped; that so-called loyalist troops had also committed such atrocities in towns and villages through which they had passed. Russia had gone mad, in her opinion, and it would take a very long time for the madness to abate.

Sasha had been angry with them both and said so. Did they doubt the loyalty of forty men because of one Bolshevik spy? Such men were planted, dispatched everywhere, to rouse up good, loyal people to their evil cause: They spoke of rewards, gave wild promises of sharing the great estates of the nobility equally amongst the workers. Any man with intelligence knew it could not be done. Give one hundred men a field each and by the following day some would have turned their property to better account than the others. Men could never all be equal: it went against human nature. But the peasants were simple folk, and the spies, the agitators, hoped to dazzle them with ideas designed to give their masters power over the whole of Russia. There was no question of *equality* for them—they wanted to rule. He thanked God the traitor had betrayed himself so quickly. An army fought best when united.

Looking back on the quarrel now, Sasha realised Irina had brought calm to the tent, as she usually did. Yet they, too, had ended by quarrelling, and over such a ridiculous issue. That stiff-necked fool of a British officer intended burying the traitor with pomp and ceremony, and Irina was going to attend. To his furious condemnation of her words she had said that although he had been right to shoot the man, it was still a human soul to be commended to his Maker. She would not accept his bitter words about the way the Reds had dismissed God. She saw it as all the more reason for someone to intercede on behalf of a lost soul. Greatly incensed by then, he had forbidden her to attend the funeral. It would be disloyal to him and to those of his men who fully supported the cause against the Reds. For an astounding moment he had believed she meant to defy him, but no more was said on the matter and she had readily accompanied him on the ride that morning.

For several minutes they rode in silence, the horses treading through the lapping water of the shore, until Irina gave a sudden exclamation and slid from her saddle to hurry forward. There was something on the ground among the small smooth rocks that littered the shoreline, and she knelt quickly over it.

"What is it, Irusha?" he called, urging his mount forward. She put up a cautioning arm and spoke softly. "An *utyonok*—a little duck that is caught and held. Shhh!" she said crossly as he arrived beside her. "See, you have frightened it, and it begins to peck."

It was a little brown creature of no more than four inches in length that could have been mistaken for a large pebble or a bunch of weed from the lake, yet she was crouching over it as if it were the most precious thing on earth. He watched as she held it steady with hands that were infinitely gentle, crooning a Russian lullaby under her breath as her fingers unwound from its minute webbed feet the trails of seaweed and slime that prevented it from moving.

A strange guilt beset him. They had been married for three years, although the time they had spent together could be counted in weeks. By now, there should have been a child, perhaps two, if times were normal. It would be fine to have a son. He would have, when Russia was a fit place for Swarovsky children. No man would wish to father sons at such a time as this. But the feeling of culpability increased. Two days for a honeymoon, a week snatched from life and death at the Galacian Front when both were too full of the tragedy to relax. A whole month in the Crimea when both had managed to coax leave from their superiors—a month of blue sea, bodies kissed by the sun and each other's lips, love and youth. But even there he had been cautious . . . and there it had ended. The next time they had met had been at the height of the October Revolution, when he had snatched her and Olga away in a dangerous escape from his home and from the Reds who were closing in. Since then, they had lived the life of gypsies, roaming where it was necessary to go—three together.

He slid from the saddle as she lifted the fluffy duckling free and, cradling it in her hands, took it to the edge of the water to set it down on the gentle eddies. It went off like a swift ball of feathers, tiny feet paddling madly, and he walked softly to stand beside her as she watched the creature go.

Without taking her gaze from the sight she said, "Do you never feel like that duckling, Sasha? Do you never pray for someone to set you free so you can discover a world of sunshine, and water that mirrors everything so that it appears beautiful?"

He could not find the words she needed as an answer and stood numbly with the water washing over his boots as she turned to him. Her eyes were misty, and she looked at him with an appeal that hit him over the heart.

"Do you never consider escape?" she whispered.

The sound of movement behind made him turn in automatic defence, but it was merely Olga trotting away. She was being tactful, but her departure had broken the moment, and Irina was walking back to her horse when he turned back again.

"Irusha!" He started after her, but she did not wait for him. Only when he caught up and began walking beside her did he notice the faraway look had returned to her face. Once able to charm a woman from a strange mood, he now found himself at a loss. It was so long since they had been lovers it seemed almost shocking to speak endearments to her—as if she were one of his sisters. Had he ever held her against him in passion, kissed that sweet mouth, whispered words that put a rose-blush on her cheeks?

Taking him by surprise, desire stirred deep within. It was a sensation he had not so much forgotten, but neglected. During the war that the *Bolsheviki* had prematurely ended as part of their plan for a "free" Russia, he had grown accustomed to suppressing his natural longings—as had most men. This war that was raging between his own people had almost put these longings from his life completely. He was a man of pride and culture, he did not take women with animal zest in any corner of a field, like the peasants. Passion was beautiful, and he was only stirred by it when the conditions surrounding it were the same. Soft lights, a scented boudoir, a woman's body soft and fragrant upon a silken couch, banks of flowers in porcelain jardinieres standing about the room, champagne and caviar.

For a moment his mind went back to Lyudmilla Zapalova, his last mistress, and, inevitably, to those days when he had been a young lieutenant with money in his pocket and gaiety in his heart. He remembered the parties; the vodka; the reckless horseplay with his fellow officers; the magnificent ceremonial of state occasions when Tsar Nicholas had reviewed his loyal troops. Now the visions shattered like glass, and the heaviness returned. All that was gone forever—the Tsar brutally murdered with his family, and the beautiful stately Russia of his youth tattered and torn.

He must have made some sound, because Irina put her hand on his arm and brought them both to a halt.

"Sasha, on such a beautiful day," she admonished, referring to his obvious sadness.

Putting his hand over hers, he shook his head. "*Nichevo, golubchik*. It is nothing."

"But yes," she insisted. "You must forget it. You did right to kill a traitor, but does it matter so much that another man honours his death?"

She had misread his thoughts, but it was better that she had. He had been regretting the loss of an era in which she had played no part in his life.

"He does not understand our ways," he said bluntly.

"Why should he? He is a stranger to Russia and her people. Do you understand him any better? What do you know of England?"

"It is not I who am in his country," he reminded her none too gently. "A visitor should always follow the customs of his host nation."

She gave the calm smile he had seen bestowed on those in the hospital ward around him. "And would Alexander Ivanovich happily eat his friends for dinner if in a cannibal country? No, Sasha, a man must do what his conscience demands, wherever he is. You should know that, for are you not doing so at the risk of your life at this very moment?"

Irritated at her attempt to jolly him out of his mood, he confessed something that had not consciously bothered him until that moment. "Risk . . . what risk? This is not fighting for a cause, this . . . playing with railways! You saw how we worked to train those men to become something near to able soldiers. Now what are they doing?" He threw up his hands in disgust. "Cutting trees, digging, laying railway track! Is it any wonder they grow discontented? I roused them to arms with the promise of a powerful and glorious Russia, with peace for themselves and their families. Do they see it here, helping an Englishman fulfil his dreams?"

She sighed and put a hand up to touch his cheek. "I think they were roused to arms by the promise of food and a rifle of their own, that is all. They are not Swarovskys; do not endow them with virtues their background does not allow them to possess."

"But . . . their country!" he protested.

"Their country—their whole world—consists of the dozen or so *versts* each side of the hovels in which they live," she said patiently. "To them Lenin is a mere name, to rank with the Tsar and God. If they are told he rules Russia, they will accept him as a great and revered man. Sasha, they do not understand why they are doing what they are doing."

Her quiet emphasis irritated him further. "Do you think I have no understanding of men—of the simple men who have been in the service of my family for generations? *Gospodi,* I have commanded them for more than fifteen years."

"I only know you were stunned and heartbroken when they spat on your uniform and left you to face the enemy alone. You did not understand them then. You still do not understand."

It was cruel and unlike her. He stared at the lovely upturned face and saw that she had meant him to be hurt. It was like looking at a stranger.

He turned from her and began leading his horse back the way they had come.

"Sasha . . . *please*." She was there clinging to him, and brightness was shimmering in her eyes. "Don't you see what I am trying to tell you? They were unhappy, ignorant, bewildered men who were desperate enough to follow a star promised to them by a man with a gift for oratory. He gave them hope, an escape from the terrible nightmare they were going through in the trenches. Sasha, I *saw* them, *saw* what they suffered. I am not Olga, who speaks from fear, but a woman who understands that they were driven beyond their endurance. Can you not see that, also? And can you not see that the slightest thing could spark off the same with our men here?"

"*Nyet*," he said sharply. "Not with them. They remained loyal even through the Bolshevik invasion of their villages last year."

"Was it remaining loyal to stand helplessly by while the Red troops took all they had away from them? When you came offering something, they had no hesitation, but if they come face-to-face with the *Bolsheviki* again and are offered more to turn on you and fight on the other side, *they will probably do it*." Her hands gripped his arms tighter. "Don't be blinded by dreams."

Perturbed by her obvious tears, he drew her against him much as a father comforts an overwrought child. "*Izvini*, Irusha. I am sorry. The sun shines, yet I make you cry. Alexander Ivanovich is a villain—indeed, a great villain." Tilting her face upward with his finger, he began wiping away the tears with his handkerchief. "For a moment you were like the duckling caught in the weeds, eh? Caught on a rocky shore and frightened, so you attacked the one who was nearest to you."

She drooped in defeat. "The winter will come all too soon. Can we not build the railway and be happy for a while . . . until the summer passes?"

"When we have won back our beautiful homeland, we shall be happier than you have ever known," he promised, kissing her gently. If he noticed the insistent pressing of her body against his, he thought of it as no more than a seeking of comfort and reassurance.

The funeral had been held to honour a principle, not a man: the rifle volley was more a means of reaching those who had stayed away than an essential part of a military burial.

Swarovsky's brutal justice had offended Paul's every inbred instinct, and when the Russian had followed up the killing with a refusal to inter the man, it was more than Paul could accept. So strongly did he feel, he helped his two men dig the grave beside the track. Used to impromptu burials in France, he recited all the appropriate words and prayers, then, feeling there should be something Russian to send the man on his way to his eventual destination, he walked across to Yagutov for a simple phrase he could repeat at the graveside. The engine-driver, who had been an interested but distant spectator, surprised Paul by offering to sing "*Vechnaya Pamyat*," an old Russian funeral chant.

His rich bass was a moving sound in the stillness of the clearing, and Paul found himself swamped with a longing to see Irina again. The chant was part of her life and background, and its incomprehensibility to him highlighted his own isolation. Only if she spoke in English would he ever understand her, yet she could mingle with her own group and speak in a tongue that made her completely out of his reach.

The recent outrage committed by Swarovsky increased Paul's violent jealousy of him in relation to Irina. How could she be tied to such an insensitive brute? Dammit, she was not much more than a girl, and he was . . . he was . . . *her husband,* came the heavy voice of truth. No, much better not to see her again. Get on with the job, then he could leave and get them all out of his system.

After the formality of conducting the burial, he took off his jacket and tie, rolled up his sleeves, and poured himself a brandy before getting down to the job of writing up his daily reports. By the time he returned to civilisation, the file would be as thick as a book. He supposed someone would put all his files into an even larger file to be stored with every other piece of paper filled in by soldiers in all parts of the globe. That anyone would ever read them he doubted very much, but they had to be written.

For a moment he toyed with the idea of filling the page with an erotic description of adventures with the maidens from the nearby settlement—perish the thought—then decided the effort would be wasted if no one ever read it and dropped his monocle in shock. Still, it might relieve his sense of sexual frustration. Full of such thoughts he rose almost in guilt as a girl on a horse appeared through the trees. But his racing heart slowed painfully. It was not Irina, but Swarovsky's sister.

Remembering how she had laughed along with Irina that day with the fluttering petticoats all around him, he decided to send her packing right away. Luckily, his men and Yagutov were engaged in a game of cards the Russian was teaching and were too absorbed to give more than an initial glance at the girl. He stepped onto the track to forestall her before she was able to walk around his territory, as Irina had.

"Good morning, Captain Anderson."

"Good morning. Is there something you particularly wanted? I am rather busy with an important report," he said pointedly.

Her smile was wide and instantly turned her vivid face into one of sensuality which, combined with the deep blue of her eyes, her softly disarrayed hair, and the white heavy silk blouse with full peasant sleeves, was heady stuff to a man who had just swallowed several brandies rather quickly in the pure arctic air.

"You did not look very busy, Captain. I would have said you were day-dreaming," Her glance lingered on him, travelling from his face down across the open neck of his shirt to his waist. "Do you always wear a gun?"

"Yes," he said tautly, not knowing what to do about her.

"Even when you sleep?"

Was she teasing him again, trying to make him appear *earnest* and *serious*? He felt his colour begin to rise and turned away so that she would not see it. "I have just finished burying one of your countrymen. Now I have some paperwork to do. If you have come to chat, I'm afraid I cannot spare the time."

"I really came so that they could be alone," she said softly. "A sister can be in the way when a man looks at his wife in a certain manner."

Heat truly burned in his face at that. That she should have come with that admission at a time when he had just been tormented by such thoughts!

"They had quarrelled, you know. She wanted to come to your funeral, but he forbade it."

He turned quickly. "She did?"

The girl brought her leg in the long, divided skirt gracefully over the pommel and held out her arms to him. Responding instinctively, he caught her at the waist as she jumped from the saddle to stand close to him with her hands on his shoulders.

"She said it was a human soul, whether it was Red or White. Is that how you view it?"

Hard riding had heated her body so that he felt her warmth against his palms, and there was a beading of perspiration on her forehead and in the hollow of her throat. The curve beneath his hands was firm and exciting; her lips were moist and enough apart to show her teeth gleaming in the sunlight.

"Is it, Captain Anderson?" she asked again, very softly.

Letting her go, he stepped back quickly, but his movement brought her hands off his shoulders in a brushing motion that touched his bare skin in fractional intimate contact.

"Something like that, yes," he said through a tight throat.

She began walking along the side of the track, and he found himself staying beside her. "You don't like my brother, do you?"

Hating Swarovsky with jealous fury at that moment when he had been left alone with his wife, Paul said, "Does it matter how I feel about him?"

"It does if you hope to have any understanding of why he is here working on your railway with you."

"It is not *my* railway," he told her with emphasis. "What I am doing here will be of no future benefit to me or my own country—such is not the case with Colonel Swarovsky."

She ignored the taunt. "He has much to worry him. Our brother and sister were caught in Moscow when the Red armies took control. We do not know if they are alive or were murdered along with hundreds of other aristocrats. Ekaterina was married to a doctor—one of the intelligentsia. Of course, they might have forced him to work for them—God knows they have enough need for healers of the human body—but she would have been arrested because she was a Swarovsky. Either arrested, or forced to clean out public lavatories beneath the mocking gaze of 'workers' who push and insult those who cannot retaliate."

The swing of her conversation had taken him unawares, but he had his wits together enough to say, "The man I buried this morning had no chance to retaliate. We have a saying about the pot calling the kettle black. I'm sorry about your relations, but such treatment seems to be the general rule in Russia."

"The man was a Bolshevik," she flung at him. "My brother Valodya was caught by men like him. Do you know what they did to loyal officers returning from the Front where they had continued to fight until the end of the war? Caught them as they stepped from trucks and trains, tied them together in groups, then threw them into the sea with heavy stones attached to their feet. Mass murder of loyalists!"

Paul had forgotten his surroundings in this argument, which had him as heated and emotional as the girl. "Do you know what some 'loyalists' did to my countrymen? After being fed, clothed, and supplied with arms by Britain, they rose up in the night and murdered the five British officers who had volunteered, after four years of war, to come out here and help an ally who had left them in the lurch. They then went over to the Reds with all the arms and equipment. I am expecting this lot to do the same at any time."

She swung in a flare of skirts to stand in his path. "And I. The man you buried was only the first. We are aristocrats, the noble class they hate. Do you know what they will do to us?"

Halted by her, he said roughly, "You should have thought of that before assembling that ragged gang."

"I did," she cried with passion. "But Sasha believes in them—believes in the return of the old regime. He even sees another tsar at the Imperial Palace when this is all over. What can I—a woman—do with such a man?"

Unable to keep his eyes from the rise and fall of her breast beneath the heavy silk, Paul thought wildly that she could probably do quite a lot with a man.

"What made him bring you on this dangerous venture?"

"He had no choice." With another swirl of skirts, she went across to the stump of a tree that had been felled for engine fuel and sat on it, looking up at him. "He risked his life in coming to Moscow for me. We escaped by night and went to our summer estate, where Irina was already waiting." She put up her head in a proud gesture. "For two days we were safe, then there was news that the Reds were entering the nearby village. Our servants, those who had worked with our family for years, came under cover of darkness and smashed all the windows with stones."

Caught up in the story so dramatically told, Paul moved nearer and stood with one boot on an adjacent tree-stump as he listened. The scent of her skin teased his senses, and the open neck of her blouse revealed the pale skin of her shoulders as she moved her hands expressively.

"Sasha took us to an upstairs room and stood guard at the door. But they were content just to desecrate our house and heritage, raiding the cellars and drunkenly smashing everything in sight." Her eyes grew even darker with the memory of that night. "We heard them come up to our bedrooms, but we were in the attic. They dressed up in our clothes, pulled down the silken bed-curtains, defiled the walls. We saw it all on our way out," she told him with such intensity that he shared her outrage. "It did not take them long to exhaust themselves, and we crept out with as much as we could take on the horses mercifully still in the stables." She drew a deep breath. "Since then we have stayed with Sasha." Her lashes lay thickly against her cheeks as she looked down. "There is nowhere else for us to go."

Caught up in something he had never before encountered, it was a moment or so before he realised she was looking up again and studying him in a manner that set a pulse thudding in his throat. He drew up, taking his foot from the stump.

"I'm sorry. I had no idea. It must have been a terrible experience, as well as one that implanted a permanent hatred against those who mistreated your home and possessions."

She made no move, just continued her deep study of him. "You can't yet be twenty-five, yet you are so full of human understanding! Why do you put on that air of impassive detachment, Captain?"

Before he had time to absorb her words, she was up and touching his arm with a gentle hand. "Life is so short. Why waste it by walking around each other like snarling dogs?"

"I . . . snarling dogs?" he queried in a daze, finding her nearness very disturbing.

"You will return to England when the railway is finished. I know very little about your country and customs; you plainly know no more of mine. Can we not teach each other something during this time?"

With his head full of the possibilities of what she could teach him, he caught himself saying. "Yes . . . yes, I suppose so."

"Then we shall start by introductions. I cannot call you Captain Anderson all the time. What is your other name?"

"Paul."

"Ha, a Russian name!"

He smiled. "If you say so."

A low laugh added to the provocation of her next words. "You really look quite handsome when you smile. You should do it more often."

With another swirl of skirts, she was walking away from him, but he crashed down to earth at her next remark.

"I think the lovers have had long enough to make up their quarrel, so I can safely and tactfully return."

He had forgotten her reason for coming, and the ache was intensified by the response Olga had aroused in him. Oh, God, why would they not stay down by the lake as he had decreed!

Silently he helped her to mount, then said the words that killed his own wishes. "Tell your brother that I have revised my orders regarding yourself and your sister-in-law. I now think it would be safer if we all stayed together. I intend taking the train up the line at five A.M. Please be ready to go with it."

She turned in the saddle, smiling widely, "Thank you, it will be so much better if we accompany you. The first step in our new friendship!"

He did not disillusion her and say that he had made the decision after hearing that the men had spoken of attacking the women by the lake. Her smile did not touch him any longer. All he could think of was those two who had been repairing a quarrel. Far from wishing to extend his knowledge of Russian customs, he wished himself on the train back to Murmansk en route to England.

Paul's plans for an early morning start had to be altered due to a signal telling him an extra train was on its way southward with some urgent equipment needed for the seaplane haven at the lake down the line. Since it would be pointless going off for two hours before having to return to the siding, he delayed his own departure until the through train had passed.

Besides his regular supplies, the through train brought a bundle of letters for the three English soldiers, and Paul read his whilst the train was being fed with water and logs. There were two from friends who had left the army and were finding life anything but easy in peacetime England. The letters from his mother he tossed aside half-read. They were full of complaints and news of Nora's latest "young man." He felt they came from another world. Gazing around him at isolation and clean peacefulness, he wondered if he could ever bear to return to that red brick house, even for a visit.

He settled down on his camp bed with the hope of catching an hour's rest, but his mind remained active. Mrs. Anderson had asked if he could send a little extra each month, as Nora had had to leave the corner shop due to the manager's disgusting advances. (He wondered how much his flighty sister had encouraged them.) She was helping in the pet store now, but the wages were lower, and they were finding it hard to make ends meet.

Unfastening the money belt he always wore, he thought how easy it would be to slip some of the money into an envelope and send it to himself poste restante until he returned to England. He could claim it as legitimate payment for food he never bought, or labour that was not available. Who would ever know? He could fiddle some kind of piece of paper that would serve as a receipt. He gave a caustic grunt, knowing he would never do it. Perhaps it was inborn honesty, perhaps it was his fierce determination to get everything by his own labours, come what may.

He sighed as he put his hands up behind his head on the pillow. Somehow he would have to manage an extra allowance to his mother and sister. Here, he had no need of money except for a supply of brandy and a few necessities that came down on the trains—but when he got home he would like *something* left in his bank account.

When he got home. It was something he did not wish to think of, especially after the letters from his friends. What of the future? All he had heard of the progress of the war against the Reds was encouraging, and once the Bolshevik threat had been crushed, the Allies would leave. Would he then be considered unnecessary? Funds to the Army were already being diminished. Would he, also, be considered dispensable once he had built his railway in Russia?

The weather was still perfect when the train got up steam and puffed out of the siding an hour later. That part of Russia might be hell in winter, but it was beautiful just then.

The women now sat in the supply-truck with the two officers, but Paul pretended to be occupied with his paperwork. There had been a scene at the siding in which he had just come off worst.

Paul had not imagined the full consequences of his new ruling that the women stay with the party. When they had assembled at the siding prior to setting off, he had been astounded to see a string of horses arrive laden with baggage and tents. Swarovsky had appeared surprised at his angry reaction and said stiffly that surely he had not expected them to leave their belongings at the mercy of villainous peasants in the settlement. Nor could he surely have imagined that the ladies could spend thirty-six hours or more with the working party on the track without a tent to give them privacy, and the normal accessories that would ensure their comfort, as far as it was possible.

It was then Paul realised he had not only the addition of two women to consider, but the entire bizarre collection of silver-backed brushes, perfumes, expensive rugs, and leather trunks full of petticoats. His protests were weakened by lack of alternative suggestions and the presence of the laden horses as a *fait accompli*. Feeling he had been overtaken by something from the *Arabian Nights,* he had been forced to accept the Russian's dictates. Now, his truck was carrying the paraphernalia of aristocrats along with the explosives. Three of Swarovsky's men were bringing the horses up the line behind them. Small wonder Paul preferred to be busy rather than make small talk!

But try as he might, their presence made itself felt. Their quiet conversation in a language he did not understand added to the feeling of isolation, and seeing Irina beside her husband did Paul no good at all. She wore the usual pale blouse—creamy fine lawn, this time—and dark skirt, and her air of quiet dignity showed up the contrast between her and her sister-in-law. In retrospect, Paul supposed Olga to be what his friends would have described as a "damned voluptuous wench" and felt uneasy. Personalities like hers were dangerously volatile, at the best of times. In the present situation, she could add to the difficulties very easily. He regretted having been so . . . relaxed . . . in her company. It would not be so easy to avoid her now that she was to be with him all the time. Neither would it be easy to avoid Irina—and that was even more essential if he was to have any peace of mind.

Apart from thanking him for allowing them to come on the train, Irina had said nothing to him that day, but that one short moment had been enough to confirm his fears. She was as lovely as he remembered, as challengingly changeable in mood, as fatal to his system as in the two previous meetings. He was swamped with jealousy as he thought of the lovers making up their quarrel after the funeral.

Once at the site, Paul's thoughts were completely taken up with the job, and he left the colourful Russians to their own devices while he went up the line to the place where he hoped to drive the cutting. Leaving Yagutov with his beloved engine, Paul and Corporal Banks began the business of taking bores, testing surfaces, measuring and estimating, taking sectional surveys of the whole area.

It was warm work, and Paul took off his jacket and tie. The two Engineers had taken water bottles and large chunks of cheese together with slices of Sapper Stevens's range-baked bread so, barely stopping long enough to eat their provisions, they worked through the day until the changing light of midnight made it difficult to see their instruments. Then they climbed down the slope to the train, where Yagutov was fast asleep on the footplate.

Giving his corporal a wink, Paul swung himself up and began checking the pressure gauge for signs that the Russian driver had worked up enough steam to set off, then pulled the handle of the warning whistle. A shrill, feminine hoot rent the air, and Yagutov came out of sleep like a startled cat, nearly falling from the footplate onto the track at the side. The two Englishmen laughed heartily, and the Russian joined them when he had collected his wits.

"That is funnies," he said, then assured Paul he had only dozed for a minute. "She ready, as Yusuv Mikhaylovich has asked."

As Paul looked puzzled, Corporal Banks explained a little sheepishly that Yusuv Mikhaylovich was his Russian name, worked out by his friend Yagutov. "Something to tell them back home, when we go, sir." "Yes."

Paul was silent for the short journey. What would he tell his people at home, when he went back? That he had built a railway better than the Russians? That he had lived in the midst of a coniferous forest and found it beautiful? That he had fallen in love with the wife of a Russian colonel?

It was then he knew he wished he could stay as he was forever. He wished the railway construction would never be finished, so that he must never return home. There was nothing awaiting him in England except a greedy family and the prospect of unemployment. He gripped the side of the cab. This was the best part of his life so far. If he failed in this command, he would never get another. Whatever happened, he *must* make this a success. The Murmansk to Petrograd line was *his* railway for a few short months. What he did with it would live on after he had left. It might be that Irina would travel it one day in the future and remember him. If only for that he would put all his skill and dedication into each day he spent working here.

F o u r

For Irina, the days that followed were full of interest. She became used to sleeping through the sound of sledgehammers rhythmically driving spikes onto the rails, through the rasping noise of two-handled saws slicing through trees and the clamour of men shovelling shingle. After the days she and Olga had spent dallying at the lake, there was a sense of purpose about the present burst of activity that suited her. Her four years of nursing had been hectic and exhausting, always on the move with the troops, and filled with professional occupation. She had the honesty to admit that her work, though terrible and undesirable, had given her a sense of fulfilment. A sense of *living*. These last weeks, apart from bandaging a cut hand or administering a dose of quinine, she had drifted through the hours with no sense of purpose. In view of her plea to Sasha to make the most of their respite before the winter came, it was a contradiction of feelings, and perhaps her honesty did not stretch as far as understanding the real cause for her listlessness.

But she was concerned for their future—it was impossible not to be. This spell on the railway was the eye of the storm. All around them the war was raging, all around their tiny semblance of normality. But they could not remain in the eye forever. She knew the storm would overtake them again before long, and who could tell what would be left when it had blown itself out?

Russia would never be the same again, she acknowledged that as Sasha never would. She knew the last of the tsars had graced the beautiful palaces of a proud land, but she would not abandon her country as Olga seemed to have done. The Swarovskys were nobles, owners of large estates, defenders of royalty. There could only be one kind of Russia for them.

Irina came from a more liberal family, consisting of artists and intellectuals. They also had wealth and estates but had seen for some years that the peasant revolution was inevitable. That it had been so ill-timed they all deplored, but of them all, Irina was probably the only member who could explain the rebellion. She had been there to see the simple people of Russia bear the straw that had broken their backs during those first two terrible years of war and had the greatest sympathy with them.

When the Tsar was forced to abdicate and the new provisional government had taken the reins, the people those ministers had to govern had been at the limits of endurance, desperate, irrational, ready to snatch at anything that would improve their lot. The great reformer, Alexander Feodorovich Kerensky had, like most idealists, underestimated the effect his sweeping attempts at liberalisation would have on those trying to hold a giant enemy at bay—underestimated the effect, or mistimed the moment. His army reforms, designed to abolish the extremely harsh discipline meted out to soldiers by their officers, were interpreted as an invitation to complete disobedience by the rank and file. When the ignorant bullies began to kill their superiors and desert, it was not long before the rest followed suit: It had been hopeless before, but with their numbers halved, the remaining soldiers feared they would be instantly slaughtered by the enemy. Deluded into believing they no longer had to obey any order given them, they also walked away from misery at the Front.

Appalled at what was happening, Kerensky had struggled to restore order and rouse the soldiers to further battle on behalf of their country. They lionised him, they cheered his speeches, they shouted that they would die for their beloved motherland . . . but the scent of freedom was too strong. When the civilian population rose in bloody revolution in response to a smooth tongue whispering of unimagined plenty for all, the peasant soldiers did not use their rifles in the name of Russia—they used them in the name of personal survival. Kerensky and his moderate government were smashed, and Lenin walked into the resulting chaos with deadly effect.

Irina had seen loyal folk who were the salt of the earth turn into vicious, grasping murderers with no comprehension of what they were doing to their country. She had also ministered to those aristocratic officers who had been shot or assaulted by their men, and seen them cry, not with the pain of their wounds, but for the ignorance that now ruled Russia. The Bolshevik method was not designed to bridge the gap but to destroy the other side altogether.

Olga, in her dramatic fashion, accepted that wholeheartedly and lived in fear of the day of destruction. Sasha, intensely loyal, seeing only what he wanted to see, believed it could never be done and saw only the solid top surface, with none of the subterranean crumbling. He would never accept that some of the officers and aristocrats had thrown in their lot with the Reds without duress because they hoped to be there when the crash came, to shore up what remained. Irina admired their courage. They were dicing with death in a game where the Chekka, the new secret police, could arrest anyone at a moment's notice and without justification. Those men and their families were not safe from hour to hour.

Irina was beginning to feel the strain of living with the flash quarrels between brother and sister. In consequence, she tried to throw herself into the absorbing subject of railway construction. That it was absorbing only because there was nothing else to occupy her might have been true, but she did find the subject interesting and did her best to find out all it involved. During their journeys to and from the siding the English officer held aloof, concentrating on his sketches and diagrams and being so pointedly busy that even Olga gave up the attempt to make conversation after the first few minutes. Irina admitted to being puzzled. She had thought she understood men in all their moods and guises, but this one did not conform. The hurt she had inflicted on him at their first meeting had surely been mitigated by her subsequent apologetic approach. Yet he remained stiff in manner on those few occasions that she addressed him.

Irina tackled her husband when he came across to the tent to eat after a long session with the Englishman, hoping to mend relations between two stubborn men who treated each other with polite, icy dislike. Sasha she understood only too well, the other must not be allowed to remain a mystery if she hoped to overcome the present situation.

"What is happening that is of such great importance?" she asked casually as her husband washed his hands before sinking dispiritedly into the chair.

Brushing his moustache into place with the back of his hand, Sasha gave her a dark look. "Our ally has made a great decision, there *will* be a cutting. After long and careful deliberation he has decided it can be done, and the work will go ahead tomorrow." He yawned and stretched his body. "I think he believed there should have been an instant church service to give thanks to God for giving him such wisdom."

Olga laughed. "Poor man! He takes everything so seriously."

"There is little about constructing a cutting that stimulates amusement, surely?" commented Irina.

Sasha, catching some of his sister's amusement, said, "There is nothing about constructing a cutting that stimulates *anything*, Irusha." He leant forward, rubbing his hands together eagerly. "Come, what has Slabov to offer us tonight? Not Captain Anderson's dreadful tinned meat, I trust."

"Why do you hate him so much?" Irina could not help asking the question.

The answer was unexpected. "Because he is a fraud."

"A . . . *fraud?*"

"He wears the uniform of a soldier, yet becomes irrationally emotional over a railway." Sasha looked from beneath his lashes, after studying the meal Slabov put on the table before him. "He condemns us for ending our war against the Germans too soon, yet I doubt he knows what war really is. Playing trains in France hardly makes him a soldier. One only has to look at that spotless uniform to guess where he was when the guns were firing."

"He certainly was not in *Madame's* boudoir," put in Olga pertly. "I would guess he does not know what such a place is like."

Sasha grinned again. "I am not surprised, *sestrushka*. It would take him until the morning hours to describe *exactly* how he will make the cutting through the hill. By that time, any woman would be soundly asleep."

Olga's eyes narrowed as she looked across the short open stretch to where Paul Anderson was eating his own meal, with an open book on the table beside his plate.

"It might be interesting to find out."

Sasha looked at her with a slight frown. "I trust you are not serious."

Her vivid blue eyes opened wide in feigned innocence. "But you gave me your blessing, *bratishka*. You said a hard lesson in seduction would do him good and keep him off your hands."

The frown deepened. "It was merely a figure of speech. You are a Swarovsky. Who is he?"

"That is what I ought to find out . . . and there is only one way to do it."

Sasha put down his knife and fork. "Now, let us get this straight."

"No, Sasha, this is one thing you cannot get straight," was the angry answer. "You had your years of dalliance whilst I was tied to *mamochka*. If I do not seize my chances now, it might be too late for me."

He was equally angry now. "What ridiculous drama! You are but twenty-four. There is plenty of time."

"Is there?" Olga jumped to her feet, full of passion. "How soon will it be before the Reds catch up with us? Wouldn't you rather your sister were ravished by one English ally than a dozen drunken *Bolsheviki*?"

Sasha rapped the table, making everything on it jump. "That is enough."

Olga gave a derisive, defiant smile. "Is it? Before you try to rule my emotional life, I suggest you look to your own. Hardly perfect, is it?"

She went from the tent with angry impatience, leaving behind a silence that hung between those two remaining. Irina found she was trembling as Sasha looked across at her, visibly searching for words. Finally he shrugged and tried a faint smile.

"She is young."

"I am even younger," Irina reminded him quietly.

The frown returned as he looked away from her gaze and fiddled with his fork on the white tablecloth. "This life we lead, it is unnatural. A tent, a few meagre possessions . . ." He sighed heavily. "That the wife of a Swarovsky has to come to this!"

Irina sat very still, wanting to help him, yet knowing it would only be sweet if it came spontaneously. But when he continued, it was almost as if he were speaking to himself.

"All those treasures, the beautiful elegant rooms, the collections of generations of Swarovskys—all gone beneath the boots of fools. Can they not see that they are destroying the heritage of Russia, not just that of those they have been told to hate?"

He looked up at her then, and there was a shimmer in his blue eyes that caught at her in the way such distress in a man's eyes had done on many an occasion. "My wife has only known khaki uniforms, mud, and suffering."

She put out her hand and covered his to still the nervous tracery with the fork.

"Even the summer estate was torn apart and defiled before your eyes," he went on huskily. "It was all yours by right. For centuries my family had owned that beautiful house." The shimmer increased, making his eyes brilliant. "We had our own theatre, you know, where actors and travelling dancing troupes performed for us and our friends. Afterward, the performers sat around large wooden tables in the courtyard and ate a feast with all those who served on the estate. When that was finished, there would be an impromptu festival. The accordions would play, and the dancers would draw into their circle all the peasants—the girls in their kerchiefs and the young men with fire in their blood." He gripped her hand as it gripped his. "How they would dance, Irusha—dance to the old tunes of Russia, the music of their ancestors. We watched from the windows and threw sweets to them at the end of every dance. I shall never forget how they would shout; 'Bless you, Highness,' then, at the end, *'Bozhe Tsarya khrani'* . . . 'God save the Tsar.'" He looked at her with questioning sadness. "How could they . . . how could they destroy what had given them all that?"

She chose her words carefully. "You were on the inside looking out. Perhaps the view was clouded for those outside looking in, *serdechko. moyo.*"

Her sudden use of the endearment he had spoken so fervently during that month in the Crimea broke his control. Getting to his feet, he pulled her into his arms. "Irusha . . . *Irusha!*"

Elated, full of the urge within her, she abandoned herself to his kiss. But it lasted no more than a few seconds. Thrusting her away, he turned to look out through the open tent flaps at the soldiers swarming over the ground beside the track.

"*Poberi!* Must I embrace my wife before the eyes of the world? Is that what we have come to?" he asked with heavy bitterness. "I tell you, a Swarovsky does not make love in a field like the peasants."

Suffering from the swift sword of rejection, Irina answered equally bitterly, "Olga is right. If we do not seize our chances now, it might be too late. I fell in love with you when you lay in a bed helpless and dependent on me for everything. You were covered in blood and moaning in your agony. It was not a Swarovsky in glittering full dress uniform gracing the salons of his grand houses I saw, but a man who rose above the degradation he had suffered." She took a deep breath. "Where has he gone, Sasha?"

He just stared at her, his throat working with emotion. She left him, unable to stand his incomprehension any longer.

Providing his calculations were correct, nothing could go wrong, and Paul knew he had made no mistakes. Even so, he had gone over his figures many times, checking with his engineering manuals until, finally satisfied, he had decided the proposed cutting was within the time and possibility factor. Now, he was nervous and keyed up, wanting to begin. It would be a stepping-stone in his career. It would prove to himself and his superiors that he was a good engineer, one worth keeping, perhaps . . . and it would strengthen his standing with all those around him. So much depended on its success.

He had declared a short break before moving the whole train up the line, and the Russians were making full use of it, sprawling over every yard of open ground beside the track, chatting and laughing together in their usual robust manner. Paul could not relax, however. He felt peculiarly conspicuous, sitting alone eating the meal Sapper Stevens had prepared for him. If he were with his own company, it would be natural to enjoy the surrounding scene whilst tucking into a hearty meal he was more than ready for. But with the Russian tent no more than twenty-five yards away, he was supremely conscious of the three occupants, and propping a book against his cruet, he pretended to read.

He had almost finished his meal and was thankfully contemplating retirement to a closed tent for an hour's sleep when a sudden movement in the Swarovsky tent caught his eye. Glancing up, he saw Olga walking purposefully in his direction. His heart sank. He could hardly walk away or plead pressure of work when so obviously in the middle of a meal. And it was so open there, with the soldiers full of curiosity and her brother able to witness every move he made. But Swarovsky had other things on his mind, Paul noticed, looking beyond Olga's shoulder at husband and wife holding hands across the dinner table. His response to the girl's greeting was clumsy.

"You look very lonely over here."

He rose quickly, jerking the table, so that a small jug of sauce spilled onto the book. "No . . . I was studying, as a matter of fact."

She looked down and read: "*Steel Girder Cantilever Bridges*. Is that what you plan to build on this railway?"

Wiping the sauce from the page with his napkin, he tried to get out of the question by mumbling something about advanced theories of engineering.

She was smiling warmly when he looked up at her again. "It means a lot to you, doesn't it?"

"Yes."

Her hand went up gracefully to push back a strand of hair, and he could not help noticing the full curve of her breast beneath the sheen of heavy, expensive silk. "I hear you are to begin on the cutting. How very exciting."

"Hardly exciting," he protested. 'The work is heavy, noisy and dangerous."

The blue eyes widened. "Dangerous?"

"Blasting is always tricky. Explosives are volatile and need careful, expert handling."

"Then I cannot wait to watch you engage in it."

He could think of nothing more to say to her and stood awkwardly, well aware that she was playing havoc with his senses. If only he could handle her as expertly as he handled explosives, she would be on her way back to her Russian relatives at the double.

She smiled again, which did not help him. "I didn't wish to interrupt your meal. Please carry on."

What, sit there eating while she watched! "No . . . I . . . actually, I had just finished."

"Bravo. Then you can tell me all about the cutting." She twisted her body so that the top half was in profile. "I feel the need for exercise. Shall we stroll along the track while we talk?"

On the point of determinedly saying he had work to do, Paul caught sight of Swarovsky getting to his feet and pulling his wife into a close embrace. She looked particularly fragile in the arms of the tall Russian, and heat washed over Paul.

"Yes . . . Why not?" he said defiantly and went round the table to join Olga. "Let's walk this way. There is more room at the top of the bank."

He walked resolutely around the curve away from the train, his mind full of the scene in that other tent. How could she submit to such an arrogant, brutal man? But that fierce embrace he had glimpsed had made him conscious of his own height and strength as he moved beside the girl walking with him. A painful crescendo of loneliness overwhelmed him.

"Sasha says the men will have to work hard because you have given a completion day for the cutting that must be met," she was saying. "How will you begin on it?"

In an aggressive flash of insight, he had the feeling she was being tactful again, leaving the lovers alone to kiss and make up after a quarrel. Why the hell should he always be used as an excuse to break up the unwelcome threesome? He was tempted to launch into a long, detailed technical account of the work involved that would bore her to tears and serve her right for pretending interest in something she did not give a damn about. Then, he changed his mind.

"You don't really want to know about the cutting, do you?" he challenged grimly. "That's not why you came across just now."

She turned and studied his profile during half a dozen paces, then began to laugh. "So, he is wrong!"

"What does that mean?" he asked, turning to her.

The blue eyes teased him with their amused luminosity. "Sasha said that all you would talk to a woman about would be your cutting."

It was the last thing he wanted to hear at that moment, and his anger rocketed. Coming to a halt he said, "My God, you Russians are beyond belief! You tell a sad story about being dispossessed and homeless, yet travel about like Persian princes in silken tents. Your brother sobs and stamps alternately, giving passionate speeches about his country and shooting out of hand any man who says the wrong thing. Now, he has apparently sent you out on an infantile prank to test my conversational prowess whilst he makes love to his wife." He put his hands on his hips and leant toward her to emphasise his point. "I am here on a mission vitally important for *your* country. Play your silly and melodramatic part, if you must, but do not take me for a fool or waste my valuable time, Miss Swarovskaya."

She took a deep breath, which tightened the silk blouse across her breasts, then let it out slowly while searching his expression as if to look beyond what was written on his face.

"I thought we had decided to be friends, Paul."

He wanted to slap her and knew he could not. Instead, he turned away and ran his hand through his hair in exasperation. "Look . . . what are you doing here, anyway? Why doesn't he send you to Murmansk . . . or Archangel?"

"There are Bolshevik agents there . . . Yes, they are there," she insisted as he turned back to her. "They would use me to catch him. We are only safe when we are together."

He felt suddenly weary. All this tension and suspicion, all this drama and Slavic intensity! For a moment he longed to be back with his own people, who always faced emergencies with calm capability.

"But the Allies hold both ports," he said with heavy patience. "*We* are there—of course you would be safe. It seems to me you all exaggerate this business of Bolshevik spies."

She sprung into defence. "You do not know what it is like to live in fear of your life."

"Don't I?" he asked bitterly. "For four years I was never certain I would see the next dawn."

She moved close to him—disturbingly close—and there was a fiery challenge in her eyes. "Then hasn't it left you with the need to live each day to the full while you can?"

She was so close he had to fight to keep his hands off her. "I do."

"Making your cuttings? Tell me about it."

"To hell with cuttings! I told you to stop those damned, silly games."

Her hands slid up to his shoulders, and she leant against him, tilting her head back. "Can you think of a better one?"

It was vastly different from kissing Lila Reynolds: Olga used her body to incite him further. With his free hand he began exploring the curve of her breast, with heady results. His arms tightened around her, and his mouth pursued hers hungrily, as she teased him. The exploration ceased the next minute, when an insistent noise penetrated the abstract pleasure he felt. He brought up his head to find Corporal Banks standing a discreet distance away, clearing his throat noisily and regarding them with the unshakeable aplomb of the British N.C.O.

"What the hell is it?" Paul's voice was thick and full of embarrassed reaction. He lowered his arms and stood away from Olga in an instant. "What do you want, man?"

"Beg pardon, sir, but an urgent message has just come through. An unscheduled express is heading south with reinforcements and will pass in two hours' time. I thought you'd want to know, sir," Banks finished with a poker face and immaculate military bearing. "I've started them on packing up already."

"Yes . . . er, yes. Good man. We shall have to move off as soon as possible."

Torn by indecision on what to do about the girl he had just been kissing so violently, Paul finally turned to her and said as formally as he could, "I'd be obliged if you'd pack your things right away. We shall have to go back to the siding."

Then he walked off with Corporal Banks, feeling like a boy who had been caught stealing apples, and wondering how the hell the whole thing had happened.

The return to the siding brought an atmosphere of gloom to the whole party. Paul was acutely annoyed at being caught *flagrante delicto* by one of his men, plus at the delay to his plans when the need for haste became clear. For the Russians, the news that the reinforcements were being rushed south, due to a serious breakthrough in the vicinity of Lake Onega in which the Reds had killed or recruited almost the entire White Russian force, was enough to throw them all into the depths of despair.

Not least unsettled was their commander, who ranted and raved (in English for Paul's benefit) all the way back to the siding. The Russian declared his intention of arranging for himself and his men to join the southbound train to swell the numbers of the reinforcements, and when they reached the siding, he told Paul to signal the express train to stop for them as it came through.

"That I won't," was Paul's tightlipped reply. "Your men have been given orders to help me on the railway."

"Tsk . . . a railway! What is a railway?" Swarovsky retorted. "South of here men are being killed for want of numbers." His tall figure in battle-worn uniform paced up and down beside the train. "You made it plain from the beginning that you had no wish to help us. Why should we help you with your selfish ambitions whilst our countrymen are dying? Why?"

Leaning back against the truck and folding his arms, Paul declined to answer that question. "The message was clear enough, surely: those who were not killed went over to the Bolsheviks. If you take this lot down there, they will most probably do the same. Are you so anxious to be deserted by your men a second time?"

Swarovsky's face flooded with angry colour, and Paul suspected for an unbelievable moment that the man was about to hit him across the face as he had some of the Russian soldiers. A tirade of vicious Russian was flung at Paul instead, until a slight figure dropped from within the truck and went to stand between them, facing the Russian. Paul had forgotten the presence of the two women and felt like pulling Irina away to tell her to keep out of the affair. But she was holding her husband's arms and talking to him urgently in their own language as she looked up into his face.

Paul could watch no longer. Walking along the rough wooden platform, he stepped off the end and stood looking at the pines. Lost in thought, he was surprised when heavy footsteps approached from behind and the Russian Colonel called his name. Had she failed to placate him, after all?

"Yes?" He turned to face a determined man.

"As senior officer, I demand access to the Morse telegraph apparatus that is in your train. It is in no way part of the actual railway, and the message I wish to send concerns my own company. There is no transgression of our agreement, I believe."

Paul took his time in answering. "Very well. If you insist, I must bow to your senior rank." He began walking back beside the Russian. "You know how to operate the signalling device, of course, and are familiar with the code that certifies our messages as genuine to those in Murmansk and Archangel?"

"But . . . your man . . ."

"Unfortunately, I need my corporal for the next hour or so. *On work connected with the railway,*" he added with emphasis. They had reached the supply truck, and he put out a hand to indicate the field telegraph. "There it is."

The Russian stopped and summed him up in a long look, then nodded slowly. "Yes, I now see why you were given this command. You are clever and determined. But you are also rather young, and youth is too easily swayed by passions. You will bring about your own downfall, because this conflict will catch you up and overtake you when you are least prepared."

As the Russian was walking away, Paul said, "You could always form up your company on the track just prior to the arrival of the train."

Over his shoulder, the Russian said, "My men will be no use to you dead, Captain Anderson. The train is an express. In a war, a man is supposed to fight his enemies, not his allies." He headed through the trees to the rest of his countrymen.

The express passed, and they all returned up the line again. It took some time for the whole group to get organised there, for the bivouac to be set up, the two tents to be erected, and a meal to be prepared. Paul took advantage of the activity to climb up the hill and give a final look at the ground he was hoping to split in two very shortly. He called up Corporal Banks, who was chatting to Yagutov, and told him to count out the explosives in readiness. Then he followed his man down and went across to the Russian tent, where he imagined Swarovsky would be. But there was only one person there, and she did not look pleased to see him.

He pulled up sharply. "I . . . I'm sorry. I was hoping to find your husband here."

Irina finished spreading an exotic rug over one of the beds. "He is not, as you see."

He looked away across the clearing, finding the contents of the tent, clothes scattered over the beds, a man's brushes and feminine lotions side-by-side, too much to take.

"Has he gone far?"

"He is worried about the horses. They have not yet arrived."

Paul knew the men with the horses had set out for this place when the train went back to the siding. They should have covered the short distance long before this. But horses were not his worry, and he was annoyed that the Russian should be searching for them just when he was wanted.

"Couldn't he have sent one of his men? I can do nothing until he returns, and a start ought to be made."

She came to the tent entrance, and her perfume filled his mind with notions it had no right to hold. "If it is so urgent, I will send someone to find him. What is it you want of him now?"

A touch of sharpness in her voice made him face her. The lovely eyes were sparked with an indefinable flash of anger that prompted a rush of excitement through his limbs.

"His men have to be told where to drill the holes for the dynamite," he said with only half his mind on what he was saying. "I need him to translate for me."

"Oh, so you *need* him!"

The first glimmerings of her hostility got through to him then. "I think I have always admitted that," he said stiffly.

"I am glad to hear it, Captain Anderson. Coming from you, that must be quite a compliment."

Feeling the back of his neck begin to grow warm, he decided to get away while he could. "Perhaps you would ask him to come over when he gets back."

In the act of going he was stopped by her sharp, "*No.* If you need him, you must come yourself when you see him return."

The cursed colour was about to creep into his face, he knew, and knowing it made things worse. "Very well."

Turning on his heel, he was soon stopped by her hand on his arm. With a rustle of skirts and a drift of perfume, she was barring his way, looking up at him with such appeal his head swam.

"Was it necessary to say such a thing to him? You are an officer. Can't you imagine the feelings of another who has been deserted by those under his command? Would it cost you too much to accord him just a semblance of respect?"

"Look, he . . . can't he face the fact that these ruffians here are going to sell out to the Reds the minute the incentive is high enough?" Paul countered raggedly. "The only thing that is keeping them together now is this job that holds them away from the conflict. Isn't that what you were trying to tell him back there?"

"How can anyone tell a man such a thing?"

Conscious of her hand still on his arm and the pale threads of her hair lying against the curve of her neck, he spoke wildly. "I don't know. Isn't a wife supposed to be able to cope with things like that?"

To his intense pain-delight, her own face became tinged with the palest blush. "You are too much like him, that is the trouble."

"Too much . . . That is ridiculous!"

Her hand slid from his arm. "Two men who are determined to do what they want no matter who tries to stop them. One must build a railway; the other needs to fight a crusade. Neither will bend in his chosen path, and the result is a needless confrontation of allies. That is what you are supposed to be, isn't it?"

The thrust made him kick out. "I'm someone who has already been let down by your countrymen. I have orders to make this railway a safe and fast run."

"He has orders to defend his country at all costs."

"Do you have similar orders to defend him?" It was out before he knew, and it produced a shattering response.

"I am part of this small army, Captain Anderson. From the age of seventeen, I have been attached to the Russian fighting forces. Give me your orders, and I will translate to our men. You need not delay your work. We are all dedicated to our duty, whatever it might be."

With that she walked out to where the Russians were gathered in their usual noisy, disorganised sprawl and had them on their feet, alert and smiling, with one short sentence.

Hoist with his own petard, Paul had no alternative but to follow her and bluster his way through a military directive in an unprecedented fashion. Calmly and clearly, she translated all he managed to say, in a manner he would use, whilst the phenomenon of a beautiful young girl in long skirt and embroidered cambric blouse walking beside him as he indicated rock structures and drilling angles so bemused him all his anger drained away.

The Russians appeared to find nothing odd in the situation, the devoted Sergeant Gromov even saluting Irina at the end. Paul had no such opportunity. Turning swiftly to him, she said, "They are ready to start the work whenever you give the word. Now, if you will excuse me, I have other things to do."

She walked off, leaving him feeling he had met with a blast from one of his own explosives. But once they all began, he had no time to think of her and all she had said to him, for he had to concentrate on what he was doing. It was slow, careful work, placing the explosives, then running out fuses. The sun was hot on the back of his neck as he squatted to twist the fuses together and feed them into the exploder.

All was ready, and he motioned to Corporal Banks to blow the whistle signalling everyone to retire behind the train. They took their time, which had him on edge, but it was essential that safety came first in cases like this. He hoped Swarovsky would not appear with the horses just as the hill blew asunder. He could do without stampeding animals—a bloody nuisance, as it was, on a railway—to add to his problems.

When he was certain the area was clear, he nodded to his N.C.O., said the little prayer that had become part of his ritual in France, and depressed the plunger.

There was a low rumbling, a tremble beneath his feet, then a gigantic subterranean roar as the hillside split into a wide crack spewing rocks and earth out in a hurtling cascade. Visibility became obscured by the clouds of brown dust that rose and hung over the spot, and it seemed an age before the sound of falling debris ceased. Paul straightened up and began walking forward to check the situation, when the most bloodcurdling noise came from the collapsed hillside. With a prickle of fear touching his spine, he peered through the brown mist of settling earth, to see a series of large grey shapes, like demons of the underworld, jaws apart and eyes enlarged with fright, rush past and into the forest beyond.

The whole incident shocked him into a halt. It was unnerving. Used to hearing the screams of men after such explosions, there was something about this that made him break out in a sweat. Only sheer willpower kept him from turning tail and getting as far from the spot as possible.

With heart thumping still, he suddenly caught sight of some movement in the obscurity ahead. In the general tumble and slither of settling rock, something was alive and struggling. He saw a head of attractive shape and a pale body twitching to be free of the weight upon it. It looked like a young dog. Its yelping cries were pitiful.

Without further thought, he ran forward and took hold of the animal, pulling it free. Its fur was full of earth, fine rock dust, and pine needles. It smelt warm and pungent as he gently picked it up, but even as he turned, the head dropped and the eyes went blank. He looked up and became aware that the Russians were all standing around looking at him strangely.

Irina came toward him, her face pale and intent. She touched the animal's fur with gentle loving fingers, but when she looked up at him, Paul was shaken by her expression.

"It's dead," he said unnecessarily.

"When one kills the child of a wolf, it is an ill omen. You have driven them from their home. Now they will gather and drive you from yours," she told him in awed tones.

F i v e

The construction of the cutting went ahead with slow but steady progress. It was hard physical grind for the men, but the two officers played their parts with equal effort, the Russian driving the soldiers throughout the twenty-four hours, and the Englishman never letting up on his supervision and encouragement of those taking his orders.

Sasha had become quiet and morose since the news of the lost battle in the south, doing what he had to do with a thoroughness that was almost a scourge. The young British officer was growing blear-eyed and weary from his constant study, calculations, and excursions over the hillock to take sitings. One of them would crack before long, and Irina did not think it would be Sasha. Her husband had an outlet for his tension in a temperament that allowed him to let free his emotions. Paul Anderson held his so tightly beneath his control that there was bound to be an eruption of some sort if he went on as he was at present. What kind of man would be revealed then, she wondered. In her experience, the person who hid his emotions did so because when unleashed they ran high.

With the situation unstable enough as it was, and with Olga determined on experimenting with sexual passions, there were hidden dangers ahead for them all. Irina's highly strung sister-in-law had already commented with secretive casualness that Paul Anderson might be inexperienced with women but he was an instinctive lover, by which remark Irina could only guess the girl had begun her ill-advised approaches to the Englishman. It made her very angry. Not only would such an alliance anger Sasha, it would further widen the gap between the two men, and heaven knew, it was too wide already!

But there was another aspect that made Irina uneasy during the days that followed. She could not forget the incident with the wolves, to which she had reacted so automatically when he had stood there holding the dead cub. Into her mind at that moment had come a memory from childhood that she had thought long forgotten.

Her *babushka* had come from a Siberian village where, she had claimed, the wolves began to gather after the death of one of their pack. The old nanny had told how a child of the village had disappeared soon afterward and was never found. The village men had gone out searching the forest, leaving their homes sometimes never to return. It was some years after the incident that reports began coming in of a strange creature spotted in the forest by various hunters—a creature with long, golden hair and human features who ran on all fours and howled like the wolves, with whom it lived.

The story had lodged in the mind of the child Irina and served to frighten her when nights were wild and windy on the family summer estate. Now that old legend had returned to bring the same sense of unease, of feeling that somewhere out in the beyond was a menace of which she dare not think. The English officer had apparently dismissed her words from his mind, and Sasha had not been there to hear them.

But the men were restless. She heard them talking together as they worked. They were peasants, full of superstition and folklore. Brought up on stories such as the one of the wolf-child, they were easily ruled by signs and superstitions. They had heard of the gathering wolves; their great-grandfathers had seen strange half-humans, half-beasts when out hunting in this very forest. One of these had been captured, related a soldier, and taken to a nearby village, but it bit anyone who went near and howled all night in captivity. The *starosta*—headman of the village— had sold it to a travelling circus. Another man told of mad wolves who had rushed through villages with eyes red as fire, savaging the inhabitants and dragging off the livestock. The villagers never recovered from the terror, remaining as mad as the wolves until they died.

Because of her vague and irrational fear of something that was only legend, Irina found her thoughts dwelling more and more on the young foreigner of whom none of them knew very much. Did he have a family, perhaps vast estates back in England? She had never been there and had as little idea of the country and her people as he had of Russia. They had been thrown together, yet he would probably go away as much an enigma as when he first walked up to her tent by the lake that morning, so angry because Sasha was out fishing.

One day, she was up on the hillock watching him as he talked with great earnestness to Sasha and the N.C.O.s of both sides, and she found herself wishing there were some way of approaching him that he would accept. Sasha aroused opposition in him; God knew what Olga would arouse. But there must be a common ground on which understanding, if not friendship, could grow. Life was so short, its opportunities should not be neglected, and she was the only one who could break the ice.

The Englishman broke away and began walking toward the hillock, then caught sight of her above him. For a moment he just looked at her as she leant against a tree, and she saw again how strained and exhausted he was. If only . . .

"Everyone back behind the train," he called sharply. "I am about to place explosives, and I want the area cleared."

Sighing, she descended the slope just as the whistle began blowing its warning. From the safety of the train she watched the familiar scene as the charges were prepared and placed by the engineer officer and his corporal. The N.C.O. was sent back to a place of safety whilst the fuses were played out, twisted together and attached to the exploder. Completely absorbed in his task, the Englishman bent his head over the equipment as he squatted to make the connection. Up ahead in the cutting all was still and silent, yet one thrust of the plunger would create havoc amongst the rock and trees.

The whistle sounded. He straightened, turned to give a thumbs-up signal to his man, then activated the fuses. As usual, there came a great muffled roar, a trembling underfoot, then an upsurge of dust and rock debris that flew through the air as easily as leaves tossed by a wind.

The noise died gradually, the echo rolling away into the distance in diminishing sounds, and the brown haze thinned as rocks and shattered tree trunks stopped slithering down the newly made slopes of the cutting. Irina held her breath, but no grey shapes hurtled from the devastation— no small creature lay twitching in the aftermath. Gradually, peace and silence descended again, and she turned thankfully to Olga as the tension went from her body.

She smiled. "It is over."

The girl did not return her smile. "*Da, Da.* It is one step nearer the end. Then he will go back to England."

Irina was taken by surprise. Was Olga so attached to him? "You will be unhappy when he goes?"

Olga's eyes flashed. "He will be going back to freedom. That word is gone forever here. How will it feel, do you think, to see him get on his train and leave, knowing we must remain to face what will come? Will you not long to be on that train as it slowly disappears along the track until all we are left with is its echo and a puff of smoke above the pines?"

Irina turned back to where the Englishman was walking forward to join Sasha and several of his men. "I no longer look ahead. For the moment, I am content to be here watching a railway grow. It is the creation of something . . . and I have seen too much destruction not to enjoy the sight of a man endeavouring to build for the future."

Irina had seen Sasha turn back to speak with a soldier at the end of the train whilst the others walked into the cutting to inspect the results of the blasting. But hardly had she finished speaking than there was another compressed roar, a fresh trembling of the ground, and to her horror, the top of the freshly made gash blew apart to fall in a shower of earth and rocks onto the men just passing beneath.

Irina saw everything in one of those flash moments that occur during a disaster. Paul Anderson was tossed backward like a cardboard figure in a sudden draught, flung against the shored-up section with great force before disappearing beneath a slide of debris. The English corporal, who was some distance behind, flung himself face down and covered his head with his hands. The two Russian N.C.O.s who had been walking with the Engineer vanished beneath the landslide.

It could only have been a moment before the English officer emerged from the earth pile, rose, staggered forward, and fell to his knees, then rose again to run with an awkward gait to the spot where the two Russians had been. He was shouting at the top of his voice; it was a terrible sound in the silence that followed shock. He continued to shout as he tore at the mound like one possessed, his left arm hanging uselessly by his side.

She was running forward, caught in the sudden inexplicable tragedy. It seemed that she was the only other moving figure in that stunned tableau, but only for a short while. Her own rush helped to set off a concerted effort, and she reached the scene only seconds before the rest. Her hands grew torn and scratched as she searched beside the Englishman, who was still shouting abuse. Subconsciously registering that she had heard a similar sound many times before, she paid him no heed until he lost his footing and fell. Then, his cry of agony made her turn from what appeared a hopeless task.

It was immediately obvious that he was in immense pain. The evidence was in his face, yellow and beaded with sweat, and in his involuntary moans as he tried to get to his feet again. The left arm hung useless from a shoulder that was grotesquely misshapen; his left cheek was cut and bleeding, the crimson streaks cutting through the coating of dirt and dust like scores from a knife. But in his dark eyes was the madness of shock. He did not even see her there.

Turning to divert two men, she spoke to them sharply, giving orders to take the injured man as gently as possible to the clearing, where she could attend to him. Another she sent for the medical chest kept in the supply-truck. But the instinct to uncover the buried men kept her patient fighting against those who tried to lead him away, until agony overrode shock when his arm was knocked and he all but fainted away. The two brawny Russians picked him up and carried him away to a spot not far from the train, where they laid him on the ground.

Irina was calm and full of purpose as she knelt beside him, but it did not occur to her that her reassuring words were all in a language he did not understand. It did not seem to matter. He lay acquiescent now, too full of pain to know where he was or who he was with. Tearing away the khaki shirt, she was thankful he had not been wearing his jacket at the time. One glance confirmed her suspicions. The left shoulder was completely dislocated. How he had got to his feet, much less attacked that mound so strongly in the acute agony he must be in, left her marvelling at his fortitude. But he would need it all in the next few minutes.

Quick instructions in Russian to the soldiers told them they must hold the injured man still whilst she manipulated the joint back into place. It was brutal, necessary, and if he struggled it would take longer and draw out his ordeal. They looked at her in blank assent. Only when they had coaxed him gently into a sitting position with the left arm clear did she realise what a big man he was. It required another man's strength to force that jutting shoulder blade back into position with any ease. Her hands were small, if competent, and it was a formidable task. However, there was no doctor to call now, and she was the only one with skill enough to help him and attempt it. Taking a deep breath she said in English, "I shall have to hurt you, I fear. I am sorry."

Then, giving a quick nod to the men and offering up a prayer, she put her hands on his back and began to apply pressure. He yelled and tried to twist away, but the soldiers held him down until he could stand no more and passed out. With an inert body it was not as harrowing, and Irina exerted all her strength until she felt the joint slip back into position. Only then did she give a shaky laugh and acknowledge that her first case of dislocation had gone successfully.

Somewhat drained herself, she took her time making a sling for the arm and fixed it into position, tying the material at the back of his neck in the most comfortable position. He came round whilst she was doing this, although it was only semi-consciousness, she felt. He looked at her hazily and was unable to form words properly. It made her anxious. Was he concussed from the explosion? Getting the soldiers to prop him against a box, she began cleansing the cuts on his face, intending to watch him for the next few minutes for signs of shock.

"I apologise for this," she told him gently. "The antiseptic will sting a little, at first."

There was little reaction from him, so she busied herself with swabs and iodine, carefully picking from the gashes any tiny fragments of grit that might cause infection. He looked a villainous sight—hair full of dirt and dust, bloodshot eyes, face yellow and already swelling around the cuts—yet there was nothing villainous about his demeanour. All the fight had gone out of him. He was completely spent.

As Irina was in the midst of applying a sterile pad over one gash that would not stop bleeding, the sound of someone approaching made her glance over her shoulder. Sasha was striding along and looked as ill as the man on the ground.

"*They are both dead,*" he exploded in a rasping voice as he arrived beside her, but he was speaking to the Englishman as if she were not there. "Those two men have been with me for seven years. Sergeant Gromov carried me to safety when I was wounded. Now your incompetence has killed them. *Bozhe moy!* They survive the war and rally to the cause at my side, only to be murdered by an egotist who cares nothing for our struggle for survival, only for his game with trains that he plays with arrogant ineptitude." He looked at the seated man with utter contempt. "This is the end. I withdraw my men. If they are to die, it will be bravely and honourably, not because a hostile ally makes a fatal professional error."

The following hours were the worst Paul had ever spent. The Russian Colonel insisted that the two men be buried within sight of the cause of their death. The graves were dug side by side, and every shovel that struck the earth metaphorically dug into Paul's conscience.

The burial was conducted with full honours, as far as the situation allowed, and with interminable recitation of chants, murmuring of prayers, and singing of songs that held an almost unbearable sadness in their melodies. The rough peasant-soldiers sang like a trained choir, with more feeling than choristers normally displayed, and Paul stood dazed and swaying with pain at the gravesides throughout the ceremony.

Corporal Banks helped him into his jacket and tie and fetched the peaked cap from the train, yet when Paul saluted the blanket-wrapped bodies as they were lowered into the earth, he felt like a hypocrite. He was virtually a murderer honouring the bodies of his victims. For some reason he felt insufferably pompous standing to attention, presenting a salute in true British textbook manner. The Russian officer, openly weeping, appeared more manly.

The business over, everyone climbed onto the train. There was no alternative but to tell Yagutov to take it back to the siding. After being helped into the truck by his corporal, Paul spent the journey trying desperately not to slip into unconsciousness. The three Russians sat like silent accusers. Their faces came and went as waves of pain washed over him, and the interior of the truck seemed to swing dizzily around, backward and forward, and sometimes right over. The sweat coursed down his face and body as he fought the need to throw up.

His eyes closed, but all he could see was a trench running with mud and a man buried beneath it. He was sobbing and dragging the body free, only to have it snatched from him and flung into the air like a broken rag doll. Everything was exploding around him. His lids shot up, but the faces of his companions were going up and around like balls thrown up into the air by a juggler. He swivelled his glance to the open door. The straight trunks flashing past one after the other made him feel even dizzier, and the noise of the wheels was turning into a roar that filled his head.

Vaguely he became aware that the dark figures with him were going, dropping over a precipice and disappearing. It seemed a long time later, when his loneliness was becoming unbearable, that voices floated through the roar in his head—one high and gentle, the other a familiar masculine one. A man he knew was beside him, then another. He gazed at them. No power on earth was going to get his body to move. It weighed inestimable pounds. Yet he was standing somehow, and going clumsy-footed to the entrance of the truck. They were holding him as he stepped onto the box there outside. His rubbery legs buckled almost immediately, but they did not let him fall. Beneath his blurred vision was a row of planks and the toes of his own boots as they shuffled forward. And all the time he could hear the gentle feminine voice encouraging him.

Then he was lying on a bed with a pillow and blankets in a world that spun round and round. There were shells exploding everywhere, men screaming. Some had hideous rubber faces and walked about through a layer of gas that hung everywhere. There was a girl with red hair who was crying, but he did not know how to comfort her. Then the shells came from the air with a spurt of flame, and everything went dark with the agony of oblivion.

There was no way of telling what time it was when he next opened his eyes and felt rational. The Russian "white nights" threw routine out of the window. With practically no hours of darkness to signify the passing of time, he could have been in his horror-filled limbo a few hours or a few days. His first overwhelming thought was gratitude that it had passed. A few minutes later he knew that being fully conscious was not the joyful experience he imagined. His body was stiff and bruised so that any movement was painful, his shoulder had burning claws digging into it, and one side of his face was so swollen his eye was half closed.

Sapper Stevens brought him a bowl of soup, then another when he saw how quickly the first had vanished. Paul discovered he was famished, which suggested he had been out for some time.

"How long have I been on my bed, Stevens?" he asked carefully through his bruised mouth as the batman put the soup on the box that served as a low bedside table.

"More than thirty-six hours, sir. We thought you was never going to come round, but the young lady said we wasn't to worry, as it was quite normal in cases like yours."

"The young lady?" Paul queried through a mouthful of soup.

"The Colonel's wife, sir. Seems she's a nurse and knows all about shock and things like concussion."

He almost choked. "She . . . she has been here to see me?"

"Every few hours right the way through. She was most worried about that shoulder. You was throwing yourself about, at times . . . and muttering." The long, sorrowful face creased into a smile. "Some of it was not fit for ladies' ears, sir, but she didn't bat an eyelid. Seems she's used to it, serving in army hospitals during the war."

"Oh, God," said Paul, recollection beginning to return in full. He left the soup; his appetite had gone.

"The other young lady come once and sat with you. She said Mrs. Svaroff . . . Svar . . . " He gave up trying to get his tongue round the Russian name. " . . . said she had been sent to keep an eye on the patient." His grin widened. "Pity you was in no condition to appreciate the attention you was getting, Captain Anderson."

The jibe went over Paul's head. Memory had returned in a flash, and he wished himself back in a coma. He had made a fatal calculation and killed two men!

"They are still here then . . . the Russians?"

Stevens sobered. "The ladies **are**, yes, sir . . . so I s'pose the rest are down there by the lake." He put on what Paul called his "valet's" look. "I never go down there, sir. Corporal Banks gets on with them a real treat, but I don't take to them, somehow. The ladies are different, mind—graciousness itself—but the rest are like them explosives, liable to go up at any time. And, begging your pardon, sir, but it seems to me the Colonel is the worst of the lot. Look how he shot that man down, quick as you like. And he had no call to say what he did to you. After all, you was half dead yourself when he ups and starts shouting insults."

"That's quite enough, Stevens," said Paul with a stupid sense of loyalty to his fellow officer.

"Well, I say anyone can make a mistake, and if you wasn't certain it was safe, you wouldn't have walked in there yourself," continued Stevens with unusual persistence. "It was only chance that you was blown back and not buried along with those other two."

Leaden-hearted, Paul put an end to the conversation by saying that he would like a wash and shave and a change of clothes right away, which sent Stevens running off for hot water, a laundered shirt, and underwear.

Corporal Banks approached to express his pleasure at Paul's recovery and to offer any assistance. He was met with a curt assurance that it was perfectly possible to wash and shave one-handed, although Paul knew he was making a terrible job of it.

They then discussed the messages that had come through from Murmansk and Lake Onega regarding trains and supplies.

"They asked for a progress report on the cutting, sir," the N.C.O. told him. "I said there'd been an accident—a landslip—and you were hurt. They want you to report as soon as you are able," He paused significantly. "I didn't say anything about the Russians moving out. Thought it best to leave that to you, Captain Anderson."

Paul looked round sharply, hurting his shoulder. "Ouch! Are they? Moving out, I mean?"

"They're packing up the bivouac. I think it's only the Colonel's lady who stopped them going off right away. She wouldn't leave while you were out cold, sir, with no medical help."

Abandoning the shaving session, Paul reached for the clean shirt and began to ease himself painfully into it.

"I see. So he meant what he said." It was more to himself than the other man.

"I was going to ask headquarters for permission to return, but the lady said you were not fit to be moved yet."

"*You what?*" shouted Paul. "*Permission to return?*"

Banks looked taken aback. "There's no point in stopping here on our own. When they go, the job's off."

"I will decide when the job is off, Corporal," said Paul with quiet fury. "No one else. Is that understood?"

The man stiffened. "Yes, sir . . . *quite* understood."

"We are here to perfect a railway, and I have no intention of leaving until it is done."

The silent N.C.O.'s expression made Paul lose some of his heat in a return of depression. "They will have to be persuaded to remain, somehow." He looked searchingly at Banks. "You've been down there, I take it? What is the general attitude amongst the men themselves?"

"Not exactly cheerful, sir. I'd say they were more confused than anything. That shooting last week shook them up, and they don't like this work at the best of times. Colonel Swarovsky treats them a bit harsh, as you've seen for yourself, sir, and seeing their mates killed one after the other . . . Well, to put it bluntly, sir, they say they're soldiers, not navvies. They're simple people, full of superstition. That affair with the wolves upset them, gave them the notion it was an ill omen. It was unfortunate coming just before the accident. They naturally linked the two together and don't like it."

"Yes, I suppose so." Paul was feeling extremely weak now he was on his feet, and the problems facing him seemed insurmountable. "All right, Corporal, let me think about it for a while, will you?"

"Very well, sir. Sure there's nothing I can do?"

Paul tried to smile, but it was too painful. "No, nothing. But thank you for keeping things running whilst I was out of action. You're a good man."

Banks looked pleased. "That's all right, sir. Glad to do it. Oh . . . there's just one other thing. Headquarters spoke of sending down another officer to take over. He's coming on Wednesday's train." With a smart salute he took himself off.

That last piece of information was all it needed to break Paul's last remnant of confidence. He knew the new man was only being sent to replace a medically unfit officer, but it sounded the last knell of failure. His dream of bridges and embankments was lost. This command had meant so much to him, this chance to use his skill for good rather than destruction. But when his replacement arrived, Paul would have to report that the Russians had gone, refusing to work with him any longer due to a professional error that had killed two of their men.

His hand stilled in the act of trying to knot his tie—a hopeless task with one arm in a sling. Dear God, how had it happened? How *could* it have happened after he had gone over and over his calculations and surveyed the ground with such thoroughness? But it had; two men were dead!

Sick inside, he threw the tie aside and turned away from the mirror that showed him a failure. But he had to face himself and the memory of that day. It was difficult. All that stood out in his mind was Swarovsky standing above him accusing him of criminal professional negligence, and the interminable funeral that followed. Apart from that, he had only a hazy impression of being thrown backward with great violence, and excruciating pain in his shoulder, a girl—probably Irina—making him shout in agony whilst men held him down, and a train journey that made him ill.

He felt the sweat break on his body as he tried to think back over what had happened earlier. There seemed to be a block in his mind that would not clear. Shaking slightly, he sat on a box, because he could no longer trust his legs, and put all his efforts into pinpointing those moments he could still recall with clarity. He had placed the charges himself, as usual. Yes, he had a clear picture of running out the fuses and connecting them to the exploder. He remembered stooping over it and the sun hot on his neck. Yes, he had checked that everyone was clear of the area, then given the thumbs-up to Banks before depressing the plunger.

He saw nothing of the ground in front of his boots as he stared at it, heard none of the chatter between his two men and Yagutov as they idled beside the engine, because that moment of recall had told him there could have been no error. The charges were all linked together and went off simultaneously. He knew enough of explosives to hear that they were right and to judge by the resulting fall if they had been rightly placed.

His heart began to thud and dizziness returned. He would never have walked forward into danger, led other men into danger, if there had been any indication that something was not quite right. In his mind's eye he went over that walk as they had advanced to inspect the successful blasting. He was saying something over his shoulder and walking up to join the Russians who were coming over from the train. Swarovsky turned and went back for something, but his two N.C.O.s had gone on, until about twenty yards inside the cutting . . .

For a long time Paul sat staring at the ground as he accepted what his senses and intellect told him. Going through the sequence once more in his mind, he knew he was right. Then, he slowly got to his feet and went across to the supply-truck, knowing what he would find.

It took Paul longer than usual to walk to the lake. With the sight in one eye limited, he went carefully on legs that were none too steady. He stopped once, wondering if he could make it, then pushed on with determination. If the bivouac was breaking up, the sooner he saw Swarovsky the better. As luck would have it, he ran slap-bang into the one person he would rather avoid, just as he emerged from the trees. It was pointless changing direction, because Irina spotted him and hurried forward.

"This is very foolish!"

"Perhaps . . . but very necessary."

She put her hand on his arm. "I was on my way to see you. Three hours ago you were still unconscious. You are in no fit state to be on your feet even. There may be . . ."

"I have a vital job to do on this railway. I must speak to your husband."

He began to move forward, but she barred his path. "It will do no good. He will have nothing to do with you."

"He will when he knows what this is about."

He tried to pass, but she would not give way. "Captain Anderson, do you not understand? He is in a mood of great bitterness."

"Is he? That is nothing to the mood I am in," he replied crisply.

She began to plead. "You are still in a state of shock. Now is no time to act hastily. Perhaps he should not have said what he did to you when you were suffering yourself, but nothing you do now will help. It is too late for apologies."

His rush of inflamed resentment that she should believe so easily that he was guilty came out in his tone.

"I was not intending to ask him for one."

The lovely eyes widened, and a tiny frown appeared on her brow beneath the sweep of pale hair. He took a vicious delight in knowing he had disconcerted her.

"I do not quite understand."

"Neither did I, at first."

"But you suggest . . ."

"That your husband is wrong," he finished for her. "Is that so difficult to believe?"

She shook her head slowly. "No."

"Then you find it difficult to believe *I* could be right," he concluded with obvious bitterness.

"I do not know you well enough to judge, Captain Anderson. Do not accuse me when you have been at such great pains to remain aloof." She stood aside, looking at him with some kind of reluctant sadness. "You cannot bring yourself to accept him, but he is a good man—loyal, courageous, and idealistic. He has been through the horror and anguish of war."

"So have I," he said thickly.

"He was wounded twice."

"So was I . . . and gassed."

She put out her hand in appeal. "His men deserted him."

"Mine were all killed before my eyes."

They seemed to be locked in some kind of battle he did not understand, yet when she moved so close he could feel her breath fanning his throat, he had never felt less like an enemy.

"But you have fought your war and won. His is still going on."

It was defeat. He realised he really did feel very weak and should have stayed in bed. It was imperative to get away before he succumbed right before her eyes. But he found himself unable to stop one last thrust at her.

"I am the one with cuts and bruises, yet you speak as if *he* were your patient. I wonder why."

He walked on, leaving her standing at the edge of the trees. As Corporal Banks had said, the bivouac was broken. The men were sitting around just waiting for the word to move off. They looked at him with belligerence as he made his unsteady way past them. But he had spotted the Russian with his sister beside the horses, and concentrated on reaching them before he had to sit down.

Olga saw him approaching and drew her brother's attention to the fact, but the Colonel turned back to his horses. Paul clamped his lips together. So he was still fighting his war, was he? Then he had a serious battle on hand!

"I'd like a word with you, Colonel Swarovsky . . . in private," Paul said as he drew near. "And it is not to offer an apology," he added, thinking of grey-green eyes and a face that haunted him.

"I have no time for conversation, either professional or personal. I am preparing to leave."

Conscious that Olga was watching him closely, he snapped, "Then you are taking a traitor with you."

As he guessed, the other man lost all interest in the horses. "The liaison is over. I made that clear two days ago. I request that you leave and return to your own camp."

Paul looked at the fine, strong face, with its soft moustache and eyes that were too expressive for a man who wanted to be a warrior, and saw all those who had walked out on a war leaving their allies to fight on.

"I am English. We see a job through to its end. You Russians are prone to giving up halfway, I've noticed."

He thought the riding-whip was going to cut across his face but assumed his opponent had been prevented from hitting a man because he already had cuts and bandages. Rapid Russian sent Olga away, and they faced each other across a patch of shoreline.

"You are in my country, at your own admission, not to fight but to pursue your profession. You have derided my rank and my right to command these men. You buried with full honours a traitor I shot as he deserved. You have killed two of my most loyal men with professional incompetence." He took a deep breath. "By any rules, it is widsom to withdraw when one's supposed ally begins to fight on the side of the enemy."

Paul immediately retaliated. "By the rules, it is also of first importance to fight the enemy within rather than the one who makes no secret of his opposition. I did not kill your men. They were victims of a clever plot."

Despite the contempt in the other's face, Paul went on to explain how he knew the second explosion had been carefully planned, ending with the fact that he had checked his supplies and found explosive material missing. "Anyone could have taken it when we were at the cutting. Theoretically it is under guard all the time, but so many people come and go whilst work is in progress it would not be difficult to slip something inside a shirt without being seen—especially when one assumes every man can be trusted. Damn it all, I have had your men guarding that truck from the enemy! It seems he was in their ranks all along."

"If you knew the true spirit of my men, you would not attempt this pathetic lie in order to cover your ineptitude," was the icy comment.

"And if you knew anything about engineering, you'd know that landslide was caused by an explosion too high and far back to be my work," Paul said equally coldly. "You discovered one traitor in your ranks. I suggest you have another."

"That one was a Bolshevik spy planted to cause unrest. They are sent everywhere—to each village and town, to every loyal group. That is how they work, how they hope to undermine the true spirit of Russia. You are helping them by this stand."

Paul turned away in disgust. "To hell with the Bolsheviks! It is immaterial to me who triumphs in your bloody war, but if all your side are dogmatically blind to the truth when it stares them in the face, then I'd back the Reds to win by a knockout!"

The reaction to that remark was so sharply reflected in Swarovsky's face, Paul tried another approach. "All right, look at it this way. If you had not turned back and returned to the train for something *you* would now be lying in a grave alongside your loyal Sergeant Gromov. It's only by a lucky chance that I am still alive. That explosion was designed to wipe out both officers and the senior N.C.O.s. It was placed with full knowledge of what we would all do after the blasting."

The Russian stared at him expressionlessly for a moment. "Who are you suggesting laid this . . . plot?"

"How the hell do I know?" said Paul savagely. "You are their commander, as you so often remind me. Which of them is most likely?"

Swarovsky gave a grim smile. "I would trust every one of them with my life."

"Right," said Paul, losing his temper completely. "Then I suggest you do. I need your men to finish my railway. Let them do so, and perhaps we shall catch him the next time he tries to kill us—because he will, I promise you."

S i x

The relief officer was never sent from Murmansk. Paul telegraphed such a vehement reassurance that everything was going splendidly, minimising his own injuries and explaining away the landslide as careless banking by inexperienced men, that headquarters declared themselves satisfied. In truth, they were glad to leave the matter in the hands of the young officer. There were more serious matters in other parts of North Russia which were presenting grave problems to the Allied Commanders in Murmansk, and in Archangel, where the hastily conceived White Russian government had made its home.

All was not going as well as expected, although there was a general reluctance to admit it. The British and their allies had been overtaken by something they were not sure they wanted, after all. The murder of the Russian Imperial Family by the Bolsheviks was looked upon with horror in the western world, and the purge of the nobles, the wealthy, and the intellectual citizens—always an act that brought out chivalrous instincts in others—inspired the desire to support those who were standing fast in the path of revolution in order to save a great nation. But if all this encouraged active sympathy, it also had come at a time when the Allies were war-weary, mourning the loss of their sons, and financially near-broke. Whilst one section of the British and American nations urged the need to stamp out Bolshevism, Communism, and any doctrines that threatened democracy, the other half campaigned to bring back soldiers who had miraculously escaped death in Europe and were now risking their lives in someone else's war.

Governments were divided, ministers uncertain. Those in high places had just realised they had mistaken the situation. It was not just a case of dissatisfied workers in the big cities being incited to violence by a few powerful orators. Those who had gone over to the Reds were staying with them . . . and recruiting hundreds more every week. The Bolsheviks were not the disorganised rabble they had been at the start. Most of the deserting army had been re-organised to fight for a "people's" Russia, and many of the officers forced to serve the new regime. It was that or death for themselves or their families if they refused. Initial victories by the White Armies were now being reversed as the Red numbers multiplied and order was being brought out of chaos. The situation in "free" North Russia was not being helped by the multitudinous small bands of troops, of widely assorted nationalities, under the command of foreign officers, mostly British, who were forced to act independently of each other due to the terrain.

It was becoming clear to the Allies that the "show of strength" they had envisaged had to be a mighty one if it was to succeed, and as large numbers of British and Allied troops had already been killed whilst fighting for the Whites, it was no easy task to approve the commitment of thousands more to those already in the area.

The Allied generals were worried, and so were the politicians. But not nearly as worried as those officers stationed out in the heart of the arctic tundra and forests. They were a long way from civilisation if they needed to reach it in a hurry, and the only means of getting there was by the railway. More than ever it had become a vital part of the campaign.

But to those isolated halfway down the line at a siding, little of this was known. Orders from headquarters merely urged that the work progress with all possible speed, and the snippets of information gleaned from those on passing trains gave no serious cause for worry. At Archangel, it was known, balls were being enjoyed by the titled and influential despite the fact that the town had been no more than a cluster of rough wooden buildings, in former times. At Lake Onega, the landing-strip was completed, the sea plane haven already in use. To Paul it seemed that everything was under control.

Work on the cutting went slowly ahead, but the tension brought on by pressures of physical exertion, lack of relaxation or emotional outlet, and conflicting personalities being held under control put an air of unrest over the group.

Irina was well aware of the various undercurrents amongst the group and found no comfort for her unease. Sasha would say nothing of the reason why he reversed his decision to leave, after his conversation with Paul Anderson. Olga had said the Englishman referred to a "traitor in their midst" before Sasha had told her to go away, but more than that she did not know.

Irina noticed, with curiosity, that their ally had moved his tent to a position beside the supply-truck and now had his corporal sleeping inside the truck. What he could wish to guard so carefully, she could not imagine, but there was also a bewildering determination on the part of her husband to remain in easy distance of that truck. Had something of great value come down on one of the trains? If it had, they were only drawing the attention of everyone to the fact by their persistent guardianship. Paul Anderson seemed to make a show of it. Already, as the Englishman moved about the site, Sasha's men watched him resentfully, working only because their own officer had decreed that they should do so. But it was apparent they had little stomach for it now and distrusted the foreigner who gave all the orders. Sasha watched the young officer, as if hoping he would make another mistake, and Olga's eyes practically never looked at anything other than the movements of a man she hoped to coax into some kind of relationship. All in all, Irina felt all those watching eyes isolated even further someone for whom she felt a kind of piqued sympathy. In all her dealings with him, she had come up against resentment and downright aggression, yet something told her he needed more than medical care in the days to come.

With that in mind, she strolled over to him late one evening when they were camped at the cutting, telling the others she must see how her patient's arm was progressing. He was sitting beside the supply-truck, writing on a sheet of official paper, so she stood waiting until he should finish. Her shadow fell across the page, and he looked up.

"Busy, as usual, Captain Anderson?"

He got to his feet, screwing the top on the bottle of ink as he did so. "There's a lot to do."

"It was not my intention to disturb you."

He held onto his pen at that. "What can I do for you?"

It was oh-so-polite, but she persevered. "I thought it time I enquired how you are feeling now. I told you to keep your arm in that sling for some days, yet you have been walking about today waving it at every opportunity."

"It's in there now," he said quickly.

She smiled. "I suspect only because it is so painful you need to support it. At this early stage, it could so easily slip out again, you know."

He fidgetted with the pen. "I have never thanked you for patching me up."

"There is no need. I told you at the start that I am with the group for such things." She smiled again encouragingly. "My efforts have made you look quite villainous, I fear, but the cuts should heal without leaving deep scars. Your wife will not be upset at your appearance."

"I . . . I am not married," he replied too quickly.

"I see. Your sweetheart, then."

"Er . . . yes."

As she had guessed, a faint flush crept over his face at the forthright words. It was a strangely pleasant experience to make a tall, strong man betray his emotions so involuntarily and know she could do it again at any time she wished. He might hide behind an aggressive role, but she could reach the man with feminine guile. Whilst he was vulnerable, she ventured further.

"I have also come across to ask you to a party. One of the men celebrates his Name Day today, and we must give him presents and a feast." She saw the obvious uncertainty in his dark eyes and pushed on. "When we are at the lake, I accept that you prefer to remain by the train, but here we are all together. Would it not be foolish for England to sit aside when Russia is celebrating twenty yards away?"

Quite plainly in a quandary, he mumbled, "Does your husband . . . I mean . . . What exactly is a Name Day?"

Feeling that she had the advantage, she put her hands behind her onto the truck and gave a little jump so that she was sitting in the doorway of the open truck with her feet swinging free. There was a curious warm smell of metal, straw, and foodstuffs inside the truck, and she realised it had become part of her life now, where flowers, perfume, and furniture polish had dominated her childhood. In a fey moment she grew chilled. Would those pleasures ever return to her? Life, that wild, wide expanse of years, had suddenly compressed into a ball that consisted of pain, sweat, and the smell that was in that truck.

Coming out of it she was aware that he was looking at her with an expression in his brown eyes that made her long to cry out to him all that she had felt in that moment. There was a haven of comfort in his youth and strength, a glimpse of something she had once known centuries ago in the softly working jaw that could be so stubbornly set, and an unbearable offer in his eyes—unbearable because it was all she wanted yet could not accept.

"Is it the same as a christening anniversary?"

She stared at him, trembling with her new knowledge. "A . . . a . . . christening anniversary?"

"Are you feeling all right?" He moved toward her with concern, but she had to stop him. It would be fatal.

"Yes . . . I had forgotten . . . the Name Day, you said. Oh, it is very exciting—more than a birthday." Somehow she managed to talk on, despite the fact that she was remembering all he had ever said to her; how he had attacked her with words on so many occasions; how she had ministered to him whilst in a coma, thinking he was just another patient. How could she have been so blind all this time? She should have been appalled, should have got up right then and walked away, but the moment was too sweet, the nearness of this man who had put a pulse-beat back into a frozen heart too precious, the vivid evening sunlight too beautiful to banish by common sense. For once, she wanted to be free, young, and beautiful for someone she only now recognised.

So she launched into a description of the celebration of the day of the saint for whom a Russian is named—and there were many saints. But tonight there was music in her voice, magic in the slight breeze that lifted her hair, isolation in that railway truck that made a mockery of the presence of forty other people busily engaged in their own activities. There had never been a more enchanted place nor any more beautiful scene on earth than a cutting through pine trees and a young man in khaki uniform sitting on the edge of a wooden box as he looked across the four feet that separated them.

"The one who is honoured receives gifts and congratulations, and an official blessing is read to him by the senior person present," she told him. "The celebrations vary according to where the party is being held. In Russian villages there is music and singing with a feast spread out upon the grass. The *barishnyi* . . . the village girls . . . all in traditional dress will put garlands of flowers around the necks of the guests. Then the girls will dance. Such dancing is magnificent, the glory of Russia, you know. The accordions play the old melodies everyone knows, and when the girls have finished their graceful dancing, it will be the turn of the men." She smiled, caught up in memories, and leaned toward him to try to put the mental vision into his mind by her words. "Each young man is strong and proud. He will try to better any other with the height of his leaps and the frenzy of his acrobatics. There is much to drink at such celebrations, and this stimulates the efforts of those in the dance. It becomes more than a dance. Perhaps an attempt to establish superiority in the eyes of the village girls."

"It must be quite an event," Paul said, lost in something that was certainly not the mental visions she was trying to pass to him.

Irina felt her own cheeks growing warm. "In the city it is different," she said in a rush, to cover her weakness. "For my sisters and me there was always a dinner party for our friends and sometimes troika rides across the snowy squares or skating on the River Neva when we were in St. Petersburg. There were flowers arriving all day, and chocolates. It was always a most exciting time, and everyone was happy. If there had been a quarrel, it was put aside and forgotten on that day. Even lovers' tiffs were mended. I remember my sisters receiving posies from young men they had not seen for months."

"And you . . . Did you receive posies?"

Unable to help herself, she continued to hold his gaze even when the depth of painful warmth in his eyes should have warned her it was time to walk away.

"I was too young. I last celebrated my Name Day with my family five years ago."

"Five years!" It was said with protective indignation.

"It was my own doing. I defied my father and went off to become a nurse. My father is an eminent professor of philosophy whose work ensures that he moves from place to place, hardly ever having time to stay at home. For those times I had leave, he seemed always to be away, giving lectures, advising at teaching institutions. He now lives in Switzerland with my mother and sisters. They all left Russia before the purge of intellectuals, I am thankful to say." She put her hands behind her knees to cushion her legs from the sharp edge of the truck. "What of your family?"

A slight frown appeared on the freckled forehead. "I have a mother and one sister. My father was killed during the first months of the war."

"Then you are head of the family?"

"That's a strange way of putting it, but I suppose you could say that."

She needed to know more, to share as much of him as was possible. "Do you miss them very much? You are far away from them here."

He looked down at the pen still in his hand. "I've only seen them twice since 1914. We don't have a lot in common." His gaze came up to meet hers again, and there was a curious lift inside her breast as he smiled faintly. It made him look younger, that small contact with the softer emotions. She realised it was the first time he had smiled at her, and treasured it.

"All I share with my family now is the same blood. How about you? Do you miss yours?"

"Yes, but I have only just realised it," she told him with exciting honesty. With this man she could make such confessions and hope for understanding.

"Perhaps you haven't had time before. This place is very peaceful."

She looked away across the clearing to where the cutting scored through the rock and trees of the hillock. The sun was catching one bank and turning it pale gold as it began its downward slope. "The memories are too strong today," she said softly, almost afraid to look back at him. "For a while it was as if I were back there."

It was a moment before he asked, "Why doesn't he send you to join your family in Switzerland?"

It startled her. The visions faded, and she turned back sharply. "He needs me."

Their glances locked. "But what do you need?"

It was broken. What on earth was she doing here with a man who had been known to her barely a month? What mad notions had travelled through her head and senses whilst sitting in an unreal world of memory pictures and things that could not be?

Jumping from her perch, she found herself, for the first time in her memory, unable to hold on to her composure.

"This is not a time when a person considers his own needs, Captain Anderson. Perhaps that is the reason why you do not get on with Sasha. He considers the cause, not his personal ambitions and desires."

Colour flooded his face, but it was born of anger, not embarrassment. "Many a good man has fallen for the sake of a cause that dies with him. My work will still be here a hundred years from now. I lost my idealism in the mud of France, Madame Swarovskaya. There, it was more important to act than dream."

Unaccountably, she wanted to hit him. Suddenly depressed, she turned and began to walk back across the clearing. Passing the entrance to the cutting she shivered. Soon, it would be finished. How much longer before all the work was completed? Where would they all go then? She remembered Olga asking how they would feel when the Englishman got on that train and went off, leaving them with only a distant echo and a puff of smoke over the trees. At the time she had answered that she did not think of the future, but at that moment she was afraid the present might not last long enough.

Paul took his arm out of the sling to shave. There seemed to be a need to make an extra effort, as if he were going to a Russian state occasion as the official representative of his country, instead of merely walking across a clearing to share a makeshift picnic with a group of people he saw every hour of the twenty-four.

It had taken him a long time to decide on going, but Corporal Banks and Sapper Stevens were all set to join in the festivities, so it would only make him appear ridiculous to sit alone. He soon realised it would be better to suffer the arrows of jealousy in their midst than burn with it as he watched her laughing and talking twenty yards away.

Even so, he consigned to the devil the man whose Name Day it happened to be. He wanted no part of their national customs and festivities, knowing one of them was doing his utmost to sabotage their work, to the extent of killing those in command. Although Swarovsky had reversed his decision to leave, Paul felt it was more for the sake of watching for another mistake to be made than any belief in Paul's story of planned murder. Admittedly, the Russian kept his eye on the stores now, but it could have been only because Corporal Banks had been told of the theft of explosives and slept in the truck.

Completing his dressing, Paul felt somewhat like a man going to the scaffold. Swarovsky was bound to be icily correct on such an occasion; Olga would probably make things damned uncomfortable with her unpredictable behaviour. Since that day he had been caught kissing her, he had been careful to prevent the possibility of a repetition. The very last thing he wanted was any kind of involvement with her, for it would almost certainly run away with him. That one occasion had shown him how easily she had awoken in him a basic response that now slumbered uneasily. It would be all too satisfying to take up her offer, if it were not for all the other things involved. She was the aristocratic sister of a man to whom Paul must never show weakness or be in debt. She was not a village courtesan—even if she behaved like one—but a high-born foreigner, and he would be leaving her to her fate the minute his job was done.

If they were not enough reasons, there was the one outstanding barrier to an emotional adventure with Olga Swarovskaya. *Irina.* After their meeting several hours earlier, he was bewildered and angry. She had approached, taken him unawares with a new relaxed friendliness that had stifled his attempts to remain aloof. Then, suddenly, the competent nurse, the gentle dignified aristocrat, had turned into a young girl full of warmth, merriment, and a strange yearning that touched his own and joined hands for a few moments. He could have sworn she was appealing to him for something he longed to give, that she had sensed the truth and accepted it. His dislike and jealousy of that one man had crashed into the moment and taken away the girl. The return of the woman of experience had brought a return of an opinion of him she shared with her husband. When she walked away, he had felt viciously resentful. He was a target for both women, unable by convention and the protection of Swarovsky to treat them as they deserved. He wondered rather desperately whether he could signal headquarters that they were hampering the work and request their removal to Murmansk as soon as possible.

After checking once more that the door on the supply-truck was firmly padlocked, he set off for the group with the air of being the British ambassador at the court of the tsar. But, of course, there was no tsar, and Russia was in a state of civil war. How easy it was to forget that!

They had lit a fire—strictly against safety regulations—but Paul wisely decided to say nothing on the subject. Looking at all the rough, bearded faces clustering around he felt, for the first time, his own vulnerability in their midst. If the Bolshevik amongst them was doing his work on their minds with any success, his own life would be the first to be forfeited in any uprising. He went further in thought, imagining what they might do to Swarovsky. His death would not be quick or easy at the hands of brutal peasants who had been treated as such by the Russian officer. They were not so cut off that they had not heard of the atrocities committed by both sides in the war, and these men lived by the same laws. Fear flooded through him at the next thought. What would be the fate of the two women?

Swallowing down the sickness of the grim pictures that filled his head, he realised very forcibly that every day the women spent here was an act of courage. Olga so obviously was afraid, but Irina never showed it. How could he ensure their safety with only an N.C.O. and a batman to back him up? His mind raced with the knowledge that he must prepare an emergency plan in case the whole company decided to go over to the Reds *before* linking up with them. Somehow the women must be defended.

It was not the best frame of mind to be in for a party, and Paul tried to wipe out such thoughts as he walked over to his host to offer a quiet greeting.

"Good evening. Thank you for asking me to join you."

Swarovsky stood up, tall and formal in the worn uniform. "In Russia it is the custom to extend hospitality to everyone." He indicated a rug-covered box next to his sister. "Will you sit here?"

Damn, thought Paul, just what I did not want! Feeling somewhat self-conscious he made a clumsy effort at a bow, feeling that it was expected of him by the ladies, then sat down, having avoided looking directly at Irina. But he was aware that the occasion had led her and Olga to take from their large leather trunks dresses that looked entirely incongruous against a background of steam engines, piled railway lines, and dark coniferous trees. Both were softly feminine with frills and embroidery, Olga's being blue, and Irina's the colour of shade-sheltering primroses. It affected him strangely to sit there with them at a bright midnight party, for they somehow managed to create an atmosphere of dignified elegance in the heart of an arctic forest. He could not help wondering if an Englishwoman could do the same. These Russians had an exotic ability to do the bizarre and make it perfectly acceptable. Not only that, they made the normal appear stuffy.

Olga put her hand on his and smiled warmly up at him, which made him feel anything but stuffy.

"We must thank you for the brandy you sent over. It was very kind of you, Paul."

"Not at all, Iri . . . your sister-in-law said it was usual to . . . well, to give presents . . . things like that."

He made a hash of the sentence because he had so nearly spoken Irina's name. He thought of her so often, it had been a dangerous slip of the tongue. But Olga had noticed. He could tell by the way the blue of her eyes grew sharper.

"How much more did she tell you?"

"All of it . . . about the Name Day, I mean."

"Yes . . . She spent so much time with you, Sasha and I guessed she could not have been the whole time talking about your health. Are you back to full strength now?"

"Oh, yes," he assured her, falling straight into the trap.

"Good. You must prove it to me sometime." She smiled teasingly, but with a sharp challenge in her eyes. "Although, with one arm in a sling, you might be slightly hampered."

Cursing again the necessity for a guest to sit next to the host's sister, he made a brave attempt to retaliate. "Look, I think there is something we should get straight. I . . . "

"Shhh!" she told him softly. "Sasha is going to read the address. Did Irina tell you of that?"

Silence fell as the Colonel got to his feet, and Paul had to abandon his attempt to put Olga right about his intentions.

"She mentioned it, but not what it contained," he said.

She leant closer. "Then I will translate for you."

Not for the first time did Paul curse his lack of knowledge of the Russian language. But from then on, the evening turned into a fascinating fantasy that caught him up against his will. After the address, read with great ceremony, there were a series of short chants shouted with verve and enthusiasm by almost forty male voices in chorus. The celebrant was slapped on the back, shaken by the hand, kissed and hugged by his fellows to the accompaniment of wishes for a long life, a good woman, and a full belly.

Then, the man walked forward and knelt before his officer, head bent, to receive a blessing. Still on his knees, he bowed his head before the ladies and displayed almost grovelling appreciation of the murmured words they offered. Paul was uncomfortably aware that such a practice of homage to a man's superiors was still rife in Russia. He could not imagine any of his countrymen giving or accepting simple respect in such exaggerated manner, yet he had seen it on several occasions here in this forest.

The man was getting to his feet when Paul said to Olga, "Ask him to stay a moment." She spoke sharply, and the man turned back, looking apprehensive as she said more to him. Getting to his feet, Paul asked the girl to translate as he explained that he had had no time to prepare a gift for the occasion, but hoped the man would accept a memento taken from the hut of a German officer in France two years ago.

When he guessed she had passed all that on, he took a couple of steps forward, offering to shake the man by the hand. For a moment or two the blunt, bearded face stared at him, then the hand came up in automatic response. Paul gripped it and smiled his congratulations before reaching into his pocket to hold out an egg-timer of Bavarian carved wood. The Russian appeared to be in a trance of amazed disbelief at what was happening and almost afraid of the consequences of such strange behaviour on the part of a man who had given orders to them all ever since they arrived. It took some persuasion to make the soldier take the gift, which he did only after Olga had passed on Paul's message that it was the usual way English people gave and received presents and that Paul would be much offended if the customs of his country were ignored.

Muttering into his beard, the peasant-soldier backed away clutching the egg-timer and was soon surrounded by his fellows, all much taken with the gift. In childish delight they turned it over and over, watching the sand run through the glass. As Paul had guessed, they had never seen such a thing before and had no idea what it was, but all found it intriguing.

Then he became conscious of Swarovsky's thundercloud expression and knew the reason for it. It was Olga who put it into words, however.

"That was a mistake. You will get no respect from any of them now."

"That is a risk I shall have to take," he replied calmly, looking at her brother. "If you ever come to England, you will find it is not necessary to make men kneel before they will obey you."

Almost before he had finished speaking, there came the sound of clapping—slow, rhythmic, increasing in volume. He turned to find the Russians clustering around the fire, smiling in his direction, showing their friendliness and appreciation in their own inimitable manner.

Someone began to sing. It was the start of a celebration Paul would never forget, for music and song to Russians is irresistible. How they sang, accelerating the rhythms with clapping hands and stamping feet! Each man was worthy of a concert platform, with the added virtue of singing purely for the pleasure of expressing his emotions. At first, the songs were melodious, happy; the dancing graceful expressions of the body. But as the minutes passed and thirsts were continuously quenched, the singing became wild, passionate, and martial. The dancing, too, took on a flavour of challenge, each man endeavouring to outdo the others with his feats. Paul was caught up in their exuberance, marvelling at the acrobatic prowess as they leapt, twirled, turned somersaults, and walked on their hands.

The amount of alcohol consumed was formidable—their entire present stock, Paul estimated with resignation—and the daring increased. One man made a brave leap across the fire, and there began a dangerous bid to better it. Logs were flung on and the flames shot higher. So did the Russians. It became a heady and breathtaking experience to watch such a thing for the first time in his life. The midnight sun, the tall surrounding pines, the clearing by an isolated railway track, a great fire moving with tongues of flames, the ancient steam-engine standing on the line behind the dancers, bronzed by the glow from the fire and representing their only means of escape, the clapping and stamping, the great baritone chants of encouragement, and the sheer vitality of emotion engendered by those he watched had Paul's own emotions surging to escape.

Soon he was drinking glass for glass with them, the warmth of the brandy reaching every part of him, speeding his pulse and slowing his thoughts. When a request was made for the two officers' swords, he surrendered his with no thought of danger. But they were used in a demonstration of a hazardous Russian sword-dance, and he found himself joining in the virile shout of "Hi-ya!" each time a particular feat was accomplished.

When one of the horses was employed by an N.C.O. of Swarovsky's late regiment to demonstrate an amazing performance of trick riding, Paul even rose to his feet in acclamation. More brandy and he had reached the stage where he might well have embraced his fellows as they did, with no thought of embarrassment. All at once, they were splendid people. Suspicion and distrust had fled. Bolshevik spies and saboteurs were far from his mind.

They began to eat. Strange pancakes filled with rich mixtures, cooked as near to perfection as their rations would allow, and spicy meat toasted in the fire on sticks. A servant brought things to the officers and ladies, bowing low and placing the plates on a spotless white cloth. It was all part of the fantasy, the china and damask in the midst of a forest, and persuaded Paul that he was living in a place somewhere between waking and sleeping.

His brandy had long ago run out, and the Russian Colonel was pouring his own vodka into their glasses. It was as if the two officers were now locked in their own competitive demonstration of manly prowess as Swarovsky tossed back glass after glass, challenging his guest to match him. But there was more than a drinking contest between them; they were well aware of that. Each had something to prove to the other, and at that moment, there was no other way to do it.

The colourless vodka seemed quite innocuous to Paul, and he wondered vaguely why the Russians set such store by it. A bottle was emptied between them, and his unsmiling opponent opened another with deliberation. When the Russian held it out, Paul put up his glass to be refilled yet again.

Another wild dance was begun, and he found himself stamping his feet to the rhythm. But the dancers seemed to be turning twice as many somersaults now. It made him giddy, so he looked away from the group by the fire. Somehow his arm had crept along the back of Olga's chair, and she was against him, laughing up with sapphire-sparkled eyes. But it was at the girl beside her he gazed with such longing. Irina was flushed and laughing, back to the young girl of their earlier meeting and as much part of his dream state as the rest.

His gaze travelled hungrily across her pale, shining hair, down the cheek to her throat curving into the soft primrose-pale frills. His heart began to hammer as he imagined her bare shoulders beneath his hands, her mouth parting beneath his own. He imagined . . . It was then he realised he was very decidedly drunk. But she must have been in the same condition, for a slight turn of her head brought her gaze on a collision course with his own. At once, he felt as strong as the leaping men, as fearless as the acrobatic horseman, as full of daring as those who had dodged the flashing swords. There in her eyes was an echo of what he had glimpsed earlier that day, but this time there was no hesitant, unbelieving wonder. This time there was total commitment. That mutual recognition was so painful in its unspoken acknowledgement, he identified it with all those throbbing songs of Russia that had tonight softened his soul.

Finally dragging her gaze away to answer the man beside her, Irina broke the magnetic contact, and Paul returned to find Olga staring up at him from the curve of his arm.

"You will be safer playing your game of trains than that one," she whispered savagely.

He could only stare at her, trying to prevent the image of Irina's face from imprinting itself on the other girl's features. The two kept changing in bewildering fashion until he realised the whole place was swaying before his eyes. Instinct told him he had no head for Russian celebrations, and retreat was essential whilst he could still walk.

The soldiers were too busy to notice his departure, but he managed a mumbled thank you and a clumsy bow to his host and hostesses. As he walked unsteadily across the clearing, Irina's eyes haunted him. That final look as he bade them all goodnight seemed to be asking—no, *begging*—him to do something. He was not sure what, but it made him heavy-hearted. She had looked anything but happy then.

Reaching his tent, he loosened his tie, pulled it off, unbuttoned the neck of his shirt, then sank onto his bed with a groan. The emotional elation of the night had gone. He just felt heavy with brandy and the problems ahead. Now there was a new one. What in God's name did she expect him to do now?

Maudlin with self-pity and sexual frustration, he rolled back onto his pillow and reached for the brandy bottle. Might as well have complete oblivion now that he was almost there. With the bottle to his lips and brandy running down his chin, he was brought up into a sitting position with heart thudding painfully. It sounded like all the beasts of hell let loose out there, for the air was rent by strident and chilling howls that could not have been made by the Russian soldiers.

Hardly aware of moving, he found himself at the tent entrance, clutching the pole for support as he stared in muddled fashion across the clearing.

For a moment it was nothing but a blur, but gradually he made out the moving pattern of great grey bodies—five or six of them—in the outskirts of the pines. Restless, pacing, they seemed intent on those assembled in the clearing who had frozen into immobility and were staring back at the creatures. The singing and stamping had stopped. The fire lit the animals' eyes with a bright yellow reflection as the Russians watched in awed apprehension.

Outside the Swarovsky tent, all three were mesmerised by the repeated howls, Olga gripping the back of her chair as she stared wild-eyed across the clearing. But Irina was protected by her husband's arm held around her in a possessive manner, keeping her close against his body. That embrace brought out all the emotion the evening's frenzy had released in Paul. That embrace shut him out completely. He remembered the way she had looked at him a moment ago, and how she had once said, "You have driven them from their home. Now they will gather and drive you from yours."

It was too much. Drawing his revolver, he began firing into the air and muttering, "Clear off, you bloody great wolves. You'll never drive me away from anywhere."

Through badly focused vision, he saw a sea of faces turn his way, so he waved the gun wildly in their direction.

"They don't frighten *me*," he boasted drunkenly, then slowly slid down the supporting tent pole to pass out on the ground of that clearing he had created.

S e v e n

The repercussions of that night were soon brought home to Paul. Such unwise drinking in his weakened state combined with lack of sleep and rich Russian food to make him feel extremely ill during the next twenty-four hours. Unable even to lift his head from the pillow, he nevertheless flatly refused to let Irina anywhere near him. Sapper Stevens, already much put out by the giving away of the egg-timer, was even more disapproving of his officer's decision to turn the Russian nurse away, but Paul used such forceful language the batman did not argue for long and made an embarrassed apology to the visitor.

By halfway through the day, Paul was able to identify the separate aches and pains sufficiently to realise he must have jarred his shoulder in falling. But even that acute throbbing pain was preferable to letting her see him in his present state. As he lay moaning and miserable on his bed, he knew he had made a colossal fool of himself in front of them all and chalked one up to Alexander Ivanovich Swarovsky. For long minutes he lay accepting the fact that the Russian officer had deliberately set out to drink him off his feet with the intention of bringing him down before the assembled company. It must have been a delightful bonus for Swarovsky when the wolves put in an appearance.

Frowning, Paul tried to remember exactly what had happened, but his head was too sore for such definite thought. He had a vague recollection of shouting—no, *swearing*—and firing his revolver rather wildly. There had been an intention on his part to show all the scared Russians his own great courage in front of the beasts, but . . . oh, God, his foot had caught on the tent pole and he had collapsed face first onto the ground. Groaning with humiliation, he turned his face against the pillow. The men he did not care about, but how would he face the two women after this? Then he groaned louder as a new thought hit him. Had they been in on the plan? Was that why Irina had issued the invitation? Closing his eyes, he drifted into uneasy sleep convinced that while Olga could very well have taken part in a conspiracy to lower his confidence, Irina could never have done so. There was no difficulty in remembering how she had looked at him with a world of longing in her eyes. . . .

When he awoke, he could tell by the angle of the sun that it was late in the evening, but his head still had knives stabbing it and his shoulder began to throb the minute he moved it. Depressed and full of self-condemnation, he told himself he had learned a lesson he would never forget. In future, the Russians would celebrate Name Days without him.

Outside, as if to mock him, he heard the sounds of work being continued normally—shovelling, digging, stone-breaking, wheelbarrows trundling along the wooden walkways, horses dragging rocks to the edge of the forest. He heard the soldiers shouting to each other, singing with trueness of tone, laughing as they relaxed and ate. Apparently, everyone else was feeling fine. He closed his eyes and sighed heavily. He doubted he could even sit up, much less stand. The engineer-in-charge was laid flat by a mammoth hangover while the navvies got on with the job. What a recommendation for his ability to command!

There was a rustle, and he opened his eyes to see Olga standing inside the tent arranging the flaps so that they covered the entrance. His blood pressure shot up, setting his heart racing with the anger and mortification her blatant intrusion on his privacy aroused.

"Are you *mad?*" he choked, struggling up from his pillow. "My God, this is ridiculous! Get out of here at once!" Giddy, supremely conscious of his undressed state, and feeling trapped, he let his temper run high. "I told my batman to let no one in. How did you get past him?"

She smiled. "He is not there. Would you like me to call him for you so that you can have me thrown out?" She came to sit on the box beside his bed, taking up the watch Stevens had put there when he removed Paul's discarded clothes. "This is silver, isn't it?" Catching sight of the engraving on the back, she read, "Paul Anderson. From the staff and pupils of Oakwood on the occasion of his winning for the third time the Shelldrake Swimming Cup. Mmm, you add swimming to your many talents, do you?"

Having run through the possibilities of calling his batman, ordering her out at gun-point, or physically ejecting her, he realised the first two would make him look ridiculous and the other was impossible dressed only in underpants. She would go only when she was ready. The fact heaped coals onto the fire of his fury.

"*Haven't you got any sense at all?*" He winced as his head began to thud even more, and he lowered his voice. "I imagine your brother does not know you are here. If he finds you in my tent like this . . ."

"Sasha does not rule my life," she flashed, "and if he is happy to let his wife into your tent, why should he object to my presence here?"

"She is a nurse," he fumed.

"You are not wounded, Paul, just feeling the effects of too much vodka on top of too much work." From her pocket she took a bottle of tablets, which she dropped onto his blanket. "I was the family nurse, you know, until our mother died. I know quite enough about sore heads and sorry stomachs to dispense advice. Take two of these with water, and they will make you forget your discomfort for several hours." She patted his pillow. "I should lie back if I were you. You do look most unwell."

Unable to do anything but fume, aching all over, and longing to throw her pills at her, he said, "I was feeling perfectly all right until you came." Clutching his hair, he cried, "Look, can't you see you are making a hellish situation worse? Your brother will walk off, taking his men with him, at the slightest provocation. If he saw you come in here . . ."

"That's all you ever think about, isn't it—*work!*' Getting to her feet, she launched into one of her flash-angry moods that always aroused equally heated response in him. "Instead of nursing you, I could talk about your precious cutting, if you wish. Or the explosion that killed Gromov and Petrikov." She moved her arms expressively, emphasising the striking lines of her body. "Perhaps you'd rather discuss death and destruction. They seem to be very popular, at the moment."

"I did not kill those two!"

His vehement defence brought an unexpected response in her, for her passionate outburst changed into one of almost complete despair.

"*Bozhe moy!*" she moaned, sinking to her knees beside him. "I do not *care* whether you killed them or not. I do not care about any of it but this."

Next minute she was kissing his mouth with provocative insistence whilst her fingers curled into his dark springy hair, holding his head in an aching tilt toward her. Quite unprepared, he found all remaining sense of balance leaving him, together with cohesive thought.

"Paul," she whispered against his mouth, "we are the same, you and I. We know nothing of youth, and soon it will be too late. We have one short summer. Do you never realise it might be our last?"

She drew slightly away, and his scattered senses registered that there were tears in her eyes. "Dear heaven, do you never see me as just a woman and forget about your railway?" Her finger traced a pattern down his chest, and she implored him with her eyes to recognise what she was asking of him.

He recognised it, even in the state of sickness that presently assailed him. But half naked and alone with her in the intimacy of a small tent, he knew that any hint of recognition would be highly dangerous. Besides, even the most lascivious man on earth would think twice about it if he were as ill as Paul felt that day. All he wanted was to get rid of her and ease his aching body into oblivion. If he had been less angry, he might have recognised the deeper need behind her obvious plea, or if he had been more experienced, he might have handled the situation with soothing finesse. As it was, he simply put her away from him with firm hands on her arms.

"I can't forget the railway. The job has to be finished before the snows arrive. Then I have to go back to England," he added harshly. "You already know that."

She got to her feet jerkily, a strange contempt crossing her face. "Yes, you will go back to England and leave us all here. But it is not that, is it? I saw it plainly last night. You were too intoxicated to hide it." Snatching up the bottle of pills, she told him, "She is my brother's wife, have you forgotten? But I can tell you you would get no pleasure from her. It is so long since Sasha last took her into his bed, she has forgotten what she must do."

He lay thinking for a long time after she had gone. Somehow he would have to persuade Swarovsky to send the two women to Murmansk.

The response to Paul's suggestion was immediate and emphatic. The Russian officer would not even discuss it, saying with malicious finality that the ladies were used to the sight of drunken soldiers and had not been upset by the wild behaviour of the night before last. Paul realised he would get nowhere with his proposal and, since headquarters did not even know of the presence of two Russian women with the party, decided it would be an impotent gesture to attempt to get them forcibly sent to Murmansk.

Although still feeling very fragile, Paul realised that the only possible thing to do was throw himself into the job once more, and the next two days were spent working on the steep inclines that would form the sides of the cutting.

The following day, Paul found he must return to the siding to allow a hospital train through to pick up wounded from the battles that had been fought several days before in the area south of Lake Onega. Since the hospital train had priority in both directions, Paul had no alternative but to take his train back to the siding until the operation had been completed. In one way, he welcomed the opportunity to get really fit again, and felt it would be good to have all the Russians out of sight down by the lake. He had had his fill of their exotic temperament for a while.

The break allowed him time for the reams of paperwork that were his lot as commander and sole British officer on the job, and time to answer the letters from his friends. He made a start on the futile daily reports in the truck on the way back to the siding. It saved him from the embarrassment he felt in Irina's presence now. Apart from a mumbled greeting as he climbed aboard, he took care to avoid looking directly at her. He was afraid of what he might see in her expression.

When the hospital train arrived on its return trip, Paul handed the post-bag to the British N.C.O. who rode the footplate with the driver, then asked him about the wounded who were lying in the straw-covered trucks.

"Who are they, Sergeant?"

"Quite a few are ours, sir," said the man, walking along the rough platform beside Paul. "There's a few Serbs, some Czechs who managed to get along the Trans-Siberian without being caught by the Reds, quite a few Cossacks who have thrown in their lot with the Whites—bloody fools, most of them, sir, charging around swinging their knouts and mostly getting in everyone's way—and about a hundred-and-twenty Russians." He nodded at the trucks that had their doors open whilst the train was at the siding taking on fuel and water. "They withstood the temptation to change sides this time, but they'll do it eventually. I just hope I'm not with the bastards when it happens."

Paul frowned. "How many went over this time, would you say?"

"Most of them, by all accounts. Two of our officers were murdered by one company, and another was disarmed and told to clear off before they cut his throat." The man looked around, then lowered his voice. "I don't much envy you, sir."

"Thanks a lot!" said Paul dryly.

The Sergeant, a big, no-nonsense man in his forties, smiled. "Only joking, Captain Anderson. You'll be safe enough up here with us down at the lake holding them off. I don't think much of these Russians as fighters. Couldn't beat a tin soldier with a wooden sword; take my word for it." He walked on in silence for a moment, looking at the wounded men lying in the trucks. "God knows what will happen when we pull out and leave them to it."

"Eh?" Paul's head turned sharply. "How do you mean?"

The man's face screwed up into a noncommittal expression. "Nothing definite, of course, but there seems to be something afoot, sir. Word is we are going earlier than was expected—government and public pressure, I understand. If you want my opinion, it'll just be a bloody free-for-all the minute we make a move to evacuate the area. With their ideas of discipline, it'll mean men chopping each other to bits without needing any reason for doing it."

"But that's ridiculous! I came out here with several shiploads of reinforcements not much more than a month ago. There's no intention of pulling out, Sergeant—quite the reverse."

The Sergeant screwed up his face again. "I did say it was only a rumour, sir. It's probably put around by some of the lads who are feeling mutinous. To put it in a nutshell, sir, they believe the Reds are doing for the Russian working man what the Labour movement at home is doing for their folks."

"Christ!" exploded Paul in unusually profane manner. "The Reds are slaughtering the wealthy and intellectual in a bid to make Russia a nation of peasant workers. They have abolished religion, and there is a rumour that they have also abolished marriage. Labour is controlled and directed by them; they have sent out food armies to commandeer any crops grown on the farms, and people are starving in their hundreds. How can any man in his right mind ally Bolshevism with the British Labour movement?"

The N.C.O. looked greatly taken aback but managed to say, "Maybe because no one has bothered to tell them what you have just told me, sir."

"But, good God, don't they *read*; don't they bother to find out?"

"They . . . well, they're only ordinary men."

"Yes, working-class, you said. So am I, Sergeant. My father was a wheelwright in the local railway works. My mother and sister live in a house in a terrace and find it hard to make ends meet since my father was killed at the beginning of the war. The Labour movement might improve their lot—it remains to be seen—but they are free to live as they please, follow their own beliefs and customs, benefit from the fruits of their labours. They will not starve, neither will anyone rush through the streets of their town burning, plundering, raping, and torturing all those they drag from their houses. That will never happen in England, Sergeant, Labour movement or not. But it is happening here . . . and they are seeing it for themselves. Isn't that education enough?"

Paul, coming out of his unprecedented tirade, wished he had kept more control over his reactions to what the Sergeant had told him. For a while he had sounded like Swarovsky. He put it down to the disturbing suggestion that the British might be pulling out soon. His command, the railway project, would be abandoned in that event.

It was close on twelve o'clock when the hospital train departed, and Paul had to think whether it was midday or midnight. Deciding on the latter, he still could see no reason for further delay and told Yagutov to prepare to move off within the hour.

The genial Russian grinned but shrugged his shoulders. "She giving troubles."

"What kind of troubles?" asked Paul, unconsciously adopting the same idiom.

Yagutov put his hand on his stomach. "In here. She make not hot enoughs."

"Oh Lord! You mean she can't get up enough steam just to reach the cutting?" asked Paul in disgruntled mood, the prospect of further delay sitting heavily on him.

"She want to go," was the dignified response, "but too many hills stops her."

"Some of the bloody awful inclines on this line would stop even the Orient Express," swore Paul. "I intend getting back there as soon as possible, even if it means taking the trucks one at a time." At the slow shake of the driver's head, he went on, "Well, let's have a look at the trouble. Two heads are better than one."

Yagutov's caricature of a face was enlivened by a slow smile. "That very clevers. You great man, Captain."

"Unfortunately, another great man thought of it before I did," said Paul dryly, "but thanks for the compliment."

He pulled himself onto the footplate and watched while Yagutov demonstrated with all the compassion of a mother for her sick child why the little engine would never make the ascent of two inclines between the siding and the cutting. Paul understood enough about engines to appreciate the trouble but did not think the repair would take long.

"You can fix that up within an hour, surely? It's not like you to stand around doing nothing. We have to get back. Too much time has been lost already."

Yagutov shrugged his shoulders again as he wiped his hands on a dirty rag. "I want to go; she want to go—but repairings all vanish."

Paul stopped on the brink of jumping from the footplate and turned sharply back. "What do you mean—vanished?"

The big shaggy head wagged. "Someone took. I not lose my own repairings."

"Why the hell didn't you say this at the outset?" demanded Paul, losing more of his patience. "When did you discover this?"

"One moment—only one moment. They there when I go to eat . . ."

Paul heard no more of Yagutov's bewailing. It was all too clear *why* they had been taken. He just wished he could put a finger on *who* had taken them. But if it was an attempt to keep the train at the siding for some reason, the traitor had miscalculated this time. There were enough tools in Paul's own gear to cope with the problem, provided Yagutov could compromise.

"All right," said Paul, breaking into the tirade of comical English. "Let's not get too dramatic about it. I can give you all you need, for the moment. Your job is to get this engine in good running order. Let me worry about what has happened to your tools."

He jumped down onto the platform and was striding along it toward the supply-truck when his attention was taken by movement at the edge of trees leading from the lake. Colonel Swarovsky and the women came quickly across the line toward him. His initial determination to ignore them was brushed aside when he saw their faces. Olga was riding through some kind of terror; Irina was pale and tense. But the Russian officer glowed as if lit by excitement within.

Changing direction, Paul went to meet them, sensing trouble. "What is it?"

Swarovsky almost thrust the women toward him. "Our great opportunity! The *Bolsheviki* have broken through and are attacking the settlement on the far side of the lake."

It was so contrary to anything Paul had expected to hear, so far beyond his plans, so typically, dramatically Russian that his reaction was swift and angry.

"That's ridiculous! There are no Reds within miles of this place."

"Do not argue," snapped the Russian officer. "At such a time, I take command. You are to remain with your men to guard the train. I leave my kinswomen under your protection."

He was in the act of turning away when Paul cried, "Now wait a minute: just what is going on?" Another look at the women's faces collected his startled thoughts. Waving a pointing finger at the siding, he said, "That hospital train only left fifteen minutes ago, and the Sergeant on it told me the nearest Reds were south of Lake Onega when it set out from there. They could not possibly be at this settlement," he finished with determination. "It would mean they travelled faster than the train— which is bloody impossible."

The Russian idealist's handsome face was far from dreamy now. For the first time, Paul saw the warrior inborn in the man who threw him a look of unquestioning superiority. The dream had become reality, the "cause" was all-demanding.

"Do as you are told! The houses are being burnt, the women violated, the men dragged away as recruits for their vile ranks. Two peasants from the settlement escaped and came with the news."

The world appeared to have gone crazy. Every instinct and all his common sense told Paul there was something wrong with what was happening. With no time to analyse his doubts, all he could do was protest once more.

"Two peasants from . . . You believe those villainous devils?"

Olga flung herself against him, and he saw all her brother had just described mirrored in the fear-glow of her eyes.

"Paul, *please.* They are there, believe me," she said hoarsely. "If they take us . . ."

A shaft of apprehension stirred the deep-rooted incredulity from his brain, and he frowned. A moment ago he had been concerned with a stolen bag of tools, now . . . It was too much. Swarovsky was bringing his lurid exaggerations into the open; Olga was clinging to Paul with a drama so genuine she had become sexless—a terrified creature wanting more from him than ever before.

As Paul still hesitated, Irina stepped up to him, her face pale but calm. Her words shocked him into action.

"Our lives are in danger. Can you really not put aside personal pride and take orders, for once?"

It hit the target true and hard. Dragging his gaze from her eyes that were now stormy grey, he asked raggedly, "How many are there?"

"My men will handle them," was the brief, noncommittal answer. "I will leave a small rearguard at the bivouac in case any of the enemy break through to the railway." He had become the battle leader now. "You have guns enough to defend the train?"

"Yes, naturally."

"Good. You will remain here until we return."

"I have to," Paul countered stiffly. "My orders have always been to defend the railway from possible sabotage."

They exchanged only the briefest of challenging looks before the Russian spoke quickly to the women in their own language, then strode away through the trees to collect his men.

Next minute, Paul was jerked back to an emotion he thought belonged in his past, when the sudden sound of screams and cries of agony broke from the stillness across the lake. There was an immediate rattle of gunfire and the cry of battling men he knew so well, then, creeping into the pale blueness of midnight, came curls of black smoke to hang just above the far pines. His heart started pumping with the nerve-fear that activated pure animal hatred.

Olga was still clinging to him with frenzied hands, so he put an arm behind her to lead her over the track to the siding. Irina walked quietly beside him.

"Corporal Banks! Stevens!" he yelled. "Double quick!"

They came, understanding too well the sight of the smoke and the sounds that had never quite gone from their ears since muddy, bloody France. Both men ignored the women.

"Trouble, sir?" asked the N.C.O., his face full of curious concern.

Paul nodded. "Reds at the settlement. God knows how many . . . or how they got here." Halting beside the train, Paul visually assessed the best means of defence as he went on. "The Colonel has taken his men to encircle the place. If he sites them well and uses surprise, there should be no trouble." Conscious of the women beside him, he gave the Corporal a significant optical message. "Our priority is to defend the railway—is that quite clear?"

The man's eyes swivelled toward the women, then back again to his commander. "Er . . . yes, sir."

"Good! Unfortunately, Yagutov can't take the train up the line to safety. Our Bolshevik friend has chosen this moment to make another move—probably designed to coincide with the attack—and tried to sabotage the engine. His not-too-bright action means *they* can't take it away, either, so we shall have every opportunity to defend it, should the need arise." His gaze travelled from one to the other of his men. "Nobody leaves the siding. Understood?"

The two nodded. In France, it had meant succeed or die at your post. They guessed it meant the same in Russia.

Paul smiled his recognition. "Thanks. While you take up positions, I'll take the ladies to a place of safety in the forest. After it is over, you'll know where to find them." *If I am unable to do so* was the unspoken implication.

Olga resisted his attempt to lead her over the siding into the trees on the far side, behind the train. "No, Paul."

He tried to be patient. "It is the safest place."

"Can't we hide in the truck. *Please*?"

"And be blown to pieces if they hit the explosives?" he retaliated savagely, feeling his fears for them marching nearer and nearer with heavy boots.

Irina looked up at him swiftly. "Can't you understand that she cannot help being afraid. This is the first time she has seen outright war."

Seizing their arms, he marched them both determinedly where they had to go. "This isn't war, just a few men who have lost their way in the forest," he snapped, then added, "And it is your turn to take orders, Madame Swarovskaya."

Yet when he left them well-hidden and assured them there was no danger whatever, Irina gave him a pleading message with eyes no longer stormy. It shook him to the core. Pushing his way back to the siding, he groaned inwardly. Just what was she trying to do to him? If only he understood women better.

But there was no time to think of such things once he got back to the train. Seeing Yagutov lounging against the engine, he called, "Can you fire a rifle?"

The man looked startled. "Me?"

"If someone tried to take away your engine, would you shoot him?"

It was blunt enough for the Russian to understand. He grinned and straightened up. "I shoots."

Paul nodded as he walked away. "Good. Corporal Banks, give Yagutov a rifle and ammunition, on the double!"

A minute or so later the whole place was still and seemingly deserted. Paul had taken his position behind the flat-car containing piled rails.

The minutes passed. Nothing stirred. Slowly, Paul's tensed muscles eased. He flexed his shoulders carefully. He had only abandoned the sling for good that morning and wanted no trouble with the weakened joint. Shifting his stance, he wiped the sweat from his eyes. It was too damned quiet all of a sudden, and all he could think of was the two women back in the trees. He had never had to defend women before. It was not something he liked, for it increased his fear.

Still they waited, four silent, unmoving men watching the sentinel trees for any sign of creeping figures.

Paul's eyes began to ache—he remembered the sensation from other times, in France—and his imagination created enemies behind every tree, in every dark shadow. Waiting was the worst of all. Once the order to advance had been given, once the reality of armed killers appeared through the mist, there was no time to think, *or be afraid.* Even after four years, he felt it. It lay in his stomach like sickness, ready to surge up. He fought to keep it down. There was a hot, prickling sensation that he was back in something he had thought gone forever.

Swallowing hard, he squinted through the narrow opening formed by the piled rails and acknowledged that he was preparing to kill like a machine. He had given three other men orders to do the same thing. It was madness. He broke out in a sweat. The days of hard honest labour, the serenity of sun on tall pines, the hopes and pride he had had were gone. They had been a lightning emergence from darkness into sunshine—an illusion, a blind stupid pretence. Like a fool, he had refused to face the true reason for what he was doing. He swallowed again, and it was bitter this time. A train had passed through less than an hour ago, filled with broken men, yet still he had refused to think about it in an objective manner. He was part of a British force that was fighting a war. Down there, they had no forest illusions, no blind professional dreams of cuttings and bridges that would stand as monuments to him who built them.

Down there. The words hung in his maudlin thoughts to take priority over others. *Down there.* Lake Onega was two days' journey by train; two days ago the Red troops were *south* of that lake. How could they be here now? All his doubts rushed back. It was not possible for men on foot to travel faster than a train through coniferous forest. In winter, on skis, it would be out of the question; in summer the forest floor was turned into huge stretches of bog and marshland that were impassable.

His heartbeat increased slowly. There *was* something wrong about this whole affair. A moment later, he knew what it was. The Russian Colonel had arrived to say the houses were being burned, the women violated, and men dragged away. Two peasants had escaped from the settlement to tell of it . . . And yet, the screams, yells, shots and smoke had only begun *after* Swarovsky had walked off to collect his men for the attack. Paul was in the act of turning toward Corporal Banks when something crashed against the back of his head, turning everything to blackness as he crumpled to the ground.

When vision and sound returned, Paul found himself sprawled face down on the warm wood of the platform. He could smell the sun-soaked pine planks and the metallic heaviness of oiled wheels beside his left arm. The back of his head was full of the stinging pain of an open cut; he could see only muzzy shapes walking about ahead of his ground-level vision. There was a great deal of hoarse chatter in Russian, and thumps reverberated in his face as it rested against the platform. His thoughts still hazy, he raised his head and saw a group of bearded men with long hair, dressed in an assortment of garments that ranged from baggy trousers and fur-lined waistcoats to long shirt-frocks belted with metal-studded leather. They were all filthy and wild looking.

Then it dawned on him what they were doing. From the supply-truck, the boxes of stores were being thrown onto the platform, opened up, and emptied. Into the pockets of the men, thrust into the fronts of the loose shirts, pushed into the tops of high boots, and bundled into stretchy woollen caps and capacious neck-scarves, the foodstuffs and provisions were disappearing with great speed and glee. The remainder was being thrown into two large sacks fixed to the back of an exhausted mule standing in sad dejection beside the train.

Fighting the instinct to confront them immediately, Paul lay where he was and cautiously looked around him. It was a relief to find his corporal and batman still alive, but they were being guarded by a man holding one of their own rifles. The other lay on the shale beneath the platform. Six feet away from them, Yagutov leaned against his engine in a philosophical pose, the rifle he had been given leaning at his side. There were no guards by him. For a mad moment, Paul considered trying to reach the Russian and grab the rifle, but he quickly realised such a gesture could cost the lives of his men.

Trying to marshal his thoughts, he realised the filthy group could not be Bolshevik soldiers. The only rifles they held were the British ones issued to Paul in Murmansk, and there was definitely no order or discipline amongst them. It was every man for himself as they plundered the train, and a great deal of quarrelling went on. He reckoned that he had been attacked from *behind*, which meant Swarovsky's men had been lured across to the far side of the lake. But the thieves could not be peasants from the settlement. The peasants were simple, but not so simple they would not realise the soldiers had only to search their huts to take back the stolen food; besides, they would have done it a long time ago if they had thought it worth trying.

So, who were these rough Russians? It was difficult to think of any action that would help the situation, so he lay racking his brains for a solution that would not involve hasty, impetuous movement to draw their attention to him. There was not a hope that his revolver would be anywhere within reach, and without a weapon, he could not hope to do much to improve the plight of his men. The only thing that did lay in his power was to attempt to delay the thieves until Swarovsky's men returned. He estimated it would be at least two hours. Whatever could he do that would keep them at the siding that long? Under the circumstances, nothing, but he thought it high time he made a start.

Groaning as loudly as he could, he began to struggle up in a manner that would suggest to nobody that he was about to make an attack—or was even fit to attempt one. It was quite a performance, but he hoped Banks was quick enough to read it correctly. He did not want his men ruining everything.

Two of the Russians caught sight of him and nudged others, who stopped what they were doing to watch his slow, unsteady progress forward.

But it was Paul himself who ruined the part he was playing. A few yards took him past the piled rails on the wagon and into sight of the clearing beyond his tent. There, held by a great grinning brute, were Irina and Olga. Paul gave an exclamation and lunged forward, only to be brought to a halt by one of the band who held a knife in threatening manner.

"*Ostorozhno!*" It was the mumble of an illiterate man.

"Be careful, sir. They're a touchy bunch," called Corporal Banks. "The ladies are unharmed . . . so far."

Paul felt sicker than when waiting for an enemy that would not appear, but he knew he was powerless. As the Russian pushed him forward to join his men, all Paul could do was gaze across at the women in the hope that it would help him see some obvious way of enabling them to run to safety. Both their faces were pale and turned to him in appeal. Irina stood still and curiously limp, but Olga was like an unstable explosive liable to break apart with uncertain force at any time. He prayed she would control herself, for Irina's sake if not her own.

Keeping his gaze on the women, he asked his N.C.O. quietly, "What is all this about?"

"I can't understand any of their lingo, I'm afraid. It must be a dialect. But Yagutov is acting as go-between and says they're a gang of convicts who walked out of jail as free men during the revolution."

"Ex-prisoners—so they have nothing to do with the war?"

"Not so far as I understand it, sir. Seems they have been roaming the country, living off what they can steal, and have taken a fancy to gypsy-style life. After the Russian jails, fresh air and freedom appeals to them very much, and they are not eager to run the risk of re-arrest. All they want is the stores, sir . . . so they say! They've heard what is going on in the cities and hope for a new life up north with others of their kind who just want to be left alone. Shouldn't think this lot stand much chance, sir, if the others are like them."

Conscious of the knife-point inches from his chest, Paul said in the same tone, "Do any of them understand English?"

"Well, I called them dirty bastards to their faces, and they didn't turn a hair, so I should say not, sir."

"Right. Tell me quickly how the hell this happened. I take it you and Stevens were overcome without violence?"

"Just came up from behind and grabbed us, I'm afraid. You were clubbed with a great chunk of wood, from what I could see from the corner of my eye." Banks jerked his thumb at the man standing before Paul. "That one seems to be the leader . . . if they have one at all. *All right*," he said sharply, as the man guarding him and Stevens showed aggression. "I'm only cocking my thumb. I hope you know how to handle that properly, or it's liable to go off."

"How did they get the truck open?" Paul asked guardedly, realising their captors were uneasy about the length of their conversation.

"They took the key from your pocket. I had to tell them where it was," he added hastily. "They were threatening to cut your throat . . . and they had the two ladies, sir. They had been hiding in the forest and saw you take them in there."

"Oh, God!" said Paul heavily.

"There never was any Reds, sir," put in Sapper Stevens. "This lot comes upon the settlement, but the headman gets crafty and offers to draw off our soldiers so's the train could be attacked, on condition that they let his people and property alone. He tells them there's far more worth taking here, then plans that little demonstration of screaming and shots to fool us. Meantime, they crossed the line further down round the bend and come up behind us. Really caught us napping!"

"Yes," said Paul, "I had just realised that the timing was all wrong when . . ." He broke off, realising it was too late for post mortems. It was more important to think of all the implications of what he had just been told.

There was a chance the gang would go when they had taken all they wanted, leaving them all unharmed. If they had been instinctive killers, they would surely have knifed him instead of knocking him unconscious, and the others would not still be alive to tell him the tale. Giving himself an opportunity to get a clearer view of the women, he pretended to stagger and sought support from the end of the supply truck. From there he had an open run to where they were being held, but there was little chance of it with a knife still only three inches from his chest and odds of twenty against three. It seemed Yagutov could not be relied upon unless his engine were threatened; he was watching everything with interested neutrality. Paul supposed he could not be blamed for saving his own skin or for being reluctant to fight his own people. He was only an engine-driver, not a soldier.

So, whilst the ex-prisoners filled their sacks, Paul was forced to lean against the truck several feet from his own men and offer no opposition to the robbery of all his supplies and those few remaining items in his own personal store. They made no attempt to take rifles or ammunition, seeming content with the knives each carried. But his mind was working furiously. It would be impossible to hold them until Swarovsky discovered the deception and returned, because the longer the ruffians remained the worse became the plight of the women. He could see now that the brute holding them was taking patent delight in their fear and was already stroking Irina's arms in a way that made Paul afire with a violent emotion. It led him to consider getting Banks and Stevens to join him in some kind of loud vocal exchange that would reach the ears of the rearguard at the bivouac, but he reasoned that they had been ordered to guard against Reds breaking through from the direction of the settlement and would be unlikely to leave their posts out of curiosity. In any case, if shots began to fly, there was a chance of Irina and Olga being caught in the thick of it. No, he must bank on the possibility of their attackers vanishing as they had come, deciding it would serve no useful purpose to harm them.

Ten minutes later, it seemed his hopes were to be realised. The volatile man with the knife grinned and gave thanks with dialectic bravado, signalled to his brothers to move off, then indicated that the Englishmen should get into the supply-truck, which would then be locked. Corporal Banks and Stevens gave sighs of relief, turned, and began climbing into the truck. But Paul had caught sight of Irina and Olga being led off as if they were to be taken with the supplies, and everything in him responded automatically. Shouting, waving his arms in a threatening manner, he lunged forward, oblivious of those around him. They closed in, forcing him back toward the open door of the truck.

"Yagutov!" he yelled, as they tried to push him in. "Tell them they have the wife and sister of a great nobleman—not village *barishnyi*. Tell them who they are, for God's sake."

Above the din and struggle, he heard the engine-driver shouting, and the others shouting back. Then Yagutov was in his view, standing on tiptoes to call to him.

"They say noblemans much betters. These they hate."

"*Do* something, damn you!" Paul ordered desperately as he felt himself being lifted bodily onto the straw-covered floor of the truck. "You have a gun. *Use* it!"

"I shoots; I kill one. Many kill me, Captain," explained Yagutov, as if the terrible fate of two women meant nothing to him.

Gripping the metal sides of the truck with his hands, Paul kicked out with all his strength, but his legs were seized and used as levers to force him further into the truck. Still he fought, keeping his body across the opening to prevent the door being pushed across and locked, whilst holding, with hands that were beginning to slip, the sides of the opening that was being narrowed by the closing door. From the corner of his eye, he saw Stevens pick up a rifle, but the Corporal knocked it from his hands saying, "You fool, you might hit *him* by mistake."

Paul wondered wildly why his opponents did not attempt to kill him, then realised they were winning without doing so. It made him increase his efforts, but slowly he was overcome and thrust back into the dimness, to fall against one of the boxes. The door was slammed across, leaving a darkness that was so significant of his defeat, he felt sobs rise in his throat.

But his fall had brought the sharp corner of a box right against his side—a sharp corner that had not hurt him. In a flash he realised why and was on his hands and knees over to the door, knocking frantically and calling to Yagutov.

"Yagutov . . . Yagutov! Are you there? For God's sake, *Yagutov*, listen to me. I have money. Tell them . . . tell them I'll *buy* the women. *I have money, I tell you.* Yagutov!" He beat on the door with his fists, and his voice was almost a scream, his throat had become so dry with fear. "I will give them money in exchange for the women. It will be more use to them. Tell them, for Christ's sake . . . *tell them!*"

Beside himself with desperation, he thumped with bruised fists and shouted it all again, forcing his cracked voice to retain an authority he no longer felt.

Suddenly, the door opened a crack, and Paul fell forward, jamming his arm in the gap to prevent it from being shut again. "Yagutov, are you there?"

The engine-driver peered through at him. Behind him stood the assumed leader of the convict group, full of doubts. Yagutov looked almost embarrassed.

"Much sorrows, Captain, but they want *much* moneys."

Almost weak with relief, Paul said recklessly, "Tell them I have as much as they could want, providing they hand over the two women unharmed." As he spoke, he shifted his feet to the gap in the doorway as extra resistance to it being closed. A hasty conversation in Russian, then Yagutov peered back at him. *"Give!"*

Paul shook his head. "Oh, no, not until I have the ladies in here with me. Tell them not to waste time, or I might change my mind and keep it myself."

The sudden reversal of tactics took all concerned by surprise, and the leader took out his knife rather pointedly.

"I am the only one who knows where the money is hidden," said Paul to his go-between, and Yagutov spoke quickly in his own tongue. The knife disappeared again.

There was a shouted argument amongst the group that seemed to go on forever, to the man waiting in the truck, but there came the sound of footsteps along the platform, then Irina and Olga were standing there before him. Heart still racing, he held out a hand to help them into the truck in which they had travelled so many silent miles together. He had time only to notice large, dark eyes in faces that seemed unbelievably beautiful in that moment before he thrust them behind him to the protection of his men. With hands that were unsteady, he pulled his shirt loose and unfastened the money-belt from his waist.

Dragging the sliding door across to just a slit, he pushed the belt through to Yagutov, then slammed the door and dropped the bolt into the waiting socket on the inside, to ensure there was no chance the women would be dragged out again.

"Give them the money," he called. "There is enough there to pay for *all* our lives and their journey as far from here as possible."

From outside came a great cheer, and Paul heard the rattle as the padlock was fastened once more on the door. For several minutes he leaned against the wood listening for the sounds that would tell him the men were departing. Gradually the voices grew fainter, the shuffling ceased. He turned, leaning back against the door.

"They have gone."

Olga ran into his arms, crying in shuddering spasms as she clung to his strength with the frenzy of near collapse. He held her automatically, the unreal quality of aftermath filling his mind. But his eyes were growing accustomed to the dimness within the truck, where sunlight was penetrating the cracks. He saw nothing of the two men, only the slender girl against the pile of boxes. Irina was looking at him with such dedication and feeling, his pulse almost stopped.

"Thank you," Irina whispered. "With all my heart, I thank you."

E i g h t

No words could describe how Sasha felt on reaching the settlement to discover he had been tricked. The *starosta* had grovelled at his feet explaining that he was sure His Excellency would understand that he had to save the lives of his people, that he had had no choice. He felt sure His Honour's soldiers would catch the thieves if they hurried back.

Hurried back! It had taken them a good hour to skirt around the lake, keeping under cover and advancing with stealth as they neared the settlement. Sasha had taken time and trouble to place his men strategically for a surprise attack, before creeping forward himself, only to discover an old barn burning and groups of peasants gleefully indulging in bouts of screaming on given signals. No matter how fast he hurried back, he would be too late to prevent a robbery that had been so carefully planned and an attack on the train and all those with it. In blind rage he had struck the headman with the butt of his revolver, pouring curses on him that were designed to blight his descendants for generations to come.

He had left, full of fear for the two women so dear to him. Would Anderson be able to protect them with only two men of his own? His wife and sister came to him from the tent as he drew near. Relief had brought tears as he embraced them, holding them close in each of his arms and kissing their hair. Olga was overwrought and clung to him, but Irina was still and distant, in a world of her own.

It was she who told him how they had been seized from behind and forced to watch whilst the English officer had been clubbed unconscious and his men overpowered before any of them had realised anyone was behind them. With growing anger and mortification, Sasha heard of the robbery and the heroic attempt of Paul Anderson to prevent their being taken off, ending with the surrender of a great deal of money in a belt worn around his waist beneath his shirt. How well Sasha recalled his counterpart angrily demanding guards for all he had in his supply-truck including "a great deal of money." At the time Sasha had thought it an exaggeration, but that sum had bought the lives of two women destined for unimaginable degradation and danger. At that thought, he pulled them both close again, thanking God for their safety.

"I think you must not forget also to thank Captain Anderson," Irina had said in a strange voice.

He demanded to know the rest, and she had told him what they had discovered once all danger had passed. As roaming vagabonds the ex-prisoners wished no harm to Yagutov or the British soldiers. They had no quarrel with them, needing only the bonanza of stores contained in the truck. But no such consideration was shown to two ladies obviously of the old regime. Twenty men in the heart of an arctic forest had great plans for the beautiful members of the noble class, which had always treated them like dirt on the road. Their hatred was so intense, it was touch and go whether they would forgo their revenge even for a large sum of money.

"I think it must have been considerable," Irina had told him. "The money-belt was bulging with notes."

Once the convicts had gone, Yagutov had been sent to the lake to fetch the rearguard. To their rather doubtful credit, only one consented to investigate the tale and leave his post. It was he who shot off the padlock to free those imprisoned in the truck. It had been pointless to pursue the thieves, since they had been on scraggy horses and could disappear within minutes in the forest, so Irina had attended to a bad cut on the Englishman's head before they returned to the bivouac to await the return of those who had been sent on a false mission.

Sasha heard the whole story in silence. It took him no time at all to realise that his own impetuous and foolish response to the story told by the men of the settlement had resulted in exposing his wife and sister to danger of the most hideous nature, risked the lives of the Englishmen, and enabled their stock of food and supplies to be stolen. He had been the ridiculous victim of a peasants' trap. Not only that, he now owed an enormous debt of gratitude to a man he regarded as arrogant, swamped with self-interest, and culturally immature—a despised subordinate.

As Sasha walked through the pines on his way to the siding, he acknowledged that it would be one of the most mortifying things he had ever had to do—to express his sincere thanks and gratitude in the knowledge that his own hasty action had endangered the lives of the two women, plus those of the Englishmen.

He trod wearily, reaction from a battle-that-had-never-been bowing his shoulders. After waiting and praying for a chance to fight those who had seized his country, he had been so sure they were nearby. He had not heard—had not wanted to hear—Anderson's avowal that they could not be so far north. It had been his moment, his escape from what he considered an ignominious command. But he had been made to look a fool in front of his own men, his wife and sister . . . and that insufferable whelp.

As Sasha broke through the trees and saw the familiar siding, he sighed heavily. Anderson was sitting at a table writing . . . or calculating. Sasha scowled. The damned fellow was always writing or adding up columns of figures. How could he have acted as Irina described, launching himself against overwhelming numbers, fighting and kicking, risking his life in an attempt to save two Russian women? Why, he had almost thrown up because a traitor had been shot on the spot, had passed out halfway through the Name Day celebrations, and most probably had never even had a woman, if all Olga and Irina said was true. There was nothing about him to suggest a warrior, a man of action. Dammit, he shied from all talk or prospect of battle.

Perhaps Irina had elaborated the fellow's part in the affair. Stress and an attempt to present the Englishman in a favourable light (she was always attempting to mend the breach in their liaison Anderson had made at the outset) had led her to paint a picture of gallantry. He had most likely done no more than hand over the money in exchange for them, his inbred sense of chivalry coming to the fore, for once.

At the Russian's approach, Anderson looked up from his paperwork and got to his feet. It was his one consistent deference to senior rank, Sasha had noted.

"I'm afraid I have bad news," he said at once, forestalling Sasha's careful opening words and putting a lurch into his heartbeat.

"The war is going badly?"

"I have no idea how the war is progressing." A shadow crossed a face that showed signs of strain and premature age. Sasha realised, with surprise, that the events of the day made him seem thirty or more, instead of in his early twenties.

"I have been in touch with Murmansk. They can send no more supplies through to us. A bridge has been destroyed three miles north of the next siding, and nothing can get down the line. That hospital train only just made it." He threw his pen onto the table. "I was in the midst of listing our requirements when the news came over the wire. My corporal is now getting through to Lake Onega. There's a chance they could send up some rations flown in from Murmansk, but it will be three or four days before they could get them up to us on the line. All we have left, meanwhile, is a small sack of flour and some forage for your horses. It makes things very tricky," explained the Englishman. "We can't expect the men to work with nothing inside them, yet that bridge must be reconstructed before the trains can get down to us." His dark eyes looked at the Russian frankly. "You know your men better than I. How do you think they'll take it?"

"I do not quite follow you." It was rather cool, due to his jumbled concentration. Anderson was somehow dismissing the greater events of the day as if they had been unimportant.

"I . . . I should have told you first that I have received orders to cease work on the cutting and effect a repair of the bridge as speedily as possible. We are the nearest group on the line, and it is of top priority."

Now Sasha understood and shared the other man's doubts on the willingness of the men to work with empty bellies. He took off his cap and wiped his brow with a silk handkerchief, finding the interview going more favourably than he had feared.

"Three or four days, you say, before we get any rations? That is a long time to go hungry . . . for any men."

"They'll survive," was the uncompromising answer that reminded Sasha of Anderson's arrogance.

His mouth tightened. "No doubt, but you cannot expect to get heavy work from them, under such circumstances."

The Englishman looked uncomfortable. "Bread of a kind can be made—enough to last until the train arrives. Our only other resource is fish. I understand these rivers are full of them, and we shall be working across a large one up there."

Sasha was still lost in the contemplation of catching enough fish to feed forty people when Anderson's next words shook him considerably.

"Since I am responsible for the loss of the stores, I shall do everything in my power to make things as easy as possible. Unfortunately, I had to surrender all the cash I was given to buy extras from the peasants. Judging by the treachery of these at the lake, I think it unlikely that any others we might come across near the bridge would give us anything on credit."

With confidence pumping back into him every minute, Sasha realised his ally was making some kind of admission of guilt. Far from having to apologise himself, it seemed likely the reverse was about to happen.

"Also, your wife and sister were placed under my protection, and I led them into a hiding place right under the noses of those men. I am not proud of my performance." Anderson turned away, running a hand through his hair and speaking as if to himself. "It seems incredible that I made no allowance for an attack from the rear."

Sasha stood almost overcome with astonishment. This "boy," usually so full of bombast and false importance, was admitting that he had made a mistake . . . admitting it freely with no pressure from the Russian. Sasha swept the tall, solid figure with a keen glance and saw that the Englishman was pretty well spent. Sasha had seen young subalterns like that. So the affair had shaken the young fool, had it?

"This bridge, Captain . . . the one we are to repair."

He looked back quickly. "Yes?"

"It has been partially destroyed, you said."

"That's right."

"By whom?"

Anderson took his time in answering, and Sasha enjoyed the waiting.

"There is no definite evidence, but there has been increased Bolshevik activity along the White Sea coast, and Murmansk thinks an isolated group could have penetrated as far as the railway. Or, of course, it could have been local Bolshevik sympathisers."

It gave Sasha almost as much satisfaction as when the young officer had fallen in a drunken stupor whilst shouting at the wolves.

"So, those at headquarters agree with *me* that it is not 'bloody impossible' for *Bolsheviki* to be in this area?"

They faced each other for a silent moment, and Sasha felt the pleasure known by experienced men who have finally brought down the young upstart.

"I . . . yes, I suppose so."

It was difficult to hold back a smile of triumph, but Sasha managed it. "Then we must be far more vigilant, Captain. I will reorganise the shifts to allow for a twenty-four-hour picket."

The freckled face was full of protest. "But that will . . ."

"That will ensure that we do not have another surprise attack from the rear," Sasha continued, rubbing salt into Anderson's wound. "There are no 'buts' to be considered. The men are under *my* command. I will explain the problem regarding rations and detail a certain number to catch fish, when we get up there." Getting into his stride, he went on. "If we are properly organised, there should be no trouble in ensuring that we are guarded from attack in all directions, fed, and rested."

"But the work," came the protest. "This bridge repair is a priority job."

"The priority, Captain, is to fight the *Bolsheviki* . . . or they will destroy *all* the bridges on the railway. Your cutting will be pointless then."

It quenched any remaining flicker of fire in the younger man's approach, and Sasha recognised that the tables had turned in his favour, at last.

"There are one or two items, happily undiscovered by the thieves, still in my tent. We shall, of course, invite you to share them with us." He smiled magnanimously. "I think we shall not suffer unpalatable bread as our only diet until the train arrives."

"That's hardly politic, is it?" Brown eyes, deepened to near black by their present mood, stared morosely back at the Russian. "The men are going to be unhappy, to say the least, and it won't help if they see us eating normally whilst they are issued with nothing but some kind of cooked dough."

"Tsk!" exclaimed Sasha impatiently. "There is not enough for forty . . . and who else should have it?"

"Those who are doing the hardest work," was the slow, careful answer.

Beginning to wish he had not made his generous offer, Sasha asked, "And the ladies? Do you expect them to eat *some kind of cooked dough?*"

Anderson coloured, something Sasha had noticed before with contempt. "Since they can spend all their time resting in a tent, yes. It will only be for a few days."

"I take a different view. If anyone should suffer, it should be those whose incompetence resulted in the loss of the stores. The ladies can hardly be counted under that description." It was savage, meant to hit where it hurt most. There was no doubt it succeeded.

"I . . . I'm doing my best to get something up here at the earliest opportunity."

A loud clatter and a shout of triumph caught Sasha's attention, and they both turned toward the engine. Yagutov was waving a spanner and wrench, grinning as he hung over the side of the driver's cab.

"She goings, Captain. You say any times, she ready."

Anderson waved an acknowledgement, then turned to Sasha, still in chastened mood. "Yagutov has worked wonders on that engine. His tools have been taken, but I had one or two things in my truck he could use. Whoever did it thought he would keep us here for a long while. He was way off the mark this time, fortunately for us."

It was impossible to ignore the man's inference, and Sasha lost even more patience with him. Was he still suggesting there was a saboteur amongst his men? He gave a thin smile.

"Rather pathetic a move after the great explosion designed to kill us all, surely?" Dismissing the supposed sabotage with no more than that, he decided to bring the interview to a close. "Since the engine is now in working order once more, I suggest we move off in one hour."

He was turning to go when the Englishman said, "There is some urgency about this, you know. I should have thought half an hour more than enough time to pack up and prepare to move up to the next siding."

Sasha resisted the temptation to insist on the full hour. He had his own reasons for getting up to an area where Reds were known to be operating.

"Very well. I shall have my men here within half an hour."

The return walk through the narrow swathe of forest separating the siding from the lake was made in a vastly optimistic frame of mind. Anderson had shown him the whole affair in a different light, and he thanked God the man had taken the initiative, in typical fashion, before his own semi-apology had been made. For the first time in the weeks they had been with the railway, there was the prospect of doing something positive, of striking a blow against those he had sworn to attack, to avenge the unknown fate of sister and brother down in Moscow. He had trained his peasant-soldiers for that purpose, and only the misapprehension that this divided command was purely to defend the rail link with the Allies from the *Bolsheviki* had led him to agree to it.

Had he known they were merely to provide labour for an ambitious engineer who cared and knew nothing of real soldiering, he would have told his own High Command his opinion of such waste of good men. Unfortunately, the situation was so unusual, with so many divided groups of all nationalities operating all over Northern Russia, the familiar ladder of command could not be maintained, nor was it possible to communicate with anyone in possession of the complete picture.

Breaking through the trees, he took little notice of the early morning sun catching the waters of the lake and turning the breeze-whipped ripples into a shimmering movement of silver-gold. The reflection danced against his eyes as he made his way toward the tent, dazzling him so that he came upon Irina before he knew it.

"Irusha, why are you not resting?" he asked, full of concern.

She was still pale from the shock of her ordeal. "I have been trying to calm Olga. She was almost hysterical after you left—crying for you or Paul."

"Paul?" he queried sharply.

"She calls him that. They have become . . . friends . . . I think."

"Mmm. She would not think much of her friend now. He is shame-faced and hollow."

"Why?"

It came out as a cry of protest and annoyed him. After the young fool's carelessness that nearly cost her her life, she could not still be defending him.

"Even he recognises his gross mishandling of the attack. I have just accepted his apology for endangering your lives and losing all the stores." He took her arm gently and led her to a tree trunk severed by lightning and lying high on the shore beneath overhanging shade. They sat together, and he kept his arm along her shoulders as he told her what had passed between himself and Anderson. She sat upright, listening quietly and showing no reaction to his words until he said, "As soon as the bridge is repaired, I shall send you both up to Murmansk. I cannot risk my wife and sister suffering another experience like this."

She turned with puzzlement in her eyes. "Why . . . why *now?*"

It was not what he had expected. "There is danger for you."

"There has always been danger. Olga has spoken of it enough, and you have brushed her protests aside."

There was growing warmth in her voice, and a tension in her body that he put down to reaction from earlier fear. But her words struck a chord of guilt in his conscience. The accusation was true, but in his present optimism after victory against a man who had ignored every military rule of command, her criticism struck the wrong note. The sweeping mood of dominance must go on.

"My sister knows nothing of life. You have just seen how she behaves when faced with something she does not understand." He took his arm from behind her and leant forward with his arms along his knees as he stared across at the far bank where the settlement gathered. "I have tried to protect her since that night I took her from our house beneath the eyes of those who were caught in a madness of destruction. Our sister and brother might be dead—who knows—and I have tried to hold onto the one who remains, in a bid to keep a family alive . . . in all senses of that word. I did not send her away because I believed she would not go without me." He stared down at the stubby grass beneath his feet. "Perhaps I was wrong, but it is my belief that she needs someone of strength beside her—a sense of security." Turning his head sideways toward her, he added, "She and I quarrel, but there is a close bond between us."

"I know."

It sounded faraway, and he realised she had withdrawn into that distant world of which she appeared to be the only inhabitant.

"What makes you think she will go now?" Irina asked.

"Fear persuades many an obstinate mind. You say she has made friends with Anderson? It might be that she will believe there is safety with the English at Murmansk."

"And then?"

He smiled with a touch of sadness in his heart. "You must take her from Russia to Switzerland to join your family."

The silence was long, then came her cold question, "So you expect me to take over the role of protector?"

It caught him unexpectedly. "No . . . What nonsense." He turned and straightened up. "What a strange remark."

"But that is what I would be, isn't it?" She got to her feet in some kind of mixture of anger and appeal he did not understand. Her face was even paler—white, almost—and the mouth that was usually sweetly curved had grown tight. What made her so aggressive just when he had so much else on his mind?

"Irusha." He used the endearing name as a plea as he got to his feet and faced her. "Irusha, you are overwrought, and understandably so. It is not like you to be so aggressive."

"You have not asked if *I* wish to leave Russia. I am your wife, Sasha, not one of your men who receives orders. Is there no bond between *us*?" She put her fingers to her temples. "I sometimes wonder if it was ever there, if I am not just another of your sisters. *Yes,*" she cried at his sound of protest, "I might well be, in this life we lead." Her eyes were alive with a passion that surprised but stirred him. She had looked that way long ago. "Your concern is only for Olga. You say I should take her to safety . . . beneath my wing," she added heavily. "She is a woman three years older than I, with the right to make her own decisions." Irina began walking, as if the intensity inside her could not be contained any longer. "You have always impressed upon me the obligations of being head of such an impressive family. I understand that and sympathise with you over the probable loss of those two in Moscow. But I also know and share your anguish over what is happening to Russia." Spinning round to face him again, she cried, "She is my motherland, and you are my husband. There is nothing I would not face for both your sakes. My place is here. I am a skilled nurse with four years of war behind me. I do not go to pieces like Olga. I will work, carry stones or cut at trees like the peasant women, if it is needed. I am young and strong; such things would not break me."

"I know you have courage," he said helplessly, hoping it was the right thing to say at that moment.

Then she was looking at him with a message no man could misunderstand, and he realised just how beautiful she could be—how beautiful she had been as she moved between the beds in the hospital.

"There are times when I need someone of strength beside *me,* a sense of security, even so," she faltered. "Sasha, there are times when I need to be just a woman."

Desire was there in an instant, throbbing, filling him with a return of his youth. His veins glowed with it, his heart thudded as it had not done for too long, his limbs ached to hold her and feel willing surrender beneath him. It was strong—almost overwhelming—but he had been trained too well and the heedlessness of sexual hunger was overruled by voices that sang a martial song.

"Irusha," he said thickly. *"Serdechko moyo."*

Kissing her hard and following it by covering her neck with small kiss-bites that had her sighing, he struggled against the passion that threatened to claim him. Where could he take her? His sister lay in the tent, and it was unthinkable that he should carry his wife, like some peasant wench, into the forest, where one of his men might stumble across them at any time. He groaned with the need to satisfy the desire that had them both trembling, when her lips moved against his throat in a signal of submission. Burying his face in her soft hair, he felt tears well in his eyes. There was no time or place for their love. There never had been.

"I cannot . . . *slava Bogu,* I cannot," he whispered savagely. "We must leave in half an hour—less than that!"

She did not find it easy to let go her need. It was written in the fiery eyes, the smooth lovely face, in the body that quivered in his arms. "We cannot leave—not for hours. There is no one to see us, no one to disturb us. Olga is asleep, and the men are not here."

"Not here?" he repeated, only half understanding.

She was pressing against him, urging him to return to the oblivion of a moment before. "They left while you were away."

Desire vanished on the instant. *"Left!"* Holding her away, he shook her gently in his urgency. "What are you saying? Where have they gone? Tell me where they have gone!"

For a moment she gazed at him with the dark-eyed transition from passion to sudden normality. Then all vitality drained from her, leaving a shell of beauty that had no heart.

"They were angry," she told him tonelessly. "When they heard how they had been tricked so that the food could be stolen, they were angry beyond reason. I could not stop them." She half turned from him. "You could not have stopped them. They have gone to the settlement for revenge."

The bright coin of the day flipped over to reveal a dark and leaden reverse side. It stared him in the face as he grappled with all her words implied.

"But . . . but I have just told Anderson we shall move off in half an hour. He has orders of the greatest urgency. How can I go to him with this?"

Irina's face changed back to the former far off coldness as she backed away from him. "You must swallow your pride. Those men will not return until they have slaked their thirst for revenge. They are but peasants, Sasha, and behave as such. You will have to tell him so . . . and apologise, as he has just been forced to do."

She turned and walked away, but there was no will left in him to stop her.

Paul stood in his tent that had just been re-erected. There was now no hope of moving out for hours. The row he had just had with the Russian officer was one of their most bitter, and he was still caught in a blaze of frustration and fury. With the most urgent and important project of his command facing him, there was no alternative but to sweat it out until Swarovsky's men returned from their bloodthirsty riot of vengeance. Without them he could do nothing.

He clenched his fists and closed his eyes tightly in an attempt to hold onto his control. Damn the man to hell! The train was ready to go, time was of the utmost importance, the best source of food was up by the river, yet those villainous, half-trained savages had taken themselves off to pillage and rape in revenge. When he had heard, Paul had determined to set out on a mission to get them back—at gun-point, if need be. But the other man knew his people and insisted that such an action would not only prove useless, it would endanger their own lives. There was nothing to be done except wait for their return.

Mid-morning was approaching and the sun angled directly onto the siding. Paul's shirt was sweat soaked, and beads stood on his face as he acknowledged that it was more than the inability to move up the line that had him in his present state. Irina had such a hold on him now, she filled his every waking moment with wanting her. The only hope of escape from it was to throw himself into his work. Now that was denied him, and he was haunted by her, by every moment he had known her.

The sweat broke out afresh as he thought of how nearly she had been lost a few hours ago. Those bearded marauders had taken him as easily as if he had invited them. The two women he should have guarded with his life had fallen into their hands almost by his own design, and the fate planned for them was something he brutally forced himself to contemplate. His frenzy to reach them against all odds had been nothing to the frenzy within as he realised that they were being led away and he was helpless to prevent it. If it had not been for the money he had so often cursed, they would have suffered the horrors he could not get from his mind. So nearly had they been lost, his resulting guilt was driving into him mercilessly. All he could see and hear was the way she had looked at him and said, "With all my heart, I thank you."

Sinking down at the table, he put his head in his hands and leant on his elbows as he berated himself. He had not believed there could be enemy troops so far north. On the evidence it had seemed impossible, in his mind it had seemed unbearable. He had not wanted to accept the need to fight a battle. His reflexes and reactions had been limited by that resistance. Oh, he had gone through the motions, but underneath there had been an antipathy to what was being forced upon him.

His fingers curled into his hair with desperate anger. He had come to build a railway. It had seemed a godsend at a time when war had eaten away everything he had believed in and held dear. So he had blindly refused to face facts—that he was still a combatant soldier and must defend his very life along with all those beneath his command. The fear must begin again. His nerves must be stretched to the breaking point night and day, week after week, with no end in sight. He must see others look to him for vital decisions, wait for his word to save them from destruction, ask him for help no one else could give. Once more he must take on the crushing burden of life or death. There was no escape. The pioneering engineer must be subjugated by the soldier. Swarovsky had once said to him "Stay immune . . . if you can." He knew the answer now.

For some time he sat in the sick disillusion that day had brought, his mind travelling back in time to places that were wild and savage, to times that were full of the extremes of life and inhumanity. When a shadow fell across the table, he looked round with heavy unwillingness.

Corporal Banks stood with a sheet of paper in his hand. "Sorry to disturb you, sir," he said quietly. "Message just come through from Murmansk."

"Yes . . . what is it?" The words were slow and slurred.

"Well, sir, they seem . . . well, they seem a bit upset about the affair this morning . . . last night," he amended, remembering that it had occurred during a bright night.

"Upset?" queried Paul, a little stupefied. "What do you mean, *upset?*"

The N.C.O.'s face was a picture of the struggle between official nonchalance and personal liveliness. "It's the money, Captain Anderson. Someone in the Paymaster's Department has got wind of the story and wants a full account of who authorised such a sum to be in your possession, why you have sent in no weekly returns of expenditure, and on whose authority you parted with a large sum of government money in exchange for two Russian peasant women." He licked his lips nervously. "That's their words, sir. Seems there's a hornet's nest stirred up now, and they want an explanation pronto . . . and they do mean *pronto*, sir. The wire fair burnt up, I can tell you."

When no reply was immediately forthcoming, Banks ventured, "What do you want me to send back, sir?"

"Tell them to go to hell," said Paul in a dangerously quiet voice, then the day really exploded inside him. Getting to his feet, he crashed his fist down onto the table with all his strength. "Some bastard up there in a cosy hut has the bloody nerve to demand an explanation for something he cannot possibly imagine? Tell him to come down here and get it."

Paul stood leaning on his clenched fists, fighting the tide of emotion that had been seeking escape for days.

"What do you really want me to send, sir?" came the quiet voice of reason a few seconds later.

Corporal Banks became the target. "What I have just said, damn you! Clear off and do as you're told. You are not in the bloody Russian army."

The man disappeared immediately. Deprived of his target, Paul seized the inkwell and hurled it across at the sloping canvas wall. A blue-black mess splattered against the khaki and began running in long, irregular trails down the slope toward his bed. He stared at it, chest heaving, then turned and pushed his way from the tent to march over the railway track into the forest leading to the lake.

Turning in the direction opposite to the bivouac, he walked doggedly for twenty minutes or more, then stopped and pulled off his clothes. The water was chill and touched his overheated body with shocking refreshment. He swam way out from the shore with steady, untiring strokes. After a while he dived beneath the surface, enjoying the green dimness and the feeling of having left one world behind and entering another. The tension and strain gradually left his limbs, the purely physical demands of something in which he excelled having a soothing effect on nerves and overtired brain.

For nearly an hour he stayed in the water, swimming lazily, floating on his back to stare at the calm beauty of a high-summer sky, or probing beneath the surface until his lungs almost burst for want of air. Only when his left shoulder began a warning ache did he head for the shore, propelling himself with his feet. Leaving the water, he shook himself like a dog, then dressed with willing lethargy. *This* was living; *this* was life. He wanted to hold onto it indefinitely.

For some time he sat back against a tree, gazing out from his shaded spot across the scene before him. He had heard Switzerland was like this—cobalt-blue lakes, tall firs and pines, pure air and silence, blessed silence. He wanted to travel there one day, to walk through the mountain meadows and see the wonders of engineering created by brilliant minds and skills. The railways there ran across bridges that hung between mountains and clung to sheer, rocky walls. It must be a wonderful sight. He would take pencils and sketch pad to draw the bridges, as he had so long ago in his youth. What a fine holiday it would be to sit in the peaceful meadows with the sun warm on his shoulders and the breeze ruffling his hair.

"Do I disturb you?"

He turned sharply, startled from his far off visions. Irina stood just a few feet from him. Her blue skirt and soft blouse made her into a girl of his Swiss mountains.

"Please," she said quickly. "Do not get up. There is no need."

Halfway to his feet, Paul sat down again when she sunk onto a low, smooth boulder beside his tree.

"I saw you swimming and came round. Do you mind?"

"No . . . no, of course not." He glanced away across the lake to hide his reaction to the thought that she might have come across him embarrassingly earlier. As it was, his reflexes were just recovering from the unexpectedness of her appearance, and that was enough to cope with.

She followed his glance. "Here, like this, it is possible to imagine oneself anywhere and in any time. It has been like this for centuries and will remain so long after we are gone."

It seemed incredible that she should voice what he had been feeling. He turned to her and was painfully hurt by the look of sadness on her face.

"There is always an element of sadness in great beauty," he said quietly, without thinking.

Her gaze fixed on his face with an unwavering appeal that made his pulse race. The silence seemed to go on and on, then she almost whispered, "I know so little about you."

Shying from the unbearable moment, he studied the ground between his bent knees. "That's pretty well inevitable, isn't it?"

"I think not. You will not reveal yourself. Always you put on a stern military face."

It sounded so much like her first assessment of him, "so *earnest* and *serious*"—a subject for girlish giggles—that he felt heat creep into his face. He picked up a stone and flung it as far as he could into the water. It gave him something to do and kept her gaze on the stone rather than his face.

"I am here in a military capacity."

She let the ripples vanish into widening circles before she asked, "How long have you been a soldier?"

"Oh . . . all my life." He threw another stone into the water. "Nearly five years."

"It *is* all your life." A pause. "Did . . . have you all the time built railways?"

He looked at her quickly. "No . . . oh, no!"

"What, then?"

He shrugged. "The usual things one does in war."

"Please do not dismiss me in that manner. I am not a spoilt rich girl. I have seen war, I have been part of those things you have known."

His pulse raced even faster. Her eyes were clear and vividly alive, her cheeks faintly flushed from some kind of anger. In such a mood she was irresistible, and all else fell away in the joy of knowing he had aroused in her something he had so often felt himself. Sweeping over him came a steadiness, a sense of assurance that owed itself to her burst of passion. For that moment, she was his alone, and he suddenly found it easy to speak to her of things he had told no one else. Who would have listened?

The minutes passed as midday settled over that quiet lakeside, but he was lost in something that had been shut inside him for too long. Without realising it, he spoke of those four years with a sensitivity and passion that would have surprised most people who knew him. Leaning back against the tree with her beside him, he gazed across the water, seeing the imagery of guns and long weary lines of soldiers on the march. He felt again the sodden khaki weighing him down, the mud clawing at his boots, the rain battering his tin helmet. He smelt the vile trenches, the daisies and sweet grass as he lay face down whilst aircraft raked the fields with machine-guns, the choking gas. It all poured out until the vague image of Lila Reynolds's face brought him to a halt. Even the spell of that day could not bring him to speak of that.

His voice tailed off, and he turned to find a real girl instead of a ghost—a girl he loved with desperation. That she knew was all too plain. The green of her eyes had become brilliant with unshed tears for the things he could not say to her; the curve of her cheek showed a youth she could no longer deny; the sweet softness of her mouth trembled as his hungry gaze travelled over her face. They both knew he needed only one sign from her . . . but she did not give it, and the moment dragged painfully on until he could stand no more.

"I'm sorry," he managed through a tight throat. "War . . . on such a lovely day . . ."

"The day does not matter," she said in tones soft with emotion. "It was on such days as this that some of the most terrible things happened. I understand. It was the same for our soldiers."

He made an impatient gesture with his hand, churned up inside and sick with something he could only name as disappointment, for want of knowing a better description of how he felt. But she misunderstood and moved closer, looking up into his face with pleading.

"No, Paul, you are wrong . . . so very wrong. I know that you think of our soldiers as cowards, as allies who walked away and left you to fight alone. It was not like that. Please listen."

His flesh jumped as her hand rested on his knee in pleading, and he would have listened to anything she wished to say in order to keep her so close to him. Knowing it would only increase his yearning, he remained where he was, powerless to get up and walk away.

"We are a country with a history of oppression in which there are not many who did not suffer at one time or another. Those in court circles—the nobles—were most vulnerable to the whims of the rulers, and many adopted the cruelty of the court in order to preserve their own lives or to increase their possessions. But those who have suffered the most are the peasants, who form the greatest part of our population. As a result they have grown to accept brutality, subservience, and poverty. Their characters have adapted to cope with it."

Angry with her change of mood he said, "That is all too evident at this very moment."

With a quick movement, her fingers rested against his mouth for a butterfly moment. "Do not be angry. Just listen. *Please.*"

He longed to keep her hand against his lips, to kiss each finger and stroke the skin browned by the sun, but it dropped back to her lap and he had no choice but to stay against the tree, a prisoner of his own weakness.

"When the war came, our peasant-soldiers rallied to the cause bravely, offering their lives with willing patriotism to defend the country they love so well." A small frown appeared on her brow, and he sensed that she was far away from him and the cry of the wild duck way out on the lake.

"I saw them die in their thousands, saw how they upheld the pride of Russia. Then they retreated mile after mile, day after day, week after week. They were soon starving, defeated, and half-clad. They heard that their families at home were dying of starvation and cold, that the workers were on strike to improve conditions in the factories, that the cities were empty of food. They have minds of the greatest simplicity. To them, it seemed the end of Russia."

He studied her downbent head, as she paused for a while in the ardent narrative, and was captivated by this side of her.

"They were partially right." It was so low he hardly caught the words. "It was the end of Russia as I knew her."

When she flung back her head to face him, the tears he had seen unshed before were now freely on her cheeks. "They were promised freedom, but they did not know how to accept it. They thought it was a passport to disobedience. They turned on all those who gave orders, using violence to destroy anyone who tried to reason with them. Then, on the brink of returning sanity, those who snatched power from the elements of good told the peasants to get all they could for themselves—peace at any price, food and shelter for their families in the homes of nobles who were to be forced to give up all they owned, a parcel of land from the great estates, and a say in the government of the country for which they had suffered so much."

Now deeply involved in all she was saying, Paul could only sit and let her pour out everything without interruption.

"What would you have done?" she asked thickly. "They walked away from misery and unbearable defeat in the belief that to continue the war would mean the loss of everything. They were unfit to see what greater minds saw." Her eyes implored him to see the same mind pictures that still haunted her.

For a long time she sat silent, apparently back in the shadow of that time, then she said slowly. "I saw officers from some of the proudest families in Russia crying as they rode away from towns left empty for the enemy to walk in. They would have sold their souls to get back those soldiers."

The waiting silence was so evocative, Paul was completely unprepared when she turned to him and pleaded, "Do not treat us with contempt. We do not deserve it."

That plea crashed into his afternoon, breaking his peace and sending myriad lightning cracks across the surface of his total love for her. It had all been an illusion. He got to his feet feeling as cold as he had in the middle of the lake. She looked so beautiful on the ground at his feet, looking up at him with silver-bright eyes, the blue skirt spread across the stone and outlining the curve of her thigh.

"Don't you think it is time you let him make his own speeches, like a man?" he said harshly.

The creamy tan of her cheek heightened in colour. "That was very cruel."

"Well, it *was* your husband's case you were pleading, wasn't it? You make a dramatic orator, Madame Swarovskaya. For a moment I was carried away by the death of a nation, until I realised it was just another attempt to persuade me to knuckle under."

He began walking away, but she was up and running after him, taking his arm.

"Paul . . . please . . . you are wrong."

He stopped and challenged. "Am I?"

"Does . . . does there have to be a battle between you?"

He studied her, the fair silken hair, the mouth that invited capitulation, the tear-bright eyes, and knew he had to go.

"You know there has to be . . . and you know I can't win." He walked away from her, back to the train.

N i n e

The sabotaged bridge was a formidable sight. Spanning a fast-flowing river that was some fifty yards across and swollen by melted ice, it looked, at first sight, to be completely destroyed. An explosion had blown a sizeable gap in the wooden structure, leaving splintered, dangling logs at each severance. The section attached to the bank on their side had been uprooted and now tilted at an angle of fifty degrees toward the rushing water. A central section remained firm but broken, but the far end of the bridge looked no more than an irregular pile of logs where it had been lifted when the track had been wrenched from the staging by the explosion. It was being battered by the force of the water that had long ago swept away any wood that no longer formed any solid part of the wreckage. The track, still obstinately complete, hung twisted and bent, pulled from the sleepers, across what remained of the only method of crossing the river.

There being no possibility of through trains, the whole company bivouacked on the banks of the river, with the officers pitching their tents alongside the train. Yagutov always slept on the footplate to guard his engine, and the two British soldiers now used the supply-truck as their home. But no matter the situation of their quarters, no one escaped the mosquitoes that lived in clouds along the bank. The Russian soldiers, men of settlements and villages, had a certain immunity to them, but the Englishmen and high-born Russians suffered almost without ceasing.

The morale of the group had not been high before it arrived, and the extent of the work ahead did nothing to improve matters. The prospects of catching fish in the tumbling, rushing river were not as optimistic as they had been back at the lake, and with only flat scones flavoured with meat extract, and tea to drink (both provided by the Swarovsky ladies), the Russian soldiers complained loud and long over the amount of heavy physical labouring in store.

They stood in a sullen group as they listened to the translation of the Engineer's résumé. Since it was imperative to reconstruct a working bridge in the shortest possible time, he proposed to push the twisted rails straight into the river rather than expend time and energy in removing them all to dry land. Next, the tilting section nearest the bank must be pulled back into position, secured, and completed. From that section it would then be possible to throw out a truss to link with the central section still standing, and from there they would push on across to the far bank with a complete new section. It would mean a great deal of tree-felling, sawing, hammering, heaving on ropes, and scrambling over precarious structures across the river.

It sounded so exactly what they had no inclination to do, they made it noisily obvious that their English ally could go and jump in the river, for all they cared about his bridge. But they had a shock coming. Food would now only be issued to those who worked, and it had only needed a drawn pistol in Colonel Swarovsky's hand to send them all down to the river-bank ready for orders.

During those first days at the bridge, Irina was desperately unhappy. She hated leaving the lake that had given her the illusion of another life for a while. Here, she felt a desolation that bordered on fear of the encroaching forest. With nothing but trees in every direction, she brooded on dark possibilities. The sun did not flood down so much on the narrow path through dark green that stretched into the distance on both sides of the river. The water rushing past was grey, icy, and flecked with white as it tumbled forward in impatience to reach a lake or sea that would swallow it up. There was not even the siding, its comforting platform and small clearing to suggest a haven for an onward journey; there was only a band of about twenty feet each side of the track where timber had been felled for sleepers, and even this was covered in infant trees. The river-bank was marshy, the home of the wretched mosquitoes and occupied by the soldiers, who had made sleeping-platforms to raise themselves from the damp earth. That area also abounded with insects and small rodents, to which she had always had an uncontrollable aversion. In their new site, Irina felt hemmed in, oppressed by the glacial water and the evidence of the broken bridge before her. In her worst moments, she looked across at the far bank and saw it as her only escape. That she could not reach it haunted her with unreasonable fear that had never been present down at the lake.

All these things would have been bearable—she had suffered worse conditions at the fighting front—if it had not been for the battle she was fighting within. She had had no earlier experience to help her with that aspect of her present life. Paul Anderson had kindled within her a love so strong she was fighting it with every weapon she possessed, desperate to resist it. What had started as a desire to reach a young man she had unwittingly hurt, to offer him friendship, had become an unbearable yearning for someone who tossed her from tenderness to anger, from incomprehension to stunning unity. The days had become coloured by his presence. She knew so little about him, yet she was hopelessly caught in the web of his personality. Far from being the peacemaker, she was now caught in the stormy complication of each day, and her fears for Olga's sexual experiments had rebounded on her. She, the voice of wisdom, was the one who suffered the penalty of aroused emotions.

Wanting to be alone one afternoon, she wandered to a spot beyond the bivouac and sat on a pile of newly cut logs, watching the young officer as he straddled the criss-cross bars forming the truss of the tilting first section. Water rushed past only a few feet below him, but he took no notice, being too intent on instructing some soldiers where to affix the ropes that were to pull clear some mass of wreckage. Hatless, in breeches and shirt sleeves, he looked young and confident, his strength apparent in the way he moved across the swaying timbers with ease.

Yes, he was strong and full of physical courage. She had seen that during the attack on the train, and those qualities answered a present need in her. That was dangerous enough in itself, but now she was becoming captivated by another kind of strength. Here was a man who ran on rails that took a direction unknown to her. He would tackle ten times his number in an effort to save two women, yet flush in the women's presence like a schoolboy fighting shyness. He could rage and swear at men beneath his command who were old enough to be his father, yet make a complete fool of himself by drinking unwisely. He could attempt to dig out a man buried beneath a landslide even when suffering agonies himself, yet speak of war with words that betrayed a deep sensitivity to suffering and pain.

Remembering that magical afternoon beside the lake, she sighed with unhappiness. Only afterward, when he had left her standing alone at the water's edge, had she been troubled by what had happened. With eyes clear of visions, she then saw that he had somehow offered her something that she had thrown back in his face. She had trampled on his gift with the heaviness of her own fears. After accusing him of being unwilling to reveal his true self, she had countered his revelation with a plea to mend his ways. Why did every meeting with him end with shields being raised? Olga was on first-name terms and had apparently been kissed by him. How that had ever happened Irina could not imagine or contemplate. Yet when he was with Irina, he said one thing with his eyes and another with his voice.

He had turned her way now, holding with one hand the precarious tilting section and leaning out across the water to signal to someone on the bank. The sun caught his face, deeply tanned by the outdoor life, and the faint sound of his voice reached her as he shouted his commands. All her training, her experience of nursing men, fell sadly short of putting him into a comfortable category and reacting accordingly.

"Who are you, Paul Anderson?" she asked softly.

That Olga came toward her along the river bank at that precise moment was not pure coincidence, Irina felt sure. Since the attack on the train, the girl had been almost silent, withdrawn into whatever it was that went on in her head. She seemed never to sleep. During the periods both women rested on their beds, Olga would lie staring at the roof of the tent with eyes disturbingly wide open. At that thought, Irina was forced to admit she did the same herself. Troubled minds never rested, whether they were full of fear . . . or guilt!

Now that the word "guilt" came into her mind, Irina had no desire to face the sister of the man she was betraying in thought, if not in deed. But it had not been done lightly. In desperation she had tried to force Sasha to re-establish a relationship that would pull her back from the edge of betrayal, and she had defended him fiercely to Paul at every opportunity, in order to strengthen her weakening allegiance to him. Neither ploy had succeeded, and she did not know which way to turn now. The marriage that had never been allowed to grow was slipping from her grasp, and with Olga constantly making a third, there seemed little chance of holding on to it. Yet Sasha was the only person who could save her from Paul . . . and Sasha was the only person she could not approach. For once, she was lost; this time, she was the patient in need of a nurse to make everything come right.

Olga reached her and commented, "In a forest, the only way to vary the view is to stand on one's head. But since we cannot do that without losing our dignity, I suppose a change of angle will have to do." Her smile held no joy in it. "Does this place get on your nerves?"

"I preferred the lake," Irina answered carefully.

The girl sat on the pile of logs beside Irina, brushing away the small pieces of crumbling bark that clung to her skirt. It was an automatic gesture, for her gaze was on the river activity. "Does it ever strike you that we have been reduced to the life of peasants? That is their aim, you know, to bring everyone down to the lowest level."

Distracted, unwilling to talk of deep things, Irina made a mild protest. "This is hardly the life of a peasant."

"No?" It was bitter. "We have both been swallowed up by the forest, cut off from the world, subsisting on what can be caught in the river. I have just used the last of the soap, and there is no hope now of washing my hair. It will grow tangled and filthy like that of the slatterns in the factories of Moscow. Our skins will grow weatherbeaten once the last of the lotions has gone, and our clothes will never stand up to being pummelled in the river. Yukov took my best silk blouse down there this morning and treated it like the soldiers' coarse shirts. It is completely ruined. It will not be long before we present a picture of two *barishnyi*." She laughed shrilly. "The Swarovsky *barishnyi*—pride of the *Bolsheviki*."

"Don't talk such nonsense," said Irina sharply, full of her own melancholy mood. "You know nothing of *barishnyi* and peasant life. Do they sleep on beds such as ours, with rugs and pillows; do they have a trunk full of clothes? Do they have a man to cook their food, have knives, forks, tablecloths, silver brushes, and perfumes? Is that all part of what you consider to be the life of a peasant?"

She should have kept quiet, let the girl make her wild comments, for reason was the wrong approach at that moment.

"You never tire of reminding me that you have lived and moved amongst the poor people of Russia, do you?" Olga cried, turning a face working with anger toward Irina. "You think of yourself as 'the Blessed Virgin of Russia' who healed the wounds of her sons and now understands the secrets of mankind. You think you have suffered, and that suffering has put you on some kind of dais from where you see everything with the eye of pious perception."

Irina felt her anger rising but kept it hidden. Of what use would it be to defend oneself against accusations made by someone who was beyond listening to unwelcome truth?

"Have you ever thought what my life was like whilst you were with the army? Have you?" Olga challenged. "I will tell you. My days, and often the nights, were spent in the company of a selfish, demanding, slowly dying woman who had lost a beloved partner in the war against Japan and saw no reason why I should have a man when she had not. Oh, yes, you need not look so wide-eyed. That was her vow—she told me so. My sister's marriage was only allowed to take place because her husband was a doctor—someone who could take an absorbing interest in her as someone approaching death. But I was to be the whipping-boy for her despair and loneliness. By depriving me, she thought to compensate for her own misery." Olga's eyes lit with blue anger. "Like the *Bolsheviki* who seek to alleviate the misery of the peasants by bringing the nobles down to share it. It does not work, Irina, I tell you that truly. My own unhappiness and frustrated womanhood made hers no lighter, it merely sharpened her temper and hastened the last painful stages of her illness. Her mind became warped, obsessed with devising ways of spoiling my life, as hers had been spoilt. Where she could have joined in the gaiety and refreshment of my friendships and love affairs, filled the rooms with lively young company, been entertained from her bitter thoughts by sharing the fuller lives of others as they recounted them, she banned visitors from the house. Where she could have been strengthened by a daughter's fond love, she wallowed in self-pity and jealousy. I hated her. Even as she died, I hated her."

Irina could not help but be touched by the sincerity of Olga's words and the sadness of the picture she painted. Often given to dramatising, this time Olga spoke from the soul, with basic honesty. Yet Irina hesitated to comment. Olga was such a secretive girl, it would be easy to say the very thing that would fire her up in derision of sympathy or contempt of platitudes.

"You think you understand human nature, *sestritsa*?" Olga mocked, using the nursing term with scorn, "because you were present during events that are unnatural and divorced from real life. *I* have seen it more closely. I have stood as witness to grief that eats out the heart, to pain that overrides the mind, to the bitterness of jealousy that destroys. I have seen human nature in a house where domestic battles are the only form of conflict and where there are contained within its walls a group of people living out their lives at all levels—lives that are strengthened or weakened by the cankerous core."

"But that surely was unreal," put in Irina with some attempt at reason. "As war is an unnatural state in a country, so is such a situation in a household."

"I escaped it to come to *this*," Olga went on, ignoring her. "But I do not intend to be cheated any longer."

Irina followed her glance to where Paul was scrambling back across the broken bridge.

"My life might have ended two days ago. He gave it back to me and now owes me the rest of it. He knows what I want from him."

"He knows?" It came out more sharply than Irina would have wished.

Olga's blue gaze returned to study her face. "Oh, yes, he knows. But he is still afraid of it."

Irina could not help herself. "I warned you before not to play dangerous games with emotions. Isn't the situation tense enough as it is without making passions run high?" At Olga's almost amused calmness, she added impetuously, "Leave him alone . . . if you value your safety."

"Explain!" commanded the other girl, still amused.

Unable to remain on the logs, Irina pushed herself from her sitting position and walked a few paces to the water's edge, where she circled a tree with her arm and stood watching the man they were discussing. Longing for him made her cold, and she shivered beneath the dimness shed by the pines.

"Until that bridge is repaired, we are marooned on the south side. He is the only one who knows how to do it. It is essential that he be allowed to concentrate on that one vital thing, with nothing to trouble or confuse him."

"Is that your prescription as a nurse . . . or as a woman?" Olga came up beside her. "Paul is quite badly in love with you."

It shattered Irina's composure. She turned away, hating Olga for throwing it at her in such a manner, for betraying something he would not want touched by insensitive words, for putting such joy in her heart.

"That is quite ridiculous. It does not help our difficulties to be provocative."

There was a short pause, then Olga asked, "What of Sasha?"

Irina turned sharply. "What do you mean?"

The vivid face was lit by a smile of maddening malice. "I suspected it, but you have just told me it is true. This is something you cannot treat with bandages and kind words, however." Then Olga grew cruelly destructive. "You have one man, Irina, do you really have to covet every other male in sight? Perhaps you are used to captivating the soldiery wherever you go, but you should never have married my brother if you wished the practice to continue. He is a proud man from a proud family. How do you think he will take to the discovery that his wife is no better than a camp follower, with her eyes on the handsome young captain?"

The strain of the past weeks seized Irina with the same reckless anger as her sister-in-law. "I think Sasha has forgotten he ever had a wife," she blazed bitterly. "You should appreciate the truth of that—you have been with us day in, night out. I have tried, dear God, I have *tried* to remind him that I am not another of his sisters, but he is wooing a civil war now. You dare to preach to me of a proud family!" Her breast was rising and falling rapidly as she let flow all that had been held back for so long, ending finally with, "A proud family, maybe, but wrapped in self-interest."

Olga clutched her skirt until her knuckles grew white. "Do you think I enjoy playing third to a pair of frustrated lovers? It emphasises my virginity beyond acceptance."

Irina had passed the point of caution. "I warn you not to test it with Paul. It could lead to disaster."

"But my rolling with Paul would leave you free to seduce your husband, wouldn't it?"

"Now you *are* sinking to the level of the *barishnyi*." Irina flung back.

"But not to the level of adultery."

"*How dare you!*" Shaking and sick, Irina turned to lean against the tree trunk beside her. "That was unforgivable."

"I . . . I am sorry. As you said, it was unforgivable. You see what this life has made us become?"

It was a while before Irina felt sufficiently in control of herself to speak, then it was only by supreme effort. "If it can make two cultured, intelligent women behave like fishwives, think what it must do to the men who have so much more pressure upon them." She turned wearily to face Olga. "For *his* sake, I beg you to leave him alone."

"You are asking me to sacrifice everything."

Irina was appalled. "Do you love him that much?"

Olga laughed harshly. "*Love?* Does anyone do that in these brutal times? No, my dear Irina, it is not love I have in mind for Paul, but something far more dramatic. I knew it that first day."

A whole day had been lost at the lake while the soldiers took their vengeance on the people of the settlement. They not only took all the foodstuff they could find, but clothing made from the skins of animals. The huts of the *starosta* and the two who had come with the false message were entered and smashed. The elderly people were rounded up and terrorised with threats of torture if they moved from that place, then the *barishnyi* and several pretty youths were taken into the forest for an orgy of depravity. The men finally returned in twos and threes, unfit for anything but heavy sleep. But their number had decreased by two.

Sasha accepted the rape and pillage as the inevitable result of the peasants' treachery, but he was by no means philosophical about two deserters. It was useless to think about getting them back in such terrain, but it meant they were now only thirty-five strong instead of the original forty that had arrived at the lake nearly two months before.

The women were plainly uneasy. Sasha could not afford to worry over it—there were worse problems on his mind—but it did strengthen his resolve to send them up to Murmansk on the first through train across the reconstructed bridge. It would be something of a relief, in a way. Olga was becoming too melodramatic to suit his conscience. As for Irina . . .

Sasha tried to put his emotions in order and found it impossible. In his heart he knew that morning beside the lake had brought a turning point in his relationship with Irina, yet did not really appreciate what it was. She had asked him for something it was not possible to give. Sexual desire had bitten deeply into him, and had she been a wench from the settlement, he would have taken her there and then at the edge of the trees. But his wife was not a wench on whom to quench his lust. A Swarovsky did not foster sons at the edge of a forest like the peasants, and she should not have pushed him to the brink of an impossible emotion. Of late, she had changed from the calm, practical nurse to a disturbing woman of moods. Never sure whether Irina would pour oil on troubled waters or stir up a storm upon a smooth surface, Sasha felt he no longer knew her. Had he ever really known her? He pushed away the problem for another day and made his way down to the bridge.

On this, the third day at the bridge, they were expecting the train from the south with supplies for all those isolated along the line, and there was an air of relief in all quarters of the camp. There was, however, no break in the work in expectancy of the train and all it signified. The Englishman did not spare himself and expected the rest to follow his example. Strangely, they did. Sasha detected a kind of reserved respect for the young officer that was somewhat surprising. Beneath their uniforms the soldiers were peasants, men of the land, whose natures made them suspicious of those from other parts of Russia, much less a complete foreigner. But they seemed to have changed in a subtle manner since the Name Day celebrations. By rights, the way in which Anderson had offered his gift and the drunken display in front of them all should have shown him as a man with little sense of command—immature. But there was no doubt they would not be working as hard as at present, on short rations, if they did not feel some kind of comradeship with their ally they had not felt at the beginning. It seemed a violent *volte-face* after the explosion that killed his two sergeants, and Sasha told himself with disgust that one could never tell with peasants. Their blunted intellect resulted in inconsistent behaviour.

At mid-morning Sasha stood on the bank whilst an attempt was made to right that section of the broken bridge that lay at an angle on their side of the river. For over an hour they had been fixing ropes and pulleys to the vertical struts of the heavy section, then securing them to trees along the bank that were considered strong enough to take the strain when the men began to pull. It had not been an easy task, and Anderson had met with no resistance when he proposed to go himself across the swaying cross-beams in order to fix the ropes, with the help of just his corporal. None of the Russians had fancied the job that the two Englishmen managed with ease and skill just a few feet above the racing water.

It was when the job of securing pulleys and running out counterweight ropes on the bank began that Sasha saw how tense his counterpart was. It plainly irked the Englishman to be unable to convey orders direct, and he studded his instructions with automatic cries of, "No, higher, for God's sake!" or "Look out, that rope is slipping!"

Sasha did his best to pass on all that was said, becoming as heated as Anderson in his exhortations to take more care. But when all was finally fixed, the Englishman inspected and tested the security of the pulleys, the positioning of the ropes, and the soundness of the trees to which they were attached. Then he approached, brushing away a small cloud of mosquitoes attracted by the heat and sweat of endeavour.

"That should do it," he said, "although there is always an element of trial and error in this sort of operation."

"You have been cautious in the extreme," said Sasha dryly. "Could anything possibly go wrong?"

A quick, sharp glance from eyes dark with tension sufficed as a comment, then, "I had better explain the main problem to you so that you can tell your men what to expect and how to cope if it should happen."

He began moving down the bank, and Sasha followed as the Englishman indicated the main supports of the section with a wave of his hand.

"Those chords and web-members are pretty hefty trunks of pine, which means the whole thing is going to be a considerable weight to shift. Those piers I have driven into the water are designed to support the whole section once it is upright, but the dangerous time is while we are righting it. Without our knowing how secure a bedding the existing uprights still have, there is a danger that the whole thing will start to shift the moment the angle of incline is altered. The structure might only be presently held in position by the balance of its weight and the force of the current. The river is too deep and swift for positive examination. I have probed as far as I am able, but I really need a diver on a job like this."

Sasha thought he understood the problem. "You are saying that as the section comes farther upright, the weight will shift and no longer be supported by the force of the current? If there is no firm foundation, the whole thing could float away from the bed and collapse into the water."

"Not if they all do as I say," was the swift reply. "It is what they must expect *might* happen. As soon as I spot any signs of 'floating,' I shall call a halt, and they must secure their ropes until I can get some more attached to the lower struts." He frowned at Sasha. "The whole operation will depend on the instant translation of my orders. The slightest delay might jeopardise it."

Stung, Sasha replied, "To suggest that I would not co-operate to the utmost is a little insulting. I want this bridge reconstructed quite as much as you . . . and for a more praiseworthy reason."

There was immediate reaction. "Which means?"

"That crossing this river will give us the opportunity to hit back at those who destroyed the bridge. You merely see it as a feather in your engineer's cap, do you not?"

It hit the mark. Sasha felt grim satisfaction at the way Anderson turned away and began climbing the bank to speak to his corporal like a very angry man. He was soon back, anger pushed aside in the activity of the moment. The ropes were fastened at each end of the tilting section, one being pulled by a team that stood almost directly above them on the bank, the other by men some yards downstream. The orders must be shouted amongst them all and acted upon immediately if any danger was to be averted.

Sasha watched as anxiously, shouted as tautly, sweated as freely as the man on whose skill success or failure hung. The two Russian N.C.O.s stood with the English Corporal at the top of the bank, passing on the instructions given by the officers, who were the only men who could see what was happening. The ropes grew taut and squeaked with the sudden load. For a while, Sasha thought nothing was going to happen, that the manpower was insufficient, but Anderson yelled, "More—dig your heels in and heave, damn you!"

Sasha translated, putting urgency into the words that transferred itself from the man beside him. Several times the command was repeated, and the men heaved and sweated. Then, Sasha felt a lift in his breast as he detected a slight movement of the heavy section.

"She's going," croaked Anderson in a voice grown thick. "Now, don't let them run away with it, or it'll go right over the other way. Steady! *Steady!*" he finished on a yell.

"*Ostorozhno! Ostorozhno!*" called Sasha to his men on the bank, and they repeated it in sharp tones.

With a creak and a groan, the mass began to move very slowly, swinging fractionally with the current.

"Ease up on that first rope! She's twisting—hold her! For Christ's sake, hang onto that second rope or she'll capsize!"

So it went on, the Englishman's voice and actions getting more tense with each instruction and each foot the great wooden section moved. Sasha was caught up in the excitement, willing the thing to rise slowly and correctly into position. His palms grew clammy, his throat became dry, the mosquitoes bit without hindrance. All his concentration was on the river and that moving section. The water around the base of the piers grew cloudy as mud rose to the surface, stirred by the moving timbers. The criss-cross lengths of pine shivered beneath the strain, having been weakened in places by the explosion. A long strut broke away at one end, dropping like the bar on a railway signal, hanging by the bolt that held it in place; several dropped off completely and were swept downstream by the rushing water.

But very gradually and with tense guidance from the English officer, the angle between the section and the water widened. Then a new anxiety beset Sasha. Would the men be able to hold such a weight; the strain on them already must be considerable. He prayed no man weakened and the whole thing went crashing back again.

It began to slew into the current, and several frantic orders were passed amongst them all to correct it. So tense was he, Sasha jumped nervously when there was a sound like a pistol shot, followed by a peculiar, familiar whining in the air above him. Caught in that split second, his sixth sense made him alert to two things simultaneously. Disaster and danger.

Glancing swiftly at the water, Sasha saw the wooden section was out of control, slewing sideways as it swung with the current. All around him there was noise—rushing water, men shouting in alarm, creaking, cracking wood. Then he sensed something dark flying through the air toward the man standing frozen with the disaster of the moment, only a few feet from him. With instinctive and reckless response, Sasha threw himself forward, knocking the other man down and rolling with him to end half in the water as two jagged struts ripped from the structure landed right where Anderson had been standing a bare second or two before.

It all happened with a speed that defied thought. The Englishman's expression showed shock, alarm, and incomprehension as he stared at the heavy spars lying on the bank. Slowly his gaze moved to focus on Sasha's face. It spoke of gratitude, unconscious comradeship, and a life-for-a-life. But all he said was, "Thanks."

Then they were scrambling out of the water, alive to urgency. The English officer took command quickly. The farther rope was useless, having broken at the pulley attached to the tree. With the hold lost on the far end, the section could do nothing but respond to the uneven pull of current and rope. There was only one thing to be done before the structure swung right round and crashed into the bank, and Sasha translated the order to secure the rope that was still intact then lend all hands to recover the broken one.

He had hardly finished speaking before Anderson was running upstream along the bank some little distance before plunging into the river to battle his way through the ice-green water toward the great rise of timbers half out of control. It looked like the act of a madman from where he stood, and Sasha started to the brink of the water in unconscious protest. Even if Anderson could hold up his head in the relentless, tumbling pull of the current until he reached the broken bridge section, the danger from the weight of timbers hanging above him was surely enough to daunt any man. Yet, it was soon apparent that he was looking at someone who was a fearless swimmer. That, added to the sweep of the current, was swiftly closing the gap between the dark head and the far end of the structure.

Without taking his eyes from the river, Sasha shouted urgent orders to his men, the excitement of danger adding weight to the commands to be swift. Already, he was standing in water that reached the top of his boots. To attempt to follow would be pointless. There was no certainty that even as good a swimmer as Anderson could keep up his present conquest of the river; to go in after him would simply double the risk. It was one of those times when a man had to consider the greater demands on him. To lose the English officer would be a setback; to lose both officers would constitute a disaster.

The water filled Sasha's boots and lapped against his thighs in icy eddies. Even there at the edge he could feel the pull, and the noise of water breaking over the wreckage as it surged toward its outlet gave his voice a faraway sound as he continued to shout. Then, he was no longer alone. The soldiers were strung out along the bank, watching the struggle out in the river. At first, they stood awed by what they saw, then they gradually began to shout encouragement, their vigorous voices growing louder and louder, as they did when watching feats of daring at a celebration. This action met with their lustiest admiration.

From that moment on, Sasha thought of nothing but saving the bridge. He kept his eyes on the bobbing head of his ally as the Englishman reached the far end of the section and clung to it, the water buffeting both him and the wood. Sasha guessed he was searching for the broken rope and hoping to bring it to land, as their best hope of securing the section safely, but when the rope snapped under such pressure, the end would have lashed back with force enough to send it way beyond the point where it was secured to the timbers. The man's only hope was to follow it from where he had tied it earlier that day and play out the length as he moved back to the bank. The rope would now be heavy with water and surely impossible to handle in that current. Anderson would need all his strength to fight his way back. Hampered by a dead weight, his chances were greatly lessened.

With nerves keyed to top pitch, Sasha watched Anderson climb with laboured effort onto the pine trunks and drag himself clear of the water. There was a moment before he made a further move across the swaying structure, then he reached for the rope still attached to the last cross strut and began to pull it in like a fisherman playing a difficult catch. Sasha was so caught up in the moment that he even felt the physical effort that must be punishing the other man, and the virile chanting of his soldiers betrayed their longing to help the Englishman, if only in spirit.

It seemed an age while the whole length of rope was hauled until the end came from the water, and a further age as the man on the swaying timbers tied the heavy rope around his waist with hands that made a slow job of it. Then he began to pick his way back across the timbers, which shivered and swayed beneath his progress.

In a moment, the soldiers acted on Sasha's orders to prepare to take the rope the minute their ally reached the bank, drag it in, and secure it firmly around a tree at the top. Then Sasha went forward himself to offer a hand to someone who had just shown that he possessed courage besides ambition.

The young officer looked pale and was breathing in laboured fashion when he put his hand in Sasha's and their grips locked. For a moment only their glances met, but in that moment Sasha smiled with involuntary comradeship. After fractional hesitation, the other man gave a faint, weary smile in return. Then he was jumping into the water to be pulled the remaining few feet to the bank by Sasha's strong hold.

The minute he was clear of the water, someone was untying the rope from around him, and many hands seized it to pull the whole length from the river before tying it securely to a tree Sasha had considered hefty enough to take the strain. When he turned back, Sasha found the Englishman sitting on the ground, leaning forward on his bent knees, completely spent. Sasha stood looking down at him. The young fool had refused to eat anything other than rations similar to the men's, turning down the offer of luxuries left untouched in the Swarovsky tent when the convict thieves ransacked the train. After three days of hard work and meagre rations, what he had just done was a ridiculously risky thing to do. Sasha sighed. What an extraordinary fellow this Englishman was! Full of bombast and prickly pride, yet courageous to the extent of foolhardiness. Then, as Sasha continued to stand, watching the water stream from the other's hair and uniform, it came to him that he had once known a proud, stubborn, impetuous youngster very much like this Englishman: himself!

The thought shook him so much that he was drawn from the reverie only by the approach of the English Corporal, who stood beside his officer until the sight of his boots caught the attention of the recovering swimmer.

Anderson looked up slowly, his eyes bloodshot from the water. "Yes . . . What is it?"

The N.C.O. held out his hand, in which were two pieces of metal. "The shackle pin, sir." He waited until the senior man had taken the pieces and stared at them long and hard. "What do you think, sir?"

They exchanged a long, meaning look that Sasha did not understand. He thought Anderson looked even paler than before.

"By God, he's sly." It was slurred and throaty, as Anderson got to his feet, pushing back his dripping hair with his free hand. "He's also very knowledgeable. Where did you find this?"

"Not far from the tree, sir. No wonder it went with such a crack."

Sasha reminded them that he was there by asking what the conversation was about, but the Englishman took his time in answering.

"It is about the traitor you have in your ranks. This pin was sawn through almost undetectably to ensure that it snapped when strain was put upon it. It's only by good fortune that no one was caught in the whip-back when the pin parted. There could have been a tragedy similar to the explosion at the cutting." He wiped the runnels of water from his face with his forearm. "I warned you he would try again, but the dramas of the past few days have put it to the back of my mind."

"How can you say with certainty that it did not simply snap from fatigue? Those pieces tell us nothing."

"To a skilled man, they tell it all."

"Then it would take a skilled man to do such a thing. You have just said that he was knowledgeable. None of my men has had training in such things."

Anderson's fingers closed tightly over the pieces in his hand. "What are you suggesting—that I did it?"

"I suggest nothing. You are the one who seeks a traitor after every accident."

The N.C.O. walked away very tactfully, but this time there was a new reasonableness in the exchange of words, a lack of real bitterness. After the events of the day, both were too thoughtful to fly into a rage. They were simply trying each other out.

"There are too many 'accidents' on this project. You must know that as well as I do."

"And each has been perpetrated by a man who understands the work you do—you have admitted as much."

He looked at Sasha steadily, his red-rimmed eyes still registering shock and fatigue. "You are not making sense if you suggest I or my two men are concerned. I would hardly jeopardise all I am trying to achieve, and my men are anxious to finish the job and return to England. They have had four years of war and see no joy in spending the winter in a Russian forest."

"My men see no joy in it either," Sasha said firmly. "All they want is to fight their enemy. Until this railway project is finished, they cannot return to their main purpose."

The younger man came out with his next weapon. "I know my men. Can you truthfully say you know yours?"

"They are loyal Russians. That is enough."

"So loyal you were obliged to shoot one not so long ago."

They looked at each other warily, uncertain of this sudden effort at understanding and reason. Sasha took it a step further, all the same.

"Then we must share the blame, Captain. You and your people have the skill this man possesses—I and mine have already harboured one traitor. It remains to be seen who discovers this one in his ranks."

The Englishman seemed unable to think of an answer to that, and the silence might have gone on for a long time if it had not been broken by a familiar, distant sound. It was the staccato puffing of a steam-engine drawing gradually nearer.

"It's the train," said Anderson unnecessarily, and he began walking away from the river toward the track, finding in the arrival of the supplies from Lake Onega an escape from something that was too big to face, after all he had been through. Sasha let him go. In the Englishman's place, he would have done the same.

A second or two later, Sasha followed the general rush toward the track. From the men there came laughter and anticipation of food supplies and news of successes against the Reds. The train could not have chosen a more opportune moment to steam in. Tension was relieved in excitement; discontent was tempered by an iron messenger from the outside world.

Everyone in that isolated group began to converge on the track, where their own train stood twenty yards from the riverbank. Little puffs of smoke could be seen above the treetops now, and the rails began to sing. They stood, the Russians in their high boots and uniforms with shirts belted in at the waist; the Englishmen dressed not so very differently, yet conspicuously foreign in appearance, all watching the distant bend for the first sign of the engine. Even the two women had come from the tent, gazing with hands shading their eyes against the lowering sun.

A shout went up. The empty track ahead looked to be dancing in the heat haze, but there was the unmistakable solidness of a great steam engine now in view, quivering with the same haze as it puffed along the straight stretch, the tall, funnel-shaped stack sending up rhythmic belches of smoke. Gradually, the round black smokebox grew larger and clearer, the shining buffers catching the sun with subdued fire, the steam escaping from beneath with a shrill hiss, as the train neared and began to slow. The rails shook as it covered the last few yards of track to come to a halt with a great explosion of steam and billowing smoke just short of their own supply truck.

The men surged forward, crying out as if greeting an old friend, and the engine-driver shouted back with equal fervour to his brothers. Then it was all bustle and noise. The soldiers began to sing, as befitted the occasion, and many hands helped to unload the boxes.

Sasha stood watching the activity until the train suddenly faded into a background blur of dark, noisy metal as a young man swung down from one of the trucks and looked his way. Sasha's heart began thudding so fast it was difficult to breathe. Disbelief, joy, painful sobbing emotion filled him and weakened his limbs. Then he was running, running beside the track toward a fair-haired lieutenant in the uniform of the Red Army.

The other began to run, also, clearly caught in a twin emotion. They met and embraced as they had that day in a devastated village during the great retreat, brother holding brother in kinship, love, and thankfulness.

"Valodya . . . *bratishka* . . . I cannot believe . . ." Sasha's voice broke as he held the boy at arm's length, but he could not see the beloved face through the flow of his tears. "I thought . . . I thought you were dead. I thought never to see you again. Later you will tell me why you wear this uniform." He pulled him into another close embrace, slapping Valodya's back and shoulders in the fervour of his greeting. It seemed incredible, a dream he had had in the lonely night hours. A train had brought a man from the dead. It was too much to accept.

"Sasha . . . Sasha," cried Valodya, in tears himself. "So long I have waited. You, too, might have been dead. I did not know."

So, laughing and crying together, the brothers were reunited, cuffing each other with affectionate gentleness, each man victim to a blood tie that was stronger than all else at that moment.

Only when the first exultant greetings were calming did Sasha become aware of another figure standing just a few feet away. His arms dropped from holding Valodya's shoulders, and a sorely tried pulse began to labour painfully as he looked into the face of a woman he had come so close to loving four years ago.

"Lyudmilla," he breathed, drawing away from his brother. "*Milochka!*"

Black-lashed amber eyes gazed at him with that long-ago passion he had shared, bringing him a memory of a silk-hung bed and the heady perfume of camellias floating on water in alabaster bowls.

"*Bozhe moy, kakoi surprise!*" she said in her breathy voice. "So, it was not the end, as we thought."

T e n

It could only happen in Russia, thought Paul: a young Tsarist Lieutenant in the uniform of the new Red Army arriving on a supply train sent up the line by the British and bringing with him a ballerina fleeing for her life, whose only luggage is an accordion inlaid with mother-of-pearl.

And only an Englishman would accept it with resigned nonchalance such as Paul was presently displaying to the Corporal who came up with the train and was explaining who his passengers were.

"The lady's a bally-dancer who upset a top Bolshie official and had to run for it. On the Q.T., sir, it seems she's the Lieutenant's lady-friend, and he got her out of Moscow under the noses of the Reds before she could be arrested. I did hear there was some sort of a fight on a train and a Commissar was shot. Now, they are both wanted very badly by the other side . . . and it's not for the pleasure of their company, if you see what I mean." He nodded in the direction of the newcomers. "He's what I call a real gent. No side with him. Had us laughing all the way up the line. You'd never think he's been through it at the hands of the Reds."

But to a man who had been through it in France, it was more than obvious. Young Swarovsky was undoubtedly who he claimed to be. The hair was fairer, the moustache trimmer than his brother's, but there was a matching dreaminess in the blue eyes and the same sharp, aristocratic features. Paul judged him to be about his own age, but in the way he moved and smiled there was a suggestion of a lifetime already lived. It struck a chord within Paul that played a harmonious tune. As he watched the family reunion, the love and affection so unashamedly expressed, a strange pang touched him. It made his own reunion with his mother and sister on his return from France stand out as artificial and forced. They had merely gone through the accepted ritual, but it had meant next to nothing. He had sacrificed his family on the day he offered to sacrifice his life for England.

But there was a worse pang to follow when the newcomer was introduced to a sister-in-law he had never met. The young Lieutenant was a handsome devil and apparently full of panache. He saluted, pulled off his cap to give a sweeping bow, then seized her hand to take to his lips. Paul was too far from them to catch more than a murmur of Russian and a glimpse of an impudent smile before Swarovsky angled his head and kissed Irina full on the lips.

Paul turned away quickly, finding the gay laughter that followed ringing in his ears. On top of all that had happened that day, it was more than he could take. He was desperately trying to accept the sudden appearance of two more aristocratic Russians to add to the burden of his command, for, although Swarovsky suggested that only the railway was Paul's responsibility, Paul knew the whole group was ultimately dependent on him. The young officer was more than welcome, provided his temperament was not like his brother's, but a *ballerina*! Really, it was hard to see how the authorities at Lake Onega could have countenanced her joining the group here at the bridge. It was difficult enough with two women. He could not see any possibility of a temperamental artist finding any kind of compromise with them. If she *was* young Swarovsky's mistress, Paul could visualise feathers flying amongst the females and little work done by the Lieutenant. He heaved a long sigh. Women were the very devil. How did any man ever get to understand them?

"If I was those two," said the N.C.O. from the train, "I'd not feel safe till I was well shot of this country."

"And so say all of us," chorused a soldier who had come up with him. "Now we've had orders to stop fighting, we ought to be on our way home."

"Until this bridge is repaired, no one will be going anywhere," murmured Paul, feeling the strained atmosphere that had settled over the Russian group now the ballerina was being introduced. Then the man's words sunk in. "*Orders to stop fighting!* What are you talking about?"

"Just came through, sir. You probably wouldn't have heard of it yet . . . although it doesn't really apply, since all these soldiers are Ruskies, anyway."

"What is this order?" he demanded sharply.

"General order from Murmansk, sir. There's to be no more fighting by British troops. We can only 'advise and instruct' the Ruskies. It's their war, from now on."

It was like a thunderclap. The echo went round and round his exhausted brain looking for an escape in ordered thought and found none.

"Does that mean we are pulling out?" Paul's throat was hoarse after all the shouting he had done. It made the words sound almost desperate, and the Corporal looked at him strangely.

"Nothing definite, sir, but the lads sense the end is near and are beginning to agitate."

The end is near. Paul walked away past the train and up the line, treading carefully over the sleepers, wanting to be alone. *The end is near.* What end? How would it all end? In their isolation, they did not know what was happening in that vast country beyond. God knew, he had not wanted to know. It had been so easy to divorce himself from the main struggle, pretend none of it was happening. Suddenly, it was intruding, taking him by the scruff of the neck and shaking him. Suddenly, he was part of a war that had followed him up a single-track railway line with a stealth and speed that caught him as unprepared as the ragged thieves back at the siding.

He felt slightly sick as he walked, head bent, staring at his boots as they covered the yards of shingle ballast. It was not surprising. He had eaten little and worked to physical capacity over the past three days. But the sickness owed itself more to that piece of sabotage this morning that now took on a different importance. He had seen it as a blow against his work on the bridge, but it was really a blow against an era. The bridge, itself, was unimportant. The saboteur was doing what thousands of his brothers

were doing all over Russia—planting the seeds of disruption and revolution. Somewhere in the ranks of the Russian company was one man
determined to kill and destroy. Perhaps more than one man! Since the
Name Day celebrations, Paul had found himself more involved with
them as people rather than a mere work force. He had picked up a few
words of Russian and exchanged greetings with them every day. He
found them robust, savage, exasperating, emotional, and warm-hearted.
After nearly two months of their company, he had grown used to them.
He doubted he would ever understand them, but he had grown used to
their ways and attitudes and felt some kind of bond that had crept up
unawares on both sides. It was disturbing to know that behind one of
those bearded Slavic faces was a mind bent on the death and destruction
of them all.

Then he heard again Irina saying to him, *I know that you think of our
soldiers as cowards, as allies who walked away and left you to fight alone.
It was not like that.* Perhaps the Russian people—the people of the vast
wild areas—truly wanted what the Reds offered. Was that the end that
was near?

The stores were all unloaded, but the soldiers who had come up with
them were to have a meal with Paul's group before starting the return
journey. He made no attempt to get back to work; he merely walked to
the broken bridge to check that the section was still firmly held. He had
the sense to let his men enjoy relaxation over a good, solid meal. In the
long run, the work would go better.

Only when Paul got beneath his own canvas to strip off the wet
uniform and boots did weariness finally take over. His limbs refused to
obey his wishes, his eyelids drooped, his neck seemed unable to hold up
his head any longer. Almost without knowing it, he sank onto the pillow
and went out like a light. But his system was now so used to cat-naps, it
was impossible to sleep for long, and he was awake again within an hour
and a half.

His slumbering senses had allowed his body to dwell on pleasures his
waking self-control forbade, so he lay on his bed tormented by the echo of
something he had experienced just once. If only he did not have to see
Irina day after day, hear her speaking the language that shut him out,
know she was just a few yards away. If only . . . But would the longing
ease if he were out of sight and reach of her? Would he ever be able to
forget that moment in the supply-truck? *With all my heart, I thank you.*
So close had he come to holding her that afternoon at the lake, so sure had
he been that she wanted what he wanted . . . until it became plain she
was using his weakness to persuade him to toe Swarovsky's line . . . *the
man who had last taken her into his bed so long ago she had forgotten
what she must do.* Did she love the Russian so much?

Paul had kept as far from her as possible since then, but the knowledge that she was always there put a tingle in his spine that never seemed to go. He let out his breath on a groan. At the Western Front, men had gone out to dig another useless trench or take daredevil unoffical potshots at the Huns. Some had drunk themselves silly, others had told stories of bestial obscenities for hours on end. Out here, the only possible outlet was hard work, and he knew that did not succeed, in his case. Turning restlessly, his glance fell upon the bottle of brandy sent up for him by the members of the Officers' Mess at Lake Onega. That might do as a start.

The third tot was disappearing by the time he had washed and put on dry clothes prior to eating his solitary dinner, and he was pouring a fourth when a shadow fell across the tent. He looked up quickly and saw Swarovsky's brother looking in at him with a questioning smile.

"Captain Anderson?"

"Yes."

"Ah, how do you do and hallo," he said in accented English, holding out his hand. "My friends at Lake Onega said no hugs and kisses for Englishmen, so you see I shake hands very correctly."

Paul's first reaction was regret that the man was Olga's brother. He was extremely good-looking and virile—a combination that would have satisfied her provocative demands and made things a lot easier for Paul. He shook hands, noting with approval that the fellow had a firm grip.

"Vladimir Ivanovich, at your service," he said with a click of his heels. "It is permitted to enter?"

"Yes . . . yes, of course," Paul told him, standing back. "Do you drink brandy?"

"I drink almost anything when it is offered." He grinned. "It is one of the few civilised habits they have in the Red Army."

Paul smiled back. "Take a seat. There's only one, so there's no question of choosing the most comfortable." He poured two drinks and held one out for his guest. *"Vashe zdorovie!"*

His Russian met with great approval, but he lost no time in putting the record straight. "No, no. I'm no linguist. That is just one phrase in about a dozen that I know. Your family puts me to shame with their knowledge of English."

"We had a governess from England who was very strict. She once put me in the cupboard because my French was better than my English. I did not mind. In the cupboard were toys and books; the others had to continue their lessons."

Paul warmed to him instantly. His friendly, open manner was blessedly refreshing after the complex personalities of the others.

"That governess sounds very long-suffering, to me."

The brandy had vanished down a thirsty throat, so Paul poured him another and held it out. "Welcome to our ranks, although it is hardly the best time to choose to join us. It was much more pleasant at the lake."

"*Da! Da!* I would have come sooner, but something detained me. About two thousand rifles, to be exact."

Paul sat on the bed, finding himself completely at ease with someone who had established an immediate rapport, someone who spoke a language he understood.

"Your family thought you had been murdered by the Reds."

"I almost was." It was said without drama.

It could have been France again. A young officer not much more than a boy, drinking brandy from a cup without a handle and speaking of death with a throwaway nonchalance that had been acquired by necessity. Paul knew him, had known hundreds like him, *felt* like him. Something in his soul reached out to this foreigner who somehow broke down the barriers of language, culture, and beliefs to establish a bond of youth in turmoil.

Paul took a pull at his drink. "Olga said there was a sister in Moscow."

The Russian nodded. "She was shot because I initially refused to serve in their army. I was of more use to them than her." He indicated the emblems on his uniform. "That is why you see these on a Swarovsky."

It shocked Paul, made him cold with the return of something he had tried to push into the back of his mind—a young girl dying at the hands of ruthless men.

"How long have you been in their army?" he asked quietly.

Blue eyes looked back frankly. "Time I abandoned a long while ago. What is it but a record of one's humiliation? It is better not to know how the days have passed." He shifted on the camp chair and leaned forward with his arms along his thighs, holding his glass in both hands as he remembered. "It was worse than war. I thought I had seen everything and felt the depths of humiliation when my men mutinied at the Front. After the shameful peace with Germany was signed and we who were left in the trenches returned to our homes, the nightmare was only just beginning. They caught us as we stepped from trains and lorries, murdering without thought or reason. I escaped and made my way through the snowy streets to the family house. It was full of drunken louts urinating over antique furniture." He gave a strange twisted smile. "They thought such treatment would destroy its years of beauty and value. How much they still have to learn."

"Your brother had rescued Olga before they arrived, and he took her to the summer estate. She told me about it."

"I was on my way to join them when I ran into a rabble in the street. They saw my uniform, all it represented, and fell into a rage." He frowned and drank deeply before saying casually, "It does not matter what they did to me. As with the antique furniture, my heritage could not be reduced by animal bestiality to dirt beneath their feet . . . but I owe my life to an old woman who dragged me into a cellar beneath a church after they had left me." He glanced up to meet Paul's eyes. "You know how it is. Someone creeps from a pile of rubble and saves the life of a stranger for no reason other than humanity."

"Yes, I know," said Paul with feeling.

"They caught me again on the road to our summer estate." A long reflective silence preceded his next words. "Only when they shot Ekaterina did I believe they meant what they said. There were three more Swarovskys in Russia, and I had no idea whether they could be in similar danger. And so I became an officer of the new Red Army—'the army of the people.' I submitted to their authority in the hope that I might one day be of some help to the remaining members of my family, wherever they might be."

Paul held out the brandy bottle at a pouring angle, and his offer was accepted. "When did you discover they were safe and together up here?"

"When I reached Lake Onega five days ago."

"Five days . . . good God, so you have been with the Reds . . ."

"I told you, I abandoned time," said the quiet, accented voice. "My service with the 'people's army' was a . . . was a . . ." He sought for the right words, then grinned at Paul. "You see how right my governess was? What is it you call the time between two parts of a theatrical performance?"

"An interval."

"*Da! Da!* . . . an interval. A time when one waits for the next part to begin."

"And this is the next part?"

The Russian smiled. "If you will allow me to join you."

"I don't usually make so free with my brandy unless I regard someone as part of the outfit." Paul used the war term unconsciously, as part of an atmosphere he knew so well. Continuing in the understated language that overrode danger and fear, he said, "You'll find things rather dull here, by comparison. All we have to liven it up are mosquitoes and the odd wolf or two."

"*Gospodi!*" exclaimed his guest, getting to his feet. "Do you mean to tell me my friends here have not yet taught you how to be merry around a campfire?"

Paul held up his hands, laughing. "Oh, yes . . . indeed, yes. But if hugs and kisses are not for Englishmen, neither are Russian celebrations. I learnt that, to my cost."

The young Russian clapped him on the shoulder. "Ah, my friend, it takes practice, even for a Russian. It is like having a woman. After the first one, a man learns that the pleasure can be sustained if he does not put all his energy into the first hour." Up went his eyebrows in comical question. "Am I not right?"

"I'll take your word for it," said Paul, as the only kind of answer he felt capable of giving to that.

"Good. Before you return to your country, I will show you how to celebrate as we do, and even teach you how to dance the *trepak*."

Paul shook his head. "You have no idea what you are taking on."

"I think I have," was the reply that was suddenly serious. The handsome young face looked frankly at him. "In situations such as these, time is unimportant, as I said before. Sometimes it is possible for a man to live half his life in one hour. It is necessary to establish friendship quickly when one feels it. Am I not right?"

A whole procession of young faces marched through Paul's thought in that moment—faces that were now white and still. He held out his hand. "My name is Paul."

The young Lieutenant gripped it hard. "My friends call me Valodya."

They drank to friendship, then to each other, by which time the world was a rosy, cosy place to be in. Valodya put his arm around Paul's shoulders and indicated the tent flaps.

"Come, Slabov cooks something splendid for us tonight, and we must not keep him waiting."

Digging in his heels with sudden cold calmness, Paul made his excuses. "I think . . . no, not tonight. You must have so much to talk about with your family."

"*Da! Da!* But that is no reason for you to eat alone."

"I usually do."

Valodya plainly did not know what to make of the remark and frowned. "You prefer this?"

Paul hesitated. It was not the time to relate what had passed between himself and the Russians, if, indeed, it ever should be told to a man who had suffered such things. In contrast, the events of the past two months seemed petty.

"It seemed the best arrangement, under the circumstances."

A shrewd look entered the blue eyes. "Mmm. Do the circumstances demand that you refuse a direct invitation from me to join us?"

What could he say? "Of course not."

Valodya grinned. "My brother can say nothing if etiquette obliges you to sit with Olga." His grin broadened. "My sister has grown very beautiful since I last saw her . . . and it is very lonely up here. You might find things easier now, for Sasha will have other things on his mind, if I am not wrong."

He had jumped to the wrong conclusion, that Paul was being thwarted by an older brother's protection of a young, desirable girl. But the right conclusion would have been even more disastrous, so Paul had to let it go and hope Valodya would not misguidedly make the situation worse where Olga was concerned.

The little table had been extended by what were probably wooden crates and covered in white damask, as on the night of the Name Day celebrations. Six places had been laid, which told Paul he had been expected—that Valodya had set out with the intention of bringing him into the group—and he felt that same incredulous irritation at the sight of silver and glassware set out with aristocratic disregard for time and place. They were all sitting on the beds and chairs as if in an elegant drawing room, and they turned as the two men arrived at the tent entrance.

The atmosphere was immediately apparent as Paul said, "Good evening."

Swarovsky rose with relief as if, in some strange way, he was glad of masculine company. Olga was even more like an unstable explosive, ready to go off at any minute, taking them all in the fury of destruction. Her face was still and strangely colourless, her eyes dark-shadowed and glittering with something akin to hysteria. Paul almost recoiled from the silent hunger she transmitted to him as he stood on the threshold. But it was Irina who took all his attention. In the same soft dress she had worn for the Name Day, she was indescribably lovely as she looked at him with absolute commitment. He knew in that moment that she had surrendered whatever resistance had held her away from him and was trying to tell of the painful desperation she now faced. Her eyes begged him to understand and help her, her sadness implored him to take pity on her. How could he, when they were surrounded by others, when he did not know what had brought about her surrender? How could he, when her plight echoed his own? His stomach churned. Could no one else see what he read so plainly?

Valodya touched his arm, breaking into wild thoughts and lost in something he was uncertain how to handle.

"Paul, I must present you to Madame Zapalova, prima ballerina and a close friend."

Even Paul's limited knowledge of women told him here was a vastly different proposition from Olga and Irina, and the introduction that was more like being presented to royalty was so unique it dragged his attention away from the confusion in his mind. It did not strike him until several seconds later that Madame Zapalova had extended her hand to be kissed, not firmly shaken, as he had just done. Having never kissed the hand of a woman in his life, he had no intention of doing so now, with all eyes upon him. It might come naturally to Swarovskys, but he was certain it was not his style.

The confusion brought a hiatus to the proceedings that enabled Paul to study her. She plainly expected to be stared at. The dark-red garment he had thought to be a calf-length skirt was really a pair of voluminous silken Turkish trousers tucked into boots of tooled leather. Over it she wore a shirt of pale lavender satin tied, Cossack style, with a tasselled cord around her waist—a waist of incredibly tiny proportions. But, then, all her frame was tiny, almost boneless in its graceful fluidity each time she moved. But it was her head that had Paul staring. Small, balanced on a long sinewy neck, it was ornamented by masses of dark, glossy hair that swept starkly away from her face to rise in piles of plaited coils that resembled the headdress of an Egyptian goddess. The severity left her features emboldened, and Paul was fascinated yet repelled by them. Amber-coloured eyes were black-ringed and elongated by the use of sweeping upward strokes of a charcoal stick. The eyelashes were impossibly long and heavy, and her lids seemed to be touched with gold paint. The skin was stretched across her face to give it a pointed, fine-drawn abstraction of expression, yet her mouth was truly beautiful, even when in repose. Paul felt she would look magnificent when she smiled.

She did not waste a smile on him. He would have preferred it to the avaricious sexual scrutiny she gave him from head to foot.

"You have a fine, supple body," she said thickly, as if he were auditioning for her ballet partner, and he felt everyone in that tent giving him similar scrutiny.

"But my English is not good," she went on quickly. "We speak in French."

Her rapid, excellent French did not sound at all like the patois Paul had learned during his years in France, but he gleaned enough to understand that she was asking him about the bridge. Acutely embarrassed, he took a deep breath and began a laboured reply in the kind of "parley-voo" accent used by British soldiers during the war.

He got no further than two sentences before she threw up her hands and gurgled, *"Impossible! C'est le langage de cochons!"*

The language of pigs! The brandy in his system roared into action. "When I learnt it, we were living like pigs, Madame. We wallowed in mud and ate our meals surrounded by the bloated carcasses of horses and rats, huddling in foul trenches that ran with the blood of our friends. We had no time for the refinements of a linguist when a man's life depended on a quick warning of danger. When men are reduced to living like animals, it is inevitable that they speak like them."

There was a stunned silence. The gold-lidded eyes widened in excessive expression, betraying the owner's histrionic talent. Then she began to laugh, and there was nothing histrionic about that. There was pure delighted amusement in the sound.

"Captain, you make much refresh. A servant I had once, as you are. Rude he was, but so delightful attractive." Her smile made her as magnificent as he had guessed. "Do you offer forgive and say you have love for me?"

Valodya, now standing behind her, took her fragile shoulders in his hands and leant forward to say in her ear, "Paul is an Englishman. You do not ask if he loves you."

Again that transforming smile and the change from grande dame to ingénue as she studied Paul's physique with bold interest.

"Do not Englishmen know of love, Captain?"

The brandy continued to do magnificent service to his reserved nature. "Certainly, but they don't shout about it in a crowded room, and they prefer to speak of it when they are ready, not to be asked outright." Elated with his spirit-induced confidence, he went on, "But up here, there is little time for such things. There is vitally important work to be done, and you must accept that if you hope to remain with us."

"Ha," she cried, striking a pose, "The silent and strong man! There was a Prussian general once of my acquaint. He was also like this but underneath . . . ah, underneath . . . such gifts as he gave me you never did see."

"Those days are over," put in a flat voice. "The only gift you are likely to get now is a bullet in your back."

It fell like cold water on the simmering atmosphere, and Paul turned to see Olga looking at the ballerina with amazing animosity. He was not so high on brandy that he could not work out the reason. She had sustained several shocks when that train had pulled in behind their own, and her heightened emotions were not helped by the presence of her brother's mistress. It made her more than ever the odd girl out. His heart sank as he realised the implications of that.

Slabov, the Russian cook-orderly who waited on the Swarovskys, appeared to make his bow. Next minute, they were all sitting around the table as if at a dinner party, whilst a remarkable soup was brought in. Paul was seated beside Olga, as Valodya had predicted, and his worst fears were verified when she spoke to him under cover of the general business of being served.

"I cannot think how he dares bring that woman here. She is vulgar and vain. I apologise that you should be forced to welcome her." Her eyes glistened with malice. "She became a dancer and, from that, gained wealth and a position in society. But she comes from nothing. Her father was a *blacksmith*." The word was produced like a trump card in a deadly game of bridge. "You were wonderful, Paul. You put her immediately in her place."

The brandy must have been working for him, because he murmured, "Perhaps it is because I come from nothing myself. My father was a wheelwright." Looking her full in the eyes, he added roughly, "In your eyes, the Andersons would be peasants."

He knew it was wrong the minute the words had been said. Her retaliation was swift and savage. "Lyudmilla Sergeyevna is a well-known courtesan. She was Sasha's mistress for five years. Think how Irina must feel to come face-to-face with her . . . and how galling to see how much he still cares."

It hit him over the heart. Now he understood the plea in Irina's eyes, the surrender to an attraction she had previously fought. His gaze flew to where she sat beside her husband, quiet, restful, a girl with infinite courage beneath her fragility . . . and infinite compassion. She should never be hurt.

Their glances locked, and something in his own expression must have told her he knew. Stealing across her cheeks came the faintest colour, as it had across his so many cursed times, and the sight of it sent desire surging from within to flood his body as the pink flooded her face. That proof of her vulnerability at his hands set off the slumbering rocket of mastery, and the longing that had been subjugated by brandy only an hour or two before returned in full force. He had never seen her so responsive. It was almost more than he could do to restrain himself from reaching out to grip her hand.

The brandy now became his enemy. It urged him to get to his feet and tell Swarovsky he was taking his wife away from him. It urged him to lead her out of that tent, out of reach of such an impossible situation, away from one girl who had no man and another who had too damned many . . . away to sanity and England.

The brandy and memories stirred up by Valodya reminded him of the French harlot who had enabled him to test his manhood. Then, he wanted Irina so much it beat in his pulse throughout his whole body. This time he would not be a fumbling boy. He would take her with a grateful passion, and she would sigh with the ecstasy of his love . . . as he would also sigh with it. She was so beautiful, even the thought of possessing her was an agony. And all the while he must sit eating soup. It almost choked him.

"They killed our sister, yet this one was saved," continued Olga deliberately. "Valodya has put his own life, and ours, in jeopardy, by bringing her here. She is not worth saving."

"She is a human being," Paul replied savagely, his gaze still on Irina, who had turned to answer her husband. "Every human has the right to live. Your brother recognises that, as I also learnt to do."

"But not at the expense of putting four others in deadly danger. *Look at me, Paul!*"

He swung his head round automatically, still full of his need for Irina.

Always vibrant, Olga had a macabre kind of beauty that night, with pale-pale face suggesting a waxen model that had living eyes aflame with ambivalence. She rejoiced that her brother was here but rejected the circumstances that had brought him.

"Do you know what Valodya has done—what that silly, dramatic creature did to make her escape necessary?"

"I know nothing except that they are two extra to guard and provision." He spoke deliberately impersonally; it seemed to be the only hope he had of getting through the evening.

But Olga was irrepressible, determined to detonate whatever lay restive beneath her semblance of civilised normality. She caught the attention of the ballerina in a tone that betrayed her imperialistic attitude in a way Paul had not noticed before.

"Lyudmilla Sergeyevna, we have not yet heard the exciting details of your adventures—only that you defied the great General Goliapin and were on the brink of arrest when our brother took you from the house. You have a captive audience—we cannot leave until the bridge is repaired—so entertain us! We cannot pay for the gracious privilege, but you are being fed by the British. That will have to suffice in this rustic playhouse."

"It was no theatre-piece," put in Valodya quickly, " . . . and we are all being fed by the British at the moment. You do not care for your situation? Be thankful you were not in Moscow."

"Are you her spokesman . . . *as well?*" Olga finished emphatically. Paul saw the elder Swarovsky react, make as if to intervene, cast a look at Irina, then hold back irresolutely.

Paul longed to cry out, "Can't you decide between your wife and your mistress?" then clenched his teeth impotently at the look that passed between the married pair.

"I should like to hear the facts of your escape," he put in desperately, turning to Valodya. "How was it possible to get as far as Lake Onega through territory held by the Reds?"

Valodya flashed him a grateful smile. "You forget, my friend, I *am* one of the Reds. But I think Madame Zapalova should tell how it all began."

He spoke briefly to the ballerina in Russian. She gave him one of her superb smiles that finally rested on Paul as she turned to him.

"You are English. You know of love, but do not do the shout of it," she began, reminding him of his own words. "You must try to understand, my Englishman, the life of an artist." Her shoulders moved expressively. "It is unusual from another. We create this . . . mmm, you know . . . this *person* when we dance. For many, many, it is the real, and so there are many admirings." Oblique brows rose above eyes large with query. "This you say?"

"*Admirers,*" he corrected, realising as he spoke that she had a magic quality that came vividly to the fore when taking centre stage. He had never seen a ballet, but if she displayed such grace and provocation on the stage, he could well imagine men flocking around her—men like the wealthy Swarovskys.

"Admirers," she repeated, rolling the *r*'s heavily. "I am use to this from a long time, you understand, and it become necessary to my career that I have the flirts. It is much expect of a dancer." Her smile was dazzling. "You do not know any dancer, Captain?"

He shook his head, feeling no embarrassment, for once. "I have never had the time."

"*Ah, pauvre enfant!*" She flashed her great amber eyes at her former lover. "*Pauvre enfant,*" she repeated softly.

"How did Goliapin join your entourage?" asked Olga so sharply that all attention was taken from the ballerina, as she had intended. "When did you start entertaining the enemy?"

But a diversion was created by the entry of Slabov with the next course—a rich meat dish made from fresh reindeer flesh that had been sent up the line to supplement the usual bully beef in tins. Paul had momentary misgivings as he remembered the Name Day feast, but after three days of unleavened bread and toasted fish, when it could be caught, he felt it would be foolish to reject meat—not that he could do so without being thought bad-mannered in such company. He embarked upon the dish with reluctance. Irina, he noticed, fastened her gaze on her plate and seemed afraid to look his way again. Perhaps it was as well. The food was beginning to offset the bravado brought on by the brandy, and the confidence that had made her his for the taking had been replaced by a sober reminder of the true state of things. It was all looking rather hopeless again. Madame Ballerina might have been Swarovsky's mistress for *twenty* years, it still would not make the girl Paul loved any less the man's wife.

"So, for many year I have a large of *admirers,*" continued the dancer, ignoring the meal before her. "My house was always fill with men of the most distinguish. Always. So many beautiful things, and such talking as you would only find in palaces," she went on, a faraway sadness touching her features.

As she continued her story, it became clear that when the October Revolution set the workers and peasants rampaging through the streets, killing or humiliating those with status, the great Zapalova had been marked down as a prime target because of her friendship with Tsarist courtiers and officers—even the Grand Duke Dmitri had been a one-time admirer. But a dancer has no interest in political or social problems. Zapalova lived in a world of spiritual and artistic expression, and such unworldly qualities meant that she had amongst her "court" men who were also fed by dreams and ideals—of a different nature to her own, to be sure, but driven by a passion and search for perfection that was as great as hers. Through the friendship of one such man, a bubble of protection was formed around her, fragile, quivering, easy to destroy, yet remaining intact so long as she drifted with the prevailing wind.

When the protector was shot under the new Red Terror, Zapalova retained her immunity through the friendship of several high-ranking officers of the "Peoples' Army" who continued to serve the next set of leaders. Her house became an unofficial Officers' Mess once again, the reformers reducing her wealth, according to their beliefs, by the simple expedient of eating and drinking it. But men are always men, and gifts and jewels still found their way into her grateful hands. Valodya, who had been one of her admirers for several years, was able to make open visits to her house once more, in his role as Red officer. But he suspected that his movements were watched.

The situation might well have continued as it was if it had not been for a Russo-Finnish general called Goliapin, who was one of Zapalova's newest and most boorish visitors. Whilst the ballerina did not care about the political outlook of those who flocked to her home for entertainment—or what terrors they had perpetrated—she did care very much about good manners.

Paul was disgusted. "Are you saying that a mass murderer was always welcome so long as he said 'please' and 'thank you'?" he challenged.

She turned her large, compelling eyes on him in scorn. "The English, I thought, were much insist on good manners. You do not have them."

"I have always been too busy working to acquire fancy manners," Paul replied in whip-like tones. "I am a peasant. If this were Moscow, I wouldn't rate an invitation to this meal . . . but I am the only one who knows how to repair that bridge, and if you want to escape from your former houseguests, you will have to bear with my bad manners."

"Captain Anderson saved my life and that of Olga Ivanovna," put in a quiet but coldly imperious voice. "I must ask that you do not slight him at my table."

Everyone looked at Irina in surprise. Paul's heart turned over. Even in that tent she looked what she truly was—a high-born lady playing hostess to distinguished company. Distinguished with the exception of himself! The truth hit him hard. How foolish to delude himself that she was just a lovely young girl in a forest when reality placed them at the opposite ends of every scale there was.

For a moment the wife and ex-mistress engaged in optical battle, then Zapalova gave her irresistible smile as her temper vanished as quickly as it had come.

"Is truth insult?" she asked disarmingly, then broke into rapid Russian enhanced by superb movements of her arms. Suddenly, her hand went out to cover Paul's as it rested on the table, and she cooed in English, "So, you admit to peasant. But brave and beautiful cannot be ignore, my captain. You have the forgive."

"It would be more to the point to tell the rest of your story," he said, still shaken by Irina's defence.

"Why did you select my brother from all your *admirers*?" put in Olga. "He must have been the most junior in rank, besides being so many years younger than you."

Zapalova acknowledged the jibe with raised brows. "It was not *select*. There was no know of my fate until Valodya came of the night to warning me."

She went on to describe why flight had been made necessary, and Paul was dragged further into the trap of unwilling emotion as he heard something he might have dismissed as pure drama if Valodya had not been part of it.

All had been going well one evening with her salon full of the new *élite* when General Goliapin had accidentally knocked from her mantelpiece· one of a pair of figurines given her by Prince Yusupov. He had laughed and kicked the fragments carelessly into the hearth before continuing to devour a dishful of glazed cherries in chocolate. Zapalova, incensed by such behaviour, threw a tirade at him, calling him a pig and unfit to move amongst such treasures. When he retaliated by sweeping the matching ornament into the hearth, she had flown at him, smacking him around the face and ordering him to leave immediately.

At that point, Valodya was obliged to continue the story, the dancer being too upset to say any more. The General, having been humiliated before several junior officers, extracted bitter revenge. Denouncing her as an imperialist plaything who should be made to work for those she had just treated with contempt, he began an orgy of destruction. Seated in one of her beautiful velvet chairs, he directed his juniors in the breaking of every ornament and the slashing of every picture in the room, first forcing the terrified woman to name the man who had given each to her. When they left, the house was a shambles of shattered china and glass; the walls were hung with pictures in tatters. Even the exquisite porcelain chandelier that had been part of the house when she moved in had not escaped. It had been the target for the revolvers of madmen.

For a woman of Zapalova's temperament, such an act was enough to send her into a trance of despair, and she was huddled in her same corner when Valodya arrived in the early hours with the intention of getting her to safety. In his capacity as adjutant to a brewer who was now a commissar in the new regime, he had overheard the information that the ballerina was to be arrested and put on trial as a Tsarist agent the following morning.

Valodya glossed over the details of how he took Zapalova from the house and through a Moscow that never slept, but everyone in that tent knew he had put his own life in the greatest peril by doing so. He had walked for two days, with her wrapped in her cloak with the accordian, posing as his pregnant sister whom he was escorting to her home village. As a Red officer, he had commandeered a mule from a pedlar, and they had made their way to a small railway station outside Moscow, where Valodya had again used his uniform to bully a pass from the railway official.

All went smoothly until they reached Petrograd. At this major junction, it was not so easy for a mere lieutenant to browbeat the civilian officials. The days of tyranny by the officer class had gone; they had been assured of that. No fresh-faced boy speaking in aristocratic accents was going to move them. They would have to check. Come back in two or three days. There was nothing for it but to walk until they could reach another country station, north of the great city. It took them five days.

Trains on the Murmansk line were spasmodic and reserved for troops and supplies. Valodya could have mingled easily, but with Zapalova it was out of the question. Their only hope was to hide in a waggon containing food, but three more days passed before a train pulled into the tiny station, and then so many soldiers spilt onto the platform to buy bread from pedlars, the fugitives realised they would have been immediately spotted if they attempted to board it.

They were nearing desperation after two weeks of sleeping in the fields and eating little, so Valodya acted with reckless promptness when a train consisting of locked trucks and only one carriage steamed into the station. From the conversation of the four officers who got out to stretch their legs, Valodya gleaned that the main occupant of the carriage was a commissar on Lenin's personal staff—a man who was at that moment sitting alone in the compartment.

Crossing the line unseen, Valodya entered the carriage with pistol drawn, pulling the dancer in behind him. The Commissar was ordered onto the platform, and Valodya followed, telling the stunned officers he would kill his prisoner if anyone of them made a move. With that same threat, he climbed onto the footplate and ordered the train away. But they were getting steam up when one of the officers tried to reach for his pistol. Valodya shot the Commissar dead and threatened to kill them all if they as much as blinked. The death of so important an official under their escort seemed to paralyse them with thoughts of the consequences, and the train pulled away unmolested.

From then on things improved. The engine-driver revealed himself as a former high official on the railways who had been forced to share his home with seven other families and made to work as a driver, as part of the levelling process of Bolshevism. He saw his own chance of freedom and willingly took the train as far as he could, before the alarm went up and a company of troops was seen waiting at a siding ahead. Knowing he had nothing to lose, the ex-controller slowed enough to allow the great Zapalova—a beautiful creature he had admired for some years—and her young escort to jump off and head into the forest. Then, he got up steam and drove his engine at full speed toward the siding, mowing down several ranks of soldiers as the train shot the points and hurtled into the trees with a great tearing noise that almost drowned the sound of rifle shots.

The man was almost certainly dead before the soldiers reached him, Valodya said, and the resulting forest fire gave himself and the ballerina perfect cover for their escape. Three days later they met up with a band of White Finns who guided them to the Allies at Lake Onega. It was there they learnt that Valodya's brother was miraculously near, and the British gladly sent them both up on the train taking supplies.

Valodya gave Olga a smile that spoke volumes. "They did not know you were here, Olechka. It was a blessing from God when I saw you."

Only then did Paul see the depth of affection felt by a girl who always made him uneasy. Her face was almost melting with emotion.

"One we have lost. There must be no more, Valodya."

The young Russian looked at Paul. "We have a paper from your people to say we are to go on the first train over your new bridge."

"Why do you have a paper?" demanded Olga with a brittle change of tone. "Why *her*?"

Sasha broke his long silence to answer that. "I think the answer is obvious. Lyudmilla Sergeyevna escaped arrest. That is not easy to forgive. Our brother killed a member of Lenin's staff in her defence. That *must* be avenged, however long it takes."

Olga rounded on him in a blaze of passion. "And every Swarovsky is condemned to death along with him. Say it, Sasha! Let there be no more pretence. We *all* should have a paper to go on that train!"

E l e v e n

In that retreat amidst the pines, the horror, pain, and destruction of a great land was brought before Paul's eyes, ears, and soul. There was no longer any escaping it. Vladimir Ivanovich Swarovsky had brought with him something Paul had thrust aside the previous November. He had brought not only a return of the only kind of relationship in which Paul felt at ease but a way of life and death that had overshadowed the peace of Paul's first seventeen years to make them unreal and insignificant in comparison.

It might have been the affinity Paul felt for another young man who had lived a lifetime in five years or the fervent understated eloquence, so much more acceptable than the drama of the older Swarovsky. It was probably both, combined with several other indefinable qualities, that changed the whole aspect of Paul's cherished command on the Murmansk railway in an evening. Sitting in that tent with its bizarre trappings of a stately home, surrounded by Russians, he gradually became part of their agony.

Valodya told how he had been re-captured by Red troops on the road to the family summer estate where, if he had succeeded in reaching it, he would have found his brother with the two women.

"So close we came that day," he said with a reflective smile. "But it was destined that we should remain apart until now."

"What of the soldiers?" prompted the older Swarovsky.

"They would have killed me, but for the man leading them. He had been a minor official on the Water Board before the October Revolution and exempt from the war because of bad sight. He was a devoted party member, however, and considered right to command a terror squad that roamed the roads leading from Moscow to catch anyone trying to evade the regime." Valodya sighed. "The man recognised the family name and decided I was more use alive than dead." He pushed aside his plate, overcome by a mental return to that time. "They took me back to stand trial. Tsk, they do not know the first principles of justice!

"They had Ekaterina and wished to know the whereabouts of the rest of my family. It took several days before they realised I genuinely did not know." Only a slight deepening of his voice betrayed the emotions running through him as memory revived those days. "Then I was ordered to serve in their army, training men to use heavy artillery. I refused, not believing their threat to our sister."

His eyes were on his brother, and Paul could see the difference between the one who had seen and accepted and the one who could not believe. The shock of Valodya's next words made the colour drain from the older Swarovsky's face as Paul watched.

"I did not believe it, because Ekaterina had already gone over to the party."

"I always knew she was weak," said Olga with soft contempt.

Sasha rounded on her, ashen faced. "You are always quick to condemn, yet you know nothing. All your life you have lived under the protection of us all." Then he swung round to face Valodya with equal ferocity. "You have been taught to lie by your masters, but I will not have it here. There is no longer any need."

"Sasha, you do not know what it is like down there," was the vigorous reply. "All these years you have spent away . . . Moscow is no longer the city you knew. Vasily Igorovich had joined the party some years ago, and our sister was dominated by him. We have always known that from the day they first met."

"She wept, pleaded, cried that she loved him. She would have no other, she told me, and refused to eat until I agreed to the marriage. But I would never have allowed a liaison with a man who was not completely loyal," roared the older Swarovsky.

Paul was taken aback by the expression of pain and outrage on the man's face, and so, apparently, was Valodya. The young Russian got to his feet and confronted his brother across the table, strangely dignified in the uniform of their enemies as he prepared to be cruel in the gentlest way possible.

"Is it disloyal to see the truth that *we* were too blind to see? Sasha, in the comfortable serenity of our lives, we shut the door in the face of our people. For years they had been knocking on it in the hope that we would look out. In the end, they were forced to smash the the doors down." Valodya kept his gaze straight and true on his brother. "Eyes are being opened. Yours are still shut."

The older Swarovsky smashed his fist down onto the table. "*Gospodi*! You have become their disciple!"

"No, that is cruel," came an emphatic female voice.

Paul turned to see Irina's face aglow with the compassion that had made her so sadly beautiful that afternoon by the lake when she had pleaded for his understanding of her people.

"What he says is right. I have seen that bewilderment in those of the greatest loyalty. . . . I have felt it myself. I still feel it, Sasha," she added in a soft pleading tone. She turned to Valodya. "They are now in the hands of worse villains than we so innocently were . . . but how will it end?"

He spoke with confidence. "That is for a very few of us to decide. Pray God the right ones are left when it is all over, or Russia will be lost forever."

"You can speak of such things?" cried Sasha in desperation. "Where is your faith in the Almighty?"

Valodya shook his head gently. "It is my belief He is also bewildered at present. The whole world has gone mad over the past five years. Our English friend here can stand witness for the insanity in Europe, we have seen it here in the East. Is the human animal the one failure in the Divine creation? God makes man a superb creature with intelligence and strength, yet men strive to destroy each other and themselves. God preaches words of peace; the human race pays no heed. Perhaps God wonders if it will not be better to let these creatures annihilate themselves, then start again with an improved version—one which will do God's will."

Sasha got to his feet, the better to look his tall brother in the eye. His voice shook as he said, "I never thought to hear such words from you, Valodya. Always, I tried to teach you as our dear father would have wished."

Valodya defended himself. "Sasha, it is not blasphemy to think of God as a sorely tried ruler. I believe God looks down and despairs at what He sees. Our salvation will depend on what we do from now on. If we fail in these coming months, we are not worth saving. Pray, by all means, but for God's sake act, along with your prayers. The old ways are gone forever. It is better that they are. I have come to see that truth. The new way will emerge from our conflict, but we must think long and hard of what that way must be."

Valodya's handsome, fair face clouded as he saw the expression on his brother's face. "I might wear their emblems, but I have never been their disciple, Sasha. What I have done has been only for your safety. I could not risk it after they shot Ekaterina."

"Izvini . . . izvini," murmured the older Russian, making a vague gesture with his hands. "Forgive me. I spoke wildly. Ekaterina . . . our little Katya . . . a member of the party . . . shot down by those same men . . . It is a hard thing to hear." He sank down onto his chair wearily. "Please, sit down, Valodya. Tell us . . . tell us how it so happened."

But Valodya was too full of fire now to keep still. He moved about the tent as he spoke, unconscious of the effect his words were making on Paul, who had not believed, had not cared. *Now* he cared. *Now* he believed. A young man too much like himself had made him vulnerable once more.

"As I told you, I thought our sister was safe because of her association with the party, or I would have agreed to serve their army at the beginning." His hands rested on his brother's shoulders for a moment as he paused behind him. "Vasily Igorovich is a good man, and I would defy anyone to say he is not loyal to Russia. His work as a doctor has been devoted and unflinching in the service of his country. His pledge is to save life, so a man's beliefs did not matter if he was in need of healing." With a quick grip of kinship he left Sasha and walked toward Olga. Once there, he placed his hand gently against her glossy hair and bent slightly over her to impress his next words upon her.

"Ekaterina loved her husband totally, but I still believe she would not have done what she did if he had not convinced her of his own certainty that the party was working for the good of Russia. Like us, our sister was willing to die for Russia." He leant even closer and said thickly, "She did, Olechka, *she did*!"

Olga's hand went up to pull Valodya's fingers down to rest upon her cheek in an affectionate gesture as her body melted toward him. There was a moment of silence in that tent, and Paul caught himself sorrowing for that unknown girl who had been shot down merely to compel a soldier to betray his beliefs.

"Vasily Igorovich had had a rich practice before the war, we all knew," the young Russian continued, straightening up, "but when he was directed into the general hospital in 1914, his life changed. There he was brought face-to-face with so much he could not ignore that, as a man of conscience, he talked with those who knew and understood social conditions and problems. He went to see the factories and hovels for himself. What he found in those places so smote him, he was driven to pledging his energies to improving the conditions of those reduced to eating rats and filthy refuse in order to stay alive.

"It was easy to persuade a man in such a state of crusade to join the party, with the dream of a bloodless revolution to save the peasant class. Our sister was equally distressed by all he told her and became a member in the same spirit as her husband. They said nothing to us because . . ." He faltered, then went on firmly, ". . . because they knew we would never understand, that we had never seen what they had seen."

Again he moved on and stood for a moment gazing out at the tranquil scene beyond, where daylight was at last beginning somewhat to dim.

"They were wrong. We *had* seen. How is it we did not act?" he said as if to himself.

"We were fighting for survival," his brother reminded him gently. "Valodya, a man can fight only one cause at a time."

The young man turned back to face them all. "Yes, a war sweeps all else aside, until something even greater rises up from the din and tumult with a voice that *must* be heard. But the bloodless revolution lasted a mere few weeks. The elements that march with poverty ran away with the concept of freedom, and ideals were discarded for greed and power. Vasily Igorovich became disillusioned when the party began to head in a direction he had no wish to go. He became a nuisance; his protests were ignored. His wife was a Swarovsky, and her murder was designed to bring him to heel and force me to serve them."

Valodya put back his head in a gesture of resignation. "In the latter they succeeded, but the deed alienated Vasily Igorovich forever. He crossed the Finnish border to join his own family, who had gone some months before. I think he lost not only a wife, but a crusading spirit which will never be recaptured."

In the ensuing silence, Paul heard himself asking, "What of yours? Has that gone forever?"

Everyone looked at him as if he were a servant who had made an unforgivable intrusion into his employer's conversation. All except Valodya, who seemed to recover his assurance and smiled at Paul with the same frank comradeship he had shown from the start.

"Mine, my friend, is alive and well. I did what I could down there. Now, I am ready to fight for what Vasily Igorovich has despaired of attaining."

"You are saying that you support these people?" asked Sasha in a tone Paul had heard too many times.

"The *Bolsheviki*? Of course not. I support the people of Russia. They are *our* people, Sasha . . . those who worked on our estates and in our homes. They cannot save themselves. We have to do it for them, but with tolerance and understanding this time." He put out a hand and lifted the tent flap. "See those men out there? They have always done as they were told out of fear. Now they must be made to do it out of trust. Right now they do not know who is right. If a man comes tomorrow with promises of freedom and plenty, they will go with him. If you do not gain their trust before such a man comes, you will lose them, Sasha. I have seen it happen. I have been with men when they heard the nectar words. I understand too well why they go." He turned his blue gaze onto Paul. "They appear to have a rare kind of affection for you, my friend, which is something to be prized."

Paul felt a ridiculous pleasure but could think of nothing by way of answer. The evening, that whole day, had been such that he was in an emotional web that had been spun around him by these people. He had stopped struggling and was now firmly caught. Yet Valodya's next words shook the fragile encompassing bonds like the slow advance of the spider upon her victim caught in the centre.

"They are like children. They have put their complete trust in you; the news that you are going to leave them in their hour of greatest need will leave them angry and resentful. You must understand that they see only what is in front of their eyes . . . and try to forgive."

"I . . . I don't understand. What is this talk of leaving?" Paul demanded in bewilderment. "How can anyone leave? The bridge is still down."

"So are several more," was Valodya's disturbing reply.

Giving his English friend a keen look, Valodya walked back to his seat and settled into it full of thought. "I am very slow witted, Paul. I should know how it is when a man is isolated with a small command, cut off from the main events of the struggle. I should also know how easy it is for headquarters to overlook such men—often with tragic results." He frowned at Paul across the table. "I see you are quite unaware of the present situation."

"We are *all* unaware of the present situation," put in Sasha harshly. "When soldiers are put to building a railway, it is not surprising."

Valodya looked steadily at his brother, "The railway might save our lives and those of hundreds of our countrymen, Sasha. If this line is lost, so are we."

With exhaustion sweeping over him and his head now throbbing with apprehension, Paul said wearily, "I think you had better let us have the truth. Since we are vital to success, it is time *someone* let us know what we are really up against."

The last sentence was said with the dawn of bitter anger against those in higher command, yet a tiny voice of guilt made itself heard. When had he cared what was going on in the rest of Russia? When had he bothered to ask?

Valodya leant back in his chair and frowned again. "I speak only from what I heard in Moscow and from what your people at Lake Onega told me, Paul. But that is quite clearly a great deal more than you are aware of, and it distresses me to be the bearer of such news."

"Go on," prompted Paul, growing colder by the minute.

"There have been reverses; the Reds are gaining ground in all areas. They have command of the southern end of Lake Onega. We . . . we are in a tight corner."

When no one made any comment, he went on, "In Siberia they have advanced even against the most stubborn resistance. In the South the story is the same. Their numbers are growing daily, but recruitment is now due to brute force or a sense of inevitability. Soldiers change their allegiance with bewildering frequency. Many who defected from our ranks have returned at the first opportunity, finding the Red discipline unbearable. But they pay dearly for their actions when their Bolshevik brethren catch up with them again.

"Such atrocities put fear into others, who now dare not oppose the new regime. Those of our loyal troops who come face-to-face with their enemy are soon coerced into joining them by threats of torture and death to whole villages. Who will condemn a man for that? Did I not do the same for the sake of others?"

His fingers gripped the crumpled napkin beside his plate. "Thousands of Russians have been put to death—are still being murdered. Many hundreds are dying of hunger in the villages through which the Red armies have passed, for they take every item of food as they go. Children are victims of disease and neglect. Only a few get away to safety. The railways in the South are under the direction of Red Guards, the borders are heavily manned, the ports are governed by Bolshevik administrators." He stared at Paul with brightness in his eyes. "The North is only free because of our allies."

Paul's voice of guilt rose. He had concerned himself only with building a railway; he had been no ally.

"Even here we face danger," Valodya continued. "Archangel is sorely threatened; the railway from the port to Vologda is the scene of bitter fighting. The Reds forced the surrender of Onega, then burned it down when they themselves had to retreat again."

"But Onega is well north of the lake, on the coast of the White Sea," grated Swarovsky. "Does that mean we are surrounded?"

"No, they are contained in the Murmansk area. But if the British troops fail to fight their way back to Archangel before it freezes over, they are certain to be annihilated. With the withdrawal of their allies, they bear the brunt alone."

"*Withdrawal?*" asked Paul stupefied. "What withdrawal?"

Valodya turned back to him. "The Americans left some weeks ago. The French and Canadians have been shipping their men back for the past fortnight. The British have orders from their government to cease armed aggression against the Bolshevik armies. It cannot be long before they also leave."

"No!" cried Paul in quick and sincere protest. "We would never walk out on an ally."

The young Russian regarded him with the wisdom of his youthful old-age. "You may have to, my friend. When a cause is in danger of being lost, lives must be saved—especially when the cause is not one's own."

It was all the nightmares returning—the fight for survival, the heart-break and despair, the cries in the wilderness, the grim skeleton of defeat staring across daisy-dotted fields washed in sunshine.

"How can this have happened?" asked Paul in dazed tones. "I came here from England only at the beginning of May, with several hundreds of others. Now, in July, you say the Allies are leaving. It doesn't make sense."

"To those parents and wives who have lost their menfolk in this far off frozen land, it does. And to the men themselves—men who want only to return to their homes and families after five years of fighting. Why should they care what happens to us?"

Guilt drove even harder into Paul. Because of it, he tried to defend all those like himself. "If we did not care, we would have left here after the Armistice last November. We would not have sent out reinforcements and quantities of stores to support you."

Valodya smiled very faintly in a sign of understanding. "Caring can only last for so long, Paul. There was a time when just a few thousand more troops and concerted resolution from leaders unhampered by world and government opinion could have stamped out the Bolshevik threat. So close were they all, so far forward had they all pushed in each direction,

Moscow and Petrograd could have been taken. But they hesitated, their governments refused to send any more war-weary men, and the chance was lost. They know it will never occur again." He humped his shoulders with resignation. "Money and public pressure govern their actions. The interests of their own nations must come first. It is a time of poverty and hardship for the whole of Europe, and something must be saved. We can see why you must all go."

"No, I can't believe this is . . . I have heard nothing about with-drawal," cried Paul. "The whole idea is senseless. Why would I be here perfecting a railway?"

"As an escape route," said Valodya quietly. "It is the only one left to those who are still here. We shall all go north to reorganise and plan our new offensive."

"We?" Paul asked through a throat that had grown tight.

"The White Russians. It is our country; we must fight to save it."

"Alone?" he managed.

"We walked away and left you to finish the Germans off for us," put in a hollow voice from his left. "We cannot expect *you* to stay now."

As he looked at Alexander Ivanovich Swarovsky, Paul saw in the man's eyes all those other things he had said in contempt and felt then what the Russian must have felt when the words had been spoken. Never in his life had Paul experienced such remorse, such a sense of ignobility. It was so quiet around that table it was as if everyone in that tent could see right into his soul.

Then, into the moment came a sound on the still air that brought an almost sobbing quality to an atmosphere already charged with high emotion. The Russian soldiers had begun singing with soft nostalgia one of those songs of their homeland that was at once unbearably sad and hauntingly beautiful. It kept each person at that table silent; it hung in the paling night like a melancholy repetition of all that had been said. They all sat perfectly still as the voices rose and fell in the beloved melody.

It was as if they had all been petrified by a siren song that would never release them, and when the last notes died away only to be followed by another refrain from an agonised land they sat on, each in his own captive state. Gradually, a soft tenor voice took up the melody, and Paul's gaze was drawn to Valodya, who sat staring out into the pine forest, lost in the poignancy of the words he was singing.

The sound touched something in Paul that could no longer be contained. But he was alone in that tent. Lyudmilla Zapalova had her graceful head tilted back, eyes closed against all but the sound of that singing. Olga was watching her young brother as if she would never see enough of him, as tears rolled freely down her cheeks. Gone was the fear, the infant hysteria; she looked more beautiful than Paul had ever seen her, now that she was simply a girl of Russia with emotion directed in normal channels.

The older Swarovsky was similarly affected, making no secret of his silent weeping. Paul remembered the man's emotion at the graveside of his two dead sergeants at the cutting and the hand of comradeship held out to Paul that morning as he clambered back across the bridge section.

Paul looked away to the girl beside the older Swarovsky—the girl he loved so deeply. She was also crying. The tears hung on her eyelashes, and her serene face was beautiful with the echoes of compassion. But his heart quivered. She had eyes for no one but her husband. In that moment, she was trying to bear his pain along with her own.

Paul got up and pushed his way blindly through the tent flaps, the song pursuing him into the midnight dimness. He stumbled into the forest, knowing only that he must get away, away from the music before it caught him and forced the tears from his eyes, also. For several minutes he walked blindly, governed by the strong desire to escape, following no track or special direction.

Then, the trees became obscured by visions from the past. The sound of singing changed. There were English voices now floating in the still air, men singing softly in the trenches while the distant rumble of gunfire provided a background reminder.

He began to sweat as he wandered erratically in the near darkness beneath the great pines, all awareness of his surroundings buried beneath the images crowding in on him. Someone had a mouth organ: the sound of it floated on the damp air. He was playing, "There's a long, long trail a-winding," and the refrain was being taken up by a hundred unseen men sitting in pelting rain in six-foot holes in the earth. Every so often there would be a whistle, a soft thud, and one less voice.

He could smell the mud—pungent, sickly with the odours of humanity when fear made men behave like animals. He could feel the rain, the chafing of thick khaki, the itching of dark stubble on his unwashed face, the biting of lice that had worked their way onto his body. He could remember fields of poppies; picturesque villages; stretches of waving yellow corn; smiling grannies, wives, and children, all waving hand-kerchiefs as the soldiers tramped past along the dusty lanes. He also remembered the crushed red poppies that lay like blood in the fields; blackened, devastated villages; cornfields full of shell craters; women and children lying dead beside the road as the soldiers dragged back in retreat.

He began to see the soldiers' faces—blunt, ordinary, covered in grime, yet ready to break into a grin even when things were desperate. They were solid, unimaginative, dependable, happy to grumble, blunt of phrase, shy of emotion. Yet they could give a pickaback to children of French villages even when they were weighed down with equipment and drooping with fatigue. They could seduce the local wenches, yet organise a collection to enable a young consumptive French girl to enter a distant sanatorium. They cursed and swore bloody revenge on the "Hun bastards," yet had been known to give their last cigarette to a wounded German prisoner. He saw them all again as if they were before him at that moment. They were his countrymen; they would never walk out when things looked black!

Something thumped against him, and he clutched at the tree trunk with shaking hands as the visions retreated, leaving him all alone in a vast Russian forest. He stood trying to get a grip on himself, searching for that courage that had kept him going for four interminable years. Dear God, a man had arrived on a train and re-opened all Paul's wounds so that he bled again!

He stood for a long time just holding onto that tree. The silence helped him, at first, then he heard the first faint howl in the distance. Seconds later it was being echoed, seemingly all around him, eerie, threatening, infinitely desolate, growing louder and louder. The wolves were gathering!

He turned to lean back against the tree. The forest was threatened. He was not there to create an engineering memorial to the future but a desperate escape route. His peace had gone. Throughout this beautiful land of pines and lakes the wolves were gathering—but it was not the grey ones that would drive him away.

T w e l v e

Irina felt heavy and depressed. More than ever their present site seemed threatening. From the start, that broken bridge had haunted her with overtones of imprisonment on the wrong side of the river. She knew, of course, that it was possible to cross the swift-running water on the raft Paul used to reach the mid-river structure, but of what use would it be to reach the far bank without a train? And if they could cross it, so too could an enemy. Death would simply occur on a different bank.

It was not in Irina's nature to be so melancholy, so defeatist, but Valodya had brought with him a terrible reality. One short summer she had hoped for, but already in July the winter was beginning to intrude.

Valodya had brought more with him than shocking news, however. Used to coping with war reverses, Irina was defeated by the arrival of a woman who plainly still affected Sasha strongly. A woman who, it was painfully obvious, could woo him from thoughts of 'the cause' as Irina had been unable to do. Yet was it so surprising? The great Zapalova had been Sasha's mistress for five years—five years of peace and gracious imperial living. She must know his mind—and his body—better than a girl with a golden ring who had spent no more than six desperate weeks with him in the midst of war.

The moment the ballerina had arrived and Irina had seen Sasha's face as he greeted her, it had been the end of a marriage that was already dying. Sasha might not have realised it, but the last fragile threads of the loyalty she had struggled to retain broke with hardly a sound. How could a woman betray a man who wanted nothing from her?

Yet the first joyous rapture over her freedom to love Paul soon died. There was really no change, at all. Lyudmilla Sergeyevna had been taken under Valodya's protection and now owed *him* everything; Sasha was still Irina's husband. Paul would be returning to England before the snows came. The only difference Zapalova's arrival had made was that there were now six people all wanting someone they could not have.

As she walked along the riverbank the morning following Zapalova's arrival, Irina reflected heavily on the days ahead. Last night had been difficult. The two new arrivals had necessitated a re-arrangement that was anything but ideal. Sasha had naturally surrendered his bed to his ex-mistress, leaving the three women occupying his tent.

Paul had immediately insisted that the brothers take his tent, saying that he would sleep in the supply-truck. But his two soldiers already being in occupation of it made that impracticable. Then, Valodya had taken charge of the situation, making it impossible for Paul to refuse to share the tent with himself and Sasha. The young man had, of course, no notion of the situation between Paul and Sasha, and Irina could not believe that the suggestion had been made because Valodya did not wish to be alone with the brother whose mistress he had taken over. Her brother-in-law was an essentially honest person who would face anything squarely, she felt.

In many ways, he was like Paul. Except when it came to women. Valodya was a charmer of the first order, and she felt sorry for the girl who gave her heart to him. It was certain to be broken many times.

But what of the girl who gave her heart to Paul? She halted for a few moments and leaned against a tree trunk. Last night she had said a silent farewell to Sasha, but she dared not draw any closer to the man she loved and who told her so plainly he needed her. One man had fallen in love with her when he was lonely, suffering, and dazzled by a beautiful face in the midst of misery. She could not let another do the same. Paul had to return to his homeland soon—oh, much too soon—and would then be caught up in another life, another world. A girl in a Russian forest would then seem like a fantasy. He would forget quicker if words of love were never spoken between them, if they had never touched.

What of me? she then asked herself. Looking around her, she knew that every time she sat in a train travelling through the green blessedness of pines she would remember this summer and love for Paul would flare again. He would go to another land where nothing of her would be there to remind him, she would remain in Russia and never forget.

The soldiers along the riverbank looked up as she approached, and they got to their feet. The accident on the previous day had caused some minor injuries. Those on the far rope had had their hands burned when it had whipped through their palms. Irina had applied ointment, at the time, and had come down today to set about replacing the bandages.

As she worked, her patients told her of the courage of the Englishman when he had recovered the floating section. She remained silent. They lionised him now. What would they feel when he got on his train and left? What shall I feel? The question pounded in her head, and it seemed like bitter aggravation to her thoughts when the sound of voices made her look up to see Paul a short distance away in the trees, talking to his corporal. The man had apparently come after Paul with a message that was making Paul very angry. She could just catch what was being said, and she listened unashamedly.

"I thought I had already given them a satisfactory explanation," Paul was saying.

The Corporal shrugged. "Seems they're still not happy, sir. They want to know what two aristocratic Russian ladies are doing with the group, and if you have been drawing rations for them all the time."

"By all the saints," cried Paul, "there is a bloody war being fought, and they sit on their backsides worrying about rations for two extra people! Well, we have *three* ladies here now. And what the hell would it matter if we had thirty-three? We have been handing out largesse to peasants left, right, and centre since we landed."

The Corporal made a comic face. "It's not really the rations, is it, sir? It's that money you handed over to save the two ladies. The lads in the Paymaster's Office didn't take kindly to your answer and are plainly going to stir up everyone over the affair now."

"Let them stir up what the hell they like," stormed Paul. "It won't alter the fact that the money is gone. If that gang of convicts had stolen our rifles and ammunition, no one would have said a word. The 'fortunes of war' that would have been. Because it was the army's bloody cash—cash they were not aware I had until I told them I had parted with it—they are going out of their minds with righteous indignation."

"Yes, sir." The Corporal stood quietly a moment, then said, "They have asked for a full written report immediately, and a telegraph message on where the money is now so that they can negotiate its return."

"Where the money is now?" Paul laughed harshly. "My God, they haven't an idea of reality, have they? Ask them if they want a report enough to send a train four days down the line for it, because that's the only way 'they'll get it . . . and warn them to bring a rifle and something to put in it. We are playing soldiers in earnest down here."

The two stood looking at each other for a moment or two, then Paul ran his hand through his hair in an angry gesture.

"Oh, hell . . . look, I'm sorry, Corporal Banks. It isn't your fault you have to pass on such bloody silly rubbish. But it's incredible that a system that has often sent men needlessly to their deaths can be so efficient over insignificant details." He put his hands on his hips and sighed heavily. "Have they no idea of what we are trying to cope with down here?"

"Perhaps they think we should leave well alone, sir."

"Eh?" Paul looked puzzled. "That's a curious remark."

The little man stood his ground. "All the others have got out. What are we stopping here for? After all, it's obvious who's winning, isn't it?"

"Is it?" came the sharp question. "What do you know of who is winning?"

"It's no secret, Captain Anderson. Yagutov has been speaking to the engine-driver on the supply-train. Seems the Reds are likely to overrun our base at Lake Onega shortly, and Archangel can't hold out much longer. The Frogs and Ities saw it weeks ago, so did the Americans. What are we still hanging on for? It's not our war."

A staggering change came over Paul. He grew tense and seemed somehow older. "We are 'hanging on,' Corporal, to repair a bridge. We are obeying orders . . . And all the time that British soldiers are being killed by Red Russians, it *is* our war." His voice lashed like a whip; his tone was full of cold authority. "Whatever rumours you might have heard, it makes no difference to our presence here. A war is never won until one side acknowledges defeat. You should have seen enough of these people here to know they will never do that."

Paul turned on his heel and walked away into the forest with angry speed. Then, a few seconds afterward, the Corporal slowly went back to the train.

Without knowing what she was doing, Irina fastened the bandage she had been working on with a big pin, her gaze following Paul's tall figure as he disappeared into the trees bordering the bank. What she had overheard jumbled her thoughts and emotions further. To hear Paul's heated defence of them all, his unconscious betrayal of an involvement he had always maintained he did not want, made her weak with love for him. But it also seemed he was in some kind of serious trouble over the money he had surrendered in return for their lives.

She trembled suddenly. How could they have been so thoughtless, so casual in their gratitude? Why had it not occured to any one of them that such a large sum must have been given to him for military purposes and he would have to account to his superiors for his action?

Kneeling on the sleeping-platform where she had set up her nursing station, she absently packed away her medical things, hearing nothing of the soldiers' cheery chatter. They had lived in separate camps, Paul and the Russians, which had helped with the delusion that he was merely an engineer advising on the railway. Now she saw the extent of his respon- sibility as virtual commander of the entire group. Without Paul, they would have received no food or supplies, no messages from outside, no wages for the men.

She rose swiftly and went in pursuit of him through the trees that thinned alongside the river. It no longer mattered that she was the Colonel's wife and could be seen going in deliberate fashion after the English officer. What the soldiers thought was now unimportant. She must put right her terrible thoughtlessness immediately.

He was standing twenty-five yards ahead, studying the river as it raced noisily over the great rocks that had been swept down by the swell of melting ice. There, right on the bank, it was possible to feel the lingering chill of water that had come from the high snow fields. Yet Paul stood with shirt sleeves rolled up, prepared for the day's energetic work. But he was not so lost in thought that he did not become aware of her approach and turn to face her. His expression was not clear because his peaked cap shadowed his face, but his body tensed warily.

"Good morning," he greeted with careful politeness as she drew near.

When she saw his eyes bruised with anger and telling her she was the last person he needed to appear at that moment, all thought of polite formality in reply flew on the wind.

"I was dressing the men's hands. I overheard." It was jerky, blurted out because there was no way she knew of approaching him slowly on such a subject. "I did not think . . . none of us thought . . ." She put out her hands in appeal. "So many things one on top of the oth- er . . . We are not, by nature, so ill-mannered. Please believe it was thoughtlessness, not ingratitude."

When he continued to look at her as if he wished her in Siberia, she said involuntarily, "It has been your fault, you know. Why did you hold yourself apart from us? How could we guess all that you had to do? How could we?" she repeated angrily.

"I haven't the faintest idea what you are talking about." It was cold, aloof, Paul at his most British.

Irina stared at him, completely at a loss. She had never seen him like this before and sensed that he had somehow reached a point of no return. His air of unbreachable authority excited yet frightened her, because it proved once more that she could not put him into one of her comforting slots of masculine predictability.

"I overheard your conversation with the Corporal," she clarified with fast-beating heart. "Just now, when you were discussing a telegraph message."

He grew more distant, more icy. "So there is no privacy, even in the forest!"

"You are angry," she said, dismayed. "It was not deliberate, I assure you."

"No, it is just one of those damned disadvantages of language," he said with sudden, savage accusation. "You can say anything you like in Russian and be certain I shall sit there like a deaf idiot not understanding a word. Everything I do and say is noted and recorded, yet you can hide behind that barrier of language and leave me roaming around in the dark."

That was when she should have left. Now she was close enough to read his expression, she saw that his point of no return had brought him to an onward path that promised nothing but loneliness and pain. He was facing defeat and crying out against it. Yet no one was answering his cry. In that moment his eyes said it all. If he wished her in Siberia, he wished himself with her . . . for the rest of their lives and beyond that. She grew weak with the longing to ease his pain. The rushing of the water whispered of abandoning her will to something she could not fight, the chill arising from it emphasised the heat flooding her limbs. The pines around them seemed to enclose them in a world of their own, and he stood there wanting her as no other man had ever done.

Aching, desperate, yearning to surrender to the youth within her that had been suppressed for too long, she forced herself to concentrate on the decision her sleepless hours had brought. Better that they should never touch, never speak of their love. It would be easier when he had to leave forever.

"We . . . we have lost our property and estates," she told him some-how, "but you have seen that we have with us still things of value. There are the Swarovsky jewels in a casket hidden in one of the trunks. The money can be repaid to you very easily. Sasha should have arranged it with you at the time."

He could not take it. In his present mood of barely controlled desire, her words were the equivalent of a smack across his face. He hit back.

"I have already had more than enough interference from your husband in my military affairs. I will not tolerate it from you now. Right from the start I made it plain there was no place for women here. What will it take to make you understand that?"

It was her second chance to go, but her mind and her body were now completely out of tune. For once, her self-assurance had deserted her. The calm, competent woman reigned in her mind; her body was that of a girl trembling from the need to feel his touch.

As she stood captive at her own point of no return, she heard her voice say, "I know you have a great deal of pride, but do not let it become false pride. They were our lives you bought. I think we should be allowed to buy them back from you."

He turned on her then, and never had she been the target for such contempt. "So that is it! It has all been nothing more than a feeling of obligation. All those melting glances, the pleas across the few feet that separated us, the eyes that lied—all due to a sense of obligation to compensate me for that day. Now you think money will serve the purpose equally well." His mouth twisted bitterly. "Keep your jewels, Madame Swarovskaya. You owe me nothing. Your life was saved by courtesy of the British government. Think of it that way, and you'll feel much happier."

He went striding away with no purpose in mind but to put as much distance between them as possible. Irina was stunned by the joy of knowing she could finally put him into a category she knew and recognised, until the urgency of the need to follow him set her running. He was a man at the end of his endurance. Something had to break, at last, and when it did she must be there at his side. So many men had she seen at the point of breaking, her every instinct demanded that she should help him, calm him, minister to that in him that cried out for someone to guide him through his lonely maze.

His angry strides took him at such a fast pace that she was obliged to hold up her skirt clear of the underbrush in order to gain on him. He must have heard her running feet, but he did not look round. Experience told her not to call out to him; he could probably hear nothing but the voices of his own nightmare.

Suddenly, he halted sharply a few yards ahead, and Irina arrived breathless beside him a few seconds later. Then, the whole forest seemed to turn upside down as she saw what lay ahead. In a small clearing stood a fur-trapper's hut, door open invitingly. But in that doorway lay a heap of scarlet flesh that was no longer recognisable as a man. A scream began rising in her throat, and the nightmare became complete when the severed head hanging on a branch of a nearby pine began to sway in the breeze.

She was in a grey world of semi-consciousness as she turned from it and flung herself forward in a mad frenzy to escape, but she felt herself caught and held against a refuge of safety. Sobbing uncontrollably, she clung to his warm, living body with fingers that were clutching at sanity. All the terrible things she had witnessed in the hospital, the horrors of the battlefield, the heartbreak and intolerable burden she had been forced to carry were epitomised in that clearing, and she would face it no longer.

Weak to the point of fainting, she felt herself being carried away from the spot, aware only of the tall, green spread of pines above her head and the strength of arms holding her. Then she was set down and rocked softly in a cocoon of warmth while a deep voice soothed her with words that gradually drove the fear away.

"Please, everything is all right. You are safe. It has gone. Irina, you are safe . . . you are safe. I am with you."

She was held close against the solid strength of his body, and his cheek rested against the top of her head as he told her she need fear nothing, with him to hold her. It was so easy to believe him, and she remained within the circle of his arms even when the nightmare vanished and the rushing of the river sounded normal again. Tiredness had enveloped her, and she longed to sleep, just as she was, held close in his arms. In that uncertain world she had entered, he was large and steady.

Yet he was not quite as steady as she had thought. It slowly dawned on her that he was trembling as he held her, and his words thickened with emotion.

"I'll never let anything hurt you, you must know that. All I want is to . . ."

She stirred, glanced up to see why he had stopped speaking, and his mouth was on hers before she knew his intention. The kiss was infinitely tender, reflecting all the sensitivity she had glimpsed in him that day beside the lake. With that gentle salute, he gave her her youth. It was the kiss of a young man for a young girl—soft, comforting, trembling on the brink of passion. It was all the things she had never had, all the things war had taken from her. It was agonisingly nostalgic and shook the very foundations of the woman she had become. *It was impossibly dangerous!*

"No, Paul," she whispered, struggling from his hold in panic. What was she doing? Another moment and it would have been too late. *Never to touch, never to speak the words of love!*

"No, Paul," she repeated, caught in the pull of her conflicting needs. "I cannot allow you to love me."

He stood before her, chest heaving, pale with humiliation. "Allow,

Allow!" he said, as if the words were dragged from some person divorced from himself. "I am not one of your bloody peasants, to be given *permission* for his feelings." He took a step backward as if he had received a blow. "You cannot stop me from loving you. I am a man with a will of his own, not a slave who has to beg favours. This might be Russia, but don't play the outraged noblewoman with me."

Full of her own humiliation, she cried out, "You do not understand. It is for your sake; it is better for you."

"Neither am I one of your patients," he raged, growing even paler. "That's your escape, isn't it? To remain immune, you cover a man in bandages and stick a thermometer in his mouth. My God, what I want from you is not a potion . . . it's . . ." He turned away and stood leaning on one hand against a tree trunk, fighting for control of himself. "You don't heal; you just turn the knife in the wound."

Something had to break, she had known that. But it was herself who was broken by his words. She stood bereft and beyond tears.

"In my wound also. How can it ever heal?"

He turned his head slowly, and there was nothing that could stop them then.

"Do not use such words to me. I cannot bear . . . Pavlik, how can I hurt you so much when there is nothing but you?" she whispered.

"Say that again," he told her roughly. "Say it again so that I can believe it."

"See if I will allow, see if I will stop the loving," she begged in English that had gone haywire. "There is nothing but you."

His hands gripped her shoulders and pulled her against him. She went willingly, knowing it had been foolish to deny the only thing that would make her summer last a little longer. And when the summer ends? asked a little voice. But she was lost in the ardent honesty of Paul's kisses and heard nothing but his words of passion.

The sky seemed bluer, the air a little clearer. Work on the bridge progressed. The soldiers sang as they hauled on the ropes and shouted cheerfully to each other as they ate. With Valodya to help with the translating and organisation, tempers remained sweet. There was no order to withdraw; Red troops were nowhere in sight. The two camps had merged painlessly into one united group. Paul began to sleep dreamlessly when the work allowed him an hour or two of rest. He felt confident, clear-minded, and brimming with health. The world was a different place; he was a different man.

Each day, each problem was bearable now. Irina was always there. He only had to look up and her eyes would tell him all he wanted to know. In the midst of directing some operation, he would turn and see her smiling across at him; at the end of one of his obligatory and useless daily reports he would stretch in his chair and find her watching him with love and sympathy; whilst he was contemplating a problem with the bridge, she would bring him a mug of tea, and their fingers would touch lingeringly around the mug.

It appeared that no one noticed their love, but Paul would not have cared if they had. They were the happiest days of his life. Even the sight of the great Zapalova doing *barre* exercises on a pine trunk Valodya had erected for her between two trees near the women's tent made him smile where once he would have condemned. The mother-of-pearl accordian given to her by a Hungarian prince and from which she had refused to be parted also served to entertain him, after his initial impatience with such an item in his camp. Valodya was a talented musician, and the whole group was enlivened by the merry tunes he played when the women begged him to take up the instrument.

Paul acknowledged that it was not only his happiness over Irina that made those days so much better. Valodya had that rare personality that drew everyone to him and, therefore, closer to each other. The soldiers were devoted to him, responding to his grip on the shoulder or smile of comradeship with all the warmth of their natures, and his presence made what could have been an awkward situation in the two tents an easy merging of conflicting personalities.

Paul felt no sense of guilt when faced with the older Swarovsky. It was not as if Irina had betrayed her husband. Their passion had stopped short of the ultimate expression of love; Paul knowing enough not to demand from her what he knew she would not forgive him for afterward. In any case, the Russian had his own problem to sort out with his ex-mistress and his brother—if there was a problem. As for Olga, Paul hardly noticed her except as one of the group. The days when she had made him feel ill-at-ease had passed.

Happiness, he discovered, made him feel young and reckless. In that he had an enthusiastic partner in Valodya, who encouraged him in acts of tomfoolery that had the whole group laughing—the kind of energetic lark he had almost abandoned for good. The friendship between the two young men strengthened fast, each finding an outlet in the other for all that had been battened down for so long. Peace reigned for a while.

The only small cloud on the horizon of Paul's happiness was that his physical longing for Irina was stronger than ever. Each small furtive touching of fingers, each glowing look, each sweet laughing response to something he said to Valodya in jest, stirred his blood to unbearable heat. Now that he had held her in his arms and heard her confess her surrender, he wanted to bring it about in the fullest terms. Here it was almost impossible for them to be alone, and they had met just once more for a few stolen moments in the depth of the forest after that day. While her constant presence made those days so wonderful, it also increased his need to make her his own. Fortunately, the following days demanded from him maximum physical effort with a slight element of danger, and the two combined to lull the worst of his hunger. At those times when desire threatened to torment him, he conquered it by imagining them both in some distant country, at some distant time, when he was building a bridge all his own, and she was there with him in a house with windows that looked onto a lake and mountains. It was always a vague and hazy picture; it could be nothing else, under the circumstances.

The body at the fur-trapper's hut had been removed and buried by the soldiers. They all agreed the peasant had most probably been murdered by those same men who had sabotaged the bridge, and Valodya was able to tell them it was now believed that the saboteurs had been a partisan group of Red Finns who were causing isolated damage as a means of drawing attention to their own lost cause. Although they had fought so well and bravely with the British against the Germans and their White Finn brothers, now that the war in Europe was over they united with the Red Russians—which meant they were now against their former allies. Just one more complication in the forest of North Russia.

The tilting bridge section was righted after two days of careful preparation and some anxiety on the part of the three officers and their men. Talking to Valodya, explaining the basic principles of everything he did to someone who was avidly interested, Paul found his relationship with the older Swarovsky was no longer the thorn in his side it had previously been. Sharing a tent with the man—even though Valodya provided a leavening third—reduced Paul's stubborn dislike for the older Russian until he wondered why it had ever grown to such dangerous proportions. Paul still found Sasha haughty and quick to take offence, compared with his younger brother, but there was no longer the need to depend solely on the older Russian as a go-between with the soldiers and he seemed to slip into the background—a place the man himself seemed happy to occupy, for once.

Throughout the whole business of getting the tilting section back into position, Paul insisted on checking with supreme thoroughness every piece of equipment, which made the operation even longer. But the section was finally hauled into place and temporarily lashed until work could begin on making it complete and strong enough to bear the weight of trains. With it even temporarily in position, the sight of a bridge three-quarters across the river from their bank gave everyone such a feeling of release, of an escape route should they need it, that an air of celebration filled the camp.

The soldiers cheered and pranced around in comic dance, the three ladies stood clapping on the bank, pleasure and excitement flushing their lovely faces.

Swarovsky turned to Paul and held out his hand. "So, after tribulations we have success. A feather in your cap, indeed."

There was no smile to accompany the words, but Paul sensed they were sincere this time. He gripped the man's hand and shook it.

"Thank you. An allied effort, I think we should say."

Valodya, laughing and buoyant, vowed he would be the first to cross the bridge and began walking on his hands along the incomplete truss to the accompaniment of *ooh's* and *ah's* from the peasant-soldiers, who loved every minute of it.

Throughout it all, Paul stood laughing and dishevelled, a sense of triumph disproportionate to the achievement filling him to overflowing. When he turned to see the glow of pride in Irina's eyes, he thought no man had ever felt happier than at that moment.

But this achievement marked by no means the end of their difficulties with the bridge. There was still a great deal of work to be done on securing the two sections together and repairing the structure so that it would bear the weight of a train. However, Paul saw how the sight of a continuous span stretching across the water had put fresh optimism and zest into the men—it had done the same to him—and decided it would be a shrewd move to go ahead with throwing a section across to the far bank before starting the painstaking job of strengthening what already stood over the river.

He fooled himself that his decision was governed by concern for the morale of the men, but there was a subconscious urge in him to establish an escape route, even by foot. He, as much as anyone, had felt that imprisonment brought on by the broken bridge.

One night several days after the bridge section had been righted, they sat at the table for their meal, discussing the need to work by flambeaux. The period of dim light was growing longer daily; night was beginning to intrude. But the work must go on, and the only way to continue was to floodlight the river where it was exceedingly dangerous to clamber over the structure once the daylight faded. All through the discussion, Paul found his concentration wandering to Irina, and as soon as he had finished eating, he announced that he was going to the river to check that the bridge was still secure.

He strolled away into the dim midnight in the hope that she would find some way of joining him. Surely she must guess his intention? But although he waited for half an hour she did not come. He returned to the site of the two tents, kicking viciously at the track as he passed, and refused to glance at the Swarovsky tent where the women had already retired.

Swarovsky was waiting for him outside the other, and Valodya was nowhere in sight. The older Russian had a strained look and approached Paul as if he had been waiting impatiently for his return. Paul's heart thumped. Good God, had the man discovered the truth and determined upon a show-down? Was that why Irina had not come to the river? If Swarovsky had hurt her . . . !

"Something serious has occurred," the Russian began in a tone that did not really suggest an accusation.

Paul's heart thudded faster. Had something happened to Irina? Was she hurt . . . ill?

"Would you kindly come with me?" asked Swarovsky and began walking down the length of the train away from the direction of the river.

Paul followed on legs that had grown suddenly weak from the climbing and bending he had done all day. He dared not guess at what the Russian was about to reveal, but surely he would not be walking away from the tents if Irina were ill. Neither could he be intending to thrash out ownership of his wife in a place where they could be seen and heard by every peasant-soldier in the bivouac. Swarovsky was the type of man who shot first and gave his reasons afterward. I would be dead by now if he suspected anything. Paul thought wildly, then amended that. No, he would make sure I finished the bridge first. The "cause" means more to him than anything else—even his wife.

They stopped beside the flat-car, and on the piled rails was a dark, humped shape shown clearly in the light from the campfire. Paul knew it was a blanket-covered body—he had seen enough of them to recognise the sight immediately—and grew infinitely cold. Dear God, who was beneath that blanket?

Swarovsky put up a hand and threw back a corner of the covering. Paul felt sick and shocked. Familiarity with such things had never made him immune, and this was particularly gruesome. There was not a lot left to recognise, for the body had been savagely mutilated. But he had been one of the Russian soldiers. Shreds of cloth stuck to the torn body could be identified as their uniform, and there were signs of badges of rank. An N.C.O.

"Who is . . . was he?" asked Paul, swallowing the sickness he felt.

The Russian turned what remained of the head toward the light. Wincing, Paul saw the answer for himself. In some macabre fashion, the features remained in a hideous mask surrounded by a bloody pulp.

"Corporal Nensky! The last of your old regiment, Colonel."

"Yes . . . the last of the Tsar's loyal men," was the thick answer.

Wishing the man would replace the blanket over the sight, Paul forced himself not to turn from it as he asked, "How did it happen? What is this all about? Nensky was working with you on this bank all the afternoon."

"No," said Swarovsky, "he was not. I thought he had been on your side of the river . . . until some men surprised wolves around a meal. It was Nensky."

The sickness almost overcame Paul at that. "*Wolves*! I know they have been around most nights, but never close enough to attack," he exclaimed, shocked at the implications of this new threat. "We can't contend with this, as well. The men will have to be organised into a shooting-party."

"That will not be necessary, Captain. I think we should allow everyone to believe the wolves were responsible, but they were merely feeding off a dead man."

Beyond making an intelligent reply to that statement, Paul simply waited for Swarovsky to go on. The whole day had turned upside down.

"Contrary to legend, wolves rarely attack humans unless they are starving and come upon a lone, wounded man. They haunt camps for the meat that is being cooked or because they smell horses and livestock. My men are ridden with folk-lore. They believed their comrade was set upon by wolves, but I did not. Once they had gone back to their bivouac, I looked for evidence and found it." He lowered the blanket, at last. "Wolves tear flesh apart with their teeth; they do not use knives, Captain Anderson. Nensky had had his throat cut as neatly as any soldier could do it. Our traitor has been at work again, I fear."

Paul felt even colder. Icy reality had moved into the sunshine of his happy days. "Nensky was your senior N.C.O. It was a deliberate blow at command again."

"It was a deliberate blow at the old regime. Nensky served with my regiment—a regiment of the old Imperial Army. Corporal Nensky served our beloved Tsar."

Paul gave him a shrewd glance. "So, Colonel, did you."

"I have already considered that," was the steady reply. "Without me at their head, there is no guarantee that my men would remain here. I think it is time we discover which among us is the traitor and deal with him as he deserves . . . before it is too late."

Thirteen

Corporal Nensky was buried with great ceremony; Sasha saw to that. But the incident had made the men uneasy. They did not like the thought of the great, grey wolves falling upon one of their comrades and tearing him to pieces. Who would be next; who was now safe? They began to murmur again of the explosion that had killed the young wolf and driven the pack from its den. They began to look sideways at Paul Anderson. The happy camaraderie was not as evident now. Sasha regretted that it should be so, but it was preferable to telling the men the true cause of Nensky's death. That would cause distrust of every other person in the group, instead of merely a superstitious coolness toward the English officer. They had a new hero in Valodya—a man of their own blood—and such coolness now would mean less of a blow to them when the Englishman pulled out and left them to it. There was little doubt he would have to before long, and men who had lionised him would be full of bitterness.

Sasha's own bitterness had had to be subjugated. If anyone but his own brother had told him Russia was being lost day by day, he would not have believed it. If anyone but Valodya had said imperialism had gone forever, that men like Ekaterina's husband had fought to improve the lot of the peasants, that he himself believed there must be a new democratic system in Russia, Sasha would say that man was a traitor to his loyalties. If any other young officer who had begun by serving the Tsar, then the Reds, had arrived on a train saying they must abandon the campaign and go north to reorganise for the last stand, he would call that officer a coward.

But he was forced to accept his brother's words—a brother he had grieved for inwardly until a miracle had him appearing from a train. But Valodya had changed from the boy Sasha had last seen afraid and questioning in a devasted village during the retreat. Like Paul Anderson, he was a boy compelled to take on the wisdom of a lifetime in a few short years. But where the Englishman had become introverted, determined, desperate to have a future before that was also snatched from him, Valodya lived for each day as it came.

But Valodya had passed a dread of defeat on to Sasha. Not until now had he contemplated it, had he ever considered the possibility of the Red Terror completely overrunning the vastness of Russia. Less than three months ago, when he had declared his small company fit to fight and set off to rendezvous with an Englishman on the railway, everything had looked set for a runaway victory. He did not need to be told of battle reverses; the fact that all the foreign troops were leaving spoke the truth loud and clear. The ship was sinking!

Their dependence on the English Engineer officer was greater than it had ever been. That journey north could not be made until the bridge was re-built, and the only comfort was that Anderson could not leave, either, until the job was complete. To that end, Sasha was prepared to co-operate in any way necessary with the man.

After the death of Nensky, Sasha felt particularly depressed. He felt his own life was dangerously threatened. With so much activity on both banks of the river, in the forest on each side of the railway track, and around the train itself, it was impossible to keep his eyes on all his men all the time. Paul Anderson was unshaken in his conviction that the traitor was a Russian, and in truth, Sasha was forced to agree. The Englishman had asked if he trusted his men. The last of those that he would swear on his life were loyal was Nensky. The others were an unknown quantity, if he was honest with himself. That they had been prepared to fight the Reds had seemed enough to guarantee their loyalty . . . but one was wearing false colours. He hoped to God it *was* only one!

With that thought in mind, Sasha wandered through the trees to where half a dozen soldiers were felling trees with cross-saws, in the vain hope that something about one of them would suggest that he was not who he professed to be. They no longer stopped work and bowed when he approached, he noticed with irritation. Since Valodya had arrived with his liberal ways, their respect had grown much more casual. But since their work was carried out more willingly, Sasha had clamped his lips on any reprimand. The bridge must be finished. After that, he would tighten up on discipline.

The day was overcast and heavy, with a hint of chill in the air, reminding him that it would be August in a few days. The snows started in October: two months and the forest winter would grip the whole area. He shivered involuntarily. Beneath the trees it was gloomy, which intensified his mood of depression. A penetrating study of the men's faces showed him nothing more than blunt features and the peasant simplicity he always saw there.

Disgusted, he turned away. To be obliged to look for a traitor, a killer of three loyal men of his old regiment, and know that man was there laughing at him! In the old days, the whole company would suffer until the guilty man was produced. It did not take long. *In the old days!* He turned down toward the riverbank and stood in isolation, brooding on the past.

When she spoke his name and he turned to see her a few feet away, it was as if she had walked straight out of his thoughts. In that forest she looked like Giselle, a wraith from his past who had materialised from a woodland mound. The way she moved across the forest floor heightened the fancy. He took her outstretched hands and looked into eyes that could fill with any emotion she wished to display for the greatest effect. Right now they told him of five years of happiness.

"How did you know I was thinking of you?" he asked gently.

Her magnificent smile was all for him. "If you had not been, my heart would be very heavy, dearest one."

How that endearment took him back! He had been twenty-four and a newly promoted lieutenant when he had gone with a group of friends to the Maryinsky Theatre and seen her dance for the first time. Just returned from a distant posting to avoid the rapacious eyes of the Garrison-Commander's young wife, Sasha had fallen immediate victim to Zapalova's magic. She had recently taken over the principal role in *Swan Lake*, when the prima ballerina fell ill, and had taken the public by storm—in particular, the aristocratic officers of the Imperial Army.

Sasha's friends promised to present him to the "darling of St. Petersburg" if he paid for the supper and a dozen bottles of champagne. He vowed recklessly that he would pay for anything if they would present him to the only girl in the world for him. It was the fashion to pursue actresses or ballerinas with dramatic dedication, and Sasha had been more concerned with gaining the coveted distinction of having spent a night with the dancer than on easing a heart that was, by no means, aching.

He had been permitted the glittering prize of sharing her bed, not once, but whenever the fancy took her. He was wealthy, tall, and personable and possessed the finesse she found lacking in some of her admirers. Alexander Ivanovich Swarovsky was an influential nobleman and could further her career, if he so wished. So, for some months they used each other without compunction, each benefitting from the liaison. Then, Sasha began to grow jealous of those other men who shared her bed, and she surprised herself by surrendering them.

It soon became accepted in the circles in which Sasha moved that he had taken over the role of protector, rather than admirer, and the cause of his jealousy vanished. In the course of five years, however, his duties took him away from St. Petersburg, and it was only natural that the rising ballerina felt she could not afford to be "unprotected." Sasha was a military man; the hazards of his profession were well known to the fair sex. When besieged by beautiful young creatures, army officers invariably surrendered.

But such was the strength of their relationship, Zapalova abandoned her temporary "comforters" each time he returned, having had some delightful skirmishes but never having finally surrendered.

With every reunion, their relationship changed and deepened, although each knew it must end in parting and held back from the final dedication. With that in mind, they had kept their love affair extravagant, hectic, and impossibly romantic, in order to divorce it from any suggestion of permanence and reality.

Sasha was an ardent and generous lover. Zapalova's house was filled with his flowers; she always wore his jewelry when they were seen together in St. Petersburg—which was in every fashionable restaurant, at the houses of the wilder nobles of the day, and at every great event.

He wooed her in grand and reckless style. On her Name Day, he led his entire company plus the regimental band, all in their ceremonial uniforms, from the barracks to her house, where he marched them up and down in salute. She was enchanted; his colonel nearly posted him to Siberia. At Easter, a confectioner's carriage had delivered to her door a chocolate egg so large it took four men to carry it carefully inside. When she opened the two halves, it was to reveal an exquisite model of the Rose Adagio in *The Sleeping Beauty,* with Zapalova in arabesque holding a rose. The whole perfect reproduction of the set was fashioned from spun sugar, but each step of the curved staircase was a miniature bar of gold, and the "rose" a pink diamond clip for her hair.

On Midsummer Night, he had hired a launch complete with fifty gypsy musician's and banked with camellias to take her down the River Neva throughout the sun-filled midnight in his sole company. The boat attracted so much attention she spent the whole time running gracefully from side to side throwing camellias to her ecstatic public, while he stood laughing with delight at the success of his scheme.

War came; reality marched in. They both knew it was the end of an idyll. The dream ballet had to end; the curtain had come down for the last time. But he did not allow their parting to be spoilt by tears. It had to end in fitting manner. They were not a mere soldier and his girlfriend seeing each other, perhaps, for the last time.

With the great ball held by the British just before Waterloo in mind, Sasha arranged a similar event at the Swarovsky summer residence, sending in an army of servants to take off the winter covers and light fires everywhere. The chandeliers were all filled with pink candles—her favourite colour, which dominated the decor and floral arrangements. Zapalova arrived wearing her last gift from him—a sable cloak lined with pink-dyed ermine—and was cheered by the officers of his regiment and their partners. All the guests behaved with desperate gaiety and drank too much pink champagne, but it was only when the "darling of Petersburg" declared to the glittering company that she intended to retire that she discovered the officers of Sasha's regiment were no longer there . . . and neither was he.

The grand gesture touched her more than an ardent parting, and she was inconsolable for three days, except when she was dancing. But there were those who had not gone to war—garrison officers and patrons of the arts—and she still had her ambitions to fulfill.

Sasha was gone for almost two years, and yet when she had looked up to find him standing in the doorway of her salon that Christmas, it was as if life had returned. But he was different. Impetuosity had been replaced by wariness. That night he had delayed their reunion for hours on end, as if he were afraid the joy would be ended too soon if he approached it too quickly. When he went back to the Front, they said goodbye like civilised people who had never taken part in those extravagant follies of love. Romance had fled; life had turned deadly earnest. It was their final goodbye—or so they had thought, at the time. Now, she was there beside him day after day. He still had not grown accustomed to seeing her in such a place.

He led her farther through the trees, away from the curiosity of his men. "You knew I was here. Why did you consent to come up the line with Valodya?" he asked with a hint of sadness.

"He would not leave me there. Already, the camp was threatened from the southern end of the lake. Many men are in danger down there; he would not allow me to remain." She slipped her arm through his and looked up at him with incomprehension in her eyes. "They had not heard of Zapalova. Can you imagine that, Sasha?"

He smiled gently at her. "If they were Englishmen, my dear, I can understand it very well. I would not call them the most culturally perceptive of races. Young Anderson is a typical example—solid, obstinate, arrogant, and totally untouched by anything in the least aesthetic."

She continued to regard him with wide eyes that now held a hint of speculation. "Do you really think so?" Then she went on, "Valodya would not leave me at Lake Onega, and I could not hold him back there in danger." It was a few moments before she added, "I owe him my life, you know."

He stopped and turned to face her, a lump in his throat. "I am glad it was a Swarovsky who took you from danger. I . . . I thought of you often in that house you took in Moscow, and wondered . . ."

"And do you think I never wondered about you, dearest one?" she replied softly. "When Valodya first came to my house, I cried upon his shoulder for news of you. He did not know and shed tears with me."

He felt a slumbering anger stir within him. That a boy of twenty-one had been forced to accept all his brother had borne!

"He blames himself for the murder of our sister."

She clicked her tongue. "Tsk! He *feels* too much, that one. Oh, he is brave and impetuous. The smiles, the songs, the foolish tricks—they are all a way of telling the world he does not care what it does to him, but in my arms he has had dreams that tell a different story. He does not know I see the truth. It is better to let him face the world with defiance."

Something twisted inside Sasha. The ghost of another young daredevil who had faced the world with defiance stood half a pace behind him, and he recoiled from what she was saying. Something of it must have shown in his face, and she was an artist of the most sensitive nature.

"You resent it," she whispered, tears clouding the amber of her eyes. "No, Sasha, you must not do that. It means nothing. He is a boy—a young animal who needed something I could give him. That is all it has ever been with any of them. None of it mattered."

He turned away, touched by feelings he had not had for some time, feelings he did not want now. The supreme ego of an artist had read his expression so that it reflected her own image. How could he tell her it was not her but what he had once been that tormented him? She was part of everything he had known of Russia and loved so enduringly. He had been in a suspended unreality waiting for it to return; he had passionately refused to believe it would not. Olga and Irina had spoken to a deaf man. Valodya had shouted it so loudly he could not help but hear. Now, this woman who symbolised all he had clung to was completing his unbearable lesson.

"None of it mattered?" he repeated with difficulty.

"You, of all my friends, should understand that," she said dispassionately. "My body was given to art from my youth. It can belong to no man . . . no, not even you, dearest one. If men want to use it, it is of no importance to me, so long as it still moves with magic when I dance. My soul speaks through my body only when the music begins, never at the touch of a man's hand. I live to dance. All else is unimportant."

His head had begun to ache as if it would burst. "People are being murdered everyday. My own sister lies in some communal grave—who knows where?—without the rites of Christian burial . . . and you say it is *unimportant*?"

She put her hand on his arm. "Yes, that is terrible, to deny them the way to the Almighty . . . but, Sasha, people die. Every day they die of starvation, old age, illness, tragedy. A world cannot stop because of it; can Zapalova concern herself with that? A dancer must live in beauty. Whatever else happens, that must remain. Without it, I die."

The pumping of his blood roared in his head like the sound of the nearby river, and the noise seemed to be spreading over his whole body. She was turning his rosy past into a blood-stained image. His mind began to fill with images of uncouth bullies smashing the ornaments on her shelves, slashing her paintings, ripping the velvet chairs with the spurs on their boots. She had entertained those bullies in the same salons that had been graced by men of culture and wit, men with the proudest names in Russia. She had opened her sheets to butchers and taken breakfast with them afterward at the beautiful, gilt-legged boudoir table where he had sat with her at their last meeting. This magic creature, this woman of delicate sensibility, the "darling of Petersburg" had betrayed and broken his past. There was nothing left!

To his horror he felt the wetness of tears sliding down his cheeks, and his shoulders began to heave. Her thin body became distorted by his blurred vision. Unable to control the sobs that racked him, he turned blindly from her and stumbled away until a tree brought him up short. Putting up an arm against the trunk, he leant his forehead against it. The pain of a nation filled his chest; the tears of a whole people rose up in his throat.

The storm raged in him until it blew itself out and left him spent. When he felt her hand slide into the one hanging by his side, he turned to her, grateful that it had been she who had witnessed his weakness, and no one else. Then he realised that only she could have brought it about. For months he had had to appear strong before the others.

She appeared as moved to tears as he had been, as she looked up at him. "Love of my only dreams, listen, I beg you. You are a soldier; you give your life for Russia. I am an artist; I do the same. Our ways are different, that is all. I have Russia in my blood and my soul and my feet. When I dance, it is Russia speaking. That will not change, whatever else may do so. My only desire is that the spirit of Zapalova will live forever. Can I do more than that for this great land of ours?"

He was still too emotional to do more than shake his head. The twist of truth was that she would be remembered long after he was dead.

"*Pauvre enfant*," she whispered, putting up a hand to touch his cheek.

He caught it and kissed the fingers gently, recovering his composure with the gesture. "*Milochka*, I swear the spirit of Zapalova will live forever."

She smiled over her tears and tucked her arm through his, urging him to walk along the riverbank. As they walked, she spoke of her plans once she had left Russia.

"I shall go to Paris, Vienna, London, New York, and they will all love me. The darling of Petersburg will be the darling of the world. My Giselle will move them to tears; my Aurora will bring them to their feet; my Odette will force them to their knees." She cast him an imploring glance from beneath her lashes. "And, perhaps, one night somewhere, sometime, a spray of camellias will land at my feet, and I shall look up at the box and see a handsome lieutenant smiling down at me with approval and pride."

He stopped and took her hand slowly to his lips again. "Perhaps—somewhere, sometime."

With one of her staggering, quicksilver changes of mood she said, "Have you really not seen that your beautiful wife is in love with that Englishman?"

It did not wound him as it should have done. Perhaps he had known for some time. "Is it so obvious?" was all he said.

"They are both such children, they have not yet learnt to hide what they feel. Sasha, she is lovely and has that air of nobility that your wife should have but . . . *a child bride*, my dear. Whatever made you do it?"

It did not seem disloyal to speak of Irina to her. She had deliberately portrayed herself as an abstract—a woman existing only in the guise of many women. He spoke of his marriage with an air of relief.

"Desperation, I think. She came into my life at a time when there was no beauty in it at all. I knew that I had to go back to horror and fear and defeat, perhaps never to return. I fell in love with her gentleness, her courage, the smile in her eyes, her *cleanness*. I wanted desperately to hold onto it, if only for a short while. Thinking of it now, I believe there was more pity than love governing the girl who found herself unable to withstand my pleas."

He stared in at a mind picture of that hospital ward and saw a lovely young face framed by a white veil—a face soft with compassion. "I was heartlessly insistent in my pleading," he added reflectively. "We had two days together, but when next we met, we were two strangers desperately trying to be lovers. We exchanged letters—a soldier wanting only an outlet for his fears; the nurse comforting her patient, still."

He veered off to stand studying the river for a few moments, until he sensed that she had come up beside him. "Since then, we have been like that water—rushing headlong, forward in the hope of finding a tranquil lake ahead. But somewhere in that tumbling, surging journey we lost each other." He sighed. "Love cannot flourish in times like these."

"Paul has not found it so."

He turned his head slowly. *"Paul?"*

"Dearest one, it was obvious the moment he stepped into the tent on the night we arrived. I saw immediately that he was sick with wanting her. Why else did I tease him about Englishmen knowing nothing of love?"

That *did* disturb him. Anderson, of all people! The insufferable whelp, the boy who had never had a woman, the arrogant upstart who flushed every time anyone spoke to him—he had the effrontery to openly desire Irina? Damn him to eternity! Whilst it was easy to accept that his young, susceptible wife could imagine a fondness for another of her patients— the fellow had looked somewhat romantic with his arm in a sling and his face all bruised—and might reasonably hero-worship someone who had saved her from a gang of rough convicts, he could not countenance the idea of another man looking at the wife of Alexander Ivanovich Swarovsky with lust in his eyes.

He sagged wearily. What could he do about it? Shoot the fellow, as he deserved? Until that bridge was built, nothing must disturb the harmony that had settled over the group—and once the bridge was built, the Englishman would go. Times had changed; a Swarovsky must compromise. All he could do in the meantime was to ensure the fellow worked so hard he was dead on his feet all the time. Nothing was more fatal to lust than complete exhaustion—he knew that from experience.

"I think you need not worry, Sasha," said Zapalova, breaking into his thoughts. "What you are unable to do, your sister will do for you. You will see."

He opened his mouth to ask a question, but a cry went up from the trees behind them, followed by the sound of running feet. All else was immediately buried beneath the soldier's instinctive response to the alarm call. Leaving her, with no more than an upraised arm, he began to run toward the sound.

Heart thudding with the prospect of another move by the traitor amongst them, he raced through the forest, pushing aside the man who had come to fetch him and fearing what he would find when he arrived at the spot. At the scene of the tree-felling, a man lay on the ground with his arm covered in blood. A quick glance showed a wound the length of the man's forearm that was pumping out a crimson flood in alarming quantities.

Beside himself, Sasha turned on those standing around looking at the victim and roared instructions for two of them to run for the *barinya,* at once.

"Take thy worthless hides off and carry everything the *barinya* requires to tend thy comrade," he ordered in the language of master to peasant, and they went off as fast as their shaking legs would take them.

With thoughts of treachery filling his head, Sasha began flinging questions at those who remained, only to discover that one man on a cross-saw had lost his grip on the handle, and his partner had overbalanced, drawing the blade of the saw along his own arm.

So incensed was he, so governed by an excess of emotions that had been released that morning, so foolish did he feel over having been seen running to the scene of a careless accident, expecting sabotage, Sasha strode to the man responsible and struck him several times across the face in rage.

"*Merzavets! Durak!* Get to thy knees and beg forgiveness," he roared.

The man hesitated, giving him a look of dark, spitting malevolence, so Sasha gave him another blow to show him he meant what he said. "Villain! Fool!" he repeated. "Kneel!"

Seeing the man's eyes swivel to look behind him as he sank down on his knees, Sasha turned to see Irina watching the scene, accompanied by the English Corporal, who carried the medical box.

"Where are the men I sent?" he raged at the Corporal in English. "What are thou doing away from thy post?"

Corporal Banks had gone pale and answered in tones no Russian would have used to an officer. "I think they were too afraid to come back, and I can't say I blame them if that is the way they were treated. I wonder the whole lot haven't gone before now."

Sasha took a step toward him and raised his arm, but Irina spoke swiftly in French to him.

"Sasha, *no!* Strike him, and there will be terrible trouble."

He stopped, seeing her properly for the first time. Her face was ashen, the eyes dark green with mystery and shock. Slender though she was, after Zapalova she presented an image of solid, undeniable reality.

She came up to him. "A man has been hurt in an accident, and you are behaving like a madman. What is it? What has happened to you?"

He shook his head to shake out the ghosts, the fears of treachery, the remnants of five years that had passed through his thoughts that morning. Then he stood looking at her with eyes that ached.

"You would not understand," he replied in French also, so that no one else knew what they said. "You do not know the half of it."

With a sadness he did not recognise, she gazed at him for a moment longer, then went down beside the injured man to open her box. Sasha walked back to the train like an old man.

The sky grew lower and more threatening during that day, turning that place beside the broken bridge into a dark clearing isolated from the world and warmth. Paul felt heavy with unease. It could not be winter making its first overtures, yet the blotting out of the sun, the increased movement of the pines, the river which was now dark grey as it rushed through the channel it had driven through earth that must yield to its force, all suggested a forest petrified by cold within a few weeks.

But it was not only the change in the elements. The Russians were morose and sullen, as uncertain as the weather. Like the trees, there was an unsteadiness rippling through them; like that tiny clearing, there was now a suggestion of antipathy in their manner. The death of Corporal Nensky had started the backslide, and Paul guessed the accident with the saw that morning had added to their superstitious belief that the wolves had resumed their revenge.

He had been on the far side of the river most of the day and had only heard of the accident when he had finally crossed on the raft just before it grew dark. Although Swarovsky had assured him it had been a genuine accident, the affair seemed to have cast a gloom over everyone.

Paul had enough on his mind that night. Admittedly, the wind was rising fast, and the river had taken on a sinister look. But there was no real danger from the bridge. Even so, the Russians made it clear they would not work in the dark midnight hours with flambeaux that flickered dangerously or blew out altogether. For once, Swarovsky seemed reluctant to browbeat them and suggested they should concentrate on the labouring jobs that did not require them to work out over the water. Since Valodya was of the opinion that they would get more work done the following day if they indulged the soldiers that night, Paul was forced to agree. The volatile personalities of these men of the forest had swung round against him once more, and another accident at this stage might alienate them for good.

As a result, he worked through most of the night straddling the bridge trusses, with Valodya and Corporal Banks to assist him. It was tiring work, yet when Paul made his final check and wearily crossed the river on the raft that jiggled dangerously on the whipped-up water, the older Swarovsky met him as he climbed up the bank and insisted that Paul should accompany him to a place well beyond the fur-trapper's hut, where there were signs that another bridge had once been started. It was their duty to decide whether an enemy force could use it to cross farther downstream, the Russian said, and practically marched Paul off to the place before he had a chance to put forward an objection.

It was a long walk made difficult by the darkness, and Paul was soon feeling dead on his feet. There were, indeed, foundations for a bridge, and although it was unlikely that anyone could complete the structure enough to cross the river by it without being heard by those at the railway, Paul agreed it would be wise to destroy what stood there at the first opportunity.

On the return walk Sasha asked Paul if he had any ideas on how to go about discovering the identity of the traitor. Incredibly weary, blear-eyed and very wet from the river crossing, Paul tried to concentrate on the problem, knowing Swarovsky and his young brother were the most probable next targets.

"With men spread over such an area, occupied in so many different activities, it is virtually impossible to watch them all," Paul said, wiping the back of his wrist across his eyes in an attempt to clear them. "The only solution that suggests itself is that one man known to be trustworthy should be told the truth and allocated in each group to keep an eye on the others. It isn't ideal," he finished lamely.

"No, it isn't," was the uncompromising reply. "Is that all you can suggest?"

Shivering suddenly in a gust of wind and thinking of a pillow and blankets, Paul said, "They are your men, Colonel. Can you think of anything better?"

"Not when you are in command of them, as you are when it comes to the railway. It is of no use for me to work out a plan which is then negated by your requirements."

Paul sighed heavily. The Russian was in one of his obstructive and aloof moods. "I'd still welcome any suggestions."

"Does that mean you are at a loss over this?"

The other man was merely a darker shape in the night, and Paul was tired. "I do have rather important things on my mind," he said irritably. "Is it too much to ask you to handle this on your own?"

There was a pointed silence. "Are you saying that, in your opinion, this is unimportant?"

"No, of course not," Paul snapped. "But I do have a damned bridge to repair."

"And who will repair it if all my men are picked off by a traitor?"

"I suppose I shall have to do it on my own . . . as I have been doing for most of the night," he emphasised heavily and with sarcasm. "Perhaps you had not noticed. Now I have to get two hours' rest before it grows light enough to start again."

He began walking off toward the tents, but Swarovsky was right behind him.

"As it happens, I do have a few ideas on how to ensure there are no more murders like Nensky's. I also realise it is impossible to discover the identity of the traitor unless we catch him in action, but I would like to speak to you about each of my men, explain their personalities, and see if you could alter the shifts so that certain of them would no longer work together." He was striding alongside the track with Paul now and took him by the arm as they neared the women's tent. "I'll give orders for Slabov to serve dinner to us in our own tent while we go over it all."

Paul's spirits plunged. Tired though he was, the sight of Irina, cool, lovely, and full of sympathetic understanding, would have made all the difference to his day. He no longer cared about shaving carefully and putting on his full uniform before facing her. She saw him most of the time dishevelled, sweating, and half drenched by the river, and he desperatedly needed that sight of her at the end of each day.

"Can't it wait until tomorrow?" he protested strongly.

"Not really, Captain. I think you must agree it is vital when men's lives are at stake. Tomorrow, as soon as it is light, you will be back across the bridge and too busy to put your mind to this."

He had no option but to do as he asked. The problem was all important, he could not deny. The next piece of work the traitor undertook might be to delay progress on the bridge. That must be prevented, at all costs. So Paul ate his meal doggedly and tried to keep his eyes open while the Russian talked on and on about each of his soldiers. But they had not reached the stage of discussing shifts when Valodya came in laughing from the other tent and threw himself down on his makeshift bed, declaring that he was dropping from fatigue.

"I ask kindly that all conversation should cease," he said pointedly. "If it does not, I shall not ask kindly the next time; the offender will get my boot squarely against the side of his face."

Knowing Valodya never made idle threats, the other two men ended their discussion, but Swarovsky thrust the list of names at Paul and suggested he go on studying them and devising new grouping for the shifts, in time for the morning.

Silence fell in the tent, and it was soon apparent to Paul that the Swarovsky brothers were asleep. Sitting in that cramped space by the light of one pale lamp and listening to the wind outside in the trees, Paul was swept by unbearable loneliness that had his scalp prickling, for some unaccountable reason.

What are we stopping here for? After all, it's obvious who's winning, isn't it?

Corporal Banks's words returned to him at the worst possible moment. Yes, it *was* obvious who was winning. Even Swarovsky was talking about getting to Murmansk now. Once the bridge was repaired, the trains would run up from Lake Onega and leave the forest empty and silent once more . . . until the trains came steaming up from Petrograd and Moscow, full of Red troops.

His hands holding the list of names slowly lowered to his knees. He was building a bridge for the Bolsheviks. Unless they were stopped, in a few months' time that structure he was struggling to complete would bear the wheels of enemy trains, and there would be nothing to stop them until they reached a small, brave force at Murmansk. Without his realising it, his fingers crushed the paper into a small ball, as the implications of that thought stuck in his throat. It would be the end of the White Russians. Whoever commanded the railway commanded North Russia.

Filled with a need for comfort, he got to his feet and went to the tent entrance, but the lights were out in the other tent a short distance away. With foolish immaturity, he wondered if she would come out in answer to his longing if he concentrated hard enough to transfer the thought to her brain. She did not, of course, and his mood of desolation returned as he gazed into the windy darkness, hearing the ceaseless rush of the river, the creaking of pine trunks, and the first faint howls of the wolves.

The two campfires kept the animals at bay and provided comforting warmth for those on guard-duty throughout the restless night hours, but the leaping, shifting light from the flames put shadows and shapes amongst the tall trunks that suggested menace that was not there. Paul let the canvas drop over the scene and returned wearily to his bed. The list Swarovsky had left with him was so creased it was illegible by the faint yellow lamplight, so he lay down with the intention of getting some sleep that would clear his brain; but although he stretched into a comfortable position, it evaded him.

When the early dawn came, it was raining heavily, and as daylight grew, it brought a leaden sky and trees that thrashed about in a wind that carried the smell of ice from the Arctic. With no respite provided by sleep, Paul was sluggish and irritable when he pushed from the tent and went with Valodya down to the bridge, where the men should have been waiting. Even as the two men tramped alongside the train, shoulders hunched against the downpour, they could see through the curtain of rain that no one was there. When they arrived at the riverbank, one glance showed them the soldiers hunched on their sleeping-platforms, as miserable a sight as men in an open bivouac can be in a deluge of rain.

"What the hell do they think they are doing?" exclaimed Paul. "Why aren't they ready to start?"

Valodya strode across to them, his high polished boots growing even shinier as the wet undergrowth dragged across them. A few sharp questions in Russian brought a spate of replies, but they all stood as the young officer moved amongst them talking, listening to what they had to say, reasoning with them.

When he returned, he was smiling apologetically. "They are afraid."

"Oh, fine," said Paul in disgust. "That information helps me no end."

Valodya gripped his elbow and led him the few paces to the edge of the bank. "Look at that water, my friend. I understand you are as happy in it as any fish, but the sight of it turns *my* legs to a jelly." He gave his irresistible grin. "But I am an officer; I am not allowed to be the coward. Always I must be like this." He struck an exaggerated pose that so resembled the illustrations in books of Victorian daring and heroism that Paul felt his lips start to twitch with amusement. "But those men do not have to be so. It is their happy privilege to say what they truly feel, and that big rushing river is something they are unwilling to face." He flung out an arm to embrace what lay before them. "Think, Paul! If they should fall in!"

"They won't get any wetter than they are now," he said with a stubborn persistence. "That bridge is urgent."

"*Da! Da!* But most of them cannot swim."

Paul knew it to be fact. He stood with eyes screwed up against the beating wetness, looking at the river. Always fast-flowing and turbulent, this morning it was racing past in great surges of grey and white, throwing up spume around the piers of the bridge. Raising his glance Paul, saw the far bank, where work had begun on the first trusses of the section that was to push out to meet the bridge. The railway track ran away into a grey, mist-laden distance bordered by sentinels of dark, waving trees. It looked desolate, almost threatening. Suddenly, safety seemed to be on this side of the river, with the comforting presence of the train.

"Why are you always so damned reasonable, Valodya?" he asked roughly.

"Perhaps because I am always right," was the cheeky answer.

"All right, I'll give in to your peasant followers. There is plenty to get on with strengthening the bridge from this side." He looked beyond Valodya to where the men were clustering to see what was going on. "But they'll still have to work out over the water. I can't move the bridge onto dry land for them."

Valodya laughed. "You are performing miracles to get it over the river, Paul. I think no one expects more of you than that."

"Except your brother." It was an unnecessary comment born of his irritation and the feeling of desolation brought on by the hostile elements. It would have been better unsaid.

"When a man knows deep inside that he has lost everything, he is entitled to yearn for the impossible, would you not agree?" Frank blue eyes looked at Paul with friendship and understanding. "All I ask is that you do not commit the final betrayal until we are in Murmansk."

Paul looked at him, completely taken aback and unable to think of anything to say.

"If you cannot do it for me, my friend, do it for her . . . and for yourself. All you have achieved here will be nothing if you have broken a man in the process."

With a quick grip of Paul's shoulder, Valodya walked back to explain to his men what they would be working on and rallied them. Then they were there in front of Paul, dark-eyed and reluctant, and he was forced to put his mind to something that had been driven from it by the young Russian's words.

The soldiers were still not completely happy over the compromise, for it entailed a lot of time spent on the structure hanging fifteen feet above the forbidding water. However, with Valodya's encouragement and a few round curses from the older Swarovsky when he arrived shortly afterward, they set to with as much enthusiasm as they could muster on a day such as that.

The more risky operations were undertaken by Paul, assisted by Corporal Banks and Valodya, who seemed to be having no trouble with his legs reputedly turned to "a jelly." In fact, he clambered across the criss-cross beams with scant regard to safety until Paul said with exasperated amusement, "You had better be able to swim twice as well as I can if you intend to carry on like that. I tell you now, I am not going to plunge into that river to fish you out when you fall."

The good-looking face took on an air of injured pride. "I shall not fall, my friend. I am like the monkey, you know."

To prove it, he began a ridiculous "tightrope" walk across a single spar, arms outstretched to help his balance, while everyone watched with bated breath. When he slipped right at the end and snatched desperately at a pier for safety, all he did was raise his eyebrows and shout across to Paul, "The monkey has been known to slip, hey?"

The soldiers were clapping. He turned a laughing face up to them and clung with one hand to his support to fling the other out in a triumphant gesture as he shouted in Russian to them. They answered immediately in a loud baritone chorus. Next minute, they were all singing and working with a greater will than they had all day.

When Valodya returned, Paul could not help laughing. "In our army, we just tell them to get on with it, or else. I can't imagine any British officer doing such tricks to encourage his men!"

Valodya regarded him with a perfectly straight face. "Ah, but if I had fallen in and drowned, they would have refused to work at all. It was a great risk I took."

Paul shook his head in mock despair. "I can't think why I am so glad to have you here . . . but I am," he finished with sudden seriousness.

"*Da! Da!* I too," replied Valodya with equal sincerity.

A storm broke soon after midday, and work had to be abandoned. The forest took on another guise as lightning fizzed across the sky in a display that had everyone praying a forest fire would not result from it. It was a savage and lengthy attack in an area where the elements changed with extremes. The soldiers all huddled in a saturated crowd inside the supply-truck to escape the worst of the rain that had become so ferocious it was almost impossible to remain standing beneath its onslaught.

To those in the tents, the time passed slowly. Even Valodya could not lift the gloom with his tunes on the accordian. For most of the time, they drank tea dispensed by the women and sat listening to the thunder of rain on the canvas. Paul felt uncomfortable in Irina's presence. Valodya's words that morning, together with the fact that Paul had been prevented from seeing her last night, settled on him a feeling of guilt. Who else had noticed and condemned him? The thought made him inarticulate when he spoke to her. He avoided catching her eye or addressing her directly—anything that would be translated as warmer friendship than was permitted with another man's wife. It soon became too much of a strain, and he excused himself on the plea of work and went to his own tent, where he sat staring moodily at the lashing rain and the dripping forest.

What the hell *were* they doing there? It was true: it was *not* their war. Why had he been unable to hold onto his indifference? Now, he was involved with the Russians up to his neck. He cared far too much what happened to them all. And he wanted Irina so badly, he had had to come away for fear of betraying the fact to them all. Swamped with feelings he could no longer control, he fell back against the pillows and stared in frustration at the sodden canvas above his head. Slowly it shifted, grew indistinct, and his lids closed over his eyes.

When he awoke it was almost dark, yet his watch showed him it was no later than seven P.M. The rain still thundered down, and the inside of the tent had that unpleasant chill that accompanied prolonged wet weather. He told himself there was little chance of resuming work just yet. Although the storm appeared to have passed, the deluge alone was enough to settle the matter. Even should he drive the soldiers at gun-point to the bridge, hands that were wet and chilled were clumsy and the risk of accidents was too great. However, fifteen hours of continuous heavy rain threatened another hazard. If the river had swollen too much, the bridge could be in danger. Then, the men would have to turn out, grumbles or not, wet hands or not, if his inspection showed that it was necessary to secure the incomplete structure. He could not do that on his own.

The minute he put his head outside, he was glad of his decision to stay in clothes that were already wet. The path that had been worn beside the railway by their constant passing back and forth was little more than mud now, and he squelched along with difficulty. The lamps were all alight in the Swarovsky tent. He heard loud conversation as he went by—the Russians were inveterate chatterers—and felt a shaft of loneliness pass through him. He was the odd man out, whatever he might like to pretend. In the supply-truck, the peasant-soldiers were singing, as usual. The sound increased his loneliness. He did not know of what they sang; the words meant nothing to him. He was shut out by a language.

It was practically dark—an early night brought on by the oppressive atmosphere and the overhang of cloud above the tree tops. He followed the track, head bent against the beating wetness, knowing he could have walked with his eyes closed. There was nothing ahead but the river, and the increasing noise of that told him he had not far to go. Indeed, the rush of water was growing so deafening that his heartbeat quickened with apprehension. If the bridge went . . . !

He almost fell over the body of Sapper Stevens. It was lying beside the track a few yards before it ended, face down in the mud. The shock of an attack on one of his own men made Paul violently angry, and he went down on one knee beside his batman muttering, "I'll kill the bastard myself when I catch up with him."

But Stevens was still breathing. A swift examination showed he had been knocked unconscious by a blow on the side of the head. Paul stared at the large contusion in incomprehension. The person responsible must have known it would not cause death. What, then, had been his aim . . . and where was he now? His pulse quickened further. Oh, God, *the bridge!*

Getting up, he began to run like a madman, finding it difficult to keep his footing on the slimy track and being further hampered by the rain cutting into his face. It was only a matter of twenty-five yards or so, but he arrived at the edge of the river gasping for breath. Straining his eyes in the gloom and wetness, he searched the bridge quickly for any sign of movement. It stretched out before him, a familiar sight now, a half-finished path of planks with gaps where reconstruction was still awaiting completion. Right then it looked empty and forbidding, stretching across to end abruptly above the river's deepest point. Only a fool would walk out there in such weather and with the river as it was.

Paul's apprehension grew as he took in the way in which the swollen waters were now hurtling between the banks with tremendous force, flowing completely over the rocks as if they were mere pebbles on a subterranean surface and bearing debris upon its pewter surface. Great tree trunks were being swept like matchsticks in the swirl, and even as he watched the bridge began to reverberate with the punishment it was taking.

A few seconds were all he needed to absorb the scene, but so strong was Paul's conviction that whoever had clubbed Stevens had been headed for the bridge, he began walking slowly out across it, pulling out his revolver as he went. It was impossible to cross to the far bank, so the man had not had escape on his mind. There was only one alternative: sabotage!

With his throat growing dry, Paul realised he was, at last, about to discover the identity of the traitor. Caught in the act, the man would be indisputably betrayed. *Caught in the act.* In an instant, Paul dropped flat as he realised there were two ways of sabotaging a bridge—from on top and *from underneath*.

He lay for a moment or two almost driven into the wood by the power of the rain, as he tried to think clearly and in the way a saboteur would think. Where were the most vulnerable points on a structure such as this? He began inching along on his stomach, gripping the wet planks with his fingers in the cracks between them. As he moved slowly toward a large gap where the surface was broken away, his one prayer was that the man was not directly beneath him preparing to fire at point-blank range into his stomach. That he was somewhere on the trusses below Paul he had no doubts. Conditions at present were ideal for wrecking a bridge; the saboteur had everything on his side.

Feeling dangerously exposed, Paul moved on, wondering if he was about to get a bullet in the face the moment he reached the gap and peered down. It was a terrible prospect, but he had to go on until the place was reached. Then, after only momentary hesitation, he stretched his neck until his eyes were over the gap. The river was not much more than twelve feet below him now that the level had risen, and he could feel the shuddering of the piers directly beneath his body as they stood up to the battering.

At last able to see clearly without the rain blurring his vision, he edged forward until it was possible for him to poke his whole head down below the bridge surface to look along the criss-cross of pine logs stretching back toward the bank. Tense with fear-excitement, he hung upside down searching the gloom for signs of movement, knowing if the man had a rifle he was presenting a perfect target. But it seemed unlikely that anyone could clamber across the structure with anything so unwieldy in his hand. It would be far too dangerous in that weather. Anyone down there would need both hands to ensure safe passage over water that was a sure killer in its present mood. As it was, Paul had his revolver lying on the bridge to leave him free to steady himself safely.

From the point where he hung, to the bank he had just left, the supporting framework stretched out deserted. He took a deep breath, braced himself to pull back in an instant, then raised his head to look out beyond, as far as the bridge now stretched. It seemed similarly deserted.

The weakness of relief was just taking hold of him when he saw a figure clinging, only a few feet above the water, where the section on which Paul was lying was lashed to the temporary piers they had driven in. On the point of jerking back, Paul realised the man had not seen him, *would* not see him, because the man was too intent on what he was doing. The rush of the river was subduing any other sound, so Paul's approach would have been unheard by someone so near the surface of the water. The traitor had no idea he was no longer alone out there.

Paul thought fast. He had no clear idea of what the man was doing, but speed was essential in any case of sabotage. To go down through the gap would mean exposing himself for a distance of fifteen yards, yet, at first consideration, it seemed the best answer. To go along the top of the bridge until he reached the end out over the deepest point of the river would mean a shorter distance without cover, but the dangers if he slipped and fell out there were doubled.

On the point of withdrawing in order to lower himself feet first through the gap, Paul experienced an incredible feeling of anti-climax that had him almost at the point of laughing. The figure below had moved slightly, and Paul recognised a British uniform. It was Corporal Banks, strengthening the ropes lashing the piers to prevent the section from breaking away under the strain.

Paul dropped quickly through the gap onto the truss below and began clambering over the wet trunks with care. Having gone to the tent and found Paul asleep, the N.C.O. had probably decided to get on with the job alone. It was damned risky, and Paul could only be thankful once more that he had such a good man with him on this command.

He was halfway to the Corporal when Banks became aware of movement and froze in the midst of what he was doing. At the same moment, Paul froze with disbelief. The little pinch-faced man had a knife in his hand and was hacking through the rope that held the section fast.

There was a long moment of mutual shock, when each man looked at the other while thoughts chased around inside their heads. Aware that several coils of the rope had already been severed, Paul still could not summon the impulse to move forward. It was all wrong; he must be misinterpreting what he saw. He would trust Banks with his life.

You will now have to, said an inner voice as he realised the revolver was lying back on the top of the bridge beside the gap and Banks had a large kitchen knife with a sharp blade. So that was why Stevens had been knocked senseless. A lightning stream of reminscences of Corporal Banks flashed through Paul's mind—things that cried out against the evidence of his eyes. He was a loyal devoted man; he was not a Russian. This was not his war. He had said so.

Clinging there just above the level of the water, Paul cried out to him, "Why, man, *why*?"

The sound of Paul's voice, a human sound above the elements, unsettled Banks. "Keep back," he cried in a voice that was higher than usual. "I don't want to hurt anyone, but I've got to do this." He waved the knife threateningly. "Stay back there."

"The Russians are on the bank. I only have to call them," Paul shouted desperately, knowing that by the time he had climbed back for his gun the ropes could be completely severed. Once that happened, the whole section could be swept away and smashed to pieces by the water. Already, it was trembling and straining under the pressure.

"The Russians won't stop me. I'm doing it for them," came the reply, barely audible against the noise.

Sick with disillusion and all his discovery implied, Paul started forward as Banks began attacking the lashings once more. His own corporal a traitor! Banks a Bolshevik—a killer! All this time Paul had trusted implicitly a man who had tried to blow him up in a cutting, a man who had slit Nensky's throat, a man who had already tried to sabotage the bridge by sawing through a shackle pin. It twisted into Paul like a screwdriver, leaving him suffering from the one emotion he had not until now experienced. As he gripped the cross struts and sought for footings on the sloping trunks, he suffered the pain of betrayal by one of his own men. *You may never know what it is like when those you think of as good loyal men spit in your face as they hold a bayonet to your throat.* Swarovsky's words twisted the screwdriver farther. He knew now.

"Keep back. I warn you."

Banks's face came into focus again. It was now less than five yards away, and even in the gloom beneath the bridge, Paul could see the frenzied determination on the face that had always been mobile in expression.

"Banks," he cried. "If you do this, you are a traitor to your country and all you fought for in France. Throw down that knife . . . or I shall be forced to kill you."

The words were shocking to his own ears, but Banks just threw him a look of contempt.

"Like *he* kills his men without thought or emotion? He deserves what he is going to get—they all do. Ahh! Stay where you are," he cried as Paul moved up another yard, and the knife came up to point at him. "I have no quarrel with you, but this must be done now before it is too late."

Banks began hacking feverishly at the remaining coils of rope that were already beginning to fray. Once they went, it would be pointless to do anything. If Banks did not get him with the knife, Paul would be thrown from the section as it twisted violently in the current. It would be a miracle if Paul swam to safety through such turbulence.

There was only one way of saving the bridge, and Paul hesitated no longer. Conscious that one slip would be fatal, he crossed the next five yards with such skill and speed he took Banks by surprise. But he knew there was only one way the Corporal could attack him, and he was ready. When Banks swung round with the intention of slashing him across the face with the knife, Paul knocked the man's arm farther on round in an outward swing that had Banks off balance, at the same time hooking his left foot around the short legs of the N.C.O. and jerking with all the strength he could muster. Carried on by his own impetus, up against a man twice his size and strength, Banks lost his hold on the wet wood and went flying through the air to be swallowed up by the river as if he had never existed. There was no cry, no moment in which to accept death; he was wiped from the face of the earth in an instant.

Paul clung desperately to the timbers, trying to recover his own balance as he hung over the river with one hand fastened round the fabric of the bridge—*his* bridge. The truss was slippery and swaying; he was gasping, breathless, giddy to the point of sickness until he threw out his other arm and found a hold between two cross beams. Thrusting his feet onto sure surfaces, he hung there, resting his forehead against the rough pinewood until he found the courage to go back for help.

F o u r t e e n

Without Valodya, Paul would have found it impossible to go back beneath that bridge again that night. As it was, the young Russian encouraged and guided a man numbed by his own deliberate murder of someone who had been close to him by dint of the peculiar circumstances of his lonely command. All Paul did toward replacing the ropes lashing the section securely in place was purely automatic. Each time Paul's hands stilled, Valodya prompted him to continue. When Paul hesitated to return, his friend went ahead of him, showing the way.

Helped by four soldiers above on the bridge, under the older Swarovsky's command, the two young officers safeguarded all their hard work against further hazard. When they climbed back to safety, it was only the outstretched hands of the two brothers that got Paul onto the bank. He was dazed and shaking, a victim of his shocked conscience. Although his hand had been scored and bruised when shifting timbers had tightened a rope around his fingers, he felt none of the pain. Before they dispersed, he thanked the soldiers with the utmost politeness, then walked between the Swarovskys back to the tents.

Stevens had been carried to Irina for medical help, and he was lying on one of the beds, having just recovered his senses, and was drinking a cup of sweet tea when the three officers pushed their way into the tent from the rain. All the ladies gave exclamations of relief when they saw them, and towels and mugs of tea were soon forthcoming.

Paul drank his tea even though it burnt his throat; the towel he did not even notice. He just stood looking at Stevens until the poor soldier turned red and tried to struggle to his feet. Irina immediately went across to tell him to stay where he was, which made the soldier turn even redder. He was not used to being in the company of such people.

Irina turned to Paul. "Why do you look at him like that? It is better that he remains still for a while. He suffers a little still from shock."

He moved his rigid shoulders impotently. "I . . . I was thinking. I'm sorry."

She gently took the empty mug from fingers that gripped it like a vice. He did not like the pity in her eyes and turned away. Everyone seemed to be looking at him in that manner—even Valodya. He began to shake again. Olga put a blanket around his shoulders as she had done with her brothers, but he continued to shake. He knew he had to speak to Stevens, but the words would not seem to come.

A glass was put into his hands. It contained vodka. He drank that, then the refill, watching Valodya as the young Russian bent down to grip Stevens on the shoulder and smile with encouragement.

"You are ready now to speak to Captain Anderson? Good. He is very tired, so you will make it quick and clear, yes?"

Stevens nodded. "Yes, sir."

Once Paul got started, it was better. His brain began working with its usual efficiency, and the noise of the river began to leave his ears.

"Do you know who hit you, Stevens?"

"Oh yes, sir. Corporal Banks was the only one there at the time. He knew I was trying to stop him."

"I see. He told you what he was going to do?"

"No, sir. I guessed . . . at least, I thought I guessed," he added miserably, his melancholy face screwing up as he thought about the events of that night. "I knew he was going to do something wrong when he took my knife. It was a wonder I noticed, with all them Ruskies packed into the truck. But they was singing away, and you know I've never got all that pally with them. Which was why I was sitting in the corner between the boxes, and from there I saw Corporal Banks put the knife inside his jacket. Seeing the mood he was in, I got worried and followed when I saw him slip out."

"Why didn't you come straight to me?" Paul said sharply.

"I did. You was asleep, sir, and seeing as how you don't get much rest as it is, I didn't disturb you. Of course, I never thought . . ." he tailed off unhappily. "It never entered my head he'd do anything like that." He looked up at Paul in appeal. "I never thought he planned anything really bad."

"What . . . With a bloody great knife in his jacket! Come, Stevens, it must have been obvious."

"No, sir. I . . . I've known Corporal Banks a long time. He . . . well, he'd always been someone you could rely on."

Paul nodded and took his time about the next question. "Did you know he was a Bolshevik sympathiser?"

"Yes . . . no . . . yes."

"What is that supposed to mean?"

"He was always a bit *red*, sir." Stevens explained lamely. "But not any more than a lot of our chaps, mind. Out in France, he was often on about the workers and how things would have to be different when it was all over. He said if we was good enough to die for England, we was entitled to a fair deal afterward. All the usual things, Captain Anderson." Stevens looked up with faint encouragement, as if his next comment would make everything more understandable. "Of course, his dad was a big shot in the Labour Movement, but it doesn't mean Mr. Banks was caught up with this lot. I mean, the Labour Movement doesn't . . ." He broke off and cast a look at the others in the tent, seeming reluctant to go on.

Paul felt it all had to come out now and said, "I think you will have to speak quite openly, Stevens. Colonel Swarovsky and his family are as much involved in this as we are."

Stevens licked his lips nervously. "Well, I was going to say our people at home aren't exactly Bolshies, are they? They don't go around killing everybody and such like."

"By no means," Mopping his wet hair so that the runnels of water no longer ran down inside his collar, Paul approached the most difficult part of his questioning.

"What I am going to tell you now is in the strictest confidence, Stevens, and I want your word of honour that you will keep it to yourself."

The doleful eyes grew astonished. For a mere batman to be entrusted with secrets was very rare. "Yes, of course, sir."

Choosing his words carefully, Paul explained to the soldier that the explosion in the cutting, the tools stolen from Yagutov, the sawn-through shackle pin, the death of Corporal Nensky had all been deliberate acts by a traitor working for the Bolsheviks.

"We had no idea who he might have been until now. Think carefully, Stevens. Had Corporal Banks done anything unusual or suspicious before tonight—anything that is explained by what I have just told you?"

The soldier looked dumbfounded. His simple mentality could not take in the complications of political treachery and associate it with a man who had been a colleague, if not exactly a pal. The question distressed him considerably.

"Captain Anderson, if you say it is true, I have to believe you . . . but Corporal Banks wasn't like that at all. He really wasn't. Blow people up at the cutting—you with them? No, he couldn't do that, sir. He thought a lot of you and was always singing your praises. Especially after you insisted on burying that one the Colonel shot." Realising what he was saying, Stevens turned scarlet and, looking at Swarovsky said, "Sorry, sir. I forgot you was there."

"Your captain has told you to speak freely," was the dry answer. "You must do as he says."

Paul felt the cold beginning to seep right into his bones and had to struggle to keep his teeth from chattering. He did not enjoy conducting this interview before five other people, but he had no choice.

"What about Nensky?" he went on. "His throat had been cut. Could Corporal Banks have taken your knife to do that?"

"If he'd have wanted to cut anyone's throat, he would have done it with his bayonet, same as we used to do in the war. Why would he want a kitchen knife to do something a born soldier is expert at?"

Paul ignored that. "Did he have any quarrel with Corporal Nensky?"

Stevens shook his head. "Not that I know of. He got on well with them all. Talked to them for hours on end, he did. He learnt a lot of their lingo, you know, sir. I thought he was too pally with them, and it didn't help when he . . ." Stevens closed his mouth firmly as he cast a furtive glance at the Russians.

"Well, go on," prompted Paul irritably.

"I'd rather not, sir."

"*Rather not!*" Paul's frayed nerves jangled. "You'll do as you are told. We have all risked our lives tonight to undo the work of a traitor. He has killed three men, almost killed me, and sabotaged our work here. This is no time to consider your feelings, Stevens. They don't matter a damn."

The man swallowed. "It was the ladies I was thinking of, sir."

Holding onto his control with difficulty, Paul said, "The ladies have been equally at risk. They are entitled to hear all you have to tell us."

"He didn't like the way they carried on, sir," said the soldier in a rush, anxious to get it over. "He was always on about how the soldiers was treated by the Colonel—being hit and knocked about." Turning scarlet, Stevens plunged on. "He saw what the Colonel had in his tent and got really mad about the way the peasants had to live in comparison with that. He was always laying down the law about giving them a fair deal and sharing the wealth around." He gave Paul a strained look. "Even I know it's not as simple as that, sir. But all that you said just now, about blowing you up and cutting Corporal Nensky's throat . . . I don't believe it of him. He wasn't like that. He was English through and through. He wouldn't let us down, sir. I know he wouldn't."

Paul forced himself to say it. "I saw him in the act, Stevens."

The batman bent his head down for a few moments, struggling with himself, then he looked up and said thickly, "I'd like to see Mr. Banks's face when he gets the telegram saying his son was killed in the act of sabotaging a bridge that was our only way to safety. Being branded a traitor is worse than being shot for cowardice, isn't it?"

All Paul could do was nod and ask if Stevens felt up to returning to the supply-truck. The man appeared glad to go, but he left behind a highly charged atmosphere. The three women were sitting almost motionless in a group, while the three men remained standing, wrapped in blankets but still dripping water onto the ground. What had been revealed to Stevens had also been revealed to the women; none of them seemed willing to speak after such a revelation. Paul felt they sat there like a trio of silent accusers.

"I don't believe it any more than he does," Paul said angrily into the silence. "I knew that man."

"Not well enough," said Swarovsky, at once.

"But what reason would he have for that explosion in the cutting?"

"To kill."

"No, apparently he wanted to help them."

The older Russian's face was harsh in the lamplight. "He knew all about explosives. You put him in the truck to guard them from my men, if you remember."

What could Paul reply to such a point made right on target? He tried again. "But it was Banks himself who drew our attention to the shackle pin."

"There was no guarantee you would not discover it. What better way of lulling suspicion than showing you the evidence of his treachery?"

It was indisputable. Swarovsky was determined that Paul should face the fact. "You doubted my ability to know my men, Captain. Why do you find it so difficult to accept that you did not know yours? You were always so certain the traitor was Russian, yet you were the people with all the technical knowledge needed for such actions . . . and your men were constantly with the train. An easy opportunity to steal Yagutov's tools. I am amazed he did not sabotage the train right at the start. No work would then have been done at all."

"That's just the point," cried Paul, seizing on the Russian's words. "Banks worked extremely hard for me. Why would he do that if he intended to betray us all?"

Swarovsky took his time sitting down in one of the chairs near the women. He looked old, with his hair plastered to his head and wrapped in a blanket like an invalid. But his eyes were bright as if with fever as he said his last words on the subject.

"He did it for all the reasons you supposed one of *my* men was doing it. Think of those, and you have your answer."

Paul was defeated, and it was hard to take. Somehow he managed to say, "There'll be no need to change the shifts now. Work will go ahead as soon as the rain eases."

He turned and headed for the night outside, but Irina's voice rang out quickly.

"Wait! Your hand is injured and needs attention."

"It's nothing," he said over his shoulder.

But she was there beside him, holding his arm. "It has been crushed. Unless you let me put some linament on the fingers, you will find them too stiff to use in the morning."

All he could see was the sympathy in her eyes; the need to console him for the terrible mistake he had made, the pretence that he was not ultimately responsible for the deaths of three loyal Russian soldiers.

"Haven't you had enough patients for one day without adding me to the list?" he asked savagely. "Thank you for your concern, Madame Swarovskaya, but I can at least handle this."

He went out to his own tent, stripped off his wet clothes, and stretched out beneath the blankets. When the Swarovskys came in, they assisted him in his pretence of being asleep. He felt even more sick and humiliated than he had been after the Name Day celebrations.

Aside from its deeper significance, the death of Corporal Banks was a great blow to Paul. Not only had he lost the only other man who had professional knowledge, he had also lost his signaller and had to operate the telegraph himself from then on. The first signal he sent had to be the notification of Banks's death.

For long minutes he sat unmoving before the Morse key, unable to put out his hand and make contact with Murmansk. What good would it do anyone, what useful purpose would it serve to tell the truth? He had made no mention of a suspected traitor. The deaths at the cutting had been explained as an accidental landslide by Banks himself whilst Paul had been unconscious, and since the dead men had been Russians, there had been no follow-up from the British. The other incidents had been left out of his daily reports because he had not seen the point in stirring up a hornet's nest when a vital bridge had to be repaired. There was enough lunacy over the money he had paid over for the lives of Irina and Olga; why create more over something that could only be solved by those on the spot?

Now the solution was known, and still he felt there was no point in going into something about which it was so easy to remain silent. Strictly speaking, he had no evidence that would stand up in a court-martial to prove Corporal Banks had caused the deaths of three Russian soldiers and tried to sabotage their work on three separate occasions. But he did have indisputable evidence that the man had intended to wreck the bridge. If his word were not enough, the Swarovskys and four Russian soldiers had seen the frayed ropes. However, Banks had not succeeded and could not attempt any further acts of betrayal. Nothing would now be gained by starting up endless questions, the need for numerous written reports, and a court of inquiry to investigate the killing of an N.C.O. by his own officer.

If that were not enough, there was the human element to consider. Banks had a fine war record. He had been an excellent N.C.O.— intelligent, quick-witted, solid, and dependable. At that point in his thinking, Paul put his head in his hands. He had been so *sure* of Banks. There had been that kind of relationship between two men who depended on each other, the kind of aloof comradeship that was highly valued by men who managed to bridge the barrier of rank yet never completely forget it. Yet, in that moment down there under the bridge, they had each been prepared to kill the other.

Paul sat back in his chair and thought about Mr. Banks who was "a big shot in the Labour Movement." Would he be proud to hear his son had betrayed his country and the uniform he wore for the sake of the workers of Russia? Would he be pleased to boast of it at the Working Men's Club and at the factory or mine where he surely worked? Thinking of his own father who had been a wheelwright at the railway works, Paul could only remember the pride on the lined face when Paul had achieved each step that had taken him up out of the rut of apathy. Surely it would be an unnatural man who would take pride in his son's treachery against his own people—whatever the cause? And if Mr. Banks was such a man, what of Mrs. Banks? She was a woman, a mother who had worked hard all her life for little reward. Would it not destroy her more than a little to hear the truth about her son?

But the nagging voice of conscience would not be silenced. It was Paul's clear duty to make a full report on what had happened last night, with written statements from the Swarovskys and Sapper Stevens. Staring him in the face was the fact that he had personally killed one of his own subordinates. By all military rules he should face a court of inquiry into such an action. Yet he sat on staring at the Morse key while the arguments raged in his mind: You are avoiding the consequences of your actions; *the consequences if I leave this job will be harder to take.* You are influenced by personal ambition; *I have orders to build this bridge.* You will not accept your own fallibility; *I will not accept failure.*

His hand went out and began tapping the code for Murmansk. In the accepted signalling terms, he reported that his N.C.O. had been swept into the river by a storm whilst working on the reconstruction of the bridge. He tapped out name, number, and rank, adding that the man's personal effects would be put on the first available through train after the completion of the bridge. The message was accepted; the line went dead.

Paul leant back, knowing that the truth could now never be told . . . and that he was still free to build a bridge that would stand as his memorial in Russia long after he had left. He realised he was drenched in sweat and hollow inside from lack of food, but he sat on for a few moments, head tilted back and eyes closed, feeling as if he had fought a physical battle.

Quite when she entered he was not sure, but he became aware of a sweet fragrance at the same time as a faint rustle told him someone was beside him. With a great leap of his heart, he opened his eyes and sat up, so certain it was Irina that he could not at first accept that he had been mistaken.

"You cannot go without eating, Paul, whatever has happened," said Olga, putting down a square of wood on which were a plate of bread and butter, some tinned ham, tomato-filled dumplings, and a large mug of tea.

Disappointment kept him silent, so she went on, "They all agreed that I should bring this to you, so do not accuse me of causing trouble by entering your tent when you are here alone."

"No . . . no, of course not," he said and tried to smile at her. "Actually, it is no longer my tent, in effect. Shall we call it the Officers' Mess?" He looked at the breakfast. "Thanks. This looks very good."

"Do you mind if I sit with you while you eat it?"

What could he say? "I'm not very good company just now."

She took the seat on the other side of his bed. "Begin, or it will be cold."

He was hungry and the food was hot and good, but he would have preferred to eat it alone. Getting on with the business of eating, he left her to make the conversation. He could guess it would not be social chit-chat.

"I'm sorry, Paul. It was obvious how much it had upset you last night."

He remembered their faces looking at him. "Yes, no doubt."

She said nothing more for a few minutes, and he went on with his breakfast, wondering what was coming. He had never yet had a comfortable conversation with Olga.

"Now you have found out what it is like to be betrayed—to be in danger from your own people."

He put down his knife and fork. So that was it! She had come to rub salt in the wound. He turned to her slowly, feeling the onset of the aggression she always aroused in him.

"Was that really necessary?"

She faced him provocatively, and it was impossible not to notice the striking lines of her body as she sat so erect in his chair.

"You have always been so intolerant of what you considered our melodramatic fears. Now, perhaps, you will understand the feelings of those who no longer trust anyone. Now, perhaps, you will be human."

"I see." He forgot his breakfast and leant across the back of the chair. "In what manner do you consider I have been *in*human?"

"In just about every way," she replied softly, and he saw the flames begin to kindle in eyes that always expressed strong emotions. "You put things before people."

"Things have a way of remaining after people have gone," he answered immediately. "But isn't that what you have just been preaching to me? *Put not thy trust in any man.*"

She had plainly not been expecting such an answer, and his controlled counter-attack excited her. The fire in her eyes flared up, and she leant forward to make her next charge—a movement that eased the silk blouse away from her neck to allow a glimpse of a lace camisole curving over white skin. He could not pull his gaze away.

"You work as if you were a machine, with no rest."

"I had four years' practice in France."

She leant farther forward. "You must be exceptionally strong."

"It's the way I am built," he murmured, unable to hide his interest in her nearness.

"I have watched you on that bridge, Paul. You climb about without fear." Her eyes were bright with some kind of animal stimulation. "Such disregard for danger is surely inhuman."

He shook his head slowly, feeling an involuntary response to her rising up within him. "I'm a strong swimmer. Water doesn't frighten me."

She rose and moved round the bed to stand before him, putting her hands on the back of the chair so that they touched against his.

"An answer for everything, Paul, and not a blush in sight. You *have* changed."

He grew more aggressive. "If you are trying to be amusing, it is completely out of place, at the moment."

She smiled tantalisingly. "No sense of humour, either? Even in a situation like this, it is natural for a man to relax . . . in some way."

"We all relax around the dinner table," he said, irritated by the effect her nearness was having on him. He had only to move his hand up a little to feel the provocative swell of her breast beneath his palm. The idea took root and wouldn't leave him in peace.

"Don't you think this has gone on long enough? It's rather a ridiculous game, isn't it?" Paul said defensively.

"Yes, of course it's ridiculous . . . and at last you have acknowledged it," she breathed, taking in the width of his shoulders and the forearms covered with dark hairs. "It is ridiculous for us to go on like this when the alternative stares us in the face. It is more than inhuman for a man to want another man's wife so much and school himself to the extent you do. You have not yet become her lover, have you?"

He stood up in careful anger. She had touched him where he was intensely vulnerable. "I think you had better go."

"I have watched you both very carefully, and the hunger is still there day after day," she said in a strange breathy excitement. "I think you are trying to be noble and British, Paul. Compared with us, you have very bourgeois notions of morality. But such a situation must be intolerable. Unless you are completely inhuman, you must be in a state of torment, seeing her day and night and knowing she is out of reach."

He turned away and picked up his cap, intending to leave. But she caught at his arms and looked up into his face with such passion that he was halted.

"Paul, it is tearing you apart, admit it. She belongs to Sasha; Valodya has that woman. We are left—both hungry and both free. Love her with as much pure devotion as you wish, but how much longer will you resist the obvious way out of our difficulties?"

He was no longer just angry, but also full of prodding guilt that made her offer almost an insult to his manhood. If he declined he was inhuman; if he accepted he was a mere lecher. She was a virgin begging to be broken if only as a substitute for another woman. It disgusted him, yet, at the same time, aroused a strange echo of a young girl lying dead in the ruins of a hospital in France. A young girl who had been cheated of life.

As he dragged her against him and explored the firm lines from breast to thigh, she was excited by the flood of delight released by the touch of his hand.

For Paul, the woman was not Olga, or anyone in particular, just an outlet for a need that had nothing to do with emotion or personalities. He found himself wanting to hurt her and gripped her harder, bending her backward with deliberate strength, closing his mouth angrily over hers.

But he was not, by nature, a vicious man, and that burst of ferocity soon had him aware that he was getting out of his depth in a current that was too strong. He lifted his head and saw Olga's face ablaze with something that had him remembering a gentler girl with love in her heart.

There was no release this way from something Olga had not even begun to understand. He thrust her away from him so that she fell back onto his bed none too gently. Breathing hard with anger against her and himself, he snatched up his cap.

"I think that just about pays for my breakfast," he told her before pushing through the tent flaps into rain that was beginning to peter out.

His aggression was soon remarked by everyone, and the Russian soldiers, always very sensitive to moods, needed no second bidding to get to work. After the prolonged storm and wetness, they were all glad of the exercise and relief in occupation. An arctic forest in a downpour offered little by way of entertainment for idle hours.

The river was still running high, but visibility improved by the minute, until a watery sun brought brightness to everyone's thoughts, as well as the camp-site, and made work on the bridge possible. Deeming it still too risky to attempt to ferry a working party across the turbulence, Paul got everyone busy on strengthening and repairing that section attached to their bank.

However, he found himself severely hampered by the hand that had been jammed between the ropes the night before. When he almost slipped and dropped into the river, he was forced to confine himself to tasks that kept him on the steady top surface of the bridge. When the ladies appeared with tea, he remained where he was, measuring and levelling with his tape and small pegs. He had no intention of socialising.

But Irina left the others and walked out onto the bridge, where he could not avoid her. "How is your hand this morning?"

"Perfectly all right, thank you," he said, keeping his attention on what he was doing.

"Which is why you nearly fell into the river, I suppose? You need treatment for your hand."

He looked up. She seemed too lovely for the sort of day it was. "Do you have to treat everyone as a patient?"

She moved closer. "Has anyone told you how stubborn and proud you can be?"

"Oh, that makes a change from 'earnest and serious,'" he retaliated.

As he went to turn away, she put her hand on his arm.

"Why do you demand so much from yourself?" she asked sadly. "From the start you have succeeded in the impossible. You must not now blame yourself over this one thing."

He looked down into her face, so vivid with life, and felt worse. "A spoonful of medicine doesn't cure everything."

"I know. Some ills can only be cured by the patient himself. If he is determined to die, no medicine will cure him. We had little time for men like that."

It hit him where he least expected it and left him with no defences against her. For a long moment he studied her clear, youthful face.

"You might have warned me this treatment would hurt."

She drew nearer until they were almost touching. "That river is like life: it sweeps us all along in the direction we have to go. Every man makes mistakes. What is there in you that drives you to seek perfection in everything you do?"

The fight had gone out of him now. He shook his head. "If I do, it must be because there seems to be so little time and so much I want to achieve."

"You have your whole life before you."

"Have I?"

She understood, as she always did. "What you have done here is more than most men achieve before they die. You have every reason to be proud . . . as I am of you."

He swallowed. "That makes all the difference."

"I love you, Pavlik. Whatever happens, that will never change."

Unable to do more than tell her with his eyes what he felt in return, he said huskily, "About that river that sweeps us all along. It is possible to build a bridge across it and change direction."

It was her turn to be disconcerted. "Bridges are so easily destroyed, it seems" she told him.

"Not those I build." His confidence had returned, and he believed anything was possible . . . even that.

The feeling of renewed confidence that invaded the three officers was transferred to the soldiers during the first three weeks of August, and work on the bridge advanced with gratifying speed. Only now that the traitor had been removed from their midst were they aware of how heavily the problem had affected them before. Both Paul and Sasha went about with lighter hearts, their treatment of the soldiers markedly more relaxed now they were sure of them and confident that what they were doing would not suddenly collapse due to sabotage.

That isolated storm had travelled on across Russia, leaving behind clear weather once more. But the summer was ending. The temperature had dropped drastically; the darkness of night grew longer and colder almost daily. The chill made the men work with more vigour; the lengthening night meant they worked by the light of flambeaux for longer periods. The three officers worked out a shift system to cope with this, and all set about their work with the feeling of being on the home stretch.

There was nothing now to stop them going straight on to Murmansk the moment the bridge was complete. That goal put zest into all they did . . . and the soldiers caught the fever of hope, also.

Such was the feeling in the whole camp, on the day the two parts of the bridge linked up, there was celebrating fit for an occasion of world-shaking proportions. The Russian soldiers fell into a frenzy of embraces before indulging the childlike delight of running back and forth across the bridge from bank to bank, grinning and shouting in glee. One man fell into the river and had to be hauled out, grinning broadly and declaring that the bridge looked as beautiful from underneath as it did from on top.

Some of their delight faded, however, when the men realised there was still a lot to do before a train could be sent across. All the strengthening, jointing, and testing seemed a dull prospect compared with the exciting visual growth of two halves of a bridge reaching out from opposite banks. But the comfort of a complete path over something which had been a barrier kept their spirits high enough to tackle the more boring but essential task of adding the finishing touches to something they now regarded with personal pride.

Paul delayed his ultimate celebration for the day he took the train across. He had built a bridge, but if it collapsed beneath the weight of an iron engine, he would have achieved nothing. All the same, he was happy and confident in his ability. He had grown used to managing without Corporal Banks. Valodya proved an able assistant, picking up the rudiments of bridge building very quickly.

Paul's relationship with Valodya also went a long way toward improving his relationship with the elder Swarovsky. Since the discovery of their traitor, the older Russian appeared to have softened his rigid attitude a little, and the sharing of a tent with the two brothers could not but help break down some of the differences that had made their joint command so thorny.

Then there was Irina. Separated as she was, in the tent with the other women, it did not seem that she was another man's wife. They never appeared to spend any time alone together. Nor, for that matter, did Valodya and his mistress. There was really nowhere a couple could go, unless they were so desperate as to plunge into the forest like a pair of peasants. But the three officers were all working flat out and, apart from enjoying the female company during meals, fell into exhausted sleep during their rest periods. What each man thought and dreamed as he looked at the feminine charms of the ladies remained a secret unto himself. For the time being, each was fully occupied with physically exhausting work.

But in the other tent, it was a vastly different story. Three women of such differing temperaments were not in the least compatible. In a normal setting, they would have been aloof, polite when the occasion demanded, and careful to avoid meeting whenever possible. In such a situation as the present one, it was not surprising that a storm of violent proportions began to gather as week followed week.

The greatest contributor was enforced idleness in a place that offered even the most determined woman no chance for occupation. Apart from making and distributing tea to the men as they worked and trying to keep some semblance of civilised living in their own group, there was little else to occupy the long days and nights. As time passed, the three men grew less appreciative of the trouble the women had taken. More often than not, the men trooped in after a quick wash and change of uniform, talking of what they had done that day and what they planned to do on the morrow, before tackling the meal with hearty enthusiasm that suggested they would have eaten with equal zest what the soldiers had been given. To those who had waited all day for the moment, it seemed heartless and ungracious.

Of course, the ladies could have passed some time with mending—an occupation Zapalova knew nothing of and determined never to learn. Olga refused to do something she considered the ballerina, with her lowly origins, was better fitted to do, and Irina, though used to such tasks during her years as a nurse, only picked up a needle and thread when she had no choice or her conscience troubled her. But she drew the line at sewing anything for the other two. They could go about in rags, for all she cared.

Moreover, their lotions and creams were almost exhausted. They tried using them sparingly so that they would last until they reached Murmansk—not that any one of them was sure there would be such things to purchase in an arctic port created by itinerant railway workers. Their one luxury, if it could be so called, was the big wooden barrel coaxed from Paul, which they used for taking baths. Filled with warm water, it gave them great pleasure to be able to climb in and feel pampered for fifteen minutes or so.

Olga began writing a journal, with the somewhat morbid intention of leaving it to posterity as a record of her last isolated days on earth, but she soon abandoned it when she realised there was nothing of interest to record day after day. Irina tactfully suggested she should describe the progress of the bridge, to which Olga replied that Paul did that in his endless daily reports that occupied all his spare time.

Irina wrote long letters to her family in Switzerland, even though there was no way of posting them until trains began to pass through once more.

Zapalova did nothing in the least domestic, thinking it was all done by magic. Her obsessive concern for her body irked the other two occupants of the tent, who were forever being asked to change beds because of draughts or to sit elsewhere so that the ballerina could put her feet up. There were interminable exercises that demanded the clearing of enough space, and other periods when the great artist explained that she had to relax completely and clear her mind of everything but music and movement. At those times, Irina and Olga were expected to remain still and silent. They certainly did not.

Thanks to Valodya, the ballerina spent long sessions outside at her impromptu *barre,* keeping her body supple and in practice, but even the diversion of seeing her in lace-trimmed drawers, one of Corporal Banks's woollen shirts, and a pair of long woollen socks offered by Sasha lost its appeal after a while. The other two women grew impatient with her determination to carry on as if she were at some dancing academy. But she at least had something with which to pass her days, even if she did complain all the time of how long it was taking to put up a simple wooden bridge.

Irina had the occasional patient to treat, even if it was simply a cut finger or a thumb that had been hammered by mistake. And she had her love for Paul. Just once in those three weeks were they completely alone together, when Paul left the bridge to send a signal to Lake Onega and Irina had returned to her tent for a bandage. They came face-to-face as they left the tents and kissed with passionate desperation as the minutes flew past to betray them.

Whilst Olga and Zapalova watched the bridge take shape and longed for its completion, it had taken on a conflicting importance in Irina's mind. When track was laid across, it would spell freedom . . . but it would also put an end to the present life that allowed her to see Paul constantly. Each time the thought entered her head, she pushed it away. Live a little at a time, she told herself.

But whilst she and the ballerina had their professions to pursue, Olga had nothing, and it became increasingly obvious to Irina that the girl's volatile personality would soon have to find an outlet or explode. In the heart of a forest with two men who were her brothers and another who continued to ignore a tormenting physical challenge, there *was* no outlet. So Olga exploded.

It was over something trivial and far less trying than any other aspects of their forest life. In the middle of one of the shifts when they knew the officers were all up at the bridge, the women decided to take their baths. Only when the tub was up-ended did Olga discover the bar of soap, now a small pulpy mess, at the bottom.

Turning on Zapalova, who had left the soap carelessly in the water, she flew into a rage of dangerous proportions.

"That is the last tablet but one! You do not care—I doubt you can even count—but on that chest lies the dwindling supply of items that keep us human. You never look at how fast they are going, do you?"

Zapalova raised her expressive brows in haughty manner and turned away. But Olga flew at her and seized her hand, squashing the slimy remains of soap into her small palm.

"There! That is yours, Madame Ballerina. You will touch none of the others."

Shaking the hand with horrified fastidiousness, Zapalova brought up her other palm to deliver a ringing slap around Olga's left cheek. Quick as a flash, the girl retaliated by doing the same to her opponent, and they both stood pale with anger and with red colour spreading over one cheek, facing each other in battle.

"She-cat!" hissed Zapalova.

"Peasant!" Olga flung at her.

Roused into one of her most dramatic roles, the ballerina became the wicked, vengeful Odile as she destroyed the pure, yearning Odette. Her face took on a magnificent, contemptuous satisfaction.

"I do not wonder the people of Russia are in revolt. You do nothing all day but pant for a man. Olga Ivanovna Swarovskaya is a useless ornament. He will not have you; he has made it plain enough. All you can do is go off into the forest with one of the peasants—or all of them. They will be grateful for anything."

Olga was shaking and wild-eyed. "I leave that practice to women like you. You have had infinite experience at it. But these soldiers cannot give you presents, like my brothers, to whom you *sold* yourself."

Zapalova moved gracefully around to deliver her next sally. "Yes, I sold my consolation. You cannot even give yours free of charge."

Intervening hastily, Irina said, "Let us keep a semblance of civilised behaviour. We are not women of the villages."

Olga turned on her immediately. "Are you including yourself in that statement?"

She tried to remain calm. "Do not attempt to draw me into this ridiculous and disgusting quarrel."

Blue eyes were brilliant with passion. "You have no need to quarrel, you smug little nurse, gliding around with your bandages and soothing hands, thinking no one sees what you are up to. Safely separated from your husband, you are free to kiss and fondle whom you fancy. Oh, don't put on that innocent, sterile air. I have seen you fall into Paul's arms at the first chance you get, and then go straight to Valodya."

It was impossible to remain controlled. What Olga was saying with regard to her young brother was infamous.

"How dare you? Valodya needed attention. He had grazed his back very badly on rough wood."

Olga's face twisted. "Do all your patients thank you as he did?"

Irina flushed. Valodya, gay and impetuous, had pulled her onto his knee, after she had helped him on with his shirt, and kissed her with elaborate panache. It had meant nothing; it had been his way of making life a little more bearable, that was all.

"I think he does not deserve what you are suggesting," Irina said stiffly. "Think what you wish of me, but do not insult your brother by such remarks. He is worthy of the same loyalty he shows to you and Sasha."

"You leap to his defence too readily for someone who is married to his brother."

"Grow up, Olga," Irina said contemptuously. "Everyone in this camp would leap to Valodya's defence. He gives himself generously in friendship and deserves the same friendship in return. In any case, he is already committed to Lyudmilla Sergeyevna."

"I give him to you, if you want him," put in Zapalova icily. "I am disdainful of such passions for possession of a lover."

Olga flounced across the tent to face her. "Disdainful, are you? Where would you be now if Valodya had not risked his life to get you out of Moscow?" Olga stood, breast heaving, leaning against the polished chest. "You used Sasha for five years in order to further your career. You used his name and wealth to climb the social ladder, then turned to his enemies when they offered better prospects. But when your fickle, useless life was in danger, you clung to another Swarovsky to get you out of it. Now you stand there like a pathetic understudy who will never be given the star part, saying you will give him away. You heartless, skinny bitch!"

"This is doing no good to any of us," cried Irina, desperately seeking the end to something she knew could destroy the last remnants of a shaky relationship in their tent.

But Olga turned on her, swept beyond reason now by emotions battened down too long. "You are no better. You used Sasha to gain the Swarovsky name and fortune. You have no more love for him than *she* had. Now he has lost all his property and wealth, you demean him by openly seducing every man in sight."

Irina had seen people on the verge of a breakdown and realised Olga was heading that way. Even so, the woman outvoted the nurse, for once. No consideration would make her stay and listen to any more of the girl's outrageous accusations. But at the tent entrance, she was halted by Olga's next taunt.

"When the bridge is finished, Paul will go. Then you will be left with Sasha. I hope he will treat you as you deserve then. He is only silent now because he wants that bridge built . . . but he is a man with great pride. He will not let his wife's lover get away scot-free."

Irina turned and stared at Olga as the import of her words sunk in. But it was Zapalova who said matter-of-factly, "You surely did not think Sasha was blind to it. Those fingers touching around the tea cups, the smiles of encouragement, the glowing glances over the dinner-table—

even the stupidest peasant out there knows what is going on between you and that virile Englishman. Sasha cannot let it pass unpunished. You must see that. I think it is time you put an end to it."

Irina was afraid, and fear made her lash out. "And I think it is time you decided to which Swarovsky you owe your allegiance."

"The same applies to you," snapped Olga. "You are both so smug in your vanity, believing you are providing release and refreshment to men in need of it. But I can see what you are doing. It's all too easy, isn't it? You preen and smile in every direction, knowing you are safe in this tent with me." She advanced on them both, tense with the hatred she felt at that moment toward every person in that forest camp. "I have the perfect solution, which I intend to suggest to them all when they come in tonight." Her hand went up to indicate the canvas roof. "This is Sasha's tent. He should occupy it with his wife, so that he can shut out the world and seek what consolation he needs from his nurse that she is not now giving him."

Switching her gaze to Zapalova she went on, "Since you and Valodya slept in fields during your escape from Moscow, I'm sure you will feel at home on the straw in the supply-truck. Throw out that English soldier, and you can start earning all you have been paid by the Swarovsky family, at last."

She smiled maliciously. "That will leave Paul as master of his own tent . . . and me without a bed. Good manners alone will tell him what he must do. If he closes his eyes, he'll never know the difference," she told Irina with soft vindictiveness, "and at least he'll be taking no other man's woman." She took a deep breath. "That, my dear courtesans, will rid us of each other's company and put things on a completely equal footing, don't you agree? I'm certain *they* will see what a splendid scheme it is."

Irina saw that Olga was quite capable of doing what she threatened. It would be disastrous and tragic for them all. Moving forward, Irina spoke in soothing manner, as she had done with men suffering from shell shock.

"Olga, my dear, we understand what it is you are trying to say, but don't you think . . ."

She was halted as Olga turned and swept the polished chest with an outflung arm, so that everything on it flew across the tent in a shower. Then she stood facing Irina with frightening malice.

"Don't treat me like one of your patients, you damned adulterous . . ."

The rest was never said, because someone had pushed through into the tent without any warning of his entry. Irina had a quick glimpse of Paul's reaction to the scene, before he looked at her and said in urgent tones, "Will you come quickly? Your husband has met with a very bad accident."

F i f t e e n

Paul strode beside the train down toward the river, silent and stern. Irina had difficulty in keeping up with him. After snatching up the medical box now kept by her in the tent, she had followed him with all kinds of thoughts fighting for prominence.

She did not ask what had happened to Sasha, and Paul made no effort to explain as he hurried her to the spot. He must have heard Olga's last words and interpreted them the only way possible. In any case, it must have been obvious to him that they were all shouting at each other like *barishnyi* even as he approached the tent. At that thought, she realised he would have understood none of it, since they had been speaking in Russian. Was that why he was looking so strained? She knew it upset him to be cut off by a language.

But if Olga really intended to speak as she had threatened, he would understand that well enough when said in English, the language they always spoke when he was present. It would be humiliating for him—for herself, too—and the girl must be prevented from carrying out her threat. In the midst of such problems, she remained outwardly calm with regard to Sasha. An accident, injuries, men in pain were all things she understood and could deal with confidently. It was emotional undercurrents— her own, in particular—that she found so disturbing.

Valodya and several soldiers were clustered around a figure lying awkwardly on the ground fifty yards upriver, and the young officer got to his feet as they approached.

"I think it is bad," he told Irina in Russian. "We would not move him until you gave us directions. He is in great agony whenever we touch him."

She went down on her knees beside Sasha, who was lying face downward with one leg spread out at an angle. Valodya crouched beside her, his face full of youthful concern.

"He is impaled on a tree stump," he said. "The wood is embedded deep in his thigh. When we first tried to help him up, we could not, because the flesh was being torn as we pulled."

Irina saw that the leg was somehow held by the stump, but it was impossible to tell how deep the penetration was until he was turned over. There was no doubt he must be in considerable pain. She quickly took out a syringe and gave him a dose of morphia, then turned to ask Valodya how the accident had happened.

"I was down on the bridge with Paul, but these men say he was giving instructions on how best to transport these extra-long trees down to the bridge. Then, he began turning as he walked away, appeared to lose his balance, and fell. When he did not get up, they ran to him, then grew afraid when they saw he was somehow fixed to the ground. One man came for us." He wiped his brow with the back of his hand and sighed. "I fear I tried to move him myself, but he cried out so much I decided to do no more until you arrived." He pointed at the leg. "It seems to be a tree that was hit by lightning during the storm. You can see the tree itself lying just behind you. The point at where it snapped off is jagged and sharp. The other part is through Sasha's thigh."

She turned her head and saw the tree that had been riven. The stump remaining after such a split would be wicked indeed. Reaching out, she gently pushed back Sasha's soft hair. His eyes were closed. Pieces of pine needles had clung to his moustache, and there was a smear of dirt across his forehead. All she could think was that he would be so angry to receive an injury that had not been caused by an enemy bullet.

She stood up and walked a short distance away. Valodya followed. Then she saw Paul standing aside, still with that same strained expression, and called to him.

"We shall need your help," she said in English as he came across. "You must both lift him, using the greatest care. To do it too quickly will tear the thigh. It is inevitable that small pieces of bark will be left in the wound, and they will have to be removed. To do that, I shall need to take him to one of the tents—yours, if you please, Paul," she said quickly, thinking of the situation she had just left in the other.

"Of course," he agreed immediately. "Valodya, can you send one of your men to Stevens for the stretcher kept in the supply-truck?"

The young Russian gave quick instructions to the nearest soldier, then turned back to Irina. "You will need to sew up the wound?"

She nodded. "I am not a surgeon, so I beg you not to tear the flesh any more than you can help when you lift him. One more thing I must tell you. As soon as the pressure is relieved, he will bleed profusely. When he is quite clear of the stump, please set him immediately down where I can apply pads and a tourniquet. Only then can we place him on a stretcher to carry back."

She smiled confidently to ease their obvious concern. "I ask you to perform the most difficult part—that of lifting him. The morphia will deaden a lot of the pain, but he is certain to cry out. You must not consider that and continue slowly, with the greatest care. Now I will prepare pads and a tourniquet, and we can begin."

With clear and abstract efficiency, she made her preparations, giving a nod to the two officers when she was ready. Following her instructions on the best way to pull him clear, they began lifting Sasha from the stump that held him. It was as well they were both strongly built, for the patient was a big man who took some lifting as a dead weight—all the more so when they had to raise him slowly.

The peasant-soldiers stood around watching and giving a commentary, until Irina asked if they had no work to do. Then they shuffled half-heartedly back to the great pine trunks they had cut for the bridge. Sasha began to yell the moment he was moved, which must have been hard on those causing his agony, and even to Irina, who was used to such things, it seemed an age before the harrowing business was over and she could see the extent of the wound. This was not easy, because the blood came gushing from it immediately, but it looked serious enough for her to have misgivings. If she was not skilled to cope with it, the nearest hospital was at Lake Onega, two days down the line and threatened by Red troops. Sasha would refuse to go, she knew.

As she applied pads and tied the tourniquet around Sasha's upper thigh to stem the flow of blood, both Paul and Valodya offered their assistance for the operation on Sasha's thigh.

"No," she said with a little shake of her head. "You two are needed at the bridge, and that must come first. Olga can give what little help is needed. It does not take two great men to hold bandages and a bowl." Flashing a look at Paul, she told him he could go back now to his most essential work. "Thank you for what you have done. I shall keep Valodya no longer than it takes to hang all the lamps we have from the roof of your tent and help me take off Sasha's clothes. Then I'll send him back to you."

Paul nodded. "Right."

As he walked away, Irina felt again that strength in times of crisis that made him ideal for this command. Her heart lurched. He strove so hard.

Valodya instructed the men on how to carry the stretcher and where to set it down, then left Irina while he went to fetch the lamps from the women's tent and tell Olga she was wanted. While he was gone, Irina gave Sasha another dose of morphia. Probing the wound for splinters of wood would be more than any man could be expected to endure with fortitude, and he had already suffered considerably. His face was yellow tinted and aged by pain, he was muttering and restless.

When Olga arrived, still showing remnants of uncontrollable anger, Irina said sharply to her, "This is delicate work. I need your help and quick response to my instructions. Can I rely on that?"

Olga looked at her stonily. "He is my brother."

Once Irina began, it was possible to forget all else but that which she had learnt from books and from watching the doctors. When she spoke to Olga, it was impersonal and quietly efficient. She did not think anymore that the patient was her husband from whom she felt completely estranged.

It was difficult and exacting work. Even with the lamps providing so much light, she could not be certain there were no more minute splinters of wood in the wound. There were conflicting demands: even a tiny splinter could infect the wound with poisonous sap, yet too great a blood loss would weaken him and delay recovery. Time was passing. The tourniquet could only be kept on for so long, and the morphia would gradually lose its strength as she worked.

Her hands were steady and sure as she worked, but afterward, when she began clearing up swabs and pans of water, they began to shake. It was then that Olga persuaded her gently into Paul's chair beside the telegraph signaller and told Slabov to fetch tea. Feeling unusually tired, Irina did as she was told, watching with mild surprise as Olga cleared the tent of all signs of medical equipment with great calmness. When the tea was brought, the girl poured a cup and put it on the table beside Irina.

"Thank you," Irina said quietly, then added, "I could not have done all that without your support."

Olga gave a twisted smile. "You forget I waited hand and foot on an invalid for a very long time. I have no real skill, but I am very good at the menial tasks."

Not for the first time, Irina reflected on the sadness of a vibrant young girl tied to an embittered invalid during her growing-up years and her frustration at the thought of life passing her by.

It was already early evening by the time Irina had changed her clothes and returned to sit by Sasha. She had washed him and settled him comfortably on the bed, but he was restless and feverish. It made her uneasy. He had never been an easy patient in the hospital, she remembered. He was impatient with illness; inactivity made him fretful. He was still very dozy from loss of blood and the morphia, but he kept muttering about the bridge and the approaching winter.

She bent over the bed, calming him with reassurances and cooling his brow with a cloth wrung out in cold water, so intent on her task she did not hear anyone come in.

"How is he?"

She spun round nervously to find Paul standing just inside the entrance. He looked dark-eyed and stubborn.

"I'm sorry. I didn't mean to startle you," he said.

She swallowed. "It was just that I did not hear you."

"No." He looked at Sasha. "How is he?"

"Feverish. I . . . I am not sure that I did everything that was right."

He studied her closely. "That is sheer nonsense, you know very well.

When it comes to medical matters, you are sure and skilled. What would we all have done without you these past months?"

Suddenly, to her dismay, she began to cry. It was ridiculous and out of character, humiliating in front of him, yet the tears flowed freely. She felt like a lost child seeking comfort. Why did it have to happen just at that moment? A nurse did not weep at the bedside of her patient.

"This is silly . . . I cannot think . . ." she began, finding it difficult to speak through the thickness in her throat.

Paul moved in but remained more than an arm's length away as he leaned forward, holding out a handkerchief he took from a cardboard box beside his bed.

"Blow on this," he said roughly.

She took it and held it to her face, but it smelt faintly of him, which made matters worse. Her tears drenched the handkerchief, but simply holding something that belonged to him helped to bring eventual calm, and she looked up to find him watching her with an emotion that matched her own.

"You are a girl not yet twenty-two; you are entitled to cry," he said. "I think you have not done it often enough."

"I sometimes feel like an old, old woman," she whispered.

"I know."

He stayed where he was. What else could he do, with her husband lying there between them? Yet she had never felt so close to him, never drawn such strength from his nearness.

"I feel so ashamed."

"It had to come. I had mine on the night Valodya arrived."

"You . . . ?" she began.

His eyes grew darker and more brilliant, but his voice was steady as he said, "I went into the forest and cried because life would not leave me alone. I wrestled with the past and tried to turn from the future. I stayed there nearly all night."

Now she knew how close he had been to breaking that next morning when she had followed him to the fur-trapper's hut. The confession moved her beyond words. It made her special, gave her something no kisses could impart. But before she could tell him of how moved she was, he changed the subject completely.

"I have arranged that Valodya and I will sleep in the supply-truck for a few days. That will enable you to move in here, where you will be on hand if you are needed. Under all the circumstances, I think those are the best arrangements."

She stared at him. It was all too plain why he had done it. He might not understand Russian, but he understood too well that three women caught fighting cat and dog were better separated for the sake of general morale. But his action did more than protect her from Olga and the ballerina; it paired her indisputably and very definitely with Sasha. In the act of opening her mouth to comment, she was forestalled by him.

"He *is* your husband."

Now she understood the stubborn set to his mouth. In this circumstance, he had no alternative but to acknowledge that legal bond that kept them apart.

"Yes, he is my husband. Thank you for your thoughtfulness and for sacrificing your comfort for my sake."

"That's all right," he said, trying to remain impersonal and barely succeeding. "If there is anything else you want, let me know."

"You have done more than enough already," she said through stiff lips.

"I take it you'd like Slabov to serve your dinner over here . . . so that you can keep an eye on him," he said, glancing at Sasha.

She nodded slowly and turned back to her patient. Paul went out without another word.

For the next four days, everyone worked as hard as it was possible for them to do. The bridge was well-nigh complete and ready for railway track to be laid across it—an incentive to every man to bring forward that moment when the engine should steam safely across to the far bank and prove their job well done.

The soldiers were full of speculations on where they would go then. In three days it would be September. In bad years, the snows had been known to start as early as that month. Then, they would need a *dushegreychka*—a thick sheepskin—to keep them warm, a *papakha* over their ears, and a stout pair of *valenkis* to keep their feet from cold and frostbite. Who would provide them? Would the British send down a train from Murmansk with all those things now the line was soon to be open again? Or would they all go north to re-equip?

They talked about the possibilities endlessly as they hammered and sawed. If things were going well, they might even be given time to visit their families. It was almost a year since they were first parted from them by the Reds, then taken over by the Whites. Wives and parents had no way of knowing where the soldiers were or if they were still alive. Even if the soldiers knew how to write letters, there was no way of sending them. They grumbled, until one man reminded them that the English officer could write but was equally unable to send or receive letters, and *he* was very far from his homeland. They were not certain where England was but imagined it was situated on the other side of Finland somewhere and must be a land twice the size of Russia. They were not certain of the size of Russia, either, but knew it took months to cross from one side to the other. The Captain must indeed feel a lonely man.

Paul was again in favour. Each soldier was warm with admiration for a man who had created a complexity of logs and planks across the river merely from a broken wreck in the water and from the trees surrounding them. With the bridge firm and stout before them, they appreciated what the endless carpentry had been for and marvelled at the man who could see in his mind what they now saw before their eyes.

Paul was unaffected by their fluctuating loyalty toward him. Those days directing the final work prior to laying track were fully occupied with mental problems that precluded personal reactions to those around him. Even Irina was relegated to the back of his mind as he tested, checked, and studied his bridge for signs of any error. When the track was laid, he would have to take the engine across. Any mistake on his part, any weakness in the structure, could result in the whole bridge collapsing . . . and their only means of transport wrecked on the riverbed. It was not a prospect to encourage restful hours.

With the older Swarovsky out of action, Paul left Valodya in command when he took a few snatched naps, but his sleep was troubled and fitful. During those working times, he grew even closer to the young Russian, finding in him the perfect partner for an isolated command. Many a time Paul caught himself wishing it had been the younger Swarovsky who had come riding across the siding on the day he had first arrived with his small train down by the lake. How different things would have been from the start. But Valodya would not have brought Irina. Would that have been better, or not?

Irina had taken Paul's gesture to its fullest extent, remaining with her husband and taking meals in the tent with him. Paul had asked two soldiers to transfer the field telegraph to the supply-truck so that he would not be obliged to disturb them and had seen little of the pair. Valodya visited his brother frequently and so did Olga. The great Zapalova was far more interested in the approaching completion of the railway track that would enable her to use the permit she had been given at Lake Onega that authorised her passage on the first through train.

Left alone with her when the others visited their brother, Paul had more than one quarrel with the temperamental ballerina. Although he acknowledged that she had a strangely compelling attraction when she turned on her almost childish mood of repentance for what she had just done or said, Paul found himself at a loss to understand how both Swarovsky brothers had fallen victim to her. The older one might find her mixture of harlot and ingénue refreshing, but Valodya was considerably younger than she and with no romantic clouds around his head.

When Paul had cautiously broached the subject one day whilst chatting with Valodya during a break from work, the young Russian had just smiled and said, "She represents the beautiful and exotic side of Russia— a side you have never seen, Paul, and will probably never do so now. She kept me going down there in Moscow."

Paul thought it wiser not to go on and ask what would happen when they reached Murmansk. It was not his problem, and he had enough of his own.

When the ladies came to dispense tea, as usual that day, Irina came with them and made no secret of the fact that she was very unhappy over the appearance of her husband's leg. She had warned him that his wound was not healing as she had hoped. Her words were proved only too drastically when Swarovsky was overcome with pain in the late afternoon, and a dark stain spreading across his bandages showed the gash in his thigh had started to ooze once more.

When Valodya was awoken by Paul just before midnight to take over while his friend rested, the Russian gave the news that Irina was seriously considering the need to re-open the wound, which seemed to be distended with poison. Her fears that small splinters of wood had been left embedded in the flesh looked like being justified. The patient was in great pain and growing feverish once more. If his condition was not improved on the following day, she would have to contemplate cutting the stitches and dispersing the poison. There was no doubt she was very worried.

Morning brought a non-committal report on the injured man, and Paul continued to supervise the laying of track across the bridge, hoping the message meant Swarovsky was slowly improving. Then, when Valodya joined him after eating a midday snack, he told Paul his brother looked very flushed but was determined on getting on his feet later that afternoon.

"Then he is even more pig-headed than I thought," commented Paul.

"*Da! Da!* But were you not also, a short time ago? Irina has just now said you had the injured arm and behaved in the same way. You two are much alike, my friend. You also have the pig-head."

"Thanks," he said shortly. "I take it you mean it as a compliment."

Paul set about explaining to Valodya what the men were presently engaged in, then prepared to go back to the women's tent for his own light meal. But Valodya stopped him with a hand on his arm.

"It was not easy to put them together, as you did, when it is plain how she also feels about you. For myself, for my family. I thank you."

"Not a bit," Paul said brusquely. "Fate rather took it out of my hands, didn't she?"

In the middle of Paul's snack, Sapper Stevens arrived at the tent to tell

Paul there was a signal coming over the transmitter. Olga exclaimed angrily and asked if it could not wait until Captain Anderson had finished eating, but he got up wearily and went out, with an apology to the two ladies.

When he discovered the content of the signal, Paul nearly switched off and walked away. He took down the tapped Morse message with mounting fury. It was long, official, and very much to the point. It was also verging on the farcical and came at a time when he was in no mood for laughter.

In effect, he was told that since Captain Paul Edward Anderson of the Royal Engineers had failed to submit any explanation for his self-appointed authority to pay over a very large sum of government money as ransom for the lives of two unnamed female Russian nationals and had ignored orders to submit, in triplicate, full written reports on the whereabouts of said money, the identity of those to whom it had been paid, and why regular accounts of expenditure of any other monies in his possession had never been completed, said officer was summoned to a Court of Inquiry and should present himself on September fourth at the Law Court in Murmansk to answer for his actions.

For some moments he sat staring at the words he had taken down, while the signal asking for acknowledgement repeated itself over and over again. He had come across such thick-skulled behaviour in France, when men had wondered if one half of the army ever knew what the other half was doing. Some conscientious man in the Paymaster's Department had plainly got hold of the news of the ransom payment and had started asking awkward questions that now rebounded on him. Paul felt it was time someone told him the truth in terms he could not possibly ignore. If it were not tragic it would be hysterically funny, but as the word *acknowledge . . . acknowledge . . . acknowledge* went on, Paul grew savage.

Out went his hand and he began tapping furiously:

> *Captain Paul Edward Anderson, Royal Engineers, is at present putting a railway bridge over a river. He is on the wrong side of it. Until the bridge is complete, nothing can travel to Murmansk. If he is killed by advancing Red troops before September 4th, he will attempt to fly up, otherwise he is forced to decline your invitation. Acknowledge.*

After almost half a minute there came rapid signals:

> *Acknowledged. Hold.*

He tapped back:

Impossible to hold. Bridge about to collapse. End of signal.

Sighing deeply, he sat back, staring at the equipment. There would be serious repercussions when he eventually reached Murmansk. In the past, Corporal Banks had prudently edited his replies, but Paul had just now jeopardised his future with the army. The authorities would never let the matter of the money drop, and the case against him would be strengthened by this evidence of insubordination. No matter what stress he was under, an officer was expected to remain cool and rational at all times and to reply to senior authority with due respect. What Paul had just done could turn a Court of Inquiry into a Court-Martial.

A signal began to come through, and he snatched up his pencil angrily. But his anger was soon replaced by the chill thrill of action. The signal came from Lake Onega this time—a signal delayed because the line had been engaged—and was of vital concern.

He wrote down the words that set all his senses jumping with alarm, then acknowledged and affirmed that he would comply with the orders. They were quite specific. An airman flying down to the lake base had spotted and pin-pointed a small group of Reds approaching the lake where Paul and his group had been sited until just over a month ago. It was vital to prevent them from sabotaging the railway at that point. The Russian troops under command of Lieutenant-Colonel Swarovsky were instructed to intercept and attack this force of uncertain but small numbers. The message made it clear that no British troops were to be involved in the action and that completion of the bridge must now take on an urgency of the highest order.

Paul wasted no time. Running flat out alongside the line, he returned to the bridge, where Valodya was supervising the laying of track. His expression must have said it all for him, for Valodya came up to him immediately, saying, "The Reds? Where are they?"

"About thirty-five, forty miles. Your brother has orders to intercept them."

Valodya's fair face clouded. "*Gospodi!* This could not have come at a worse time."

Struggling to regulate his breathing, Paul said, "You'll have to go alone, of course."

"He will insist on going with me."

Paul stared. "That's quite out of the question."

"*Da! Da!* It is out of the question, but he will go." Seeing Paul's expression, Valodya took him by the arm and walked until they were out of hearing of the troops. Then he stopped and faced him. "My friend, you are a man with the same qualities as my brother. This bridge you would build through any adversity; a cutting you tried to make, even with one arm and in great pain. Yes," he said with a faint smile, "all that I have heard about you. And so you, of all men, must understand that Sasha *has* to fight the enemies of all he believes in. I think he has not been an easy partner in command. All he has ever wanted is to kill those men who have murdered, and plundered, and raped Mother Russia. At last, that chance has come, for *him*. Like me, he has to avenge our sister Ekaterina. He has to avenge those who were forced to bow to Germany. He has to redeem our name to men like you, Paul, who destroyed one enemy for us and find it hard to forgive. He will go . . . on his hands and knees he will go."

"He will not. A man who cannot stand, a man in fever, is not fit to command."

"We have horses. He will ride."

"But he won't go if he knows nothing about the message."

The young Russian considered Paul for a moment or two, then shook his head. "I hope you do not mean what I think you mean, my friend. Sasha is not only my brother, he is my commanding officer. I have to tell him of this."

"I am senior in rank to you and order you not to."

"You are English and no longer combatant. We Russians are fighting our own war now."

Paul sighed heavily. "All right. I'll accept that I have no voice in this matter. But answer me this. Do you want your brother along on this mission—a mission that will almost certainly kill him?"

Valodya would not give a direct answer to that. "I cannot go without informing my senior officer; if I inform him, he will go."

It was a damnable situation for a man to be in, so Paul tried to help Valodya out of it. "In cases like this, a soldier has to be ruled by his medical advisers. In any other times, your brother would be safely tucked up in hospital and command delegated to his junior. No surgeon would let him so much as get out of his bed, much less ride off forty miles into the forest."

"I know. This I know," said Valodya miserably.

"If he is declared unfit for duty, will you accept command?"

The young man ran his hand through his hair, well aware of what Paul was saying. "She is his *wife*, Paul."

"She is also the only person who can tell us the consequences for your brother if he insists on going."

"You are a hard man, my friend," was the slow answer. "To ask a woman to decide this."

"I shall ask her as our only medical adviser," Paul answered brusquely. "You underestimate her if you think she will allow personal feelings to enter her decision. Well? Time is passing, and you should be on your way."

Valodya nodded. "Very well. Let us ask Irina . . . our nurse."

She came calm, pale, and quiet, when Valodya fetched her from the tent. The patient was in a feverish sleep, she said, looking all the time at Paul. He was struck by how small and feminine she looked, standing with a white apron over her blouse and skirt, and had to steel himself to approach her with official candour. It seemed to Paul she grew paler when she heard the news, but she listened quietly until he had finished speaking.

"If he knows, he will go," she said immediately. "Somehow he will climb onto a horse. He has lived only for an opportunity such as this and will listen to no one."

"What are his chances if he goes?" asked Paul sharply.

Her frank grey-green eyes were fastened unwaveringly on him. "He will die. To attempt to ride with a wound such as he has would split it open. If he did not faint from pain and fall from the horse, the fever would bring him down." Her forehead wrinkled. "But he is determined. If he reached the place, he would be killed by the first enemy he encountered. He does not stand any chance of survival if he goes." She looked from one to the other. "And he will be of no use whatever to his men."

Valodya shrugged helplessly. "All this I already knew. But he is in command. I have to tell him."

"He is asleep," said Irina calmly.

Paul was growing irritable. "The Reds are advancing while we are standing here. We are fighting a war, not considering one man's wishes."

Irina spoke to her brother-in-law as if Paul had not intervened. "It is your duty to tell him, Valodya, but time is of the greatest importance, is it not?"

He nodded.

"If Sasha is unable to be told, you must take command?"

"*Unable* to be told?"

She went on with determination but spoke now to Paul, as if it were he she must impress with her words. "All the morning I have been trying to put off the decision to cut open the wound. There is poison in his leg, and it must be dispersed if it is not to affect the whole limb. As there is no chance of getting him to a hospital, the responsibility rests with me. I have just decided it must be done without delay. My patient will be under heavy sedation for several hours, and I can permit no one to disturb him."

If love had before consisted of fascination, the call of youth, tenderness, physical desire, it now deepened into a proud, throbbing compassion that swept through Paul unawares. There was so little of her that he knew—could possibly know, as things were. She stood there so outwardly feminine, yet showing him a strength that complemented his own.

Valodya stepped forward and kissed her cheeks, murmuring something in Russian that put a suspicious dampness into her eyes. Then Paul went off with him to prepare the troops. With the exception of six who were to remain and finish the track-laying, all the Russian soldiers fell in and prepared to march off. Three of the horses were saddled, for Valodya and the two remaining N.C.O.s promoted to replace those who had been killed. The other three horses were laden with field rations, equipment, and a number of rounds of ammunition.

Armed with a map of the known tracks in that area of forest, a compass, and Paul's field glasses, Valodya swung up into the saddle and prepared to lead his men south. He sat erect, a young man with bright eyes on the nearest horizon and a face that was strong beneath its youthful lines. He wore a khaki shirt belted at the waist, breeches tucked into polished boots, and a khaki peaked cap, yet he had that air of élan that typified all those Swarovsky ancestors in their vivid and elaborate uniforms who had swept through Russia's colourful history.

Valodya smiled down at him, and Paul was reminded of so many others who had gone off in the same crusading spirit.

"Good luck," said Paul with careful nonchalance. "The bridge will be finished in a day or two. Don't miss the train, will you?"

"I will try not," was the equally nonchalant reply.

"It will be dark long before you reach the lake. That will give you the advantage of a surprise attack." He held up his hand. *"Spokoinoi nochi."*

Valodya gripped the hand tightly. *"Spokoinoi nochi*—peaceful night, my friend."

Then he was off, leading the column of peasant-soldiers alongside the railway into the quietness of mid-afternoon.

Sasha felt he had been in a world of darkness far too long when he opened his eyes to see welcome light on the canvas above him. For a brief moment he was back in time about three years. There was the smell of antiseptic about him, a languidness in his body that suggested a lull after prolonged pain, and the quiet presence of a girl with compassion in her face. But it was not a hospital, and the girl was now his wife whom he knew less than that nurse of three years ago.

She saw that he was awake and came to him with a grave expression on her face. "Good. The fever is going. Now it will be much better."

He lay still as she took his wrist between her fingers and studied the watch pinned to her blouse. How easy it was for a man to become dependent on the woman who tended his wounds. The world of sickness was unreal and divorced from the rest of life. Had that been their mistake, or had it gone wrong for some other reason?

Irina had risen above the desert of suffering around her—perhaps because of her chosen profession—but she had also never known a time when love and desire had thrived in beauty, as he had. A young girl needed passion; he could not give it to her until life flooded sunshine in to melt the ice inside him. So was it not inevitable that she should find herself caught up in a strong physical attraction for a man she saw day after day? No one would deny Anderson was a strong, healthy male animal, whose very inaccessibility could appeal to a girl of Irina's temperament. That air of arrogant independence would present an irresistible challenge to someone whose instinct was to comfort and cosset.

Sasha was prepared to accept hero-worship for the man from his wife, but Anderson's feelings were another matter. Inexperienced with women, virile and aggressive, pushed to his limits with no chance for relaxation day or night, a man of his age could be reckless enough to do anything and to hell with the consequences. Sasha knew; he had been a young Lothario himself. The sooner the bridge was up and the fellow back with his own people, the better!

"Sasha, give me your attention, if you please."

He came out of his thoughts to see Irina watching him with a frown on her face. He tried to smile. "*Izvini* . . . forgive me, my dear. It is good to feel rested once more. How long have I been in that strange land between night and day?"

"Some while," she replied with the aggravating vagueness of a nurse. "Do you feel any pain in your leg?"

He considered for a moment. "I cannot even feel my leg."

"You will, as soon as you try to move it," was the brief comment. "This time, you will not try to get up until I say that you may. Is that understood?"

"Understanding does not mean I shall obey," he said with gentle teasing.

"Then I shall give instructions for you to be tied to the bed. Do you not understand that I mean what I say? There was poisoning and great swelling. It was necessary to cut open your thigh once more, and I am not a surgeon. The poison is going, but the wound is going to take longer to heal now. It is essential that you stay there, or the consequences could be very serious indeed."

He grew aware that she was curiously tense. His attempt at light banter had been met with over-heavy drama over his condition. There was no chance that he would attempt to get up yet. He had already tried moving his leg and regretted it. Why was she behaving with such intensity?

"Is something wrong?" he asked quickly. "The bridge?"

"The bridge will be finished by the end of today."

His pulse leapt. At last! "And Anderson will take the engine across tomorrow? I *will* be there when he does it. Valodya can bring one of the horses here, and I shall ride down to the river."

"Paul wished to speak to you on that subject. He has asked that I tell him when he can do so." Already she was walking past him, as if unwilling to hear anything else he might have to say. "I shall fetch him now."

"What has it to do with . . . ?" But she had gone.

He lay puzzling over something he sensed rather than suspected. She was afraid. For whom? Was she telling him the truth about his leg? Even in that military hospital when men lay dying, nurses always kept their light, cheerful optimism when they spoke to their patients. They never let the truth show through. What had happened to make her first and foremost a woman and secondly a nurse?

His heartbeat quickened. Had he mistaken her feelings for the English Captain? Was it not merely hero-worship but a deep attachment that had led her to already surrender to him? Was she afraid for his safety when he took the engine across the bridge . . . afraid it would plunge into the river below, taking him with it? Yes, definitely, her strange behaviour was in some way connected with Paul Anderson.

Then, he heard them approaching, their words carrying on the still air.

"I'll see him alone. You wait here."

"No. I took the responsibility. I should be there to explain why."

"Just do as I say."

"He is under my care."

"And you are under my command. Wait here!"

There was a short pause, then Irina spoke again. "Paul, please, if he should . . ."

"You worry too much," came the soft interruption. "He is a man, not a child."

Next minute the flaps were pushed open, and Anderson bent his head beneath the canvas to enter. He looked hot, dirty, and exhausted. His shirt was smeared with marks, open almost to the waist, and drenched with sweat. One could almost imagine him to be one of the peasant-soldiers. On his freckled face was one of his most obstinate expressions.

"How are you, Colonel?"

Sasha looked at him with distaste. "A great deal cleaner and more comfortable than you appear to be. Have you been cleaning the engine, by any chance?"

"No." Paul ignored the sarcasm. "I have been laying track across the bridge."

"Do you mean that literally, Captain?"

"Yes."

"You have been . . . ? What are you saying—that you have been laying track with your own hands?"

"I've done it before. In an emergency, it's a case of everyone on the job."

Now Sasha knew there was something wrong, and it had nothing to do with youthful affections. The Englishman was growing more arrogant with every clipped sentence he uttered. Sasha knew Anderson in that mood. It meant he was determined to have his own way against all opposition. Sasha struggled to raise himself but only managed to get to one elbow.

"An emergency? What has been happening, Captain?"

The Englishman wiped his brow across with his forearm. "Quite a lot. You have been out since yesterday morning. By sundown today, the bridge will be complete. I shall take the engine across as soon as it gets light again. The line can then be declared open!" He took a deep breath. "I have been laying track and so have Stevens and Yagutov. There are only six of your men here, at present, so I needed all the help I could get."

"*Six* of my men?" Sasha asked, a premonition of disaster softening his voice.

"The rest of your troops, under your brother's command, went south yesterday afternoon in answer to a signal from Lake Onega. There is a company of Red troops in the vicinity of our last campsite, by the lake. They have gone to intercept and attack."

If the Englishman had drawn his revolver and clubbed him around the head, Sasha would not have felt more dazed and shattered. The tent seemed to close in on him. The words rang in his head and exploded in his ears. Somewhere in the region of his chest, the pain of all the past few years was gathering once more.

"How dare you? How *dare* you? My men. *My* men! How dare you send them into battle on your own authority? *They are my men!*" He roared the last sentence with the bitterness of several months behind it.

"When the Colonel is unable to command, they are the Lieutenant's men."

Anderson's calm manner sent Sasha's rage soaring to the topmost heights. "Who are you to say whose men they are? You are out of this war. You British have walked out on us. All you have ever done is play trains."

"I am still playing trains," was the cold answer. "*I* have not taken your men. When the signal came through, you were under sedation and unable to be consulted. Time was paramount. Your second-in-command had to take over. I merely suggested that six men remain to finish the essential work on the bridge."

Despair, impotence, deep hatred for the man who had all the way along fought to command the group filled Sasha with the need to destroy him.

"The men who spat on me in the trenches did so for what they were led to believe was the good of Russia. You do it for your own twisted need for superiority. Contempt for my people has ruled you since you arrived in this country—contempt and your own ambitions. For that, you have spat on me at every opportunity. Do you think I cannot see that you did this deliberately to prevent what you know I have waited and prayed for? You made no attempt to present me with the signal that concerned my men . . . and my men only. You ignored my rank and sent those soldiers to battle with the deliberate intention of denying my command. You are self-centered, arrogant, base and completely dishonourable."

There was a flurry, and Irina was there standing beside the Englishman, her face white and wild.

"No, Sasha, I did it. They would have told you, but I knew and they knew that you would go if they did. It would have killed you. A doctor in a hospital would never have given permission. I, as your nurse, would not give it either."

He saw it all then, and it nearly broke him. "So it *has* come to that! You defend your lover."

"Don't speak to her like that," snapped Anderson. "And apologise for what you have just said."

"Do you deny that you are her lover?" Sasha demanded contemptuously.

"If I were, don't you think it would have been to our advantage to let you go?" was the furious reply. "You have just heard her say it would have killed you."

Sasha had reached the end. They stood like a pair of conspirators, young, strong, and in harmony. They had robbed him of all he now lived for. Fixing his eyes on the girl who stood beside the tall, dishevelled foreigner, he almost choked.

"He has never made any secret of his emnity. You have hidden yours until now. I shall never forgive you for this."

S i x t e e n

That night it was extremely cold. Paul and Sapper Stevens took turns sitting beside the field telegraph in case a message came through concerning the Reds down by the lake. But Paul had no sleep when he lay down in the straw and pulled the blankets over for warmth. The dim light of one lamp on the table threw shadows in the truck, gilding the sides of the wooden boxes and glinting dully on the tools of his trade. With the door almost fully pulled across to keep out the cold, Paul found himself saying again and again in his head those Russian words stencilled on the inside of it. They meant nothing to him; he did not even know how to pronounce words containing unrecognisable characters. There had been no time to devote to learning a strange and difficult language, no time to grow to understand those people around him with a culture so varied and exotic it would take years to study them.

The Russian soldiers with their switchback enthusiasms were at least consistent in that they put their entire warmth into whatever they felt at one particular moment. A man was either distrusted or admired by them—never treated with indifference. Paul always knew where he stood with them and knew now how to deal with each attitude.

The Swarovskys were different. He had never associated so closely with aristocrats before and was reasonably certain that, in normal times, the son of a railway wheelwright would never have been allowed even to press his nose against the windows of one of their great houses. In his own corps, of course, there were officers from noble families, but the trenches of France were as levelling as a Russian forest, and he had learnt what few social graces he possessed over mess tins in rat-ridden depths of a front-line Officers' Mess.

That night he was acutely conscious of life as it must be when times were normal. He had always been aware at Oakwood, that school to which he had been sent at great sacrifice to his parents, that he was a cockerel amongst pheasants. His fortunate prowess at sports had bridged the gap and made him popular with his fellows, some of their gilding rubbing off on him along the way, giving him a surface appearance of a gentleman. Today, Swarovsky showed him he was not.

Going straight from Oakwood into the army had protected him from the difficulties of class prejudice prevalent in pre-war Britain. His six months in the ranks had been easy because his fellow soldiers had been just like the lads in his street, and when they made him an officer, he had slipped effortlessly into the role due to those years at an expensive private school. But a velvet coat does not make a man a duke, and his whole background was solidly in a setting of red brick terraced houses. Alexander Ivanovich Swarovsky had pushed him back there that morning. Even in bed, exhausted by fever, the Russian had had a dignity that had shown up Paul's blunt announcement of a *fait accompli* as the action of a peasant.

Human pride was a strong force, and they were both men who

possessed it in abundance. Paul's part in the conspiracy had left the Russian with his pride in shreds. His conduct was all the more blameworthy since the British were no longer taking offensive action in the war. Who was he, as Swarovsky had said, to order the movement of Russian troops? Of no use to keep saying it was done in the name of expedience and humanity. The man should have been allowed to make his own decision. It was his life, after all.

As if that were not enough to highlight the Englishman's own lack of noble instincts, Paul had been charged with stealing the man's wife from under his nose. Yet, in a curious, twisted way it was almost the fact of the accusation *not* being true that somehow belittled him. Olga had said as much not long ago, and standing there beside Irina today, he had been aware of it once more.

People like the Swarovskys lived by their own rules, which often had a topsy-turvy standard of values compared with the bourgeoisie, of which Paul was one. In that terrace of red brick houses lived people of solid worth. They got drunk on Saturday nights, but gave their children a hiding if they so much as sneaked a lollipop from the local sweet-shop when the owner was looking the other way; they laid down the law about class distinction, yet stood in their Sunday best lining the streets when persons of rank and position passed in their cars, and cheered them; they were honest and hardworking—they had to be to keep their jobs. They had strict notions of behaviour. Nobody borrowed anything without returning it; they turned out in force to help a sick neighbour; and their god was respectability. Daughters were brought up to be virgins until they married; sons were lectured on not seducing "good" girls. If one such girl broke the rule, she was labelled "no good," and her shame was shared by her parents. If a lad put a "good" girl in the family way, he married her immediately, and the couple suffered the cold shoulder until gossip died down. Paul had been raised on these strict principles, the message about never abusing a decent girl having been drummed into his head by his father from the age of puberty.

In this Russian forest, Paul had come across three women of bewildering complexity. The great Zapalova had had lovers by the dozen and spoke of them with unbelievable frankness. Two men of a noble Russian family openly acknowledged that she had also been their mistress—spoke of it before a wife and sister. Olga, a girl who had spent all her life until just over a year ago in complete protection and luxury, abandoned herself quite without shame to her sexual longings and would willingly have seduced Paul weeks ago if she had found a way.

When Paul thought of Irina, he knew she was the greatest puzzle of all. From the start she had beckoned him on, then held him at arm's length. He never knew if she was nurse or wife to Swarovsky; she was a young, innocent girl one minute, a woman of wisdom the next. Time and again she had vowed her eternal love, yet managed to retain an air that suggested she was simply his for a day.

His righteous denial of being her lover had seemed to rebound on him. It had emphasised his "middle-class morality." It had made him a bourgeois prig compared with the lofty, rakish Swarovskys, had suggested that he was a pathetic figure of a man who yearned after a woman and had not enough red-blooded masculinity to take her. Swarovsky had dismissed Paul as a fool who played trains. Would the Russian have respected him as a man if Paul *had* seduced his wife?

There was a wide gulf of upbringing and beliefs between himself and the Russians. Valodya was different, but even as he thought of the young Russian's friendship, Paul knew it was really due to the meeting of two "types" created by war. Take away the last four years, and he would be left a working-class upstart trying to find a niche in society while Valodya would be a wealthy playboy gracing the salons of princes. Coming face-to-face, they would have nothing in common, and little respect for each other. We would both have been the loser for it, he thought, remembering Valodya's face with its audacious smile as the young officer had walked tightrope fashion across a spar over the raging river.

A movement in the truck made Paul turn his head. Sapper Stevens was looking at him, long face yellowed by the lamp, like a Halloween mask.

"You've been lying there just over an hour and haven't once closed your eyes, sir," Stevens accused.

Paul smiled faintly, "Big day tomorrow, Stevens. If that bridge falls down, we shall have to start all over again."

"Oh, yes, sir," Stevens said in a tone that suggested it was as likely as tigers in Hyde Park. "What would you say to a cup of tea?"

"I'd not say anything to it; I'd drink it very gratefully."

"Right-o, sir. I'll just nip and make a pot. Can you keep an ear open for this machine for a bit?"

Paul nodded. "I'm not planning on going anywhere. Close the door behind you when you go. It's damn cold in here."

When Stevens returned with the tea, Paul sat up and leant against some boxes while he drank it. There was something familiar about the dim lamplight, boxes of ammunition, and isolation with just one other man that encouraged confession.

"I reported Corporal Banks's death as an accident, Stevens."

"Oh, yes, sir?" It was said with apparent nonchalant interest.

"He fell into the river whilst working on the bridge."

"Well . . . it was very rough that night, sir."

"Yes . . . yes, it was."

"I'm glad, sir. I mean, there wasn't any use causing a rumpus un-necessary, if you see what I mean. It isn't as if we was sure he did it all."

Paul's head turned sharply. "How do you mean?"

Stevens's face looked even more weird in the yellow light as he screwed it up. "I still can't see him setting out to kill people one after the other—especially you, sir."

"He tried to at the bridge." It was harsh with irritation.

"Ah, he *was* kind of mad that night, sir. I saw it for myself. But those other things you mentioned, well, he would have to be mad all the time . . . and that he wasn't, I'd stake my life on it."

Letting out a long sigh, Paul said, "Yes, so would I have done. But it is an indisputable fact that all such activity has stopped since that night."

The soldier seemed unconvinced for a moment, then slowly nodded. "It just goes to show how strange life is!"

Silence hung between them for a while as they drank their tea, then Stevens asked, "How much longer before we go home, d'you reckon, sir?"

"Eh? Oh, I suppose before winter really sets in," Paul replied, shaken by the import of what he was saying. *A month. So soon?*

"It'll be good to see Blighty again, sir."

Paul nodded slowly. "Yes, Stevens . . . I suppose it will."

Dawn brought a morning of brilliant, chill clarity that put a beauty over that site no one had ever liked overmuch. The sky was high and coldly blue, and the pines stood unruffled by a breeze, tall, mysterious, hiding the secrets of an arctic forest within their crowding midst. The air was invigorating, filling the lungs with health. Sound travelled clearly for great distances, making those gathered near the bridge into crashing, noisy intruders on a quiet backroad of nature.

Paul ate a quick breakfast alone in the supply-truck. He had things on his mind and had no intention of socialising with a girl who wanted *him* for her breakfast and a ballerina who was making a dramatic display of anxiety over her absent young lover.

When he had finished his meal, he walked briskly alongside the track to where Yagutov was polishing the engine with cheery excitement. Paul grinned as he came up to the engine driver.

"Make sure she's spotless, Yagutov. I'm not driving a dirty engine across my nice clean bridge."

The Russian laughed. "She always clean. Today she have excite. Too long she stand here not do anything."

"Well, this is her big moment. The first engine to cross the bridge. I think she should wear a ribbon to signify the occasion."

Yagutov climbed down beside Paul and walked to the front to point. "She dress already."

There across the front of the engine was an elaborate wreath of pine branches. Paul laughed and clapped the engine-driver on the shoulder.

"Splendid. I'll make a quick walk to the other bank just to check that everything is all right, then you can give me a lesson or two on driving this engine. The last time I took the footplate was some while back and on a vastly different lady to this one."

The inspection was more than "a quick walk to the other bank." He would be risking his life and their sole means of transport very shortly, and deep in the back of Paul's mind was the conversation he had had with Stevens last night. He did, in fact, examine very thoroughly every area of the structure that lent itself to sabotage, and he even climbed over from bank to bank on the trusses beneath, looking for any signs that all was not as it should be. All through the inspection he murmured to himself that he was being foolish and imaginative, but he continued until he had covered every possibility.

When he found nothing, he berated himself further. All he had done was suggest to those watching that he had doubts over his own competence. On the contrary, his faith in his skill told him the bridge was sound and would bear the weight of any number of trains. But his faith did not prevent a tingle of excitement bordering on apprehension gripping his stomach as he walked back to the engine, where Yagutov was getting up steam. There would be a feeling of supreme anticipation as that engine inched over the bridge.

In his comical English, Yagutov explained the idiosyncrasies of his beloved charge, and Paul went over the details several times to make certain he had them right. So absorbed was he, so full of that tingling excitement, he declared himself ready to go and clean forgot his promise to let the ladies know when the moment had come.

"Right. Here goes!" he exclaimed, holding out his hand to Yagutov.

The Russian pumped his hand up and down. "You clevers! This bridge even good enough for she to cross. That great compliment."

"I know," laughed Paul, watching him climb to the ground. "Why don't you walk across and ride back on her?"

Yagutov nodded, a grin spreading across from ear to ear. "It safers coming back."

The next few moments took all Paul's attention as he unwound the brake and set the engine very slowly forward. It was exhilarating to be on the move after all those days trapped at the end of a broken line. From up on the footplate, the bridge looked the most wonderful sight he had ever seen, as it stretched out across the silvery river sparkling in the early sunshine. It was *his* bridge. A feeling akin to mastery of the world filled his breast until he thought it would burst—a feeling so supreme a man would surely experience it only rarely in his lifetime.

He had reached the start of the new track now, and a moment later, the wheels ran onto the approach to the bridge. Paul hung out from the cabin to watch as the riverbank slowly dropped away and the engine began to roll forward over the water. He was on the bridge proper now; the new wood began to creak and crack beneath the weight. In that clear stillness, it sounded as if the whole structure was breaking apart below the surface. He knew it was not. So he took the engine on out to the accompaniment of suitable sounds—the slow belching puff of smoke, the crack and groan of wood, the hiss of steam, the rushing babble of the river.

By the time he reached the centre of the bridge, he was drenched in sweat and punch-drunk with triumph. It was the greatest achievement in the world. Bells should be ringing and guns firing. White doves should be released by the hundreds. He wanted to throw back his head and laugh so that the sound echoed throughout the forest. On and on across the river puffed the engine, declaring success with little clouds of smoke that hung in the blue above him. He had flung open the Murmansk line—he alone!

When the engine ran off the bridge at the far end, Paul was still in that euphoria that made him king of the world. He wanted to go on up that track that had stretched so tauntingly inaccessible for so long. But he brought the engine to a halt fifty yards farther on, returning to normal only slowly as he leant against the side of the cab and gazed at the sky in pure elation.

He might have stayed there a very long time if he had not been jerked back to awareness by a shout and running feet. Then Yagutov bounded onto the footplate, clapping him on the back and pumping his hand up and down excitedly.

"You great man. She great engine. This great bridge. All is happys now."

"Yes. All is happys now," echoed Paul through his laughter. "She great engine, sure enough." He flung out a hand. "There you are. Take her back and enjoy every minute of it."

Yagutov could hardly believe him. "You mean I have her to myself?"

"Yes. I'm going to walk over and watch her as she goes past. It's something I couldn't do just now." He jumped down and called over his shoulder, "You can take her faster now . . . but don't get carried away and crash into the trucks at the camp. We still need them."

The Russian looked injured. "I carefuls, Captain. You know I keep she safe. No bumpings."

"Good." Paul grinned and walked off with a wave of his hand.

As he stepped onto the bridge, he heard the engine begin to puff in the distance. He wanted to get to the middle so that he could turn and watch it approach, then pass. Quickening his step, he stepped over the rail to walk along the broad width that ran alongside the track on both sides.

But Yagutov was bringing the engine faster than he expected, and a quick glance over his shoulder showed him he would not reach the centre before it passed him. He grinned to himself. Poor Yagutov had been leading a frustrated existence these past few weeks. An engine—a whole train— that had nowhere to go was a heartbreaking prospect for a man with such love of steam engines. Now the engine-driver's enthusiasm was carrying him away.

The wooden planking beneath Paul's feet began to shudder and tremble as the engine advanced, and the noisy hiss of escaping steam joined with the regular puffing to echo in the surrounding trees. It was like music to Paul's ears, and he felt the excitement begin to rise again as he turned to watch the engine's approach. Then his heart stilled, raced, and stilled again. The round, black smokebox was no more than a few yards away, advancing quickly, and Yagutov, no longer the smiling clown, was leaning from the cab, brandishing the long-handled shovel used to feed fuel to the fire.

There was no time to think, only react instinctively to sudden danger. He began to run like a madman, conscious only that the slightest deviation would have him under the train or in the river. With no real sense of surprise, he knew Yagutov was out to kill him, knew the identity of the true saboteur and traitor. Drastic revelation did away with such emotions as surprise and clarified a man's thoughts amazingly quickly.

As he raced along that no-man's land between the iron rail and a fifteen-foot drop to the deepest part of the river, something allowed him to keep his balance and footing until he realised he could not win. The steam was now swirling around his legs, and the buffers were already alongside him as he ran. The noise of the throaty puffs thumped his eardrums along with the pumping of his heart.

He threw a desperate glance behind him as the sun was momentarily blocked out by the great black engine, and his balance wavered. Yagutov, directly above him now, leant from the cab and brought the shovel crashing down. Paul staggered, fought to stay on the bridge, then fell backward into space as something thumped against the side of his head, putting the blackness and roar of fifty engines into it.

The roar closed right over his head and echoed all around him as he started to spin and tumble out of control. It had grown icy cold, and his body was unbearably heavy. He could not breathe. His lungs were bursting, and he was being pounded unmercifully as he was thrown against rocks. Everything began to grow brilliant, shimmering with diamonds. Then he was gasping in great breaths of air as he saw trees flashing past through a liquid blur. He was still spinning and swinging out of control, and the roaring was louder now. Even so, his arms began to move instinctively, and his legs kicked in rhythm until he was once more in control of his body.

Still acting more with instinct than with conscious action, he fought against the pull of the water with strong overarm strokes. But it was exhausting, gruelling work. He could not co-ordinate thoughts and actions; part of him was urging surrender to welcome oblivion. But his natural talent was too strong to bow to surrender, and after what seemed like a lifetime's struggle, there was a surface beneath his feet that set him clambering forward in a progression of slow, weary heaves as he dug his fingers into the earth of the riverbank.

With dry land beneath him once more, recollection came racing back. Chest heaving, fighting for breath, he got unsteadily to his feet and looked back toward the bridge. The engine was nowhere in sight.

Like a madman he attacked the bank, scrambling and slipping in his sodden clothes as he mounted the steep slope. There was no doubt what Yagutov intended to do next . . . and Swarovsky was helpless in bed. The women would be next, then any of those six Russians who refused to go over to his side. They would all be completely unprepared. The soldiers had been watching from their bivouac on the other side of the bridge, which meant they would not have seen the attack on him. Completely unsuspecting, as he had been, none of them would stand a chance.

He reached the top of the bank and headed off through the trees, trying to cut a corner that would bring him to the tents before Yagutov. He had no idea how much time had passed, and his sense of direction was a little vague as he raced over the forest floor, dodging trees and obstacles. Wild thoughts flew through his brain. The train had stopped—there was no longer the sound of puffing in the still air. Would Yagutov round up the soldiers first, to support his attack on their colonel? No, he would go straight to murder their commander, as an extra incentive to gaining their reversed loyalty. Then Paul's battered brain fixed on something else. In Swarovsky's tent was Irina! Surely Stevens would see Yagutov, surely *someone* would see him and raise the alarm? Dear God, let him be in time!

Bursting into the open twenty yards from the tents, Paul skidded on the loose ballast beside the track and nearly fell. As he raced on toward the tent occupied by the Russian and his wife, he saw Yagutov in the act of entering. Throwing himself forward with superhuman effort, he was still more than six yards from the tent when two shots rang out.

Blind with despair and revenge, he crashed through the opening into the tent, ready to choke the man to death with his bare hands, then swung round in a frantic turn to avoid colliding with Irina, who was standing at the end of the bed staring down at Yagutov's body by her feet. Swarovsky was sitting up in the bed with a revolver in his hand.

Paul stood reeling, a confused picture in his head. In those first seconds, he took in the blood-splattered body with a knife lying beside it, the Colonel lowering his pistol, an expression of cold calculation on his face, then, finally, Irina looking at him with eyes so large and dark they looked black in her white face—Irina miraculously alive.

"I thought you were . . . I saw him do it. You disappeared under the water," she said in agonised tones. *"I thought you were dead."*

Dear heaven, he had thought *her* dead! It was all too much. He went a little crazy with relief. "I won a watch at school for swimming, you know," he said fatuously.

His words seemed to upset her, for some reason. She turned away to the corner of the tent and stood with her head back, gripping and re-gripping the edge of the table with hands that were shaking.

But Paul's attention was taken by Swarovsky, who said calmly, "I take it the bridge proved to be perfectly sound?"

"Yes. The line is again open," Paul replied equally calmly, then became aware, when he put his hand up to wipe it away, that the trickle running down his cheek was not water.

"I seem to be bleeding rather a lot," he commented to Irina's back. "Do you think you could put a dressing on it?"

She swung round, still white and wild looking. Her gaze swung from the man setting a pistol down on the blankets to the other standing panting while water ran from his hair and clothes onto the ground around him. Then she gave a faint moan, put her hand to her mouth, and rushed from the tent.

When the truth stared them in the face, it seemed strange to everyone that the culprit could have remained hidden so long: perhaps, they thought, the reason was that Yagutov had held that unique position of being Russian, yet no part of the force commanded by Sasha; of being answerable to Paul, yet neither soldier nor navvy; of being indispensable to the group, yet forgotten for long stretches of time when the engine stood still. Friendly, genial, willing, certainly devoted to his engine, the man had just been Yagutov, the engine-driver. He wore no uniform, therefore took no sides—so they had all thought.

How could they have all been so blind? It was a well-known fact that railway workers were amongst the most passionate advocates of "power to the workers," and Yagutov had had access to the supply-truck where the explosives were kept, as well as a selection of tools and the know-how of simple engineering. Putting all the facts together, it left no one in any doubt that Yagutov had been the sole dedicated Bolshevik in the company. It was easy now to see how he had picked off those in command and most loyal to the old regime, at the same time delaying or attempting to wreck the work they were doing.

The explosion in the cutting should have killed both officers along with the N.C.O.s, but although it was only partially successful in that respect, work was held up while Paul recovered from his injuries, and the Russian soldiers had only been prevented from marching off behind their colonel through the refusal of Irina to leave a wounded man with no medical help. And Yagutov would have had no difficulty in sawing through the shackle pin on the pulley so that the section broke away. He had probably hoped for the death or injury of as many as possible.

It did not take much intelligence to work out why all sabotage had ceased in recent weeks—all, with the exception of the murder of Corporal Nensky. With the arrival of the train bringing supplies and two surprise passengers from Lake Onega had also come the news that the Allies were pulling out and the Reds advancing. The news had been kept from Sasha's men, but a fellow-Bolshevik driving that train would certainly have passed the facts on to his comrade who was working with the Whites. From then on, Yagutov would consider it essential to let the work go ahead as quickly as possible, for the Bolshevik armies would need the line to Murmansk open when they swept through North Russia. He then confined his efforts to the killing of Nensky and the spreading of the wolf threat to sow distrust amongst the soldiers.

When the bridge was complete, it was time to strike his final blow. If Paul had not seen that shovel at the last minute, if he had not been a superb swimmer, if Irina had not been watching from that side of the forest and run to warn her husband, they would most probably all be dead and the train on its way south to link up with the Reds Valodya had gone to intercept. Yagutov had been clever, but fortune had run out on him.

As for Corporal Banks, it seemed likely that Stevens's description that he had "gone sort of mad" that night had been true. After four years of war in France, the isolation in a forest with men who represented very dramatically all he had heard from his father since childhood must have proved too much for him. They had all been subjected to severe stress on this job, and each had reacted according to his own personality. Was it surprising that a little man with seemingly unshakeable command of himself should go a little berserk in the heart of a violent, savage storm? No, it was not surprising to anyone who had lived through the horrors with him.

In the man who had pushed him to his death, this realisation aroused mixed reactions. Paul was overwhelmingly thankful he had not made any charges against Banks in his report of the man's death, but he was saddened to think he had not recognised Banks's mental condition and arranged for him to go back to England before he broke up. He should have been helped not kicked from a bridge to drown. It did not make it any easier for Paul to remember that men had been shot by their officers when they had gone berserk in the midst of battle. In a case of one life against dozens, there was only one decision to make. But the man forced to make it had a conscience that continued to bother him long after danger had gone.

Sasha's conscience was quite untroubled. He had fired at Yagutov the minute he had appeared in that tent and would have gone on firing with savage satisfaction if the man had not fallen to the ground out of sight. That the traitor had, after all, been Russian did not sadden him. There were thousands who now were, and Yagutov had not been one of his own men. But it had made shooting him more satisfying. It gave Sasha a triumphant pleasure to show any man who had turned against Tsar and country what such treachery would earn him . . . and each of those shots had been fired in the name of his sister Ekaterina. Denied the opportunity to go south with Valodya, he had killed *one* of the filthy creatures who thought they could rule Russia.

But if the two men had their separate, private responses to what had happened at first light that morning, Irina was more greatly affected than either of them.

The shock of seeing Paul apparently murdered as she watched had had to be subjugated beneath the urgent need to warn Sasha. When he had asked for his revolver and shot the engine-driver before her eyes, she had still managed to hold down the demons of hysteria rising inside her. Then Paul had crashed into the tent, dripping water with blood running down one side of his face, and he had begun telling her about a watch he had won at school. As if that had not smacked of madness, he had then begun to discuss with Sasha, in matter-of-fact tones, the test on the bridge that had re-opened the line to Murmansk, just as if it were an ordinary conversation. Had they not understood? There was a blood-covered body at her feet . . . and she had thought Paul was *dead*.

She had run from the tent and had not been back since. Unaware of where she was going, she had headed over the bridge and up the railway track that led to Murmansk. There she had finally broken down, there where she was alone and betraying herself to no one. Paul had told her she was a girl of not yet twenty-two who was entitled to cry. But it was as a woman deep in an emotional web that she sobbed that morning, and her thoughts were wild and irrational.

She wanted, more than anything, to wear a camisole and drawers of silk adorned with ribbons. She wanted a pale *crêpe de Chine* dress and a matching hat with a wide, dipping brim trimmed with winter roses. She wanted furs—soft, creamy furs that would give her a semblance of fragility—and gloves of the finest suede. She wanted a ballgown that hung off her shoulders and swept out behind her in a great tumble of heavy satin. She wanted presents, baskets of flowers, and words of passion. She wanted to run laughing across meadows to be pulled into strong arms that would lower her tenderly into the wild flowers. She wanted to see dark brown eyes full of wild, exultant desire for her. She wanted to tease and tantalise. She wanted . . . oh, she wanted to forget blood, blood, *blood!*

Irina, the woman, must be allowed her turn. She must be allowed to put on airs, like Lyudmilla, and pout and plea with all the men; she must be allowed to rant and rage like Olga and press her body against Paul until he could stand no more. Why should not the new Irina demand first bath in the barrel or scream with rage over the soap? Why should she not fling her clothes at Sasha and cry that Yukov had ruined them in river water? Why could not Irina sit with her feet up while others went to mop up men's blood and stitch their torn flesh together? Why could she not give herself body and soul to Paul, as she was desperate to do? *Why, when she loved him beyond containment, was she having to question herself this way?*

It was well into afternoon when she re-crossed the bridge and began walking back alongside the track toward the tents. As she passed the supply-truck, her name was called, and Paul jumped to the ground beside her. His face was clouded with worry, and if there was not exactly "wild, exultant desire" in his brown eyes, there was certainly concern born of love burning there.

"Where have you been?" he demanded angrily, so angrily he nearly choked over the words, "I have been combing the forest for you."

There was a dressing on the side of his head, fixed so carelessly that the gauze was half hanging off.

"You have not put that on properly," she told him tonelessly.

"Damn the dressing!" he swore. "I've been nearly out of my mind with worry. Where have you been?"

"Over the river," she told him fiercely.

"Over the . . . What have you been doing all this time, for God's sake?"

"Do not speak to me like that! I do not have to account to you for everything I do."

He looked nonplussed and, realising they were within earshot of the troops, took her arm and led her across to the edge of the trees, where they were more private. There he faced her, running his hand through his hair in an awkward gesture of appeasement.

"I was only shouting because I was so relieved to see you safe and unharmed. You have been gone half a day," he told her, the muscle in his jaw working to betray his intensity. "*Half a day!* Anything could have happened to you."

"I am surprised that you even noticed."

He grew still and wary. "Are you going to tell me what I have done wrong?"

"You see, you do not even *know* what you have done," she cried, backing away from him. Why had he been there just as she passed? It was impossible not to see how weary and beaten he looked, impossible not to see the lines of fatigue on his face . . . and that crooked dressing. Yet it was that silly, stupid piece of gauze hanging askew that sparked her temper further. "You stand there asking me what you have done and have no idea what it is!"

He studied her face a moment. "Why did you run away this morning? Is it anything to do with that?"

"Anything to do with . . . *Paul, I thought you were dead,*" she cried passionately. "Don't you understand?"

"When I heard those shots, I thought *you* were dead," he told her tautly.

The cry within her grew. "And all you did was tell me about a watch you won at school!"

He looked bewildered. "A watch? I don't remember exactly what I said. I mean, those first few moments were very confused. Is that all that has upset you—something about a watch?"

She backed away even farther as the woman inside Irina remembered all those things she wanted. "No, Paul, it is not something about a watch. It is something about life and death, loving and living. Something about two men who fight like bitter enemies over a woman one day, then ignore her and pretend it never happened the next day."

He frowned, plainly upset by what she was saying. "Go on. You will have to explain to me what that means."

"Yes, I'll explain," she said with some force. "It will plainly never occur to you, otherwise. You see, I was foolish enough to want to see your great moment of achievement and share, even in secret, the culmination of your weeks of work. But from my hiding place in the forest, I saw you struck down and swallowed up by the river. Even through my grief at losing you, I knew Sasha was to be next, then the rest of us . . . so I left you for dead and ran to warn him. I had only just handed him his gun when that man came in. I saw the bullets part his flesh and the blood begin to flow. I saw his expression change from hatred to anguish before he dropped to the floor. Just then, you hurtled in like a living ghost, a fantasy conjured by my love that could not bear to let you go."

"I expected to see you and him lying dead," Paul protested harshly.

"One would not have thought so," she said with bitterness. "You spoke about the watch you had won for swimming, and then . . ." She could hardly get the words out. ". . . then you and Sasha began to talk about the bridge as if I were not there. It was as if all that had been said between you the day before was unimportant."

He moved toward her, his jaw still working. "In time of war, things have to be put aside."

"Yes, I see that *I* had to be put aside," she cried. "Sasha was right. All you think of is being an engineer."

"Irina!" He tried to take hold of her, but she avoided him. "I . . . men don't go around giving emotional displays."

"You do not," she accused quickly.

He lost his temper completely. "All right, what *should* I have done, according to you? I was so bloody thankful you were still alive I had to cover it by talking about the first thing that came into my head. I couldn't have pulled you into my arms right there in front of him, could I?"

"Why not? You stood there chatting to him about your stupid bridge as if he had never said those things yesterday."

"That bridge is vital to our safety and to the war. Personal quarrels have to be put aside."

"And I am one of them?"

He looked at her with eyes full of unhappiness. "You are all of them, you know that."

It shook her and made her angrier than ever. "So I have to be put aside for those things that are of the utmost importance? I am there when you have time and wish to be consoled, but when a bridge has been built, everything else must take second place."

He was unused to female adversaries, and she found an emotion verging on savage delight in seeing that his inexperience with women left him vulnerable to hurt from extreme feminine behaviour. As she watched, he struggled to find a way to deal with a challenge he could not meet with masculine aggression, for once.

"Irina, please, you are being irrational," he said finally.

"No, Paul, I am being a *woman*," she flung at him passionately. "I am, you know, quite as much as Olga or that vain creature who gathers men as others gather wild flowers. I am not simply a nurse in spotless uniform, ready with a bandage and soothing hand whenever it is needed."

"Then why the hell do you always act like one?" he demanded, suddenly as blazingly angry as she.

It was as if he had hit her. It hurt, and she retaliated. "He accused you of being my lover. Is that why you are not—because you do not recognise a woman when you see one?"

He stood looking at her, full of some kind of strange humiliation she did not understand. It was there in his eyes, in the very toughness of his physique, in the huskiness filling his voice as he said, "You know why I am not."

"No," she persisted cruelly. "If I knew, I would not ask. Tell me!"

Through tight lips, he said, "You are another man's wife."

"And your English manners and standards dictate . . ."

"Stop it," he ordered harshly. "You are behaving like Olga. I can't believe you have ever wanted me to drag you into the forest and force your surrender."

Too far now to stop, she snapped, "Is that what Olga wants?"

"Yes . . . if you must know."

"Then why have you never done it?" she cried. "*She* is not another man's wife."

He seemed almost to gasp, and her anger evaporated fast as she realised she was saying unforgivable things to a sensitive and exhausted man. What interpretation could he put upon her taunt?

"Paul, I did not mean that," she whispered in stricken tones. "I have been too angry and too frightened today, that is all."

That he remained where he was, cold and disillusioned, helped her to say what should have been said in calm, competent, nurse-like manner without the emotional flare-up.

"I have reached a decision this afternoon. Sasha has said he will never forgive me for keeping him here when he would rather have gone away from me to certain death. Whatever love we once had was finally destroyed by that. But my love for you is impossible here and so uncertain in the future—if we have a future. You are wrong. There have been times when I longed for you to take me into the forest and bring about my surrender. But that was my heart talking and not my head. Today, I have thought about my own feelings, for once, and decided I cannot be anything to any man while we are here. From now, I am just the nurse, as I was in the field hospital. I will soothe any man's hurts with my hands but not with my heart. I cannot bear it anymore, Pavlik," she whispered finally.

He looked even closer to complete exhaustion, and she only just caught what he said as he began to move away.

"You won't have to bear much more. I signalled Lake Onega just now. They will be sending a train up within the next three days, and I have asked that it should stop at the siding to pick up three women. You'll be in Murmansk by the end of the week."

She was left standing at the edge of the forest to make what she wished of that information.

The celebration that had been planned for the day the bridge was completed did not take place. The six soldiers drank their double ration given them by Paul and grew maudlin instead of merry. They missed their fellows and had hoped they might be back by that evening. The few songs they sang were mournful, and without Valodya's accordian music to encourage them, they soon abandoned singing altogether to sit moodily alongside the train staring into the darkness, listening to the echoing howl of the wolves.

With the onset of cold weather, the beasts were moving in nearer the glow of fires that signified human presence and food supplies. It was often possible to see the yellow glint of eyes in the darkness of the trees where the campfire picked up the large nocturnal pupils of wolves and turned them golden with reflection. At times, a watcher could catch a glimpse of grey shapes moving around or grouped still as statues, just at the edge of the trees, watching and waiting. Splendid and beautiful animals though they were, there was an element of spine-tingling menace in the sound of their concerted howls starting up in the stillness of night.

That particular evening Paul found them really getting under his skin. He missed Valodya. With the young Russian's departure, the atmosphere at the campsite had changed. There was no one to laugh and drink with, no one to make him forget his pressing problems, no one to bring unity to them all. They were now firmly in three groups—Swarovsky and his nurse, the two women in the *Arabian Nights* tent, and himself. The expectation of the three women being picked up by the first through train had increased that feeling of separation. They were busily sorting out the chests containing Swarovsky treasures to be taken with them. In spirit, they had already gone.

Paul faced the knowledge that he had lost Irina completely. Once she boarded that train, it would be the end of something he would never forget . . . and from which he did not know how to recover.

Also weighing on his mind was the knowledge that he would have to drive the engine himself now Yagutov was dead and that their present strength would be totally ineffective if attacked by Reds. All he could hope was that his young Russian friend or the train from Lake Onega came soon. He had received no orders other than to stand by at the siding for a through train across the new bridge, yet in his heart, he felt that the passing of that train would signify the end of his command.

It was in the midst of such depressing thoughts that he heard a faint cry in the distance . . . and then another. It sounded like men shouting, and his reflexes had him on his feet in an instant.

"Stevens," he cried urgently, "Grab a rifle and tell those men outside to prepare for an attack."

Stevens, scrambling to his feet gasped, "Yes, sir. But I doubt they'll understand what I'm saying."

"Use signals, man. They can hear those voices the same as we can. Come on!"

He jumped from the truck, snatching up four rifles and his gun-belt as he went. It was imperative to get the women under the train and warn

Swarovsky. But there was only time to register that the wolves had fallen silent, before the Russians pushed past him in great excitement, unarmed and shouting greetings.

Paul was level with the tents now. Olga and Lyudmilla came from theirs and looked in surprise at the way he was draped around with guns. Then Olga laughed gaily.

"It is Valodya back, not an invading army, my dear Paul."

He threw down the rifles in disgust. If only he understood their damned language! Irina came from the other tent, casting a quick glance at the rifles on the ground before asking rapid questions in Russian of the other two. He felt more alone than ever as he watched the approach of the returning force.

The six soldiers had gathered around distant figures as they emerged from the trees, and there was a great deal of vigorous shouting going on. But as Paul watched, the voices lost their strength and slowly died away, the men standing intently around the newcomers some fifty yards away. Paul moved forward. Why did Valodya not come right into the camp? Paul strode up to the silent group, pushing his way through. Then he stopped dead. Three of Valodya's men stood swaying and weary, speaking in disjointed sentences to their comrades, who were now sober with shock.

"What has happened?" he asked sharply. "Where is Lieutenant Swarovsky?"

They answered. They were almost weeping and told him with great drama and volubility . . . and he understood none of it. He felt apprehension rise up inside him. Three out of twenty-seven! What had happened to the rest, and where was Valodya? Was this an advance party? Were the others wounded and in need of help? Were the Reds following up? Should he take the train down the line to pick up wounded? Oh, God, *someone* must tell him what was going on.

"What are they saying?" he demanded, swinging round on the six beside him. But they did not understand his words any more than he understood theirs. There was no mistaking the distress on each face, however, and fear throbbed through his limbs. *Three!* Surely these were not the only survivors?

Grabbing the arm of one, he began leading him toward the tents. Swarovsky must be told, then he could translate. As the only able officer, it was essential that Paul knew the truth so that he could take appropriate action.

The women stood waiting as he approached, still and unsmiling now, sensing that the night held menace for them all.

"What has happened? What are they talking about?" Paul asked Irina desperately as he passed her. "I *have* to know."

Then they were crowding the entrance to his own tent, where Swarovsky sat with his leg up on a pillow. He looked old and yellow-faced as he barked orders at the soldier Paul had by the arm. The three women entered as the soldier went on his knees beside the bed and began to speak.

It was terrible, standing in that lamplit tent listening to a man's overwhelming misery and being the only person there who could not understand the reason for it. Something told Paul Valodya was not coming back, and he felt a return of that sickness a man was forced to swallow when a friend, a smiling young face, a familiar cheerful voice had vanished in an instant, leaving only a pile of something in khaki. He stood with his gaze riveted on that soldier's bearded face, feeling the man's anguish, yet uncomprehending of it. His body grew more tense until it ached; his throat grew dryer and dryer as the soldier became pitifully overcome and tears ran down his cheeks. Then something dropped to the ground beside Paul and he turned to see Lyudmilla in a dead faint at his feet.

"What . . . by God, what is it?" Paul asked in hoarse desperation. *"What has happened?"* But there was no one to tell him. Irina had gone to her husband and was holding him with hands that gripped his, as if forcing him to hold on to life . . . or sanity . . . or whatever was being driven from him at that moment. Irina was sobbing silently and uncontrollably as she clung to Sasha, gone away in a world that excluded everyone but herself and the man she was supporting.

Then Olga gave a great cry and rushed from the tent like a person in dementia. Paul, filled with an agony of impotence, looked once more at those in the tent, then took off in pursuit of Olga, who was running blindly down the track in the direction from which the men had come.

"Olga! Olga!" he shouted, pounding over the sleepers after her, then veering off to the right as she made for the trees. "Stop, for God's sake, stop!"

He caught up with her about ten yards farther on and grabbed her arm. "Where do you think you are going?" He shook her in his passion. "What has happened? Tell me what has happened."

She was breathing fast and shaking from head to foot. By the light of the moon, her face was dead white, her eyes as glittery as the stars. For a 834sec or two she looked at him as if she did not know him, then she flung herself against him and dragged his head down to kiss him over and over again.

Shocked at what she was doing at such a time, Paul stood dazed for some moments, before he began to pull her arms from around his neck. Her hold had become unbelievably strong; he had almost to fight free. And all the time she was covering his face with urgent kisses.

"Have you gone mad?" he choked, holding her off, but she would not leave him alone. Clinging, pulling at him, moaning his name, she resisted all his attempts to push her away, until he lost control and threw her off with a strength that had her staggering backward against a tree. Then, as he stood breathless, trying to gain some clear thought on what had become a nightmare situation, she began speaking in a high-pitched, unnatural voice.

"You're a man, aren't you? Take me! There's no one to see us. No one will care. Here in the forest . . . anywhere you like . . . Just take me!"

It sounded obscene and vile, like a harlot in the doorway of a brothel. That voice, almost whining and inhuman, revolted him. But on the point of turning away, he was halted by her voice again.

"Paul, I am a woman—as good a woman as you have ever had." Her hands began tearing at the blouse she wore, then, as the silk ripped, at the lace beneath until it hung in a jagged frill around her waist. Her breasts gleamed in the moonlight and quivered as she shook as if with tropical fever. She leant forward in grotesque pleading, doubling up as if trying to contain an anguish that was unbearable. "Look at me, Paul. You must want me now. Dear God, you *must* want me now!"

Something inside Paul curled up and made him long to retch. This bizarre evening was more than he could handle. He felt as mad as the rest as he looked at her, ugly and disgusting against the tree—a proud, aristocratic girl offering her body like a desperate camp follower. But as he watched, he saw that she had begun to cry. The silver streaks down her cheeks banished her ugliness, and her face in the moonlight was suddenly heartbreakingly beautiful in its grief. She stood in her tattered clothes, oblivious of her nakedness, returning very slowly from a bout of madness.

He began to move toward her, but now she retreated from him, asking in strangled tones, "Do you know how old he was? Twenty-three. That was all." Great glittering eyes stared right through him. "I have already lived one year more. I have already cheated them of one year. Do you know what they did to him?" she cried in a great burst of anguish that halted him. "Because he was a Swarovsky, they stripped him, tied his hands and feet together, and threw him, still living, onto their fire. And they laughed as he burned. They laughed *because he was a Swarovsky.*"

Paul stood reeling, closing his eyes against the horror of what she had conjured up in his mind. But a new sound made his lids fly open again. Olga was clutching her hair with both hands and sobbing with terrible broken moans that rose into a crescendo.

"I want to live. I want to live. I want to live."

On and on it went, until he could stand no more. Pulling his coat off, he went to her and wrapped it around her nakedness as he coaxed her to the ground. He sat against a tree, holding her tightly against him as she

lay racked with sobs. At first, he stared into the night, trying to keep his
mind a blank. But then he recalled Valodya's playing the accordion with
gaiety and panache; his reckless antics on the bridge he had helped to
build; his laughing comradeship with the men; his departure on a horse
three days ago, and his farewell then: *Spokoinoi nochi*—peaceful night.
As he recalled all that and many other things about a young man his own
age, a foreigner, a Russian who had given him and the world all of
himself, Paul felt the tears begin to slide down his own cheeks. He had
thought himself immune to death, but Valodya had penetrated the barrier
erected five years ago and shown him one could never grow immune to
it.

A long time afterward, when the tears had dried, a young girl stirred in
his arms, and two lonely, shattered people—one who had lived too little
and one who had lived too much—sought comfort from each other in that
dark, isolated forest.

S e v e n t e e n

There comes a point in most people's lives when they are forced to
recognise that no amount of hope, endeavour, fervour, or prayer will
prevent the inevitable from happening. The murder of Valodya brought
Sasha to that point. The destruction of a young man who had seen and
experienced both regimes and had learnt from them, perhaps, the only
way Russia could have lived within herself, marked the moment Sasha
knew the cause was lost. When a nation behaved as animals did, what
hope was there for peace and wisdom?

But it was not merely the barbarous killing of a young man who
represented something that was being ruthlessly stamped out, it was the
entire outcome of that disastrous foray into the forest that destroyed
Sasha's delicate dreams.

Those three who had returned told how they had reached the lakeside
near dawn, taking longer than expected because of a marshy area they
had had to circle. They had seen the light of fires near the water's edge
and had supposed it to be the enemy's bivouac, but when they drew near

it was to discover that the "campfires" were the huts of the simple settlement whose headman had led the convict-gang to rob their train nearly six weeks before. Bodies of women, naked and mutilated, lay around amongst the burning huts.

The soldiers stared from the trees at the terrible sight and wondered what had happened to the men and old people. When dawn came three-quarters of an hour later, they found their answer. The other inhabitants had been tied together inside the burning huts. The three survivors broke down as they spoke of their comrades who had been so frightened by this sight they had thrown down their rifles and walked over to the *Bolsheviki* when they were seen an hour later near the site of their own old bivouac.

Just over half their number threw in their lot with the Reds without persuasion. Seeing that, the remainder lost heart. What hope had twelve men and one officer against such butchers? But Lieutenant Swarovsky had rallied them, deployed them to best advantage, and begun picking off the enemy troops—untrained peasants, for the most part—who were on the open shore by the lake. Then the Lieutenant was hit in the shoulder and could only fire sporadically.

It was getting near noon, said the survivors, and they were hungry and tired. They had marched through the night, and their eyes were aching with the reflections of sun on water. They could not stop for any food, and their thirsts were tormented by the sight of the nearby lake. It did not help their morale to see their erstwhile comrades eating and drinking in the enemy camp. Finally, it was the blinding sun on water and general sleepiness that reduced their alertness. They were overrun. The Lieutenant, firing as long as he could, was seized and dragged to the Red Commander. The man knew of him, had heard the name. Undiscovered in their hiding places, the three watched, uncertain what to do and unable to help him or their colleagues taken with him.

However, when it became apparent their officer was about to be cruelly killed, those who had gone over to the enemy rushed at the Reds, attacking with their bare hands in a frenzy of defence for the man they all regarded with great respect and affection. But their renewed loyalty came too late. They were overpowered and marched down to the lake's edge, where they were held face down in the water until they drowned. The prisoners were then treated in similar manner, the Reds declaring they had no bullets to waste on garbage.

When Lieutenant Swarovsky was dead, the three crept away knowing all they could do was return to report what they had seen and heard. With no knowledge of how to get back, they simply stumbled upon the railway track and followed it, knowing it must lead to the bridge.

But they were heartsore and frightened. The *Bolsheviki* were superhuman, they claimed, men who walked through the forest catching everyone and killing them. When their comrades had disarmed and gone to the Reds, they had been greeted, fed and welcomed. Only when they rushed to defend their officer had they been spat upon and drowned. Would it not be better to make friends with the *Bolsheviki* than to fight them? No one who did survived, they, themselves, were full of fear for their lives if the Red troops caught up with them and knew they had shot at them down at the lake. And what of their families?

The enemy had spoken of going north to conquer the White resistance. What would happen to those in the villages whose men were away fighting with the White armies? There would be more huts burned down with people inside. Now the bridge was built, they wanted to go home. They had only agreed to fight because they had been promised freedom from oppression, and regular food.

It was obvious now that they had chosen the wrong side. It was not that they wanted to go around doing all those barbarous things, but when they saw a nobleman with a gentle courageous spirit, a *barin* who sang the songs of the Russian people with such feeling, a true and loyal officer destroyed before their very eyes, they could see that nobody and nothing was strong enough to stop the *Bolsheviki*. No, they wanted to go home now and save their families from murder.

Sasha heard all they had to say on the following morning. They spoke the death knell to his hopes. Speaking in a manner he had never used before with his troops, he told them gently, as if they were children, that he understood their fears and was grateful for their loyalty that had withstood the recent attack. But they could not return to their villages until they all went back to Murmansk. In the meantime, he would expect them to maintain their loyalty to himself and the English officer who had shown them how to build the bridge. Then he had added, equally gently, that he wanted them to know that not only his brother but a sister down in Moscow had been cruelly murdered by the *Bolsheviki*. Yet he would continue to fight the Reds as long as he lived. They were not superhuman, just bullies who ruled by terror. Lieutenant Vladimir Ivanovich Swarovsky had never been afraid of them—not even as he died—and never would *he* be.

The soldiers had gone off quiet and thoughtful, but Sasha knew they would serve their Red masters when the time came. What choice did a peasant have, what choice had he ever had? That morning, Sasha was a living frame with no centre. What had remained of his heart and soul was already in the grip of arctic winter. Valodya was dead. He accepted it but dared not think of his manner of dying. Last night he had heard it said; now his mind had shut it out or he would never again shut his eyes in sleep.

Last night! How near he had come to breaking as he had cried aloud asking *God, why?*—why the bullets had missed Valodya when so many others had been killed all around him on the German front; why he had not been shot as he escaped from Moscow; why the cholera or typhus had not claimed him victim; why, even, he had not been killed by that runaway horse at the age of seven? Why he had not been spared *this*?

Then Sasha had turned on Irina, cursing her for preventing his own presence on that march south. If he had been there, he would have saved his brother. He called her *murderess*, blamed her for Valodya's death, cried out to her that the horror would dog her to the end of her days. She had held him, accepted his curses, sobbed with him. Then she had made him sleep with one of her injections.

When he awoke, he was in a frozen state. It was the only way he would survive. Irina seemed to know this, in the strange way she had of understanding a man. There had been no protest from her when he got from the bed, dressed, and hobbled with the aid of a stick down to the train where the men were grouped. He had walked past the women's tent. Olga and Lyudmilla were asleep, Irina told him. She had given them both a sedative, also.

Only after he had spoken to his soldiers—the six who had stayed behind at the bridge joining the other three in their declaration that they wanted to go home—did Sasha attempt to locate his ally whom, he was told by Sapper Stevens, was looking the engine over. He was, indeed, on the footplate, squatting down to study some levers. He looked up when Sasha approached.

"Good morning, Captain."

"Good morning, Colonel." Paul jumped to the ground beside Sasha. "I'm trying to get the hang of this. Since I shall have to take it back to the siding to let the train through, I thought it would be as well to get in a little practice."

No mention was made of last night or of the fact that Sasha was on his feet—or *one* foot, to be more exact. The young Englishman looked sallow and dull-eyed and seemed unusually meek.

Sasha nodded. "Yes. This is a new facet to your many skills."

He had not used sarcasm, it had merely been a comment. Yet Anderson appeared disturbed by it.

"Hardly that! It's my train, after all, and I have to take responsibility for it."

"How old are you, Captain Anderson?"

The question took him aback, but after slight hesitation Paul answered. "I shall be twenty-three next month."

Twenty-three! Sasha had been close to that age when he had first gone to the theatre and watched an exciting young ballerina called Lyudmilla Zapalova throw kisses to him in his box.

"Boys. That's all they are," he murmured to himself. "Boys forced to be men."

Anderson was looking at him with apprehension, so Sasha quickly asked when the train from Lake Onega was due.

"Stevens is standing by for a message at any time. I just hope the train doesn't get blown up on its way here."

"I think not," Sasha commented unemotionally. "My men report that the Reds were not interested in sabotaging the line. It seems they are more anxious to keep it intact now, for their own advancing forces."

Anderson's mouth tightened. "That's what I guessed. All our work is . . ."

"You have agreed that the ladies may travel on the train with all their luggage?"

"Oh, yes, I think there'll be no objection to that, Colonel."

"And they will be perfectly safe?"

"In Murmansk? Yes, of course. We have an entire force still up there, you know."

"But for how long?"

The young man sighed heavily and looked at the oily rag in his hands. "God knows . . . but it won't be anywhere near long enough. It won't be anywhere near bloody long enough," he added with sudden vehemence.

Looking at him, Sasha felt a hundred years old. "One man cannot save a nation, Captain."

The freckled face was grim with emotion as he looked up. "I wish to God I could."

"To avenge a friend?" Sasha asked pointedly.

"If that were the only reason, I would have to save a hundred nations," was the slightly husky reply. Paul leant back against the engine and stared at the bridge, lost somewhere in the truth of the past four months. "Out in France, we soon abandoned vengeance—the debt proved too overwhelming—and all through those years what we were fighting for was the *spirit* of England."

His gaze swung back to Sasha, who remained as frozen as when he had awoken that day.

"When I first came here, I was still full of that. Valodya . . . Valodya showed me the spirit of Russia. I would do anything now to save that."

"At twenty-three, that is all any of us want to do, Captain. But you are two years too late. It died in October 1917."

When the message came through from Lake Onega, it contained more than the time the train was expected at the siding near the bridge. It put into words all Paul had refused to believe. The British *were* going home.

The aircraft and seaplanes were evacuating British personnel and equipment; the train was the last that would be run by the ally who had been ordered to withdraw before winter cut them off. The base at Lake Onega was to be left in the hands of a White Russian force under General Skobeltsin, who had recently been fighting alongside the British commander in some bitter battles for control of the huge inletted lake. The Royal Engineer officer and his batman were told to wait until the train had gone through, then stand by for their own orders regarding withdrawal.

Ships would be standing by at Murmansk and Archangel to take off all British personnel and any Russians who wished to leave or whose lives would be endangered by the departure of their last remaining allies. Reinforcements from England had just been landed to cover the withdrawal, and all British troops should be gone by the end of October. Ships could remain at Murmansk to deal with emergencies or stragglers from lonely forest posts, but the harbour at Archangel was normally closed by ice in October, and the last ships from there would have to leave by the middle of the month.

As if to emphasise the menace of arctic winter, the first snow began to fall as night approached, settling on the bridge to turn it into a wide white path across the darkness of the river. All at once, the bridge had taken on the aspect of a path to civilisation, the only route back to the rest of the world, and none of them wanted to leave it to travel back the two miles to the south to reach the siding on the following morning.

Paul, in particular, did not relish the idea of the trip back to the siding. The few instructions he had had from Yagutov on setting the engine in motion had been sufficient for a journey across the bridge at dead-slow speed but not enough for him to feel confident about moving back to the siding with several bad curves to negotiate on the way. Also, in the back of his mind was the thought that the train had somehow to be taken back to Murmansk by the next month . . . and who was going to do it? He had told both Murmansk and Lake Onega about Yagutov. He knew the former could do nothing, but the more southerly base had promised to send up an engine-driver on the train, *if one could be found*. He knew what that meant and was worried.

The soldiers were busy cutting piles of logs they would never use. No one tried to stop them. It kept them warm and occupied. The women stitched and packed and sorted, sorted and stitched and packed, ready for their journey to Murmansk.

Sasha wrote reports to his new Russian commander at Murmansk and the one at Lake Onega, already the acknowledged new leader of the little group by the bridge. He packed his equipment, wrote off the loss of his six horses to the Reds, and made lists of his requirements, ready for his arrival in Murmansk. He also gritted his teeth against the pain and walked around on his injured leg as much as possible. When he got to the northern port, no one was going to tell him he was unfit to fight.

Paul also occupied himself with writing reports—those that would have to be presented at the Court of Inquiry. Although it seemed that the general craziness over the affair would not extend to holding the investigation at Murmansk in the midst of a withdrawal, Paul would have to answer for his actions back in England.

Even as he wrote, he realised how it would all sound to a group of staff officers at Chatham or Aldershot—rampaging ex-convicts, two aristocratic women being dragged off to be raped, then cut to pieces, himself being clubbed on the head whilst looking the other way. Oh, yes, he could see their neat moustaches curling with disbelief, their eyebrows rising in haughty disdain, cold eyes looking him over and asking what a young jackanapes was doing in sole command of such a project. They would know nothing of what it was like here, have no notion of how a nation was dying so painfully, be incapable of understanding the Russian temperament.

He hunched farther into his thick coat and pulled the blanket closer around his shoulders as the cold of the night seemed to fill him. He stared through the narrow gap left by Stevens when he went from the truck to collect tea. The fine snow was drifting down more as a gentle prelude than a determined fall, but it increased the normal hush hanging over the forest, so that when the howl of the wolves began, the sound was even more desolate and chilling than usual. He stood it for no more than a minute, then got to his feet angrily.

"Bloody infernal row!" he swore, marching across to slam the door to. But he did not do so, because someone was peering in.

"Olga!" His heart sank. He had been dreading this meeting.

She wore fur—dark and glossy—which made her appear older and too much of a stranger for the look that was in her eyes. She gazed up at him, offering her hand, and he had no choice but to pull her into the truck. But he remained by the door, where there was no suggestion of intimacy. It did not deter her, however, and he was forced to hold her in his arms as she sank against him, clinging to his shoulders as she sought his mouth. That deliberate, prolonged kiss and the pliancy of her body reminded him of the previous night but aroused no passion in him. All it did was make his heart sink further and increase the unpleasant feeling of unwanted responsibility. It was useless now to blame himself for letting it happen; it had, and he was faced with the consequences.

"You . . . you shouldn't be here," he said, putting her firmly away from him.

"Why? This is more comfortable and cosy than the forest."

He looked at her in something akin to shock. Last night she had been bereft, unable to accept what life had dealt her, afraid that her life would end too soon. Now she spoke with sultry suggestiveness.

"How do you think it will look for you to be here like this at such a time?"

She kissed his mouth swiftly and fiercely. "Does it matter now? They must all know we are lovers."

"Look . . . Olga . . . What happened last night . . ."

"What happened last night was that you became my lover, Paul. My very first lover." She turned from him and walked to the back of the truck to face him again—a lovely, vital girl who stood like a princess addressing a commoner. "When a man takes a mistress, it is usual for him to offer her protection, you know."

"A *mistress*!" He almost choked over the word. Oh, God, it was worse than he had feared. She knew damn well it had been nothing like that, that it had been instinctive and meant to comfort her. Yet how could he stand here now and say it had merely been a means of driving the demons away? How could he infer that it had meant nothing to him, without it sounding like an insult? "You don't understand," he said lamely.

"I understand that you have taken away my virginity . . . and who knows what else you might have done?"

"What do you mean by that?" he demanded, feeling decidedly trapped.

She sat on a box and looked across at him, her smile bittersweet in the yellow light. "You were not exactly careful, Paul. It might only have been the second or third time you have had a woman, but you cannot be unaware of the penalties she might have to suffer."

Of course he was aware! Had the thought not been bothering him all day? "But, the chances of that happening . . ."

"Are fifty-fifty," she put in quickly. "What do you intend to do about it?"

He grew very angry, very speedily. Last night she had been as shattered as he, had turned to him instinctively. Now it was as if that terrible grief over Valodya, and the overwhelming fear, had vanished, to leave a cold calculating courtesan. She was speaking as if she had been seduced with wicked intent, as if she knew already that she carried his bastard child.

"I intend to do nothing about something that is pure conjecture," he said, going toward her.

"What if it turns out to be fact, Paul? Surely your middle-class morality will demand that you do the right thing?"

His anger rocketed. "You have always despised Lyudmilla Zapalova, but by God, you are no better. I have never really understood you, but now I do—so clearly that I am revolted. Last night, I thought you were torn apart by grief and terror, but now I find Valodya meant nothing to you at all. It was all a disgusting act, designed to get me to do something you have been begging for since the moment we met. Yes, it was only the second time I have had a woman, but it was vastly different from the first. She was a French harlot. I treated you with reverence, but I see now you are the same, underneath that aristocratic exterior. But there's one rule of the game you seem to have forgotten. Harlots do not expect their clients to 'do the right thing.' "

No sooner had he said it than he realised how wrong he had been. She seemed to shrink before his eyes. Her face grew pinched and full of defeat as she doubled forward and began to rock back and forth on the box. He was appalled at what he had said. What was happening between them? All his inbred gentleness and sense of respect toward women made him try to stammer an apology and plead overwork and worry as the cause of his treatment of her.

Then he put his hand on her shoulder. "I . . . I felt as close to Valodya as I have ever felt to another person. Last night, I tried to drive thoughts of him from my mind by being close to you. It was instinctive; you know it was. It should never have happened."

At that she looked up, her eyes full of the old wildness. "Yes, last night was instinctive, but I have been trying to make it happen ever since I saw that you were my escape. Oh, don't look so stricken, Paul, you know very well I have been throwing myself at you from the start. Do you really not know why I did it? You were young and very attractive, and you were out here alone with nothing to take your mind off the problems. I also knew you had had little to do with women. A perfect victim, I thought. But you fell in love with Irina, and you were much *too* inexperienced with women to even take what you could have in lieu of what you could not."

She rose from the box and began pacing restlessly up and down, her voice growing higher and more excited as she went on. "I was clever, Paul. I meant to seduce you right from the start, then tell you I was expecting your child, even if it was a lie." She flashed him a look of blue fire. "You see how beautifully you would have been caught? Your bourgeois morals would have obliged you to accept responsibility and take me back to England—my freedom from horror and death." She began to laugh. "That pale-faced nurse took your eye instead, and your bourgeois morals were stronger than I had allowed for. Don't you see how desperate I was growing?" she cried on a sobbing laugh. "I think I went a little mad last night, then, when I least expected it, you surrendered."

He was shocked by all she was saying, split between pity and the old aversion to her opulent attraction. Fear made people sink to many levels, and this girl was terrified.

She gripped his arm and gazed frenziedly into his face. "Paul, take me back to England. That is all I have ever wanted from you. As soon as we get there, I'll leave you alone, I swear. There'll never be anything between us; I know Irina rules you."

"What if you *should* have my child, after all?" he asked through stiff lips.

"I will find it a father long before it is born. I will never ask anything from you for it; that is a promise."

When he said nothing for the moment, she grew wilder. "Think of last night, Paul. If I spoke of it to Sasha, he would demand some kind of gesture from you to compensate for your treatment of his sister—his one remaining sister. Paul," she cried insistently, tugging at his arm, "you are ridiculously governed by conscience, so you must feel some sense of responsibility for what you did. After all, it might make an advantageous marriage more difficult if the man finds out I'm not a virgin."

He pulled his arm away but nothing would stop her now. "Get me to England . . . I don't care what you do, but get me to England with you, or you will have more than my seduction on your conscience. I can't get out alone." She began to laugh with a rising note of hysteria. "Another Swarovsky roasted alive!"

Sickened, he shouted, "Stop it! *Stop it!*" But she continued laughing, growing wilder and more hysterical, and he smacked her hard around the face. "Stop it, I tell you!"

The laughing expression crumpled into one of desperate misery as she threw herself against him and clung there.

"Take me away from here . . . for pity's sake, get me away!"

He held her shaking body with arms that were learning to give comfort. "There was no need for all this," he told her thickly. "You will probably be in England before me. Any Russian who wants to leave will be given passage on our ships. We may be running out, but we are prepared to take you all with us as we go."

Although it had stopped snowing by morning, there was a fine powdering everywhere, grizzling the trees and highlighting the isolation of the place where a dark double line of rails stood out against overall whiteness, running away in both directions to disappear around curves in the distance. The air was chill in the nostrils and froze the breath hanging in the surrounding stillness.

But beside the train there was activity a-plenty. The camp had been ⌐ruck, and all the equipment was being loaded into the supply-trunk, together with the Swarovsky chests, the tents and camp furniture, and even the mother-of-pearl accordian clutched by Zapalova as her most treasured possession.

Irina sat on a box in the supply-truck, wrapped in a long fur coat, and stared at the wintry scene through the open door. So it was all ending; the summer had gone!

In three hours she would be on a train to Murmansk. In three short hours she would move slowly away to the north, leaving Paul standing with his servant beside the tiny train, alone in the midst of a white wilderness. In her mind she could already visualise the scene—his tall figure dwindling as their train gathered speed and took the gradual curve that would block him from sight altogether. Then they would come to his bridge and cross it—that bridge that would symbolise forever the most painful and the most wonderful moments of her life.

They were all going and leaving the two Englishmen with their train. It had been discussed openly between the two officers in front of them all. Sasha had put forward his points with quiet reason. Work on the railway had ceased; he and his men had completed their orders to help the English engineer. The British had relinquished command in Russia, so he was now in a position to do as he thought best with his men, without reference to his erstwhile ally. Since he now had only nine men of uncertain loyalty, he intended travelling on the train with the three women to reach his new commander in Murmansk. Paul took his orders from his own retreating superiors and had nothing to do with the campaign against the Reds any longer. He had been told to await orders; he had a train for transport, with plenty of supplies. His part of the dual command had always been anything to do with the railway; Sasha's part had always been to fight for his country's freedom from the *Bolsheviki*, and that was what he was intending to do now.

Irina was appalled. They were all deserting Paul. After all he had done for their sakes, they were going to leave him alone and helpless in a forest alive with savage enemies. The men who killed Valodya were moving north, they knew. Her mind screamed at the thought of what they would do to an English officer if they caught him. What Sasha was proposing was brutal, yet both officers accepted it with calmness. Sasha was beyond feeling anything any longer. He did not need to tell her he was now dedicated to fighting, fighting, fighting, until they also killed him. But Paul she did not understand. Had she ever been able to do so? Why did he so easily accept their desertion? It could not be that he also no longer felt anything. She knew he did. At that moment she had further proof of the fact, when he appeared at the open door of the truck to tell Sasha he was ready to move off. He looked taller than ever in the long khaki coat with the collar turned up around his ears. The peaked cap left her with only an overshadowed view of his eyes, but they were turned in her direction for a swift moment before he turned away, and they told her in one glance that he felt their going very deeply.

The two miles to the siding seemed like twenty-two. Progress was slow, and when they finally reached the siding, they stopped with a violent jerk. It was a while before the door was pulled open and the two officers appeared, pulling themselves up into the comparative warmth of the straw-strewn truck. They had red cheeks and were shaking their hands to bring the life back into them.

Paul smiled much too brightly. "There is an hour or two before we can expect the train, so we have got the lads busy on lighting a fire. We might as well have some hot tea and something to eat while we wait. *No!*" he added sharply, "please don't leave the truck." Irina guessed the soldiers were posted with rifles in case of attack before the other train arrived. Somewhere out there was the force that had destroyed their own.

They all drank tea and ate slices of tinned ham toasted in the fire. It tasted smoky, and Irina almost had to abandon her brave attempt to eat when her churning stomach began to reject it. But the others were keeping up the pretence, so she forced herself to retain an outward calm while she stared out at the quiet coldness of near-noon and wondered how she would ever be able to say goodbye and leave him standing there on his own, forsaken in a frozen siding.

The tense, leaden minutes passed, until Paul said suddenly, "It might be a good thing to get the baggage outside by the track. They won't want to stop any longer than necessary."

"Yes, yes, I think that is wise," agreed Sasha.

So the pair of them began moving the two chests containing the Swarovsky possessions that were all that had been snatched from the summer estate on that terrible night of flight. Irina wondered again about repaying the money Paul had paid out as a ransom in exchange for herself and Olga. But she supposed it would all be forgotten now the British were going.

One by one, the officers carried out those things that were to be taken, the fact of their not employing the soldiers in the task giving credibility to Irina's guess that the soldiers were all on guard. Lyudmilla had been exceptionally quiet since the tragic revelation two days before, and it was difficult to tell whether she had been genuinely attached to Valodya or simply shattered because his death had been so ugly. Perhaps, if he had been cleanly shot, she would have shrugged it off as a reality of present times and nothing to do with her as an artist. Completely unable to feel any affinity with a woman like the great Zapalova, Irina noticed only that she had attached herself to Sasha since that night and he appeared to accept it as natural.

Olga had been alternately bright and tearful. When they were all together, her gaze never left Paul's face, but he seemed to avoid looking directly at her whenever possible, although there was an unusual air of gentleness in his treatment of her.

Irina, herself, was keeping to her vow to soothe a man's hurts with her hands and not her heart . . . but, oh, how she wished that she no longer had to see the desolation in Paul's eyes each time he came back to the truck and glanced automatically in her direction.

Then it was coming! One of the soldiers spotted it and let out a cry. Soon, they were all scrambling from the train to stand in a long line along the side of the track where the luggage was already lined up. Their faces were turned to the south, where, in the far distance, smoke was rising between the trees into the grey sky. The cold bit into Irina's face as she watched for an uncertain blob to turn into the round shape of the front of a great engine. The blur covering her eyes must be due to the cold making them water.

Then they could hear the puffing, and the singing in the ice-frosted rails. After so many weeks looking at empty track, the sight of this monster bearing down on them was highly emotional. The line to Murmansk was open; here came the train to freedom! When it was close enough to be seen quite clearly, Sasha turned to Paul and held out his hand.

"So our command ends much the way it began."

Paul shook the hand firmly. "In war, that is often the way it is, Colonel."

That was their goodbye. But Olga's was much more passionate. She went into Paul's arms, kissing him with fervour, and she was openly crying as she said, "Thank you, Paul, thank you for all you have done. I shall never forget it . . . *any* of it."

"Nor I," he said, then hesitated. "If you ever . . . need anything . . . you can always find me through the army authorities."

She shook her head, crying and laughing together. "I told you last night all I wanted was to get to England, and you are doing that for me."

Then he was standing before her, and Irina was lost. It proved impossible to speak to him. In that moment, she knew she had glimpsed her elusive youth in that forest and been unable to reach it. Looking into his freckled face that would haunt her for the rest of her days, she saw he knew it was goodbye to his own elusive youth once she got on that train and went off into the distance. It was evident he could not speak either, and they went on looking at each other until he suddenly took one of her hands and lifted it gently to his lips. It was so foreign to him, so much a gesture of the deep devotion in him that did not know how to let her go, so much more than a passionate embrace, she could not bear it.

Drawing her hand away, she turned and walked back toward the little train in the siding, trying to regain control of herself before she had to climb aboard that other one and leave him.

The puffing was considerably louder now, and so was the rattle of wheels on the line. Taking in a great, long breath, she turned back and began to approach the others once more. They all appeared spellbound by the nearing train. It was a long, long one, snaking out behind the great black-and-red engine with the pointed snow-plough on the front, and it now filled the stillness with a clatter and roar as it grew nearer. After their own small engine, this one was a monster. Her taut nerves jumped as a shrill whistle blast rent the air several times, and she found her heartbeat increasing as the train bore down on them. It could not be more than two hundred yards away as it continued to thunder toward them. The others were picking up small items and crowding forward to see its arrival, the soldiers getting so excited they even stepped onto the line to get a better view.

Then, suddenly, Paul was shouting and running like a madman in front of them all, waving his arms. "Get back! For Christ's sake get back! *It's not going to stop!*"

They seemed not to understand what he was saying, and he began pushing them off the track, back away from the edge of the rails like a man demented. And hardly had he done so than the engine was upon them, rushing past with a great blast of air. Then the trucks, one by one, flashing before their eyes in a dazzling pattern of dark wood and slots of pale space between them until there were no more. The train had gone, leaving only the stillness that had been there before and a dark oblong getting smaller and smaller until it disappeared into the trees to the north.

The silent tableau was broken by Olga, who gave a strange kind of moan and began running along the track after the train, holding up her skirt with one hand and reaching out with the other as she stumbled across the sleepers, as if hoping to touch her means of escape that had left her behind.

"No, no, no," she moaned again and again, until she collapsed in the middle of the track and sat huddled on the shingle, staring at the empty line ahead.

Lyudmilla was frenziedly attacking Paul with her fists against his chest, until Sasha pulled her off and began to speak sternly in Russian to her. Then her tantrum really broke. She ranted and raged, flung obscenities worthy of a village crone at both officers, using all her artistic drama to work herself up into an uncontrollable bout of screaming hysteria.

Irina just stood unbelieving. It was as if the train had never existed. They were all there as they had been ten minutes beforehand . . . and Murmansk was as distant as it had ever been.

Her trance was broken by Paul, who came to her with plenty of words to say now. There was a dark cloud of anger across his face, and the echo of a goodbye that had never been.

"I'll signal them right away. They can stop the train at the next siding, and I'll get you up there to join it. They have mistaken my message, that's all."

It was as if she were the only one to whom he could explain what had gone wrong, but she just looked at him, knowing she had been given another chance—a little more summer, after all. The thought was too fragile to be broken by words, and he strode off to the supply-truck.

Standing there in the snow, Irina felt incredibly alone. She turned and walked away from them, away from the group of soldiers, away from the pile of abandoned luggage, away from the endless empty track. Not until she reached the supply-truck did she remember Paul was signalling. On the point of altering direction, she saw him out of the truck and up near the engine, staring up the line to the north. There was something unusual about the way he stood, so still and lost to the sound of her approach, that she hesitated, then went up to him, thinking he might be watching for the train to come back for them.

But when she drew near, it was to see that he was in the grips of something quite different from anger or anxiety or expectancy of a train. She put her hand on his arm, but he took no notice. It was one of those times when she could not soothe a man's hurt with just her hands.

Moving round in front of him, she said softly, "What is it? Tell me what is wrong."

Without taking his eyes from whatever it was that he saw, he put out his hand that held a paper. It was covered in words—words Paul had written as he translated a Morse message.

> TRAIN URGENT NON-STOP MURMANSK. YOU ARE NOW SOUTHERNMOST REARGUARD. PROCEED AT ONCE MURMANSK WITH ALL PERSONNEL BLOWING UP BRIDGE AS YOU GO.

Her heart contracted. "Blowing up . . . oh, no! Not . . . not *your* bridge, Pavlik?" she cried, looking up quickly.

But she knew by the look on his face that it was.

Eighteen

The little train headed north again as soon as possible. The siding was exposed and unpleasantly unfamiliar. Everyone seemed glad to be going back to the site by the bridge, even though it had never been really popular with them all. Now, their pleasure in their earlier lakeside camp was blotted out by the horror of what had happened to Valodya and his men in that spot they had remembered as so beautiful. One day so peaceful and safe, the next a place of massacre.

The shattering blow of the train going through without stopping was alleviated by the thought that they would be following it up the line, and once the message was made known to them all, they clambered back into the trucks, anxious to be on the move from a place they all viewed with a certain amount of apprehension. Even to get two miles north would be something.

But Paul viewed the prospect with a sinking heart and grave misgivings. What he had with him was an ancient working engine. Yagutov had been madly proud of it, but it had seen years of service and was only intended now for shunting and general repair hauling. On the way down from Murmansk, Paul's small train had been towed by another full of supplies for the southern base. Now the little engine was expected to make a four-day journey up and down dangerous inclines, across unstable bridges, round treacherous bends, and through forest under attack from biting cold. The farther north they went, the more arctic the conditions would become, and there was no way of knowing how effective the small snow-plough on the front would prove to be.

But their greatest peril lay in the fact that Paul had to take them there. A trained engine-driver could do the journey without too much difficulty under such conditions, but Paul had no idea of what he might be up against. He knew the basic stop and start techniques for this particular engine and a few vague principles on power in proportion to an incline, speed on inner and outer cambers, and steam pressures. If there had been a long, straight track to Murmansk, all on one level and expertly ballasted, and plenty of time to get there in summer weather, he would have enjoyed the experience, much like a schoolboy's dream come true. As it was, he felt helplessly overwhelmed with the responsibility of the safety of seventeen people.

These problems occupied his mind all the way back to the bridge, but when he came in sight of it, all he could think of was what he must now do. All those weeks of work, all the problems and the attempts to delay its being built, all his pride in creation, all the comradeship and endeavour— all that for the sake of one train. Now it must go, and he was destroying it for the same cause that he had built it.

The snow lay thinly on the surface as he drove the train across to the far side, remembering that other time, when he had gone over with such supreme elation. A monument to his skill, he had proudly thought. Some small part of him that would remain in Russia long after he had gone. But there was no such thing as permanence; he should know that by now.

With the train halted, Paul jumped from the footplate to walk back to the supply-truck, which was at the end of the train nearest the bridge. He had suggested the Russian officer should travel back the short distance with the ladies, ostensibly to calm them, but mainly because it was obvious to Paul the man's leg was giving him pain. The last thing he wanted now was a disabled man on his hands.

However, Swarovsky jumped down gamely enough on his uninjured leg when Paul approached to outline his plans. With the unspoken agreement of the Russian, leadership was back in Paul's hands. Not only was everything now exclusively connected with the railway, but with Paul driving the train, he was indisputably the leader.

He took Swarovsky to one side, first telling the ladies they could stretch their legs if they wished, but to remain near the train and to avoid the bridge. The two officers walked to the riverbank and stood talking, knowing the longer they halted the more vulnerable they became to an advancing enemy.

"While I prepare and lay charges for the bridge, I'd like you to get your men organised on several essential tasks. I want the tender filled with as much wood as it will hold, because I don't want to stop in order to cut fuel again until we are well clear of this area. I also want three barrels filled with water from the river. Food supplies are adequate for the journey, but who knows when we shall next reach a river or lake *or* whether we shall be able to stop there? The ladies, Colonel, will be warmer and safer if we divide the supply-truck in two. A small private compartment can be made by piling the boxes around them. They will not need so much straw, so the rest can be used by the men. Oh, yes, and I shall have to ask the ladies to restrict themselves to one blanket each."

The Russian instantly objected, but Paul was ready for him.

"The decision has nothing to do with gentlemanly instincts, just pure common sense. The ladies have fur coats and boots; they are in a covered truck protected from draughts by straw on the floor and a barricade of boxes. Most important of all, they are simply passengers on this trip and in no way expected to work. The men are and should be given first consideration."

Swarovsky shook his head slowly. "You have revolutionary ideas, Captain."

With continued firmness, Paul told him, "I shall need two blankets around my own shoulders . . . and so will you if you insist on travelling on the footplate with me. I can't operate that engine with frostbite, even you must see that." He rubbed his hands together in subconscious reaction to the present cold of mid-afternoon. "In the other half of the supply-truck, I want to instal my batman and your two orderlies, along with the men, all armed as a rearguard. I take it your orderlies can fire a rifle?"

The Russian gave him a blunt look. "They are men of North Russia, Captain. Where there are reindeer, there are hunters who are excellent marksmen."

Paul smiled very faintly. "Point taken. Now, the other thing I want to say to you is that I intend to jettison the side-tip trucks and the flat-car with the remaining rails. They are of no use to us now, and the less weight we are pulling, the better, especially with some of the inclines I know lie ahead of us. Unfortunately, the dispensable trucks lie between our engine and the supply truck. We can do nothing until we reach the next siding, when I'll attempt to shunt them to the end of the train."

The Colonel looked at him sideways. "Why not just leave them in the siding?"

Paul frowned. "I rather like the idea of dropping them off along the way . . . preferably after a long curve in the track. If they do succeed in re-building the bridge, it will halt their advance a while longer if they careen around a bend straight into an abandoned truck."

Mention of the bridge brought Paul back to thoughts of what he must do, and heaviness returned. In consequence, his tone was very brusque as he finished his conversation.

"I am sure you realise, Colonel, that since I am not an engine-driver by trade, I can give no guarantee that this train will ever reach Murmansk."

Swarovsky looked at him, tight-lipped. "My soldiers are not bridge-builders by trade, Captain, but they built a bridge. You know how to make this engine move, so the train must reach Murmansk. I am not concerned with whether you ever reach England or not, but we have a war still to be fought, and you must now help us to achieve our ends, as we helped you to achieve yours."

Paul looked long at him, then began to turn away. "We have always spoken our minds to each other, Colonel. No doubt it will remain that way until our association ends."

He went his way, leaving the Russian to put into practice all he had just outlined. Paul had a bridge to destroy. It took some time to make the charges, attach the fuses, and place them all. Paul paid little heed to precise demolition practices. His supply of explosives would have no further demands made upon it by him, so he recklessly decided that, if the job had to be done, he would blow his work into such small pieces, whoever came behind him would have absolutely nothing upon which to build.

Meanwhile, his orders were being carried out to the letter, and the cook prepared a hot meal that might be their last substantial food for four days. Paul ate his while he worked, forking it into his mouth as he bent over the tricky business of attaching fuses. Placing the explosives was easy enough—there were so many there was no chance of failure.

It was beginning to grow dark by the time all was ready for the train to move off, and Paul then lit the two lamps on the front of the engine before taking the train several hundred yards up the line away from the blast of the explosives. Even he was uncertain of the result of his attempt to destroy the bridge.

Walking back along the side of the train, Paul ignored all the faces watching him—even that one sweet face that would be sure to register pity and sad understanding. He was certain he felt fine. Yet when he reached the exploder he had placed ready, and looked out ahead to the bridge, he knew he could not depress the plunger, because his hands would not move.

He stood there with the thing at his feet and felt so ill he began to shake. Time was racing past, darkness was gathering, and he *had* to do it, yet he reamined there, shaking and paralysed. To destroy that bridge would be to destroy a part of himself. It was the only thing he had ever done with pride. The cutting had never been finished; his command here had been a constant battle with another officer. But that bridge was clean and beautiful and creative. It was all his. Was it only death and destruction that lasted? His bridge had existed barely one week.

Still he stood with that exploder as a *bête noire* before him. One sharp thrust, and it would all be gone. Just one sharp thrust . . . but he could not do it. So many memories it held, that bridge. Into those wooden struts and chords was woven a drama that would soon be forgotten by most of the Russian soldiers. But he would remember it forever.

The bridge he had always wanted to build! Into it was woven his love for a woman to whom his skill had all been dedicated. Into it was also woven the sadness of a little corporal who served his conscience too faithfully at the end, and the warm inexplicable contrariness of the peasants who sang their mood in the beautiful melodies of Russia. And into that structure was woven the spirit of Valodya, laughing, reckless, as true to himself as he was to the world.

Paul's throat tightened as he saw again that merry, fair-haired young man balancing along a narrow strut across the rushing river. But it was that pale ghost that freed his hands. Valodya had been destroyed after so short a life, yet it did not make his existence worthless. Whilst he had lived, he had been as clean and beautiful and creative as that bridge. Paul recalled that night Valodya had first walked into the tent and told of how he had been caught in Moscow.

It does not matter what they did to me. As with the antique furniture, animal bestiality could not reduce my heritage to dirt beneath their feet.

He knew then that it did not matter whether the bridge had been there a week or an eternity. He had built it and a train had passed across it to freedom; that was the important thing. Like Valodya, it had been with him only a short time, but it would influence him for a lifetime. Slowly he raised his hand in signal, then pushed the plunger down.

It was if the forest was being riven apart when everything ahead of him rose up in an umbrella of debris and soil and water. He had thrown himself flat and covered his ears, but the roar slammed against his eardrums unmercifully, and he felt the tail end of the blast whistle across his head. It seemed as if the shower of pieces would never stop, but when he eventually walked forward to the torn riverbank, there was nothing left there but a great pile of broken logs that would soon be swept away on the current like the flotsam of splinters that covered the surface now as it raced past. Of the track there was nothing but a twisted mass of rail that hung obstinately on the far bank where their camp had once been.

He blinked as he stared at that sight. Even the bank had great holes in it, and there was nothing there on which to put the foundations of another bridge. Completely gone! No one could use his bridge, or even part of it. It had had its moment of glory, and no one could touch it now.

"Goodbye," he breathed, and he walked away, but the farewell was made to much more than a wooden bridge.

The enormity of what lay before him was obvious the minute the train began to move. Night, that arctic darkness that increased daily with amazing speed, had already fallen. Night brought a drop in temperature that frosted the snow and petrified the pines on each side of the track into grizzled sentinels, mysterious and threatening in the dim light thrown by the two lamps on the front of the engine.

"Dim light" was all too true. Whilst a lamp sufficed quite well when walking through darkness, even two were hopelessly inadequate for a man unused to driving a steam engine and driving it through unknown country on difficult track made treacherous by snow. So Paul found his speed regulated by the length of the lamps' beams, at a time when haste was essential. The snow-plough made very little difference, the covering being far too light to be affected by the pointed metal grid, but the universal whiteness hid the track so well it also hid the bends and inclines until the train was virtually upon them.

It was a strange experience, standing on the footplate with blankets around his shoulders to prevent the coldness from settling into every part of his body, the silence around him broken only by the sound of their slow progress through the snowy night. But imperative though haste would appear to be, Paul was prepared to allow his apprehension full rein.

What danger they could expect from Reds could only be from men in the forest. Trains could not follow now the bridge had gone, and if there were any ahead they could only be run by the Whites. That there were groups of enemy troops in the forest ahead of them was known. Archangel had been under threat for some time, and the fact that it had held out meant that Reds and assorted sympathisers had moved west around the White Sea coast to penetrate the forest and recruit villagers in readiness for the moment when all loyalists were abandoned by the last of their allies.

With that in mind, Paul felt it would be more prudent to go ahead with caution than race along risking an accident that would make them a stationary target for an enemy that emerged from the trees.

With the blowing of that bridge, all Paul had achieved had gone. Now he was filled with the iron determination to get them all to Murmansk, if it was the last thing he did in life. The Russian stood beside him, almost inhuman in his lack of emotion, having no idea what lay ahead for a novice railwayman. All the odds were against him, but those were the odds Paul understood best.

He said nothing to the Russian officer, as they rattled through the early night, but concentrated on the pressure gauges and the ghostly path between the trees ahead that became yellowed by the lamplight yard by yard as they moved north. He sensed a change in the man beside him since the death of Valodya. Even more unapproachable than before, the Russian was nevertheless easier to understand now for a man like Paul: his motivation was less idealistic than basically human. In those blackest months in France, Paul had fought for basic survival—ideals had flown on the wind—and he recognised that Swarovsky had reached a point even beyond that. The Russian was fighting toward the moment of his own death, which he knew was not far off.

Paul was jerked into sudden action as a curve in the track led straight into an upward incline without warning, and the train began to lose speed almost immediately.

"*Hell!*" he exploded quietly and opened the regulator with more haste than judgement.

But the incline was a formidable one, and the train had been travelling too slowly for the required steam pressure to be obtained in an instant. Paul felt the wheels begin to slip, and his clumsy action with the regulator put too much strain on the engine, which then seemed to shudder, groan, and almost stand on end, whilst he stared helplessly at the gauges and levers wondering what to do next. In the grips of terrible shuddering, the little engine ground to a halt, exuding steam, and there was an unpleasant smell of burning metal that filled Paul with apprehension. Looking ahead at the great white ramp rising ahead into darkness, he did the only thing possible and slammed the lever over to allow the train to roll back, praying as he did so that the icing on the rails would not mean they would slide back helter-skelter to the bottom and end up in a pile on the curve.

Only when they were safely back around the curve and sufficiently withdrawn along the straight stretch did Paul stop to consider the situation anew. It had been a nasty incident that served to emphasise once more how inept he was at driving an engine for more than a simple test run across a bridge or new stretch of track. This time he had been lucky, but he could not afford to take risks when so much was at stake. So he decided on caution rather than haste.

"I'm going to take a look before I try again," he said to Swarovsky. "I shouldn't be gone much longer than twenty minutes."

"Gone?" echoed the Russian, his pale eyes silvery in the reflections from the lamp. "What are you talking about?"

Paul recognised aggression and responded. "I'm talking about walking ahead to find out just what I am dealing with here. We couldn't see the top of that incline just now. It might go on up getting steeper as it goes, or it might level out just a few yards further on. There might be another curve to negotiate; there might be an equally steep downward incline almost immediately. Before I get up more steam and go hurtling up into a stiff climb, I want to know what I am going to have to cope with at the top of it."

"Are you telling me you propose to walk along the track for half a mile or so just to find out what lies ahead? You will be doing that at every turn in the track and every slight hill. We have urgent orders to get to Murmansk, Captain. This is no time for faintheartedness."

"Neither is it the time for foolhardiness," Paul snapped. "I refuse to take this train forward until I know what I must be prepared to do with it."

Swarovsky moved toward him. "I'll send two of my men. You remain at your post! If anything happens to you, we have no driver."

"And if anything happens to the train, we have no *hope*," Paul said with savage emphasis. "Anything to do with the railway has always been my command, Colonel. I have to drive this train, and I am the one who should see how best to do it." He was already swinging to the ground and looked up to say through a cloud of icy breath. "You and your men stay at your posts. Your job is to defend the train and its occupants, not me."

He tramped off into the darkness following the track that was clearly defined by their own earlier progress. But it was a spine-tingling sensation walking out into frozen wilderness with the frail light of one lamp as sole company, even though he knew that following the track would ensure that he could not get lost.

Faintheartedness, he thought grimly. Swarovsky was concerned only with arriving at Murmansk, not with the hazards of getting there. The engine had to be nursed and protected as their sole means of survival. Yagutov could make it as tame as a kitten, but right now it was a wild tiger liable to do anything to an untrained keeper. Paul had no wish to give it its head to go up a hill, only to find the ground dropping away again immediately or be hurled into a counter curve that could have them running off the rails at a crazy speed.

He walked briskly to offset the cold, but he missed the comfort of the fire on the footplate. The temperature made him short of breath; the cold pinched in his nostrils. He began to pant on the uphill climb, and it worsened when he went beyond the point where the engine had rebelled. The space between the rails had not been cleared by the snow-plough, and his boots began to slip on the frozen surface.

It seemed he had been walking half the night by the time he felt the ground level out before starting a very gradual downward incline that ran straight for a hundred yards or more and seemed likely to go on that way. In reality he had been away just over ten minutes, which meant his estimation to Swarovsky had not been far out. Just at that moment, his boot slipped on the snow as he turned, and he fell heavily, rolling back down the hill until a collision with the rails thumped his shoulder and brought him to a halt.

He got to his feet and went painfully on his way around the curve. Not until the small, yellow glow of the lamps on the engine became visible did Paul realise how little he had enjoyed that lone walk and how cheering it was to be in sight of fellow travellers again. But he merely reported what he had seen in a crisp tone, before outlining what action he was going to take.

"So, we are on the move again, at last," was the dry comment. "The ladies had no idea of what was happening when we ran backward and stopped for so long. They are right at the end of the train and, naturally, very apprehensive."

Paul flashed him a look. "Not half as apprehensive as I am up here at the front of the train, Colonel. Now, will you put some more wood on the fire while I open these valves?"

After only slight hesitation, the Russian did as he was asked, pulling open the fire-box door with the tongs to expose the fire glowing there. But Paul was conscious that the man's eyes were on him all the time.

"It wouldn't be a bad idea for you to learn some of this," Paul commented, his eyes on the steam gauge. "If anything *should* happen to me before we arrive in Murmansk, you would have the basic knowledge to set this thing in motion and avoid attack."

"Yes."

It was non-committal, and Paul decided to let it go at that. Perhaps it would be wiser to have only one engine-driver on this trip. It was during the ascent of the incline—this time successful, although with unwelcome groans and noises that suggested complaints from the engine—that Paul decided on something else that would be wiser for the trip. At the very next siding, he would shunt off the three extra trucks, instead of trying to drop them off to block the tracks. Without their weight, it was possible that the first ascent of the incline could have been made with no trouble. Those trucks were slowing them down and should be dropped off as soon as possible.

But they passed several sidings without stopping. In the darkness, he was upon them before he was prepared, the curving branch line only visible as he passed the swathe through the trees, and the returning curve joining the main track some hundred or so yards ahead. Apart from that, the train was now running fairly straight and level, the engine having settled into a speed that suited it. Paul therefore felt a reluctance to break the pattern while everything was going well, hoping there was not another hazard like that hill awaiting him.

They had also spotted what they thought might be campfires glowing in the darkness, soon after they had rattled across a bridge, and could not believe there were any remaining White troops in the area. It could have been the camp of huntsmen, of course, or another group of ex-convicts such as that which had attacked their train. But that sign of possible human presence made Paul uneasy and loath to stop. When he shunted off those trucks, there would be a time when the supply-truck was standing uncoupled and completely vulnerable on the track. In the case of sudden attack, there would be no chance to pull it away. No, he would wait for daylight that would allow him to post lookouts all around the siding.

With the coming of winter, dawn was arriving later and later, and Paul was bleary-eyed from staring into darkness at the pool of yellow light on snow by the time he realised it was possible to see for some distance ahead. But daylight brought more snow, this time falling in great flurries that further hampered vision, and Paul still hesitated about stopping in a siding. Lookouts would be no use in a snowstorm.

Swarovsky reminded him that soldiers travelling through forest areas always bivouacked beside water, so any siding in the vicinity of one of the numerous lakes or rivers was potentially dangerous. If they could find one that offered no lures to travellers, he thought the risk of stopping should be taken.

"We have also had nothing to eat or drink for twelve hours, Captain. That should be taken into consideration."

"I think we are nowhere near starving yet, Colonel. You said yourself, we have urgent orders to reach Murmansk."

"I was thinking more of the ladies," was the stiff reply.

"I suggest it's time they take care of themselves," Paul retorted sharply. "All the food supplies are in the truck with them. If they are hungry, let them open some tins."

Yet when they eventually came to a siding that was remote, used purely as a passing place for through trains and apparently deserted, Paul jumped from the footplate and walked back with instructions that tea and some kind of food be prepared whilst he did the shunting.

The halt was longer than anyone had anticipated, due to frozen points that had to be plied with hot ash and hammered energetically before they could be moved with any success. This had to be done at each end of the siding, and it took more than half an hour before Paul and Sapper Stevens could shift the heavy levers that swung the rail across.

Meantime, the ice on top of the water barrels had been broken and tea successfully brewed. Irina brought him a mug of steaming liquid, together with a thick slice of bully-beef between two pieces of dry biscuit.

"This is the best we can manage," she said to him, looking up to the footplate.

He jumped down and stood beside her, noticing how incredibly tired she looked. There were lines around her eyes and mouth that suggested a middle-aged woman.

"Are you all right?" he asked tautly, remembering that she wanted nothing from any man until she reached Murmansk.

"Yes, thank you." She passed him the tea and strange sandwich, then began to turn away.

He could not leave it at that. "Irina!"

"Yes?" She did not even twist her head to look at him.

"I'll get you there, I swear."

She nodded. "I know you will."

He watched her walk away, a small figure in furs that had cost a great deal of Swarovsky money. God, what a world she was forced to live in!

Sapper Stevens ran up puffing and panting. "They have uncoupled the supply-truck, sir."

"Good man. I'll take the train into the siding, and while the Russians uncouple the remaining three trucks, you switch the southerly points back."

The manoeuvre entailed leaving the supply-truck standing alone on the track just south of the points while Paul took the train into the siding, shed everything but the tender, then drove it out again at the northern end of the siding, ready to back onto the supply-truck once more, along the main track. He felt it was a dangerous time, with the entire train split into sections—a time when any enemy with intelligence would choose to attack. So he asked Swarovsky to post all men who were not engaged in uncoupling the trucks in places that would cover all directions of approach, their rifles at the ready.

It was a nervy time, which was reflected in what he was doing. He made a clumsy job of the shunting, backing along the track too fast so that he contacted with the supply-truck too heavily and pushed it some distance back instead of gently re-coupling with it. The Russian soldiers waiting to slip the locking bar into position jumped back in alarm and shouted at him.

"Try doing it yourself, you noisy bastards," he growled under his breath, easing the heavy lever once more and conscious of the flying minutes.

When he succeeded at the second attempt, his temper was still understandably short, so when his curt orders to get aboard immediately were met with general complaint, he told the whole group in no uncertain terms what he thought of them. In the event, only Swarovsky and the ladies understood what he had said, and the ladies took exception to a dressing-down they felt they did not deserve.

"There is no need to display your temper in front of these men. We are not peasants," snapped Olga. "We have been crouching in a tiny space for over twelve hours without even a hot drink. It has been extremely cold and uncomfortable."

"You have at least three more days and nights yet to go," he returned quickly. "And you will have even less space. The men are going to need sleeping space."

"But that is ridicule!" cried Zapalova dramatically. "I cannot have these . . . *creatures* . . . all the time with me."

"Then stay here!" was his icy advice. "I'm leaving now, and anyone who prefers a cup of tea to safety is welcome to settle down for a long stay."

With that he marched off to climb back on the footplate prior to moving off. A loud escape of steam and several blasts on the whistle were enough to have everyone scrambling for the trucks, and Paul noted with grim amusement that the ballerina was the first in. While he was waiting for them to board, he decided on a plan to make things awkward for anyone coming up behind him. After their train had passed over the northerly set of points, he would switch the points back to the siding. Any train rushing up the main track from the south would almost certainly be derailed unless his trick was spotted in time. In snow, that was unlikely, but in any case, the points would have to be unfrozen again before they could be moved, which would cause considerable delay and inconvenience to Reds on their way to Murmansk.

But as he began to take his own little train past the points, Swarovsky swung up onto the footplate, saying grimly, "Just because you are playing the part of engine-driver, there is no need to adopt the manners of one. There was no need for such behaviour just now."

Paul rounded on him. "How do you suggest I behave, under the circumstances?"

"Madame Zapalova is afraid."

"*So am I.*"

The well-bred face twisted in disgust. "Then I suggest you hide it a little better—especially in front of the ladies."

"Damn the ladies! I am afraid only that this engine will pack up on us before we get to Murmansk. If it does, we shall have to walk—which will be a damn sight more uncomfortable than their pile of straw in that closed truck. I might have a little sympathy with their grumbles then. If they want courtesy and general pampering, I suggest you stay back there with them. There is no need for you to play engine-driver, also. I'd sooner have Stevens. He's not so insistent on impeccable manners."

With that, he stopped the engine and left the cab to alter the points. When Paul climbed back, Swarovsky was sitting on a pile of logs in the corner of the cabin, with his injured leg held stiffly in front of him. Paul took no notice of him. The display of courage and fortitude, when the leg was so obviously giving the man hell, left him cold. He would still rather have Sapper Stevens on the footplate with him.

When the train got up steam, it ran off along the track with great willingness, and Paul realised he would have to adjust his attitude now the load was lighter. Learn my trade all over again, he told himself with bitter humour.

For a while the snow was a great nuisance, blocking the small window so that Paul had to keep putting his head outside the cab to look ahead. Each time he did so, the snow bit into his eyes with icy insistence. But then the train ran out of the snow into a clear area, and Paul had to decide whether or not it was worth stopping to clear the window now the engine was running so well. He decided against it. Sooner or later he would have to stop at a siding to take on more water. Far better to wait until then.

All the time, he was searching for boulders across the track, or uprooted trees—anything that would derail the train. Now the news of the British withdrawal was out, all kinds of groups would emerge from the forest where they had waited, to take a hand in hampering the retreat of those they considered interfering foreigners.

So the short hours of daylight passed, and Paul began to feel the strain very badly. Lack of sleep was affecting his powers of concentration, he felt unkempt and unshaven, and flitting around in his head were thoughts of the coming cold of night and pangs of hunger. They all depended on him to get them to Murmansk, yet he could not go on for four days and nights without rest. With himself in a state of collapse, he could prove to be their biggest hazard. When, then, would be the best time to stop? Where would they be safest?

It was decided for him. They grew low on water, and he knew he would have to stop at the water tank he saw just ahead. But where there was water, there was a river or lake, and men could be encamped there. Thanking providence that it was still too early in the year for the tank to be frozen up completely, Paul waited only long enough to fill up with water, then moved well up the line away from the siding. Then he halted for a snatched sleep and something to eat. It should be safe enough to stop in the middle of the forest.

In the event, Paul ate very little of the hastily prepared scratch meal. Two cups of tea went down his throat very quickly, but sleep must have overtaken him at that point because he remembered nothing more until Swarovsky shook him by the shoulder, and he came to, lying in the straw on the floor of the truck.

"We have been here over an hour, Captain, and the snow appears to be worsening."

Paul pushed himself up, feeling leaden headed and filthy. "Yes, yes. It's time we got going."

They all looked at him like accusers as he got unsteadily to his feet and tried to get his wits in some kind of order—at least, that is how he thought they looked at him. The women seemed like pale ghosts as they watched him from their corner of the truck, pieces of straw sticking to their expensive furs. Sapper Stevens had stubble around his face that gave him the appearance of a sad dog. Swarovsky, normally very spruce, also had growth around his chin, but since it was fair, it hardly showed. Paul was certain his own very dark stubble made him look as villainous as some of the Russian soldiers. His mouth felt dry and stale, and he longed for a bath and fresh clothes. The very last thing he wanted to do was climb up on that footplate again with the thought of another eternity of staring at yellow pools of light on the snow ahead of him. But that was what they expected, and he made his way to the door to jump down into the snow-filled night, feeling the loneliest man on earth.

He had grown used to that feeling by the dawn of the second day, and all his earlier pleasure in the peace and escape of a vast coniferous forest had deteriorated into a conviction that if he saw much more of snow-covered trees he would go mildly mad. The combination of stress, lack of sleep, snatched unsuitable food, unending boredom of scenery, and the company of a group of sullen, complaining people who had no idea what he was coping with as they sat hour after hour in their closed truck was playing on his morale. And there was the cold. The farther north they travelled, the more intense it grew and the more snow they encountered.

But despite all that, Paul saw danger and reacted with swift instinct when it was suddenly there before him. Seeing it all through eyes dazzled with snow, Paul's brain still worked quickly enough to send an urgent message through to his hands, so that he brought the engine to a halt several yards from the torn track.

"What is it?" asked Swarovsky sharply, getting up from the pile of logs to look from the cab.

"Sabotage."

Whoever had been responsible for it had not used much intelligence. Instead of choosing a bend or incline where a train would be almost certain to come upon it suddenly with no chance of warning, they had blown the gap in the track plumb in the middle of a long straight stretch, easily visible in daylight. It might have been a different thing if they had approached it at night.

The Russian stared out at it in silence, visibly defeated by the thought that their journey had come to an end. But Paul had encountered this kind of thing before in France. It could be the perfect ambush!

Drawing his revolver and staring around him at the trees, he said, "The through train passed successfully and can't be much more than six hours ahead of us. This is recent work, and whoever did it could be there in the trees still. I'll alert the men, and you be ready to take the train back at the first sign of trouble. You know what to do?"

Swarovsky nodded. "I have not been wasting my time up here, Captain."

At that, Paul climbed warily down from the footplate, watching the trees closely and ready to drop to the ground the minute he saw movement. He edged first to the supply-truck to thump on the side and call out to Stevens a brief account of the situation, telling him to get one of the ladies to translate to the Russian soldiers. Then he walked slowly forward again, watchful and apprehensive, until he reached the break in the line. The whole area remained silent except for the hissing steam from the engine, but he had seen such apparent peace broken by a horde of men appearing from innocent woodland before and did not trust it.

He could not have stood gazing around him for much longer than half a minute, but it seemed much, much longer as the silence continued and the expected rattle of rifle fire did not come. Only then did he risk breaking his scrutiny of the encompassing forest and putting his attention to the broken rails. Whoever had blown the track either did not have enough explosive material or knew very little about railways. There was a small crater in the ground, and the track was severed and twisted right in the midst of a length of rail. Hardly the work of a good saboteur! But it served its purpose, which was all that was needed.

Thinking of that truck containing rails that he had left way back in a siding, Paul strode back with less caution than he had shown earlier. By now, the Russians had spilled from the truck to stand staring at the gap ahead that meant they could go no further. Voices were raised in agitation, fast-flowing Russian (probably conflicting suggestions on what they should do now) was exchanged amongst them, and the soldiers all seemed ready to throw down their arms there and then. But worst of all, the women were climbing down from the truck in all stages of reaction. Irina just stood staring at the gap in silence, holding herself tightly with her arms wrapped around her fur coat. Olga ranted loudly about wasting their time in such a ridiculous journey when they should all have gone down to Lake Onega and demanded a seat on one of the aircraft leaving from there.

"She is right," said Swarovsky beside him. "We are hundreds of miles from Murmansk."

Paul swung round on him in mounting rage. "Just thank providence that I have encountered this sort of thing before, Colonel. We now have to take up track behind us to replace that broken section. It isn't easy work, and we have far too few pairs of hands . . . but it is the only way we are going to get to Murmansk. Now, get everyone lined up here while I explain what has to be done."

With a set expression, the Russian officer barked orders to his men and soon had them all quietly ranged along the side of the train. Then Paul outlined the work. First, the twisted track and broken sleepers must be removed, and the crater filled in and made level again. Then a section from behind the train must be taken up, together with the sleepers, and laid ahead of them. It would be a long job and there was a chance that they would be overtaken by darkness before it was finished. Fourteen men, including the two officers, were nowhere near enough to easily cope with the heavy sleepers and the transfer of lengths of rail, but it had to be done, and everyone must put his total energy into it. Since all the men were needed for hauling and lifting, it would be left to the ladies to fill in the crater with shovels from the truck. It would be hard digging, but they were all perfectly capable of doing it.

Ignoring the stir of protest from the ladies, he went on, "Because we have not immediately come under attack, it does not mean we are safe. Whoever did this might be under the leadership of a very intelligent man. Once we take up that track behind us, we are effectively immobilised. I think you will agree, Colonel, that that is the time a clever enemy would choose to attack."

Paul walked away before any protest or comment could be made. They demanded that he should take them to safety; they would work damned hard to give him every assistance.

If anyone had had doubts on the seriousness of their position, the doubts were removed as soon as work began. It was all made more difficult by bolts and spikes that were frozen in, and ground that was iron hard around the bedded sleepers. All this, with the threat of possible attack hanging over them and night approaching fast.

With their original work force, Paul could have accomplished it without too much concern, but with so few men, it was punishing work. Conscious of time flying, he drove them to their limits, shouting, swearing, and demanding as much from them as he did from himself. His voice grew hoarse, and his head swam with tiredness. So it was not surprising that he lost his temper completely when he noticed the women had stopped digging and some kind of altercation was taking place between them. Until that hole was filled in, nothing could be done about re-laying the track.

He flung down his pick and strode across to them, demanding in furious tones what they thought they were doing. "We are working like slaves over there," he added hoarsely. "You have the easiest job of all and can't even do that."

Olga looked at him with loathing. "We are not *barishnyi* so do not speak to us in that tone. *She* is the one who needs a lecture," Olga said, pointing to Zapalova. "Give your orders to *her*, you great bully, before I push her into this hole and cover her with earth. Perhaps you could twist her arm. I'm sure you are capable of it just to get your way."

Irina began gamely shovelling again at the rock-hard earth, but Zapalova threw her shovel at him and said with eyes glittering with rebellion. "I do no more. It is finish! I say all along you have the manner of a servant."

"And you have the manner of a spoilt child," he flashed back. "Pick up that shovel and dig!"

"No," she cried. "I do no more. My hands will be ruined. I am prima ballerina."

"You'll be a dead one if we don't get away from here soon," he told her with deadly finality. "Pick up that shovel and do as you are told."

Drawing herself up in a histrionic fury, she spat at him in French, *"Cochon! Cochon!"*

Without hesitation, he dealt her a resounding slap around the left cheek that had her staggering backwards. "Before we get to Murmansk, you might have to do worse than this when I tell you to. I'd rather save any one of those peasant-soldiers than you, so if you want to be on the train when it moves off, you will work as hard as they are. Judging by the number of lovers you are constantly bragging about, you have extraordinary stamina, so a little digging should come quite easily to you. In fact, you should be able to keep it up long after everyone else has become exhausted. Now, pick up that shovel and get to work . . . and if you ever call me a pig again, I shall hit you a damn sight harder than I did just then."

She had turned ashen with shock at his treatment. "You would not leave me here to starve in the forest."

"No," he said harshly, taking out his revolver and pointing it at her. "I would shoot you before I left. You wouldn't feel the wolves tearing you apart then."

She stared at the gun, then gave a strange kind of moan and picked up her shovel. Olga laughed with a touch of hysteria.

"The same applies to you," he told her, trying to keep a grip on himself. "If you put your energy into digging instead of female spite, this kind of thing would never occur."

She flared up at once. "Do not start on me! You owe me particular respect."

"I owe you nothing. Stop thinking of yourself for once in your life and do something for the good of us all. If we are attacked before this job is finished, now might be your last chance to do so."

When he got back to the train and looked over his shoulder, all three women were working furiously. It was surprising what a little hatred of him did for their muscles!

After several more hours of work, the most vital time in the whole operation had come. The two lengths of rail had somehow to be dragged and manhandled from their position at the rear of the train to the site just ahead of it. Even with the ground levelled and the sleepers bedded, there was still a lot to be done before Paul dare take the train across it. One wheel off the track and that *would* be the end of their journey. The distance between the rails must be tested with a track gauge, then they must be spiked to the sleepers. Even by risking only alternate spikes it would take some time, and darkness was now only two hours off.

Giving a brief glance to the two women who were now up on the footplate posted as lookouts with rifles, and at Olga posted just inside the supply-truck, Paul nodded to Swarovsky.

"Let's go, but be prepared to run for cover the minute they give us a warning."

With that terrible feeling of expecting a bullet in the back at any moment, Paul went about the tricky task, remembering other times when he had struggled in knee-high mud to do the same thing under shell-fire. He hammered and measured and tested until he suddenly realised it was difficult to see with any clarity. When he got wearily to his feet, he saw there was now a complete track running ahead of him into the fast-gathering darkness.

It was while he was staring at it in a bemused manner that someone appeared beside him with a steaming mug. Trying to collect his thoughts after his concentrated efforts, he looked at Irina through bleary eyes.

"What's that?"

"Soup. I heated several of those big tins in the truck."

"*Heated?*" He turned and saw a big fire blazing merrily some yards away and the men now clustering round it to drink the soup with ravenous appetite.

"I gave no permission for a fire to be lit . . . and you were supposed to be on guard," he accused angrily.

In the twilight, her eyes were just large shining blobs in a face still palely impassive.

"I am the medical adviser of this group, if you remember. The health of us all is my concern alone. It did not need your permission to prepare some kind of hot meal for those who are cold and exhausted and must face another night of hardship."

"But . . . the fire! It betrays our position."

"To whom?" she asked quietly. "Do you know how long we have been here? Five hours. An enemy who will sit for so long watching us would now be too affected by cold to attack. Am I not right?"

Still bemused, he gazed back into her eyes. "Yes, you are right."

"And if we do not put some warm sustenance inside our bodies, we shall also be too affected by cold to continue." Her gaze slid past him to the track. "Is it done?"

Feeling remarkably light-headed all at once, he said with a laugh of relief. "Yes, it's done."

She looked back at him, and her eyes were glowing with something he ought to recognise. "Thank you."

He was warmed by more than the soup. Suddenly that snowy, isolated night scene was aglow like her eyes. It was if they were united and able to conquer anything together. He would achieve, and she would be there with quiet, unshakeable comfort to support him. The exhaustion, the dirt and grime, the ache in his limbs and head dropped away.

"I promised I would get you there," he said softly.

She nodded. "I trusted you to know your profession. You must allow me to know mine. You are not angry that I lit a fire?"

"Angry? No . . . no," he said fervently with a voice that was rough with shouting.

But the moment of union was broken by her next words. "As a nurse, I must ask that Sasha remains in the truck with me when we move off. All this has been too much of a strain on his leg. If he is to be of any assistance to you, he must be allowed to rest until the terrible pain has diminished."

"I . . . yes, of course." He let her walk away, cursing himself for thinking anything had changed. Until they reached Murmansk, personal feelings must be put aside. Yet when he eventually pulled himself up onto the footplate beside Sapper Stevens and faced the night ahead of him, he could not help feeling the burden on his shoulders at present would be much lighter if he knew Irina would be his when they were away from all this.

But they had yet to get up to the northern port, so he pushed aside his own unhappiness and mentally squared his shoulders as he prepared to take the train across the new piece of track they had just put down with such exhaustive effort.

"Slowly does it," he said to Stevens as he carefully opened the regulator, then smiled briefly by way of encouragement. "At least, you can see what you are heading into from up here . . . and you won't have to mind your language because of the ladies."

Stevens smiled faintly back. "I didn't notice you paying much attention to that back there, sir."

Feeling at ease in the company of the only other Englishman in the group, Paul took the engine gradually forward, satisfied when the wheels rolled smoothly over the joints and onto the original track beyond.

"Ah," he breathed, "we are still in business, Stevens."

"If you get this train and all of them back to Murmansk, it'll be a miracle, sir."

He turned sharply. "What makes you think that?"

The long, mournful face creased into a calculating expression. "There's a long, long way to go yet, sir, and there's too many wolves in this forest for my liking."

Although Paul did his best to cheer up his batman, the words stuck in his mind through the early part of the night as he stared out at the inadequate light of yellow lamps on the snow. The night was clear, which was something to be thankful for when he had to negotiate two sudden nasty curves and an embankment that seemed dangerously narrow in the surrounding darkness.

He felt as if he had been driving a train for an eternity, and now had the feel of it, even if the last incline had come within a yard of getting the better of him. But the feeling of greater familiarity with the engine gave him no more enthusiasm for the journey. He knew their progress was slow because he was putting caution before speed, and the through-train could be a whole day ahead of them by now. What had taken four days on the journey down would probably take five and nearing six at his present rate. The prospect appalled him. How could he keep this up for three more days and nights?

Staring moodily into the darkness for hour after hour, he found that the only things that broke into his depression were the requests to Stevens to stoke up the fire-box.

"We're running low on wood, sir," Stevens said at some time during the middle of the night.

"Mmm, we shall have to stop and cut more before tomorrow is out, I suppose. Tomorrow, Stevens," he mused. "Tomorrow will be exactly like today, and yesterday—snow, forest, railway-track . . . snow, forest, railway-track. What wouldn't I give for a tropical beach, palm trees, and a blue lagoon."

"And girls in grass skirts?"

He turned to grin at the soldier. "Yes, a few of them wouldn't come amiss, either. But I'd trade even the girls for a pot of your jolly good tea right now."

"Me too, sir."

With thoughts of tea in his head, Paul turned away to look ahead through the cab window, and his pulse gave a great lurch that sent cold fear rushing through him.

"*Christ!*" he breathed and flung himself into action that demanded the impossible from an engine rattling along at an easy and contented speed.

The night became filled with the agonised scream of metal on metal as spinning wheels were forced to slow against a forward impulse that was too overpowering. Paul's arms felt as if they were being torn from their sockets as he feverishly wound the brake and hauled on the heavy levers, praying for strength he did not have. Rocking from side to side, the little engine roared its way forward against all his efforts to stop it, until it seemed almost to skid along the rails to grind to a screeching halt within two feet of disaster.

Sweating and shaking with the strength of his own pumping heartbeat, Paul let out his breath slowly as he stared from the cab.

"It's over, Stevens," he said in defeated tones. "We'll never get to Murmansk now."

N *i n e t e e n*

Inside the supply-truck there was pandemonium and panic. The whole place rocked violently, sending boxes from their piles and scattering equipment across the straw at the feet of those inside. Several of the soldiers were thrown off balance to land in a pile in one corner, their stacked rifles rattled along the wooden side of the truck before falling splayed across the floor.

The terrible screech of wheels on the track beneath them added to the fear of not knowing what was happening. The two lamps hanging from the roof miraculously did not fall, although they swung madly from side to side to put changing shadows on the faces turned inward in questioning fright. Lyudmilla began to scream. Olga clung, a tight ball of misery, to one of the heavy wooden Swarovsky chests, her face chalky white.

She will not stand much more, thought Irina as she put up her hands quickly to prevent a box from falling on Sasha, who was sleeping. Of us all, Olga will be the first to crack on this journey. But her own heart was thumping against her ribs as the train seemed to struggle to combat a force that was holding it back. It was three A.M., but it did not seem to her that ten hours had passed since they left the place where the rails had been lifted. She must have slept, yet it seemed she had been sitting staring at the pile of boxes the whole time. So quiet, so monotonous it had been, then suddenly the night had been shattered.

Sasha awoke and struggled up, looking twice his age in the dim light. "What is happening?"

She could hardly hear him above the din. "We are stopping—very urgently. We do not know why."

He got to his feet but was thrown when the train gave a last lurch, and he lay rolling in pain in the straw. She did not attempt to go to him, there was nothing she could do, and the train had now come to a screeching, grinding halt. The ballerina stopped screaming, the soldiers fell quiet, and everyone looked at the door. The silence was unnerving. Having expected a crash as they hit something, or the sound of guns, the normality seemed *abnormal*.

Holding herself tense, Irina strained her ears. At first, all she could hear was the high-pitched escape of steam, then thought she recognised another sound faintly in the background. Water! Her blood seemed to freeze in her veins as she remembered Sasha saying soldiers always bivouacked beside water. She also remembered the three survivors saying the Reds did not waste bullets on prisoners. Her stomach crawled as she thought of how they were possibly outside now, preparing to set the truck alight to burn them all inside it.

Clambering to her feet with thoughts of what they might be doing to Paul, she knew she could not stay where she was. The horror of Valodya's death swept over her, and she ran at the door to tug at it with all her might. If she jumped from the truck and ran, they would be forced to shoot her.

Sensing her terror, the soldiers also grew desperate to get out of that small truck, whatever might be awaiting them outside, and they soon had the heavy sliding door open. Jumping out onto the snow with scant care, Irina lost her footing and fell, thinking only that she had lost her chance of a clean bullet as her blessed end. But even through such nightmare thoughts the peaceful scene made its impact, and she sat up, still trembling, to gaze at the sight of the engine with its two headlamps and the tall figure outlined inside the cab, slumped across the levers in an attitude of defeat. There was no movement, no sign of soldiers, no suggestion that Paul and his companion were prisoners. They certainly were not dead, for as she watched, Paul straightened up and climbed clumsily from the engine to stand leaning against it, staring into space.

Sasha came up, limping badly, but walked right past her to the English officer. She heard him demanding an explanation in a voice taut with fear. But Sasha's fear was only that he would arrive in Murmansk too late to be part of the new White Russian Army. That was all he lived for now.

She struggled up from the snow and tramped across the sloping ground toward the two men, who were standing beside the train staring out ahead. When Irina arrived beside them she realised they were virtually standing on a riverbank, and what she saw made her gasp. No more than two feet from them, the track ended in a twist of iron that hung grotesquely out over space. The light from the lamps showed spikes of wood and debris clinging to the bank, then nothing but an abyss of blackness with the sound of rushing water below.

"There was a sudden void ahead," Paul was saying to Sasha. "I never thought I'd stop in time. The whole train would have plunged into the river."

"It might just as well have done," said Sasha tonelessly.

Paul continued to stare out at the twisted rails. "Build a bridge; knock it down. Rebuild it; knock it down again. The whole world has gone mad."

"So that is the end?" asked Sasha.

Paul still had his gaze on the blackness. "There's nothing more I can do."

"There must be," cried a voice beside Irina, and she turned to see Olga had come up to them. "We must go back to Lake Onega for an aircraft."

Paul swivelled in a daze to stare at Olga as if he had no idea who she was. "We have taken up track and blown a bridge. We can't go back."

She stepped nearer him. "You can put the track in front of us again and rebuild the bridge."

"It takes weeks to rebuild a bridge." It was lifeless, an automatic answer to a ridiculous statement.

"You have done it before. Do it again!"

"I can't."

"Yes, you can. You must. It is up to you to get us out of here," she cried. "All this only to stop now! You *have* to get us to safety."

Paul put his hand across his brow in a gesture of exhaustion. "There is nothing I can do."

The girl's face became ugly in its hostility as she kept battering him with words. "Then *think* of something. You have always wanted to command us all. *Do it!*"

He seemed to rouse from his stupor of reaction at that and became sharply defensive. "If there was anything to be done, I'd do it. My God, do you think *I* want to be stranded here in this forest?"

"You promised to take me to England," she raged, stepping up to confront him face-to-face. "You promised!"

"*England!* We can't even get to Murmansk."

"Then you lied. All of it was lies," Olga accused with high-pitched hysteria. "You promised to get me to England. It was our agreement. You *have* to take me; you have an obligation."

Irina could stand no more. "Keep quiet, you silly, immature fool, and leave him alone," she snapped. "He has done more than any man could be expected to do. He'll never get to England himself—his own country—so you cannot demand that he takes you. And why should he?"

Olga fell on her like a wolf with its prey. "Because he is my lover. I could be carrying his child." Swept away with her own desperation, she spoke more and more wildly. "When a man takes a mistress, he looks after her, doesn't he? Valodya saved that whore of his." She rounded on her brother in a welter of sobbing, clinging to his thick coat and trying to shake him in her insistence. "Tell him, Sasha. *Tell him!* You have had mistresses. Tell him what a man must do after he has taken a woman in the forest."

But Sasha just looked from her to Paul, prised her fingers from his coat, and limped away to the end of the train, where he stood, a tall figure in the very faint light seeping from the supply-truck. There was movement as Stevens walked quietly away from the engine to join the Russians who were gathering to look at the broken bridge. Olga, her ungovernable desperation completely mastering her, stumbled away to drop sobbing into the snow, a sprawling, pathetic figure that everyone tried to ignore.

Her departure left Irina and Paul facing each other with a world of unspoken pain between them. She saw by the dark confession in his eyes and the broken expression on his face, aged by dark ragged growth, that Olga had not lied. As she gazed up at him, the nurse vanished and the young girl she had denied so few days ago came throbbingly alive again. There in that desolate place, then, at that moment of helplessness, she was filled with the agony of the youth she had refused to snatch when it had been within her grasp. It was now too late—banished by lust in a forest.

Paul seemed unable to say anything to her, and she knew there was nothing he could say that would override words that so brutally separated them. Yet she could not pull away from that moment. She asked with her eyes, "Why?" yet knew the answer. Had she not challenged him to take Olga instead of herself? How could she have known he would?

It was plain he recognised her optical question but was too shattered to begin to answer. She looked at a tall young man, unshaven and bleary eyed, in a long khaki greatcoat and a peaked cap that shadowed his face, and knew he was accepting defeat by his very silence and stillness. Those brown eyes that had been so warm with love for her now looked back with guilt and the echoes of failure. She could stand no more and turned away to join the Russians, who were now by the supply-tuck, leaving Paul standing alone by the rushing, invisible river.

It was incomprehensible that now, in the moment of her greatest peril when they all recognised that survival was no more than a faint miracle, she should be overtaken by an emotion that played no part in the life she had become used to living. It was something completely new to her, this driving, tearing jealousy, and it raged through her while the others sat listlessly on the straw-covered floor of the truck, drinking tea made by the two orderlies, who could think of no better way to face the inevitable.

As she gazed at the piled boxes around her, Irina could see only Paul and Olga lying in each other's arms in the peace of the forest. She thought of his mouth on Olga's voluptuous body as her sister-in-law drove him further into passion, and his hands touching that creamy skin with exciting caresses. Tormented by memories of those things a man can do to excite a woman, she thought of how much more heady and ecstatic it would be with Paul. How Olga must have teased and enticed him, her blue eyes afire with seduction! An instinctive lover, she had once called him. How he must have responded to her lures, his strength gradually subduing and capturing Olga's bared, curving body!

She bit her lip until it hurt, but the pain inside her was still there. Why, why had she *now* to come so vitally alive to those things that had been thrust from her life four years ago? Why now, when all freedom was gone? Had she truly believed that youth would come eventually? Had she ever hoped for any life other than the one she had been living for an eternity? *Yes, yes*, she cried inwardly. Underneath my acceptance, my preoccupation with easing pain, my dedication to greater things, I hoped . . . dear God, I *hoped* . . . for love and happiness. Yet, when I could have had it for one short beautiful summer, I could not grasp it. Loyalty to Sasha, too much love for Paul who had to go back to his own country at the end of it, devotion to the title of wife—all those I put before my own selfish desires, and I am the loser all along the line. Sasha did not need my loyalty, after all, and the title of wife also meant nothing to him. Paul has found a mistress who would have gone back to England with him.

Sestritsa, Olga called me—Sister of Mercy—but, God in heaven, there is anything but mercy inside my heart at this moment. I want only to beat him to the ground with my contempt of his professed love. It did not even withstand the first test.

Then she was looking at him again, across the width of the truck as he appeared by the narrow opening in the door. Only for a moment did he hold her gaze with that same air of defeat, before he climbed into the truck and crossed to squat beside Sasha with a folded map in his hand.

"I'm going to move back right away," he said in a voice grown scratchy with tension. "I've been looking around, and there's a chance that others are still in this vicinity. I don't think we should risk staying here, even though it seems unlikely that the Reds did this. Why blow a bridge when they believe we have all gone through? They want the railway intact for their own use. It could be some damn fools of our own who had no idea we were still south of here, or it could more likely be the work of White Finns. They have been roaming about making themselves a general nuisance to our commanders, and probably now feel free to continue harrassing the Reds to promote their own cause. I think it was Finns, because they have also cut the telegraph wires. Our people wouldn't have done that when they know there are still isolated groups scattered in the forest . . . and the Reds need the communication system as much as they need the railway."

Sasha listened with interest, but it was plain he still did not understand what Paul was leading up to. "What is the advantage of moving back when we know we are cut off?"

Paul put up a hand. "I'll explain in a moment. First, I want to make our position clear. With no telegraph, all hope of sending a message for help is out. We might have crossed the river on a raft if they sent down a train to pick us up, but it is pointless going on with no means of letting anyone know we are moving north on foot. We'd all die of cold and exposure before we reached any place of safety. We can't go back and hope for a seaplane to pick us up because I blew the bridge as we left. So, unable to go forward or back, there is only one alternative—to cut across country." He opened the map and spread it out on the straw. "I estimate that we are in this area," he said, pointing with his finger to make a circle. "Here is the railway crossing the river. If we strike out to the northeast, we shall eventually reach the White Sea coast."

Irina saw that Sasha had grown intensely interested now that Paul was talking about another chance to be on the move . . . any move that would get him nearer Murmansk. Already, he had thrust aside his disgust over what had gone before with Olga, and Paul had overridden his defeat to speak as if it would be the easiest thing in the world to walk off across arctic forest to the coast. Men were the strangest creatures. They were faced with defeat and despair, and the next minute they behaved as if nothing else but their present ideas mattered. They seemed to live in a world where emotion did not exist.

Racked by it herself, she hit out at them both. "Face reality," she cried in English for Paul's benefit. "You both sit there talking of the impossible because it suits your dreams. Sasha will get to Murmansk if he has to crawl through the snow. And you," she blazed at Paul, "now have a desperate desire to get *her* to England. But have you thought of everyone else? *Have you?*" Her anger was all for Paul now. "Of course we shall reach the White Sea eventually . . . or we could go on to Siberia, you know. You fool! How long do you think we should last out there?" She got to her feet to look down on him contemptuously. "This is not England. It is not possible to *walk* to the White Sea through Russian forest. Have you not learnt *that* much since you came to our country?"

He winced a little from her attack but just said quietly, "I'm hoping to take the train across."

"*The train?*" Sasha leant forward eagerly. "How is that possible?"

Paul's dark head tilted down again as he indicated on the map the various sidings marked all along the railway. "I'm not sure it *is* possible, yet. But in thinking about what we should do next, something came into my head that I think is worth following up. See, here are the sidings we have already passed. I marked them off as a means of checking our progress."

Sasha studied the map, then looked across at Paul. "Yes, I see that we can tell our present position, but I still do not understand what makes you think you can take the train across the forest."

"I might be wrong. Until I take the train back, I won't be certain. But I think it is worth a try. At some time during the night—I think not too long before we reached this river—I saw what I thought was a siding leading off from the track, but I didn't remember seeing it link back again. At the time, I was surprised and told myself I must have passed the other end without noticing. It was unusual because of the monotony of the scenery, which was only relieved by the advent of a siding, but looking on the map just now, I find there is not one marked to correspond with what I saw."

"Perhaps you imagined you saw it," suggested Sasha.

Paul shook his head. "No. A line was definitely there, leading off to the east. I recall thinking that if someone had played my own trick with the points, we would be in trouble." He looked seriously at Sasha. "I believe it could have been a branch line. Up in Murmansk, I heard some talk of a proposed link with the Archangel–Valogda railway that would run through Onega on the White Sea coast. It was only a proposal, as I understood it, but it could be that a start has already been made. I think we should go back to investigate."

"And I," said Sasha immediately.

Paul got carefully to his feet. "You must understand that I am not certain how far back it was. In the darkness, I shall have to go slowly so that I don't pass it in error."

Sasha stood beside him. "I will come on the footplate and watch with you."

"Fair enough." Paul began to fold the map abstractedly. "But once we find it, I want to wait until it gets light enough to see what we have actually stumbled upon. It might be merely a half-finished siding, or it might be a long loop-line that will take us some miles south and rejoin the main track."

"And if it *is* one of those things?" demanded Irina loudly, cheated of her revenge on them both.

Paul said nothing, but Sasha shrugged his shoulders. "We think of something else. That is the only thing that must concern us, at the moment. I rely on you to help."

"No! I have decided to copy everyone else on this train and think only of myself from now on," Irina cried, finding herself shaking with temper. "I am going to be the first to snatch a cup of tea, the one to take the most straw, the loudest in demanding attention. I am going to complain of the cold, cry that the peasants are filthy uncouth creatures because they urinate in the straw . . ." Her gaze slid to Paul. "And throw down my shovel when my back aches. So, gentlemen, do not rely on me for anything."

They both looked distinctly shaken by her words. Then Sasha walked away to explain to the soldiers what they were planning to do, leaving Paul still there in front of her. But she deliberately turned her back on him, and he moved away to jump from the truck. A few moments later, the door was drawn across, then the train began moving slowly back, away from the scene of their near disaster. But there was only one disaster she could think of, and when the slow steady clicking of wheels on rails settled into a pattern, she leant against the rough wood while the tears trembled on her eyelashes.

There was nothing now in either of the two officers except the fanatical determination to succeed, and both of them stood silently on the footplate as the train travelled slowly backward in search of a way to achieve that success. Both of them knew their new destination was Archangel and were prepared to use each other in order to get there before the White Sea froze across and the last ships had left.

Paul's mind was working furiously on impossible plans, in case he had been mistaken about the branch line. Could sledges be made from the wood of the supply-truck? But who would pull them? How long could a man survive in the forest at this time of the year? Was it possible to create some kind of vehicle on wheels that could be driven by foot pedals? If he deliberately derailed the tender, could they get the wheels off to attach to some kind of crude cabin? How long would it take to construct such a thing? How far would they have to travel in it . . . at what speed? Would the food supplies last out, how would they keep warm, would they arrive at the coast only to find a sea of solid ice? On and on went the questions, pounding in his head and finding no sensible answers.

He no longer cared about anything but defying those who were trying to prevent him from reaching safety. He recognised the feeling, he had had it once before in France, when he had arrived at a hospital to visit a nurse and found only a blackened ruin. In the forest he had made the mistake of coming alive again. Now that was over, and he had nothing to lose once more.

It was not a sensation he liked, heading backward with no idea what was behind him, but that was another reason for going slowly; when they came upon a bend, the short train followed the curve gently round, and he could not remember any difficult inclines on that particular stretch that might halt them. But he grew more and more tense as time went past, and he told himself he *could* not have been mistaken. Yet he was conscious of Swarovsky's avid concentration that seemed prepared to condemn him at any moment.

His eyes ached from staring at snow-covered trees for mile after mile, so when there was a sudden break, he was not even certain that he had seen it in reality. His tense nerves reacted immediately, and he brought the engine to a halt with a clanking of buffers.

"There it is," he said sharply. "I was not mistaken, and it definitely isn't a siding."

The headlamps shone out on a curving track going away into the forest to the east. Their frail light showed only part of the branch line before it was swallowed up by dark forest, so there was no way of telling if it was a possible escape route or something that ended fifty yards inside the trees.

"Let us go straight along it," urged Swarovsky.

"Not until it is light enough to see what we have found."

"That is wasting valuable time."

Paul looked at him across the cabin. "If it is merely a railhead put there when the main line was laid, with the object of extending it at a later date, it will be senseless to go onto it. In any case, the points will be frozen solid and need thawing out. Better to stay where we are until we can investigate further."

Swarovsky leant back against the side of the cab. "What advantage is there in remaining on the main track? We cannot go forward or back on it, so there is nothing to lose by leaving it."

"I suppose it will be better than sitting here doing nothing until daylight comes," Paul agreed recklessly. "But unfreezing those points will take a hell of a time, so I suggest the ladies get busy organising a meal of some kind. There's no knowing what lies ahead, and we are all hungry, I imagine? It will also keep them occupied. Hysterics help no one and are bad for the general morale of the men."

After a brief, expressive glare, the Russian nodded. "I will speak to them."

Unfreezing the points seemed, at first, to be a task that would defeat them. Paul grew more and more pessimistic as successive applications of hot ash followed by lubrication failed to shift them. The lever eventually responded, but the points themselves would not budge, which suggested they had not been used for a very long time—if ever. Hardly an encouraging theme for his hopes.

A fire had been lit, everyone now feeling he was in the hands of Fate and caution could be thrown to the winds. The smell of cooking sharpened the hunger of those hammering at the points, and they grew impatient to be relieved by those taking a short rest. Paul kept well away from the supply-truck, where the women were busily finding plates and spoons for a meal they considered fitting for "the condemned." He was now merely the engine-driver, as far as those three were concerned, so he would keep to the part.

Wanting to keep warm while the others were hammering, he took a couple of lamps, called Sapper Stevens, and set off along the branch line to investigate. They tramped at a good pace and after ten minutes saw no reason to suppose the track did not continue as they hoped. Turning back, Paul expressed his feelings on the subject to the man who was as far from his homeland as he was himself.

"Well, Stevens, we seem to have found ourselves a nice little back exit." When the soldier said nothing, Paul looked at him shrewdly. "Not too overjoyed, eh?"

"If you want the truth, sir, I don't think we've got a hope in hell."

"I'll remind you of those words when we all troop into Archangel," said Paul. "Now I suggest we break into a trot before we freeze on the spot. Something smells good back at the train."

As they came into sight of the main track again, it was quite extraordinary to see a blazing fire with figures moving around it as tinned foods were heated into something approaching a banquet. It reminded Paul of one New Year's Eve when he had been a boy, and an unusually heavy fall of snow had instigated an impromptu party in the garden of his home. Time had banished the boyhood memory, until now. It must be the snow and the women in their long coats bustling around the fire with cooking utensils.

His return coincided with the announcement that the points were stiff, but movable, and the meal was ready. With that sense of mild amazement he had never overcome at the changeability of the Russian temperament, Paul saw them all set about the serving and eating of a hot meal with all the excitement that suggested his long-ago New Year's Eve party. Optimism reigned once more.

But Paul had no intention of joining the group sitting inside the supply-truck with the door open to get the warmth from the fire. Together with Stevens, he returned to the engine, ready to move off as soon as they had eaten. One of the Russian cooks brought them food and great mugs of hot tea. Irina had always done so before, but Paul knew that was all over.

There was no doubt that warmth and a semblance of normality was doing their morale inestimable good, and Paul's own spirits rose as he ate. They were not beaten yet. But he was not so relaxed that he did not stiffen and reach slowly for his revolver when he saw unmistakable movement in the trees beyond the fire. The flamelight had caught at something that glinted as it moved, then at something else a little farther along.

"Stevens," he said quietly, "there's someone out there. Have you got your rifle handy?"

"Yes, sir."

"Don't move quickly," he advised, gently putting down the plate on the metal floor of the cab. "Those in the truck must be clearly outlined by the fire, but we are in semi-darkness here. Whoever it is will be concentrating on the others but might spot us if we make sudden or noisy movements."

"Right, sir . . . but what do we do?"

Heart thudding, Paul thought quickly. "We'll get out at the back of the train and split up to cross the line out of range of the firelight. You go north, I'll go south, and we'll circle up behind them. If we fire off enough rounds, they'll think there's a whole company of us. After looking at the brightness of the fire, they won't be able to see a thing when they turn back. On the other hand, they will be beautifully outlined for us to pick off."

"I'm not exactly a crack shot, sir."

"Just make a lot of noise, Stevens . . . but for God's sake, don't hit one of our own people."

With great care, they got to their feet, both now satisfied that whoever was out there was creeping up for the attack with too much confidence that they were effecting complete surprise. Yet Paul had got no farther than putting his foot on the step, when the night was rent by the blood-curdling howl of wolves that seemed to come from all around the train. For a moment, his heart raced, then the shock passed and left him weak with anti-climax.

But the terrible chorus brought silence and stillness to those in the supply-truck, who could now see the great grey shapes slinking between the trees, their eyes golden-bright with the reflection of flames. There were more than ever before—a large pack hunting together because of the hardness of approaching winter. They were hungry. The smell of food had drawn them to the train, and they were not going to be driven away until the temptation was satisfied or withdrawn.

As Paul watched, the pack leader and two of the dominant males moved forward out of cover of the trees to fix their human tormentors with bold, determined stares. The firelight caught their thick grey pelts and gilded them, turning the wolves into creatures of fable and legend— masters of the forest. But the howling chorus continued and echoed all around as the ringleaders closed in to sniff out the source of food.

"Blimey, they're going to attack us," breathed Stevens, eyes wide with fright.

"It's the smell of the cooking," said Paul, trying to sound reassuring in the face of something in which he was inexperienced. "They're not after us—just the food."

"As far as wolves are concerned, that's just what we are."

"Then they're mistaken," he said shortly. "Why don't the Russians do something? They come from this kind of terrain. They ought to know how to deal with this."

"Not now. Not since you blew that little lot up. They are convinced the wolves are out for revenge. They won't do anything, I'll wager."

"Damn them and their revenge!" swore Paul, thoroughly rattled by the howling and the feeling that he was expected to deal with everything on this nightmare journey. "I'll soon scare them off."

In the act of raising his revolver, he saw movement to his right. It was Swarovsky with a flaming branch, which he hurled across at the leading wolves with a great crying curse. The stick whistled through the air toward the animals, and as if by magic, the howling stopped instantly. Then there was a rustling as the wolves all rushed back into the trees like fleeing agile spectres, to vanish into the darkness.

But hunger was stronger than fear, and it was no time before the glint of yellow eyes could be seen out there in the night and the cry that spoke of desolate wilderness rose again in increasing chorus. Paul had had enough. Walking along close to the train, revolver at the ready, he arrived at the supply-truck, only to receive a battery of accusing glances from those inside. Losing patience and forgetting that the soldiers could not understand him, he shouted at them.

"Let's get this straight, shall we? Even if animals had brains enough to decide on personal vengeance for that dead cub in the cutting, these wolves are not the same ones we saw several hundred miles south of here. They are just plain hungry, and we have food."

No one spoke, and Paul turned on Swarovsky. "They don't really believe these creatures are trailing me with the idea of vengeance, surely?"

He shrugged. "They are peasants—people of the forest. Superstition is part of their lives."

Paul saw the three women looking at him, and his anger flared up. "Well, I am not offering myself as a wolves' supper just to make everything come right. I'm moving off *now*. Anything that is not inside this truck within two minutes will be left behind. Tell them, will you?"

He put the revolver away and strode back to the engine carelessly, to show everyone who cared to watch that he was not afraid of wolves. But he was acutely aware of the creatures only a few feet from the other side of the fire, who watched his every movement.

"Steam up, Stevens," he said loudly, as he rejoined the soldier. "We'll show them we're no Red Riding Hoods."

"What about the Colonel, sir?"

"We'll show him, too."

Stevens grinned nervously. "I meant, is he coming up front?"

Paul unwound the brake viciously. "If he is, he'll have to step on it—unless the wolves get him on the way here, by way of revenge."

The Russian officer did, in fact, climb painfully onto the footplate as Paul opened the regulator just enough to get the train on the move. But neither man said anything as the first belching puff silenced the howling once more and sent the wolves running for cover.

The silence continued on the footplate as the light from the fire faded into the distance behind them, and the little engine pushed forward over the points that took it and its passengers onto the branch line and into the unknown.

T w e n t y

They stopped soon after daylight broke. Both fuel and water were low, and there was no certainty that there would be a convenient siding to provide either. Although they were still on a single track, they had seen no passing-places along the route. It was the only sign that they were no longer on the main track. For the rest, it was still snow, trees, and railway lines for mile after mile.

Paul got busy with maps and his compass to see if he could pinpoint his position and spot any likely rivers or lakes that would provide water. It was essential to hold back some for drinking, and what the contents of the barrels could provide was only temporary assistance. The little engine drank a lot and needed topping right up.

By estimating their speed and the time they had been on the move, he was able, with the aid of the compass, to get a rough idea of where they now stood. As he studied the estimated line of their progress, he frowned. The track had travelled due east for some distance, which suggested it would meet the White Sea coast and run along to the little town of Onega before linking with the Archangel–Valogda line. But according to his estimated present position, it would seem the branch line was curving southward. Surely it could not be going down to link with Valogda—way south of Lake Onega? Valogda was in the hands of the Reds. North was the only direction to safety.

He was worried. At present, they were only forty or so miles from the White Sea coast. He did not want to take the train farther if it meant widening that distance. Tempted to confide in Swarovsky, he decided against it. It was *his* train, so the decision must also be his. He temporised by deciding to go until there was strong enough evidence to show that they were heading inexorably south. If that happened, he would return to this place, and suggest they strike off across country, on foot. It would be their last resort.

They got on the move again with Paul deep in thought. He had not seen lakes or rivers in the immediate vicinity on the map, but only the more important ones were marked, and there were innumerable small rivulets running through the forest and smaller lakes not recorded on the maps that had been available to him in Murmansk. At the first sign of a water supply, he must stop. He must also mark very carefully the curves in the track and keep an eye on the compass needle. If it swung round the way he feared it might, he must put the engine in reverse. It would be disastrous to chug straight into enemy-held territory.

Two hours later, in the midst of such thoughts, he realised the matter was out of his hands. Up ahead, along a beautiful straight stretch of track, stood a black-and-white barrier denoting a railhead. The track had come to an end in the heart of the forest. They had been following a line to nowhere.

He turned to Swarovsky as he slowed prior to bringing the engine to a halt. "Well, Colonel, unless you have spotted another branch line, this is as far as we can go on the North Russian Railways."

The Russian nodded, tight-lipped. "You once accused us of walking out before something was finished. We Russians seem to have a habit of doing so."

It was not exactly a helpful remark, but Paul realised he was himself hiding the gravity of the situation they now faced beneath surface calm as he stopped the engine and remarked, "It solves one of our difficulties. We don't need the water now."

He jumped down into the crisp snow and looked around him. Perfect for a calendar picture, he thought, as he took in the dazzling whiteness, the frosted pine needles touched by sunshine, and a blue sky above. How amazing that nature should be unaffected by war! Right now the scene looked temptingly attractive for a brisk country walk, but forty-odd miles through arctic forest was a different proposition when temperatures dropped and snow blotted out all hazards.

"The sooner we get on the move, the better," he remarked as the Russian came up to him. "This clear weather might not last, and it will be dark by four—or even earlier."

"I agree."

Paul turned to give him the facts they had to face. "There are between forty and fifty miles to cover before we reach the coast. I can give you a more accurate figure when I have done a few calculations with the map. We have enough food and water, plus guns and ammunition. Some kind of sledge can be made to drag the supplies, and our supply of blankets is adequate, if not ideal, for keeping out the worst of the cold. Our biggest problem is the three women—and you. Our progress will be slower than it needs to be."

Swarovsky looked him straight in the eye. "I think you are forgetting something, Captain. Anything to do with the train comes under your command, I agreed to that. But we are now leaving the railway. I am Russian. I know how to survive in my own country and how best to move through terrain such as this. Since you have only one subordinate, and I have eleven men and three women in my charge, even you cannot fail to recognise who should command this group from now on."

Paul looked at him long and hard, then nodded. "Very well, Colonel. I'll go and work out our position and my estimation of the shortest route to the coast. I take it you would like me to do so."

He walked off, realising he would be a passenger on the overland trek; he was no longer needed. His command had ended, petered out in the middle of a forest as unceremoniously as this track with its black-and-white barrier. He did not even have his own men to organise—just Stevens and the vow to make the soldier eat his words when they walked into Archangel. That would seem to be his only goal now.

He stopped in the midst of reaching for the map and thought of what lay ahead. Why bother to go? There was nothing for him in England but a grasping family and disciplinary action over that damned money. Irina now despised him, and he did not trust Olga ever to let him go if it suited her purpose. Why, then, should he not simply stay with his train, travelling up and down the line until his food ran out? The wolves would have their revenge then, without a doubt, and he would be free of life. It did not seem attractive enough to hold onto any longer.

"Are we on the move then, sir?"

"Eh?" He looked up at the footplate to see Stevens watching him with a questioning look on his face.

"Is it shanks' mare from now on?"

"Er . . . yes. Colonel Swarovsky is organising the men and equipment now. He is going to lead the overland trek."

"Good! That means you can have a bit of a rest, at last, sir. If you don't mind me saying . . ."

He never said. There was a sharp crack, and he crumpled up before toppling from the engine to lay at Paul's feet, gazing up with blank eyes at the blueness above. There was only a moment in which Paul was shocked and saddened by the death of a man with whom he had shared that comradeship peculiar to men of all classes and creeds, who find themselves side-by-side, sharing danger.

Then he slid instantly into something he understood and recognised—something he had grown up with. He ran swiftly along, shielded by the train, to where Swarovsky was struggling to bring order in the face of so unexpected an attack. It was one of those savage twists of fate that they had been prepared for at every other stopping place, yet now they had run right across the path of an unsuspecting enemy, who must be delighted at having an adversary presented on a plate in such a state of surprise. The one advantage they had on the enemy was that the firing was coming from the far side of the train, which left the open door of the truck protected for everyone to scramble inside.

Jumping in, Paul saw the Russian officer barking orders and underlining their urgency by cuffing the men into obedience. They began smashing loopholes in the side of the truck with the butts of their rifles, or kicking out the wood with their boots, and Paul realized that a bullet could rip easily through the wood and kill those behind it. But as the Russian soldiers began sighting and firing, it became plain they were holding their own.

He moved up behind Swarovsky. "Are they Reds?"

He did not look round. "They are ignorant fools, not soldiers. They choose the worst time to attack. It is so bright and clear out there, every time a man moves from behind a tree to fire, he presents the perfect target . . . and the rifles they have demand that they move into the open to see their target properly. They do not stand a chance."

Paul put his eye to a crack in the wood and saw the scene for himself. The attackers were certainly not trained soldiers, even though they wore the same kind of uniform as Valodya. It was impossible to tell how big a company it was, but they were either numerically strong or strategically stupid. Already, a large number of bodies lay in the snow, yet they continued to offer themselves as easy targets as they stepped out to fire. Paul had to acknowledge that Swarovsky's "ill-assorted peasants" were better soldiers than he had imagined. Their marksmanship was first-class. Then he remembered that they were men of North Russia, hunters and trappers who were used to forest conditions. The Reds were probably men from the South, conscripted and marched off with little training.

Above the deafening reports of the rifles, Paul became aware of high-pitched cries behind him and swung round. In the need for action, he had forgotten the women! The ballerina had her hands over her ears and was sobbing uncontrollably. Olga looked poised to jump from the truck to run into the trees so temptingly near, which would be fatal. Irina saw him looking at them, and the expression on her face sent him across to her.

"Get them into that corner, and for God's sake, don't let them run off. They'll never make it."

He began to push her into the corner, but she resisted him, pale but determined. "I cannot be responsible for them. Their lives are their own, not mine. Besides, I can fire a rifle. I was shown how to do so before I went to the front."

He pushed harder, forcing her back behind the cover of the piled boxes. "Englishmen don't expect women to fight," he told her harshly. "Get back there with the others and keep out of the way."

"You are no longer in command," she cried. "The English have stopped fighting. This is not your war."

It hit him hard. "When people shoot at me I shoot back," he said with biting force. "They have just killed Stevens. It wasn't his war, either."

She resisted, clinging to the boxes and facing up to him with her eyes large and expressive. "I am sorry . . . but that is all the more reason for me to replace him."

He took hold of her shoulders in a hard grip. *"You are replacing no one, is that understood?"* he shouted above the noise of the rifle fire. "I haven't brought you safely all this way just to let you stand up there and get killed. It might be your way in this damned upside-down country, but it isn't mine. As far as *you* are concerned, I *am* in command. Now get into that corner where I know you are safe, and stay there until I fetch you out."

She moved back in some kind of trance, staring at him. "You . . . you *do* still care!"

It was the wrong time and the wrong place, and he was in the midst of a battle. "You are the only nurse, remember? We shall need your services before we are finished."

She turned away into the corner, going to Zapalova to calm her. Paul stacked boxes quickly around them so that they were barricaded in, then went back to Swarovsky.

"I'm going to try to get to the engine," he began, but was stopped by the Russian, who was peering through a split in the wood, firing his revolver spasmodically.

"You would be instantly shot. Moving back would be useless, anyway. These men will almost certainly have horses and would follow us. We know there is nowhere else for us to go. We must stand and fight now if we hope to get to Archangel."

"All right, it's your little army," said Paul, seeing the sense in his words. "Where would you like me to operate?"

Pale eyes gave him a look of aloof coldness. "You have direct orders to withdraw and stop fighting. This battle is my concern, and mine only."

Filled with disbelief, Paul said, "Do you really expect me to stand by and . . ."

"I do not care what you do," the Colonel snapped. "Your job was to get us to the north on the train. You cannot now do that . . . and I have a battle on my hands."

He turned away to his soldiers, and Paul stood trying to master the desire to throw away his gun and walk off into the forest as far from this man as possible. Finally, he sheathed the revolver, snatched up a rifle and some rounds of ammunition before jumping from the truck to find a position beneath it where he could fire from behind the wheels. It was lonely but something with which he was familiar. He had once held a position for half an hour on his own while reinforcements were brought up.

From where he crouched on the crisp snow, he had a clearer view than those inside the truck, and he watched all around him for any signs that the enemy was attempting an encircling movement that would spell disaster. But still they continued committing suicide by attempting a disorganised frontal attack. Their commander must be an inexperienced or uncertain soldier to let the slaughter go on so long. He was losing men in large numbers. Yet, as far as Paul could tell, there was only one casualty in the truck above him: He had heard a man's cry, and the frenzied shuffling of feet. But the volley of shots still coming from the truck was encouraging.

There was a lull during early afternoon, and Paul's stomach began to churn as it always had when he had waited and watched for a row of silhouettes to rise up from the enemy trenches and rush at them. The silence was always the most unnerving. Battle noise was comforting in that it told a man where the enemy was. Silence kept him guessing . . . and fearful.

Old spectres had begun to haunt him when movement set the reflexes in his arms responding to what he saw. Trying another tactic, the Red commander was sending a charge of mounted men at the train. But any soldier worth his salt could have told him that cavalry was only effective when charging infantry. As in South Africa at the turn of the century, when the doomed British cavalry had rushed at Boer laagers, the Reds now suffered the same fate. Ten rifles from behind cover and with deadly aim brought them down one by one or sent them back into the forest after a rearing turn on their horses. One who was either stupidly heroic, or whose horse had bolted, crossed the track ahead of the train and began to gallop along toward the open supply-truck. Paul shot him in the head, and the terrified beast veered away into the forest carrying its macabre burden.

That failure brought a long pause in the exchange of shots, and Paul eased his cramped, frozen limbs. What little warmth the sun had given was going now, and the pines were being stirred by a rising wind that had the smell of ice in it. They were undoubtedly in for a bitterly cold night. Staring out across the few yards of clear ground between the track and the trees, watching for a new move by the Bolshevik troops, Paul realised their own defeat was merely a matter of time. The Red soldiers might be inexperienced, but the man who led them must by now have realised that as soon as darkness came he could rush the train and take it easily. The long cessation in firing suggested this was correct. Why waste bullets at three P.M. when another hour would mean an easy victory without any?

The thought of that galvanised Paul into action. Taking advantage of the lull in firing, he scrambled out and levered himself into the truck. A quick glance showed him that two men had been slightly wounded. Irina was tending them in her safe corner, much to the disgust of the other two women. So Paul went across to them, ignoring the Colonel and his soldiers watching keenly from their vantage points.

"Get out as many blankets as we have available," he said sharply to Olga and Lyudmilla. "Then sort out food supplies—tins, an opener, tea, and a large pan to heat water. And all the matches we possess, plus a can of lubricating oil. We'll need enough for three days. Then I want you to put it all into blankets and tie them into bundles suitable for carrying." Seeing their faces take on a comprehension of what he was saying, he added, "Jewels and money can be taken, of course, but everything else must be left behind."

Olga was looking at him as if he were a saviour, but Zapalova said, "*Nothing*, I do. Sasha has not spoke of it."

"He will," Paul told her grimly. "The minute it grows dark, we shall have to get into the forest as quickly as we can."

Her great amber eyes regarded him with loathing. "The great Zapalova do what she wish. You are nothing."

He wasted no further time on her. "Valodya risked his life to save you from the Reds. If they throw you onto their fire when they catch you, as they did to him, I just hope your last thoughts will be of him."

It silenced her very effectively, and she began to take tinned food from the wooden chests with hands that forgot to be graceful. Paul broke open boxes filled with ammunition and piled it into canvas buckets that could be carried on a pole across the shoulders, coolie-style, on a long trek.

"What are you doing?"

He saw Swarovsky's boots beside him but did not take his attention from his task. "My train, *my* supplies, I think." He went on counting bullets. "You realise they'll rush us as soon as it gets dark?"

"Of course."

"Right. While you are fighting *your* war, I'll sort out *my* supplies ready for the moment we are forced to join forces and run like hell." He glanced up then. "All right by you?"

All he received was a curious look and a nod that sufficed as a reply, before the Colonel moved away to see how the wounded were faring.

Paul glanced quickly at his watch. Three-thirty, and the sun had almost gone. Darkness would come earlier than expected. His stomach tightened. It was not simply a case of slipping away in the night. It had to be timed so that the darkness was complete enough to hide their getaway from the unseen watchers in the forest, yet not so black that the attackers came before they had gone. Who could tell the exact moment the enemy commander would choose to strike?

Then Paul's hands stilled in the midst of sorting bullets. Their chances were extremely slim. Even if they timed it perfectly, there were more than forty miles of forest to cover. In that forest were bogs, freezing temperatures, and wolves. Swarovsky might know the Russian winter and how to master it, but even his singular determination would not get twelve men and three women safely to Archangel through all that if there was a company of Reds hot in pursuit. Against a background of snow, moving figures could be easily picked off . . . and this enemy was not going to give up easily.

Paul looked up and out through the open door. Already it was growing difficult to see between the trees. Time, time, there was nowhere near enough time! Thinking desperately, he cast his glance around the truck. The supplies tied in bundles stood ready, and the Swarovsky chests had been robbed of everything that would provide warmth for someone. Silver brushes and perfume bottles lay abandoned among silk blouses, leather boots, and fine lace underwear. The china and starched linen looked incongruous amongst the straw scattered on the floor. All the fine things that had been smuggled so desperately from that house one night must be left. Paul looked at them and remembered Valodya saying, *They thought such treatment would destroy its years of beauty and value. How much they still have to learn.* He found himself nodding. Yes, all this had had its moment of glory in that forest.

Zapalova was clutching the mother-of-pearl accordian, and no one tried to wrest it from her. She would drop it soon enough in the wilderness.

Paul left the bullets. There were enough in the buckets, anyway. Swarovsky was getting his men together and explaining what lay before them, but Paul interrupted him and took him aside.

"Yes, what is it?" asked the Russian testily, his gaze on the dusk that had arrived outside.

"Are you still determined to get to Archangel?"

The pale eyes narrowed. "That is a strange question, when you are well aware of the answer."

"There is only one hope of your getting away—to stop the Reds from following and killing you all out there in the forest. You have wounded men and three women to slow you up, so I'll stop them for you."

"This is not your war, Captain."

"So I have already been told. But it is my train—that is the one thing on which we have always agreed—and I have a duty to prevent it from falling into enemy hands. Like my bridge, I am going to blow the whole thing up—preferably at the same time as you make your escape." Without allowing the other time to comment, which he plainly wished to do, Paul went on. "I shall have to improvise. Darkness is closing in fast, and those fools outside might mismanage even this by coming too early. I'll tell you briefly what I am going to do. Since there's no time to wire up charges and run out fuses to an exploder, I shall fix short, slow-burning fuses to slabs of gun-cotton. When we leave, I shall wait behind in the trees until I am certain the Reds are coming, then throw the slabs back into the train so that the whole thing goes up just as they reach it."

The Russian's face, haggard and coarsened by three days' growth around his chin, considered Paul for a moment. "You can do this with absolute safety to yourself?"

"There is a certain amount of risk involved."

"I see. Then why do it?"

Paul hesitated, then decided it was a time for truth. "The railway was my first command, which I must conclude to the best of my ability. I shall be risking no lives of subordinates . . . and perhaps I just don't like walking out on my allies in the middle of something."

Swarovsky turned away, but Paul called after him. "Colonel, whatever happens, you will go on, of course."

A brief glance over his shoulder, "Of course," and he went back to his men.

Paul worked fast, with sure fingers. The plan had sounded splendid just now, but what if he timed it wrong? What if the Reds rushed the train now, before he was ready? What if, when the time came, his aim went awry and the explosives merely threw up some ancient pines? A voice suggested that he should play safe and leave the gun-cotton on the train, lighting the fuses before he jumped out, but that might be a dismal failure. Of what use to blow up the train when the Reds were nowhere near? No, he must watch and throw the explosives at just the right time.

As he fashioned his "grenades," he thought with longing of the real kind, which would be of such advantage now. A sapper was taught to improvise, but never had he thought he would have to use his supply of engineering explosive for such a purpose. His whole purpose in Russia had been to improve a railway, never to act as an attacking commander. He could not even be certain of the results of his home-made weapons. His casual comment that there was "a certain amount of risk involved" might have been grossly understated.

But such thoughts were interrupted by Swarovsky, who told him they were preparing to leave. He looked up to find them all standing ready, with just two soldiers peering through the loopholes, guns at the ready. Time had run out!

He gathered up the crude "grenades" and walked to stand by the open door. Dark though it was in the truck, outside it would still be possible to see darker shapes moving across an open space of some twenty yards. He said as much to Swarovsky, but the Russian replied that they would all risk losing each other in the darkness if they left it much longer.

"I'll keep watch while you run for the trees. When you have all reached them safely, I'll follow," Paul said to the Russian.

"Very well."

"If they start to come before you are all away, I'll start firing. You must all keep going as fast as you can."

"And you?"

"Oh, I'll just light the fuses and run like hell. We'll meet up in the forest."

Without another word, Swarovsky called his two men away, and the group blotted out what little was left of the light as they filled the doorway. At the other side of the truck, straining his eyes through the loophole for any sign of movement, Paul heard them all leave, and his stomach tightened further. Now was the tricky moment. If a volley of shots rang out, it would mean the Reds had somehow managed to creep up unseen against the snowy background.

But the seconds passed and nothing happened. The loneliness inside the truck ate into him and set him moving toward the door and forty-odd miles of forest. Stevens had said they had not a hope in hell of reaching Archangel. Paul looked at the dark shape of the soldier's body lying beside the engine and hoped he had been wrong. Then he jumped from the train for the last time and ran for the cover of the trees, throwing himself face down as he reached them out of force of habit. Ahead of him, he heard rustling as the Russians made their way through the trees with the aid of his own compass. He was at a disadvantage when he wanted to catch up with them, but he and Swarovsky had arranged a signalling system with gun-shots, so there should be no problem.

He had retained his field glasses that were now slung around his neck, but before he took a look through them, Paul stealthily lit a taper he would need to put a flame to the four fuses. In such poor light, he would have very little time successfully to light all four from matches, then throw the "grenades," so a taper was essential. He lifted the glasses and peered through. God, it was almost impossible to see even the trees beyond the train now. How would he know when dark, creeping shapes materialised from them?

He looked down at the glowing taper. "Much longer, and the bloody thing will burn itself out," he muttered viciously. "Where the hell are you, you bastards?"

For a mad moment he wondered if they had packed up and called it a day, but then he remembered these people were tenacious. Untrained they might be, peasants though they probably were, the Red Army had grown into a savage monster that was swallowing up a country as huge as Russia. They did not pack up and call it a day.

"Come on! *Come on!*" he urged under his breath. "You can't be *that* stupid. You must know we'll make a break for it in the darkness."

Then there was the old familiar sight of shapes that were no longer shadows or figments of a man's imagination. He knew because there were dark boots against the whiteness of snow. That was all that gave them away. But they had left it much too late, and Paul had the satisfaction of knowing they had been outwitted by a Swarovsky—a White Russian, a Tsarist . . . and a good soldier, he added generously. When put to the test, the Russian had timed it beautifully and met it to the full.

"And you are going to meet *this*," Paul murmured, picking up the taper and setting the tiny flame to all four fuses at once. It was risky. By the time he threw the last one, the fuse would be nearly burnt through, but it saved on time. Now feeling quite calm, Paul stood up with the four slabs in his hand, then realised it was now too dark to see the train clearly. He hesitated, thinking furiously of ways around it, but the fuses were burning merrily in his hand, and those boots against the snow were much closer now. Hurling the first one where he thought the engine would be, he quickly rid himself of the other three in a direction he estimated the supply-truck stood.

"*Spokoinoi nochi!*" he said viciously. Peaceful night! As peaceful as Valodya's had been. Then he turned and began to run.

But it was not an open field, and running fast through a pine forest proved impossible. As he stumbled forward in the darkness from tree trunk to tree trunk, boots slipping on the frozen snow, he found himself counting and trying to resist the urge to look back. It was like one of those nightmares when he was straining and fighting to flee from danger, yet his feet would not move.

"*Four . . . three . . . two . . . one,*" he breathed, and as he blundered into another tree, the night exploded behind him. He only had time to think that he had vastly overdone it, before he was catapulted forward. The force of the blast hurled him into blackness that turned him over and over with such cruel savagery, he passed into blessed limbo.

But agony returned to prod him into awareness again, and his muddled mind told him he was in Hell. With consciousness being maintained by the terrible pain in his back and shoulders, he gazed through blurred vision at what seemed to him to be the leaping flames of Hades. Everywhere he looked was yellow light, moving like a gigantic halo of fire way above him.

I must be dead, he thought, then realised he would not be in such pain if he was. That was followed by the horror of returning intelligence. Had the Reds caught him? Was he to be burned on their fire? Surely, he was already there? He struggled, and agony gave him blessed relief from awareness once more.

When he returned to that same place, it was because he was running away from the vision of a fair-haired young man being thrown into a fire like a log of wood. Paul knew he was crying out, yet could hear no sound at all. It frightened him even more than the vivid yellow light all around. The world had gone silent and deserted him in the moment of danger.

It was growing hotter, and the flames were working their way nearer. He could not hear the roaring of fire, but he could see it well enough. His vision was clearing and adjusting, although there seemed to be blood running across one eye. What had been a blurred inferno above him focussed into a forest of blazing trees. The great, swaying branches of the pines were well alight, the needles burning quickly and passing on their leaping burden to the neighbouring trees as the wind whipped up the flames. But what had begun in the tops of the needled branches was spreading downward to the trunks, and branches were dropping like flaming arrows onto the forest floor around him, to peter out in the snow into smoking, blackened logs.

That smoke was getting thicker. It burned Paul's eyes and entered his lungs to make him cough. He knew he was coughing, yet heard nothing. Neither did he hear the crackling of burning timber or the rush of the wind.

With a great effort he put his thoughts into order. The explosion had deafened him and caused injury to his back and left leg. He had not run far enough before the train blew, and the ammunition still in the supply-truck had gone up with a force he had underestimated. The resultant fire had caught the nearby trees, and the strong wind was spreading it. Having got that far in his thoughts, he realised that they would be among his last. By gritting his teeth and praying he might get a few yards farther into the forest, but forty-odd miles was out of the question.

With difficulty he turned his head and stared at the place where the train had stood. Floodlit by the fire, the scene stood out clearly, and he even managed a painful smile. As with the destruction of his bridge, he had done the job thoroughly. Yagutov's engine lay with a broken back, smoking heavily several yards from the track that now stood up, blackened and twisted, like some kind of witches' tripod, with debris hanging from it. Of the supply-truck there was nothing but a tilted, derailed chassis and scattered wreckage all about. There were the bodies of men, also, thrown into grotesque death poses all around the clearing, touched by the reflection of the yellow flames.

His smile faded. He had wanted only to be an engineer, not to be a killer; to create, not destroy. Yet that was all he had ever done. Then his eye caught sight of something fluttering in the wind, and he realised it was a frilly petticoat caught on a piece of broken track, flying like a flag of truce over the scene of destruction.

He closed his eyes. She had been his peace for one short, beautiful summer. He would not remember her recent words to him, only those smiles across a lamplit tent, the fingers touching around a mug of tea, and her sweet accented voice calling him by his Russian name, Pavlik.

Yet he could not hear her voice. He was deaf and would never hear the sound of it again. His lids flew open. The flames were drawing nearer, yet they spoke no sound to him. Perhaps it was as well. He would not hear his own cries when the time came. Silence was golden . . . and the wolves would have their revenge after all.

Then they were pulling at him, tearing him apart in their fury. But faces appeared, and they were human. Bearded faces with dark eyes that opened and shut. It was men who were pulling at him. He tried to tell them to leave him, that every movement was agony, that they were risking their lives needlessly, but even if the words were coming out loud and clear, they did not understand him, of course. They had never understood him, nor he them. Branski and Nardoff, those were their names. He had given Branski a carved egg-timer for his Name Day. What was he doing here when he should be on his way to Archangel?

"Go back, go back!" he ordered, but they took no notice and began lifting him. He screamed silently, and the burning trees were suddenly all around him, licking at his clothes and hair until the fire dissolved into instant blessed blackness.

Then there was a hand touching his brow, cold but gentle, and he opened his eyes to blinding whiteness all around him. She was there, and she was crying. Were the tears for him?

"Are you all right?" He heard his own words way off in the distance, but when her mouth moved in reply, the sound did not reach him. Such a lovely face, full of love and compassion, with grey-green eyes sparkling with teardrops. She was dressed in fur, dark against the snow. Then someone led her away, and he felt himself rise in the air as if floating.

It was unbearably cold, and he was full of pain that urged him to relinquish life. There were tears cold against his own cheeks, because she had been there and now had gone away again.

T w e n t y - o n e

Archangel was a small port comprising wooden houses, wharves, and a seventeenth-century cathedral that dominated the town with its size and beauty. It lay on the northern bank of the River Dvina, which was negotiated by reindeer sledge between October and May, when not only the river but the White Sea was frozen to the extent of barring even ice-breakers access to the port. It stood in the surrounding tundra, an arctic outpost that spent half the year in daylight, half in darkness. Those who lived there were hardy, simple people of mixed nationalities, hunting or trapping the animals of that area, and whose only vehicle was the dog or reindeer sledge.

These were out in force toward the end of September when the undulating surrounding wilderness was already deep in snow and ice was beginning to glaze the river. But there were others driving dog-teams and coming into the town on sledges during that time: faces that were not broad with black eyes; fair skins that had no resistance to such intense cold; eyes that were dull with loneliness or defeat; faces that turned southwest toward home. The British Army was assembling.

From the forest and tundra they came, from their isolated outposts in a country they did not understand. They came, in small bands, up the river and railway. Others, caught on the Murmansk side and unable to reach that ice-free port, had been picked up by boats sent to Kem and Kandalaksha, on the White Sea coast, and brought across to Archangel in the race against the ice. But besides British soldiers, Archangel was being invaded by all manner of desperate refugees from Bolshevism, and White Russian units anxious to unite and re-form without their British allies.

The military authorities were in a ferment of activity. Ships stood in the harbour to take off all troops and any Russian or foreign refugees. The withdrawing ally had done its best to establish training centres in all branches of military warfare for the White Army that was dedicated to driving the Bolsheviks from Russia. Equipment and supplies were to be left, to this end, but the invitation to ship to safety any who wished to leave was an unspoken expression of no-confidence in a cause they recognised as all but lost.

All-in-all, the temporary population of Archangel was volatile, wary, and bitter. All three of these characteristics were evident in the man who sat through the dark morning in a wooden hut put up by the British when they had first arrived over eighteen months before. Outside in the snowy streets were the cries of Samoyeds who drove the reindeer sledges, mingling with English voices shouting orders for troops to fall in. Sasha fluctuated from anger to despair over the time that was being wasted: his increasing bitterness over the withdrawal was only held in check by his involvement in the re-organisation of the White Russian troops now in the Archangel and Murmansk areas.

Sasha had been in Archangel almost a month, following his three-and-a-half-day journey through the forest and thence by small fishing boat to Kem, where the British were picking up stragglers caught on the wrong side of broken bridges or ruptured track. The White Finns had chosen this moment to practice mild revenge on the British for political reasons of their own and had sabotaged the Murmansk line.

In his mind, he recalled that journey, which the British had tried desperately to turn into a heroic achievement on his part, by insisting that he saved the life of one of their officers. Time and again he had told them bluntly that it had been none of his doing that young Anderson was brought to Archangel. Two of his men had deliberately disobeyed him to go back when it had already been agreed with Anderson himself that the premier need was to push on.

Nonplussed by such a reply, the British authorities had tried another tack. Injured in the leg himself, they said, he had nevertheless led a group of eleven men and three women to safety with the added handicap of a man on an improvised stretcher. His reply to that had been that he was an officer in an army that knew how to survive in its own harsh country, carrying its wounded with it. Also, his wife was a trained military nurse, who had attended the wounded man throughout.

Robbed of the chance to laud one of the allies they were leaving, the British authorities then went on to praise the courage and fortitude of three aristocratic ladies, who were an example to them all. Sasha had responded to those words as they had hoped, and they went away smug and satisfied. It was a small sop for their uncomfortable minds during those last days on Russian soil.

But they would never know the truth about those three-and-a-half days. They would never know that he had held on only because he was driven by a compulsion above normality; how every dragging mile and every spasm of pain in his thigh had been measured against Valodya's suffering and counted as nothing; how he had driven the others on when they had been ready to give up.

They would never know how he had been forced to drag Lyudmilla along and even carry her in his arms when she allowed herself to collapse; how he had thrown aside the accordian wrested from her clutches, only to find one of his men carrying it still; how he had encouraged, threatened, and cursed her when she had played her dramatic scenes. Then Olga, desperate, terrified of dying out there where the wolves lurked, vowing she could go no further and refusing to eat the tasteless ration of food. Olga being sick in the snow, accusing him of leading them around in circles and threatening to walk off in the direction she was convinced led to safety.

And Irina? Who knew how she would have been if Branski and Nardoff had not gone back through that fire for Anderson? When they had heard the explosion and seen the night lit by vivid yellow light, she had begun to run back like a woman possessed. He had caught and restrained her, forcing her onward with the others as he told her there was no time. She had turned on him, sobbing curses, crying that she would never forgive him, swept by a kind of madness he understood only too well. When they brought the inert body, clothes torn and blackened, hair singed in the fire, face bruised and bloody, she had taken it immediately into her keeping, remaining alive only for that purpose, her determination to reach Archangel matching his own. Together they had succeeded.

Coming out of his thoughts, Sasha rose stiffly and walked to the window. Daylight was coming, at last. It was now early October, and the last ship must leave by the middle of the month. Lyudmilla was already in England, having been given passage on a ship leaving two days after her arrival in Archangel. Their farewell had been brief; it would have been better if they had never met again in the forest. The dream had been unable to survive. Like all his other dreams, that vivid, poignant liaison had died some time during those last months, and he had stood unmoved on the jetty as she had walked gracefully onto the deck to the applause and admiration of her future audiences.

Now, Olga and Irina were sailing the next morning on the same ship as young Anderson, who had now been declared fit to travel. The Shipping Officer had been a susceptible young man who had been easily persuaded that Olga had some kind of attachment to the good-looking Englishman she had helped to rescue and that Irina naturally wanted to remain with her husband as long as possible. Sasha's mouth twisted. The English were too damned understanding and sentimental. Little did they suspect that the wife was the one who wanted their precious young captain, and the sister, now she was safely surrounded by hundreds of armed soldiers, was bound by the blood-tie that had to be finally broken. When that ship sailed in the morning, it would be the end of his past . . . and the future would be short.

He had not been near Anderson since they got to Archangel. The women had reported on his progress in the hospital, and Sasha had been as civilised as he could in his comments. But that morning he could delay no longer and put on his thick coat and gloves before stepping out into mid-morning dawn to make his way down to those huts still retained by the British. Already, the sea had a layer of ice across it, and the wind that whistled over the tundra was arctic and threatening. He shivered and turned up his collar. Winter campaigns were always the worst.

Turning into one of the huts, he enquired where he would find Captain Anderson and was directed to a small room at the end. When invited to go in after he had knocked, he found the English officer staring moodily from the window.

"Good morning, Captain."

Paul was unprepared, that much was obvious. "Oh . . . good morning. I thought . . . well, I guessed you'd be at the jetty tomorrow. I was going to say goodbye then." He turned round completely. "I haven't been across before because I thought you'd be pretty well occupied with the re-organisation."

Sasha walked a few feet into the room, pushing the door closed behind him. "Yes, I have been."

"Would . . . would you like a seat?" Paul waved a hand at a wooden folding chair. "Not much better than the tents, I'm afraid."

"No. I do not intend to stay long." Sasha put his cap on a nearby table. "How are you now?"

"Fine."

He did not look it. His face was thinner and so pale the freckles stood out clearly. There were lines left by pain running down from the corners of his mouth, and his brow and cheek bore scars where wounds had been stitched. But it was his eyes that were so different, and Sasha knew at once the reason for that desolation and emptiness in their brown depths. The young fool was bearing the defection of an entire nation and suffering from it—that same young fool who had once arrogantly declared that he did not care if the Russians all killed each other, so long as he could build his railway.

"I would have gone on and left you, as we arranged," Sasha said with brutal bluntness.

It did not disconcert Paul. "Yes, I know you would. It was the only thing to do in a case of fifteen lives compared with one."

"Branski and Nardoff disobeyed my clear orders."

Anderson gave a faint smile. "Ill-assorted peasants! I always said you couldn't rely on them."

That channel of conversation had gone as far as it could, and Sasha had no choice but to say what he had gone there to say.

"Tomorrow, at the ship, there are some matters that cannot be broached. That is why I have called upon you this morning." Sasha was finding it more difficult than he had thought. "By the end of this week, all the British will be gone."

"I think they are wrong," was the earnest reply.

"Perhaps. Who can say? Only the future will show."

"The future? But you know what that will be?"

Sasha nodded. "We shall go on until the end. So you see, I must know what you intend to do. One is my wife, the other my sister."

It threw him, made him edgy. "Yes . . . yes, of course."

"They will both be fairly wealthy women; the Swarovsky jewels are of fine quality."

Anderson grew instantly, hotly angry. "My God, do you think I consider that?"

"I meant to imply only that they do not *need* you. In their new life, they will be independent, so what has happened here need not concern you once you are back in your own country."

"Concern me? Of course it will concern me! What kind of person do you take me for?"

"I am not certain I can answer that . . . but once that ship leaves tomorrow, my responsibility for them both ends. All the same, I should like to know whether you will claim my sister or my widow."

Anderson began shaking as if with some kind of spasm. "This is macabre . . . grotesque," he choked. "You speak as if you are settling inanimate objects in a behest."

"If you are not mature enough to discuss this, you should never have involved yourself with them," said Sasha harshly. "I think I have the right to an answer from you."

After a considerable battle with himself, the younger man looked frankly at Sasha and began. "Your sister has never been my *mistress*. Just once, on the night we heard Valodya was dead . . . that night . . . well, I don't think any of us was responsible for his actions." His eyes were unhappier than ever, and Sasha knew he still suffered over the death of a foreigner he had made his friend. Paul left the support of the chair he had been gripping and limped right up to Sasha. "If Olga ever needs anything, I will help her, of course. But I have loved Irina from the start. When she is free, I hope to marry her. How long a period of mourning would you like us to observe?" He took a deep, steadying breath. "Is that mature enough for you?"

He had parried Sasha's attack with as firm a hand as he would have wished, but still it shook him, and it was a moment or so before Sasha could say, "I think I shall never completely understand you."

The other man looked him straight in the eye. "Nor I you."

"Perhaps that is the trouble with us all."

"Perhaps it is."

Sasha held out his hand, despite himself. "But through it all, we achieved . . . and that is all we can ever hope to do. Thank you, Captain."

Anderson gripped the hand. "*Spasibo*, Colonel."

Paul hated the nights that began at two P.M. and went on until mid-morning, and that particular one was worst of all. They were sailing at first light, but it would not be the usual affair of brass-band sentimentality, streamers from deck to shore, and a sense of sailing to adventure. This time, those left on shore would never be seen again, and those on the ship would never return.

Paul did not even have the occupations of packing and saying fond farewells. All his possessions had been blown up with the train; even his uniform was borrowed and did not fit too well. As for fond farewells . . . !

The meeting with Swarovsky that morning had added to the weight already bearing Paul down. They had never understood each other— *liked* each other—yet there had always been something between them that had just revealed itself as a grudging respect. Paul had made no attempt to thank him for that journey on a stretcher across snow-bound forest, nor had Swarovsky eulogised on the blowing up of the train that had allowed them to get away. They were both soldiers and did what they had to do. Yet that meeting had left Paul with a heavy restlessness he could not conquer. Would he ever get that forest out of his system, even in years to come when he might be in some country at the bottom of the world?

Turning to his bedside cupboard, Paul took out a bottle of brandy and poured himself a stiff tot as he told himself he was lucky to be alive, so what more did he want? And he had achieved, which was all any man could hope for, as Swarovsky had said. The future must be his concern now, not the past.

He leant back on his bed and tried not to notice the cranes on the floodlit wharves outside. The business of the ransom money looked like being sorted out without too much bother, after all. The confusion of withdrawal, a harrassed Paymaster's Department in faraway Murmansk, an understanding and tactful general who still remembered his own days as a junior officer, and a decidedly battered and bruised culprit all pointed to the affair being delayed until they reached England.

Zapalova had charmed the General, who was a great patron of the arts, and so had the courage and beauty of the other two aristocratic ladies, for whose lives the money had been sacrificed. It would need only careful wording to turn a doubtful incident into one of British gallantry towards the noble victims of persecution, and since Russian lives were being saved wholesale by being shipped to safety from the Reds, there seemed little doubt that Paul's full report on the situation in which he had been placed would absolve him from any likely penalty.

However, Paul had had to appear before the General to answer for the language and content of his Morse signals. Kindly the great man might be where ladies were concerned, well might he remember his own youth, but when it came to telling off naughty boys, he had a stern eye and a lashing tongue. Paul had stood a bruised and sorry sight while his character was torn to shreds and his assurance squashed flat. Only after he had apologised very fully and admitted that he had behaved reprehensibly had the General stopped him at the door with a twinkle in his eye and the comment that they were both dashed pretty women and any man was liable to lose his head under such circumstances.

As for the other army men, they all seemed impressed with how he had handled his first sole command and suggested that he had a bright future in the army. But he was not yet ready to make plans. He was still in Russia, and everything else seemed unreal—especially that red brick house on the corner in a railway town which composed his heritage.

That house had occupied his thoughts a great deal during the past three weeks. He had this morning told Swarovsky he wanted to marry Irina, but what could he offer a girl who had a noble background and those damned family jewels that would make her "independent"? That forest had had an equalising quality which would vanish the minute they set foot in England. It was beyond him to imagine his mother and Irina together. They would have nothing in common—not even love for him, since Mrs Anderson had given him up as a disappointing stranger to devote herself to the demanding Nora.

What of Irina herself? He poured himself another drink and downed it in one draught. He was uncertain how things stood between them now. She had visited him every day in the hospital, but always in the company of Olga. Her eyes told him what he longed to hear her say, so he was not unhappy, but there was a strange quietness about her that suggested she might be ill. He gripped the glass. It was all this damned waiting! It played on everyone's nerves. Once they were on that ship and out of sight of Russia, they would all be able to think straight.

As he was in the midst of tipping the bottle over the glass once more, there was a knock on the door, and he called, "Come in."

She was alone, and he was so unprepared he stayed where he was for a few seconds, drinking in the serene dignity of her slender figure in the rich, dark furs. Somehow she made the dim wooden hut glow with life.

With his gaze still on her, he put down bottle and glass, then swung his legs to the ground beside the bed and stood up. She walked slowly across to him, and he saw then that her face was full of dreams that had flown. Growing cold, he took both the hands she held out to him, some fear he struggled to deny filling his throat so that he could not speak.

It took her a moment to say it. "Pavlik . . . I cannot come with you."

All he had struggled for meant nothing; all he had achieved broke into pieces like the bridge. Those weeks of toil and sweat, the endeavour and determination, the growth of the man who was in him now were snatched from him by her words.

"With Olga . . . It was not like she said," he told her desperately.

"I know already. She told me."

"Then . . . *why?*" he asked in a voice that was cracked and afraid.

"Because he needs me."

"*I* need you," he cried instantly.

She shook her head with gentle sadness. "You are strong, with a future before you. He has lost everything."

"He has accepted that."

"Does a man ever accept total defeat? Would you?"

It was a question to torment him. What could he answer? Was she not asking *him* to do just that?

"Do you know what you are saying . . . what you will be facing if you stay here?" he asked desperately, unable to face the translation of his words.

"I have been in deep distress for three weeks, thinking of nothing else." She stood fair and feminine before him, telling him she had greater courage than he wished to admit. "Now that this time has come to leave, I know, like Sasha, that I cannot desert Russia."

"How . . . how can I let you do it?"

She put a hand to touch his mouth gently. "By loving me, as I shall love you . . . always. Perhaps, for a while, we both saw it within our grasp, but the time for our youth has gone—swallowed up by a lifetime of five years."

He wished they had never dragged him from that fire. His fingers loosed their hold on her hands. The end of everything! Then, and only then, he saw the glint of tears in her eyes and knew what this was costing her, also. Caught and held in that moment that would not let them go, he stood irresolute for a moment. Then he walked past her to the door and turned the key in the lock.

She looked round at him as he stood with his back to the door, the lights from the wharves outside putting a shimmer on her fair hair and turning her face into one of unusual radiance. He spoke steadily, knowing the moment must not be lost or spoilt.

"If we can live a lifetime in five years, one night should give us our youth."

He moved across, as she stood in emotional bewilderment, and slipped the coat from her shoulders before leading her over to the bed. There, he sat her down and knelt on one knee beside her to look up with a smile.

"You are Irina Karlovna, that is all."

"You remembered that name?" she asked softly, still unsure of him. "After all, you remembered that name."

"How could I forget it? I said it so many times to myself, even if I was too shy to say it to you." He took one of her hands. "You are Irina Karlovna, who is very beautiful and has many suitors. But I am the fortunate one who receives your love. I have taken you to balls and picnics and showered you with presents on your Name Day." Inspired, he reached up quickly and took up a book he had been reading, to present it formally.

Wondering, half in his fantasy, she took the book with gentle hands and leant forward to touch his mouth lightly with her own. He rose and sat beside her on the bed, seeing the soft curve of her lips and the blush of a young girl on her cheeks as he touched her hair with a lover's caress.

"We have kissed like that many times throughout the summer, and your father has now given his consent to my desperate request." His hand moved slowly down her cheek, rested for a moment on her lips, then began to unfasten the buttons at her throat. He had forgotten the wharves outside, the ship ready to sail in the morning, and the snowbound forest. He was away somewhere in a land of beauty and sunshine, where lovers realise their dreams.

"You are my bride," he told her huskily as the blouse slipped from her shoulders.

Her eyes had lost their shadows of horror and war, and there was only the clear gaze of youth enthralled as they gazed up into his.

"Even in this, you must be correct," she whispered, trembling beneath his touch.

He drew her against him. "When a man loves so deeply, it is the only way he will have it—for a whole life long."

Tenderness—the sweet tenderness of young love—soon turned into passion, and the long arctic night heard their sighs. If he had hoped to change her mind, he failed. But she taught him all he would ever know about a woman. She could be a tender comforter, a temptress, a sweet laughing companion, a wanton with all the tricks of passion, a beautiful creature with hair spread across the pillow and tears of joy in her eyes, the reason for a man to live.

But she could also be courageous and incomprehensible.

When he awoke she had gone.

Epilogue

They came to a lake, winter-gripped and silent. It was only possible to tell it was a lake because the trees ended, leaving a vast open snowfield spread before them, blue and peaceful in the half-light of noon. They halted in the trees lining the frozen shore and set down their wounded. The men looked at each other with eyes that reflected their fatigue, then began the ritual of lighting a fire from wood they chopped off the nearest trees. It was hard work. The extreme temperature made the branches iron hard, and their hands, even in thick gloves, were too stiff to hold the axes steady. The frozen wood did not easily burn, and they had little will left to persevere. But a tiny flame eventually flickered, and they scooped up snow in the rusty pan to heat. Their beards glistened with ice, and what could be seen of their faces, covered with old woollen shawls, had marks of frostbite. But they were strong faces, carved by a heritage of hardship.

Irina knelt by the wounded. There was nothing she could do for them but show that she cared. The medical supplies had run out along with the food, and the cold would kill them if their wounds did not. They looked at her with warm kinship—something they had never believed possible with a *barinya*—and helped her by hiding their pain. She knew what they did and gripped their shoulders in understanding before tipping some hot water down their throats to warm their stomachs.

Then, as she remained kneeling there, a hand went beneath her elbow to raise her up and lead her away. She looked at the young Lieutenant and smiled kindly. He was no more than a boy—a foolish boy who suffered from that calf love so many felt for a nurse. She knew that winter had taken its toll of her, and she felt like a middle-aged woman who was tired to her very soul, yet his yearning for normality saw her as a young heroine. Because she understood, she treated him with gentleness that salved his pride.

But, oh, suddenly she was filled with the memory of last summer as she saw that flickering fear of rebuff cross his youthful, bearded face. Perhaps it was the lake, or perhaps it was because she sensed that Paul was also thinking of her that memories of him swept her with the need to walk out there on the snow-covered ice.

Without a pause, she moved away from the tattered company and trod the virgin snow that stretched out for several miles to the far bank. It was a long time since the yearning had been so strong, and she made no effort to resist it. As she walked, the trees grew green again, dark and grand against the cloudless heaven. Out on the sun-shimmered water there were wild duck bobbing, calling to each other in the serenity. The summer of her youth! There was a young man throwing pebbles into the water, longing to put into words something he felt so deeply; beside him was a young girl in a blue skirt, telling him of another love he did not want to understand.

Out there in that blue-whiteness, she felt immensely close to him for a while and knew it was not the length of loving but the depth that really mattered. Theirs could not have been deeper. Then she cried a little because his would be the bigger burden. The years that lay ahead of him would keep her image too long in his memory. For her it would soon be over.

A figure appeared beside her. Sasha said nothing, just put an arm behind her to lead her gently back.

"Not yet," she said softly.

So he stood, holding her against his side, two isolated figures out on that frozen lake. Her gaze wandered over the petrified pines all around, white and stiff; over the sky that hung with the curious blue arctic day above the silence; and over the pure innocence of snow all around her. It was like standing at the top of the world.

"It is beautiful, isn't it?" she whispered.

"Yes . . . yes, it is beautiful. It will always be beautiful," he answered as softly as she, as if loud voices would shatter the ice and send everything tumbling.

Then she saw the long line of dark shapes materialise on the shore, coming from the trees like wolves in the night. Shots echoed in the distance, and shouting voices rang with authority. One figure detached itself from the shore and began to run toward them, calling to her to run for her life. The Lieutenant fell twenty yards from the shore and lay still. Irina had only time to be thankful they were using bullets before she saw the dark host step out onto the ice, rifles raised.

Sasha turned her slowly round, and they walked quietly on close together, gazing at the serenity ahead. The shouts grew louder; they fired . . . and kept on firing. When she fell, she kept her gaze steadfastly on the majestic pines way off on the far bank. Her last thoughts were not for her husband sprawled beside her nor for the man she had loved so dearly. They were for Mother Russia.

* * *

The river was half a mile wide at this point. It thundered through the deep gorge, blue and foam-speckled, reflecting the African sky. On both sides of the gorge rose the lush, humid jungle that was the home of snakes, monkeys, leopard, and birds of brilliant plumage and song. There was a liquid musical chorus coming from the trees as these winged rainbows called to each, but there was another chorus coming from the navvies who hauled and strained, their black bodies glistening, as they sang the melodies of their ancestors.

Paul was straddled precariously across two struts of the lower trusses of the bridge, looking up at a splice his foreman had reported as suspect. The man was right. It would have to be strengthened. He climbed back up, sweating profusely in his tropical-kit, paying respectful attention to the two-hundred-foot drop beneath him. At the top he went across to the black foreman and told him what was wanted, indicating on the plans where the main stress would be felt when a train crossed.

While he was talking, one of the civilian engineers came up, and when Paul finished and turned to him, the man smiled as he wiped the sweat from his brow with his forearm.

"You mystify me, Major. You nearly killed yourself trying to learn their mumbo-jumbo lingo, when all the head-boys speak English anyway."

"Of a sort," he replied. "It's hopeless if you can't communicate."

"I've always managed it."

Paul smiled patiently. "If a man is about to fall, it is no use telling the head-boy, 'Look out!' is it?"

The man scratched his chest and laughed grudgingly. "You have a point. I'll tell you straight, when we heard an army engineer was going to be in charge of building this bridge, our hearts sank. We all thought you lads put planks on top of boats and called them bridges."

He smiled again. "Not always."

He turned to look at the bridge spanning the gorge—a beautiful, sturdy construction that overcame a barrier of nature and would link two garrison towns that were presently separated by a tedious three-day journey through jungle.

"I hear you are taking an engine across at the end of the week," said the man. "You don't mind if none of us accompanies you, do you?"

Paul acknowledged the taunt in the manner it was given, but he merely said, "It won't fall down."

There was a short silence as both men looked at the new rail link so high above the river, then the man said, "By the way, weren't you in that little shindig in Russia last year?"

The bridge faded away before Paul's eyes. "Yes . . . Why?"

"The mail and the newspapers have just arrived. Russia is finally lost."

Paul walked away from him out onto the bridge, where he stood leaning on the railing, staring down into the gorge. *Russia is finally lost.* There would be a letter from Olga with all the details soon. Underneath her bravado, she cared deeply about her lost country—underneath her careless treatment of the young naval officer who had fallen under her spell on the ship from Archangel and married her with haste, and underneath her constant references to her son, born prematurely, whom she had named Paul. He was still uncertain whether or not she was provocatively teasing him when he received a letter saying that the boy had surprising brown eyes when she and her husband had blue ones. But she had kept her promise to ask nothing more of him once she got to England, so he maintained a correspondence with her for his own reasons. Through that correspondence he kept his link with Russia, and felt it could not entirely slip away from him while she wrote of the group of White Russians who had made their homes in England.

Russia is finally lost. The river way below faded away as he saw again Irina's sweet serious face, with the pale hair wound around it in shimmering bands, and the grey-green eyes that had seen too much of life.

For a long time he stood reliving those five months in a forest. He thought of men like Swarovsky, who would die gladly for a cause he truly believed was right. He thought of Lyudmilla Zapalova, now the darling of Paris and London theatreland, thrilling audiences with the magic, eloquent drama of old St. Petersburg. He thought of a bridge across a river, made from pines that grew beside it. Then, inevitably, of a warm incomprehensible group of ruffians who built it whether they were loathing or loving him. He thought of Branski's Name Day, when they had danced and leapt with joyous vigour, as their ancestors had done.

The brightness of the day dimmed a little when he recalled a fair-haired young man balancing on a spar across a rushing river, arms spread wide and grinning in response to a chorus of encouragement for his daring, and in contrast, a soft tenor voice taking up the refrain of one of the old folk songs that spoke of pain and hope, while everyone was moved to tears by the beauty of such sadness.

The day grew darker as he thought again of Irina, who had loved him yet walked away for the sake of a nation and a lost cause.

For a long time he rode back in memory to those days that would be forever in his soul. Then he straightened and gazed defiantly into the far distance. No, they were wrong. That spirit was too strong . . . and all the time it was there, Russia would never be finally lost.